Perfectly Wrong

Alexandra Barnard

Contents

Chapter 1

"I fucking hate maths."

I chuckle, continuing solving the equation.

"For God's sake, Kadie, you always have your nose stuck in those notebooks," Harper says. I can hear she's joking.

"You don't mind it when I help you with studying for your exams. Maybe you should try it, too, sometime?" I reply, lifting my head to look at her.

She sticks her tongue out, grabbing another glass to polish it.

Harper Gilmore is my cousin and my closest friend. The only real friend, I could say. I talk to other people, hang out with other people, help them, but they're still not my friends. Not really. Most people at this age are just back-stabbing bitches who hang out with you because it's convenient for them. They also like to act like they're making you a favour by being your friend. Ha. As if.

Harper is working at a bar I spend most of the time at. I basically live here. The loud music, drunk people and their screaming, dancing and making out don't bother me anymore. I don't even hear or see any of it anymore. Even those few guys who dare to come and hit on the nerd studying at the bar every night don't bother me that much because I'm good at focusing on one important thing and muting everything and everyone else.

I'm not here at the bar to make friends, either. I study here. And talk to Harper. Basically, I spend most of my free time here. Once I got used to the scene, I started to like it here.

Harper scrunches her nose up, staring at the piece of paper before me as if it's going to jump up and bite her. "I would rather not. I'm too stupid for that."

I roll my eyes. Not this again. "Too lazy maybe." Harper isn't stupid. She's far from that. She's studying medicine for a reason, but she's a joker and she especially likes to joke about her smartness. Maths isn't really her forte, but it's a good thing she doesn't need it that much and when she does, she has me for that.

"Not everyone has good genes like you, smartass," Harper retorts back.

I give her a pointed glare. "Harp. We're related." I try to hold back a smile because I know how much it irks her. I know we're only cousins, so we're not that similar, not in looks and especially not in behaviour.

Harper is more of a prude and actually thinks what people think about her so she's always trying to do good by them, while I'm more of a I-don't-give-a-fuck-about-anything type of girl, but everyone thinks I'm a good girl and a nerd just because I get good grades. Boy, are they wrong!

I love studying. I know many people can't relate to that and I know a lot don't feel the same. Most people my age would rather go out to a party and get shitfaced drunk while I'd rather stay in and watch a historical drama. I just love learning about new things and I like educating myself.

People think I'm smart. But I'd say my smartness is just that. Smartness. I have a big mouth, though, and, sometimes, I don't know how to shut it. I'm basically a beast and I have to tame myself at times. I'm not afraid to speak what's on my mind, which often gets me in trouble.

The good part about being good in school is that teachers love me, so if there happens to be any drama involving me, they look through my fingers. Because I'm the good student.

If only they knew ...

"We're cousins, Kadie. Our genes aren't that similar. How come even I know that and you don't? You're supposed to be the smart one."

I can't help myself but get out a loud chuckle. "I'm messing with you."

"Uh-huh," she says, narrowing her eyes on me.

Since it's getting late, more guests seem to appear and Harper gets busy with the work, so I don't have any more distractions from my maths homework. And since it's Friday, there are some people from my school here, too, although I don't bother acknowledging them. They mostly ignore me, as well.

This is what I was talking about. They're not really friends. Just some familiar faces I occasionally talk to.

I blow a strand of hair that fell over my eye away, shaking my head a little so my hair gets off my face.

I feel a presence next to me and I don't bother lifting my head. Harper is quite busy with the guests and I feel the person will be here for some time. I sigh to myself. They're standing directly at the light, creating a shadow right on my paper.

The man places his hand on the counter, next to my notebook and it catches my attention. Or rather, his tattoos do. His hand is full of tattoos, detailed tattoos, that go up to his arm, disappearing under the sleeves of a black T-shirt he's wearing.

My eyes slowly travel upwards, landing on his face. I frown. He's staring down at my notebook, his lip curled up. He has dark eyes, I notice. They might look even darker in this light. His hair is dark and a little too long in the front so a few strands fall over his eyes. He's got sculpted cheekbones and a sharp jawline. That's one feature that always interested me on men.

He actually looks scary, dressed in all black, wearing a dark expression. My hand moves slowly, covering the glass of lemonade Harper put in front of me before.

The guy's eyes catch my movement and they fall on my hand, covering the glass. And then he looks at me. And I almost gasp. I don't even know why. He's kind of attractive, if you like scary looking guys. It's not that I'm scared of him, it's just that his eyes ... they're a different colour each.

I only notice this now when the light hits them. One is light blue. The other is dark brown. And they captivate me. I can't look away. And then he opens his mouth, "It ain't gonna be me putting anything in your glass, princess. Maybe turn your head in the other direction."

I blink. What? I look to my left to see a guy sitting next to me on the barstool while a few others surround him, all of them standing. They look a bit older, but not much. I don't find anything wrong with them, they're well-dressed and they don't even look drunk.

"That's right. The prettiest ones are usually the dirtiest," the guy on my right laughs humourlessly as if he's reading my thoughts. I look at him yet again.

"Are you trying to say he put something in my drink?" I ask, holding his stare. He doesn't seem to want to answer my question. "Are you or are you not?"

"Not trying. I'm saying," he says curtly. I notice his voice sounds gruff. Deep. I wonder how old he is.

"And you saw him?"

"Fuck's with the questions?" he says, irritably. "Yeah, sugar, saw him with my own pair of eyes."

I shake my head to myself, not knowing if I should believe him or not. I won't test my luck and I won't be stupid enough to drink it – just to be sure. But I can't tell if he's playing me or he's being serious.

I drop my eyes down on the back of his hand again that's still placed on the counter. Harper comes to him then, taking his order. "Tequila shots. Five."

My finger starts stroking the corner of my notebook, just out of a nervous habit. I look at Harper, preparing the drinks. She's still alone behind the bar, her co-worker doesn't start until 10. She smiles at the guy as she puts the shots on the counter and he pays her.

Out of curiosity, I decide to study her expression when her eyes land on him. Her pupils dilate and her movement slows down just a little bit. Her mouth falls open slightly, but she quickly composes herself, smiling as she does to everyone.

"You have inguz on your hand," I note.

The guy pauses and when I look up, he's staring down at me, his brows furrowing.

"It means man fertility, since the addition of 'ing' to an English verb represents action. It also means new beginnings, often signifies a new life or a new phase of life. It comes from Greek and it basically means 'when there's a will, there's a say.'"

The guy stares at me as if I'm crazy. He leans down to me and I smell his scent. It's not cologne, but something else ... it's pleasant, manly and not at all what boys from my school smell like. "Mind your own damn business," he hisses. He puts the change off the bar and throws it in his back pocket, grabs the shots and walks away.

I look at Harper and she gives me wide eyes. She doesn't have time for chit-chat, but I understand what she's trying to tell me. She finds him hot.

I go back to solving the equations.

She comes to me later, planting her hands right down in front of me, demanding my attention. "That was one hot piece," she tells me. "And he talked to you."

"I talked to him, basically, but yeah." I shrug, playing nonchalant.

"What did you even talk about?"

I play disinterested. "He actually warned me about the guy next to me. He said he put something in my drink."

Harper instantly eyes the guy on my left and then the glass. She raises her eyebrows at me. "Seriously?" she asks.

I shrug. "That's what he said."

Harper chuckles. "The saying states something else, but you might've just did something here. But that man, Kadie ... you don't see a fine man like that that often here in this shithole."

"He might have an attractive face, but his personality is pretty shitty."

Harper glares at me. "You talked to him for, what, five minutes? Don't be such a pessimist."

I lift my hands up. "I'm being realistic."

Harper stares into the distance. "He has the vibe of being an asshole." She sighs. "I've actually seen him in here a few times, but he never stayed long and he never came to order anything. And now he came here and talked to you. God, I'm kind of jealous."

"Harp." I glare at her. "Please, don't. You're being ridiculous."

"Just let me gush a little. He's dreamy."

I roll my eyes. "Yeah. Okay. I think I'll need a new drink since I'm afraid this one is spiked."

Harper eyes the guy on my left a little sceptically. "I should inform security about him." She nods towards him.

I shrug, not really caring that much about it, but if he spiked my drink, who says he won't spike someone else's as well?

Harper calls Josh, the security guy here, about what happened. He listens to every word she says, his muscled arms crossed over his chest. If I didn't know him, I'd be scared of him. He's big and has that mean stare, but he's actually a real sweetheart.

He comes to me. "Hey, Kadie. Having some trouble, I hear?"

I shrug, giving him a smile. "I think I successfully avoided it, but I don't know what his thing is. Better be sure than sorry, you know."

He pats my shoulder. "I'll handle it."

He steps to the group of guys and talks to them. I try to ignore the scene, pretending I have no interest in knowing what's going on. I hear a loud, "What the fuck?" from one of the guys. I look just with the corners of my eyes and see Josh is already dragging him out.

I slightly turn my head to see the guy giving me a death glare. "I didn't put anything in your drink, you bitch!" he yells.

I avert my gaze, looking back down at my notebook.

I don't know why, but I look towards where the guy that came here before went to. He's with a group of friends, I suppose. They're laughing. Looking right at the guy Josh is dragging out. I get a weird feeling.

Especially when I see him looking right at me, wearing a devilish grin. I frown at him, my eyes narrowing. He raises his glass at me and drinks everything at once, his eyes never leaving mine.

I look back down at my notebook, too distracted to focus on equations. I never get distracted. I can hear their laughter all the way to here. I try to zone it out, I try really hard to focus on anything else, but I can't. I sigh in irritation, somehow still feeling his gaze on me and it's starting to make me angry.

I switch my head into their direction yet again, not even trying to be subtle. But they're already heading towards the exit and he doesn't glance in my direction again. I loudly close my notebook and grab it in my hands, standing up. Harper notices me and I think she instantly gets what my intention is. "Kadie!" she shouts after me.

I ignore her completely, going into the same direction they went.

Chapter 2

I manage to get through the dancing bodies and drunk people, although it's tough. I'm not that tall at my 5'3" and my body is slim. I put on a mean face, ignoring all the jerks that tried to grab my attention and almost punching someone for trying to be too touchy. I might be small and appear harmless, but I can throw a mean punch. All my self-defence classes taught me that.

It's not until I come out and breathe fresh air that I realise how bad the air inside the bar is. It's more of a low budget bar and you can find a lot of people in there. And I mean a lot. That's one of the reasons I decided to take self-defence classes.

I'm not really afraid of assholes. I know how to fight. I carry a knife with me at all times, just in case. That's why I'm not afraid to go after the assholes – one in particular – and stand up against him. What he did wasn't cool and I don't want him to just get away with it.

I hear them before I see them.

"Who even was that chick, man?"

"Fuck if I know. Some rich posh princess who tried to get into my business."

I'm seething. I cross my arms over my chest, getting a good look of the scene. They're walking towards the motorcycles, all five of them and I see them holding a beer in their hands now. I didn't see any of them come to the bar to order a beer, but then again, I wasn't even paying attention to anyone else but just one of them.

"You haven't seen me trying to get into your business, but now you're really going to."

All heads turn around equally fast, all of them wearing surprised expression. Except one. He's amused. I can see it all the way from where I'm standing, the darkness not really hiding that much. "Ah. Princess- Good girls like you shouldn't hang out here. Especially not with us."

I daringly look at him. "Good thing there aren't any good girls here then."

He looks back at the boys as they all chuckle in unison. He turns back to me, shaking his head. He's still laughing. "Don't try to be something you're not just to impress us. Go back inside." He points the chin towards the bar.

I cross my arms over my chest. "Stop trying to act like you know me."

A bunch of ooohs comes from the boys. I see his jaw tick as he comes even closer to me. "Stop trying to act so tough, princess. I don't want to make you cry."

My eyebrows shoot up. "Cry? Because of you?" I snort. "Don't worry. You won't get that pleasure." I roll my eyes. "Anyone else nicer than this one? I would be really grateful for a ride home."

Everyone stays quiet, just looking at each other. The guy in front of me crosses his arms, matching my pose, and giving me a self-pleasant smile. "Maybe you should go look for a ride somewhere else. Just an idea."

I point a finger at him like he just had the brightest idea I've ever heard. "You know what? I'll go find the guy you've accused, falsely by the way, that he spiked my drink. He actually seemed like a guy who'd take me home."

His grin falls right off his face. "You're seriously asking me to take you home while you don't even know my name?"

I shrug. "I won't even ask you because I know you won't tell me."

That surprises him. "You won't even try?"

"No," I say.

"Well, I'm not taking a girl home whose name I don't know."

"I won't tell you my name, either."

He mutters something under his breath. "But you'd tell me your address?"

I chuckle. "What? Will you come and kidnap me? Rob me?" I mock him.

"Dude," someone calls in disbelief.

He eyes me, ignoring the guys behind him. I don't want him to take me home. Or any of them. I just said that to mess with him. He messed with me first.

"Did you know the guy in there?" I ask him. I'm not leaving this case alone until I get some answers.

"I'm not giving you any answers since you don't want to answer any of my questions, either."

I have to grin at this. "Man," I say, still grinning. "You have an ego this fragile, huh? Should've known you're one of those guys." I shake my head in disappointment. I see it makes him confused.

"What does my ego have to do with me not wanting to answer your questions?"

I shrug, taking a few steps back. "You should figure it out by yourself. But, honestly, if you have problems with yourself, you shouldn't cause troubles for others, too. That doesn't make you cool. It makes you pathetic."

He takes a step towards me, his eye now twitching in anger. He does have a scary look and someone else would probably fear him. But I don't. I know his kind. I live with his kind. People like him can't scare me anymore.

"It was nice meeting you. See you around." I wave in farewell before I turn around and go back into the bar at a quick pace, smiling to myself because I feel his eyes on me as I walk away.

I find Harper panicky looking around while also managing to successfully handle the crowd. When she sees me, she's instantly in front of me. "Are you fucking crazy? On drugs? Did you take something? What the hell, Kadie!"

"Relax. I'm still breathing and very well alive," I say calmly. Harper is older than me and knowing me and my life, that makes her very protective of me. She knows I can handle a lot of stuff, but she doesn't think that I should. I often bring myself in situations she doesn't approve. She loves and hates seeing me at the bar. Because there are all kinds of people and I fear no one. But she can also keep an eye on me here.

She points her finger at me. "You can't do that. You don't know him and by the things I've just heard right now, they're not people to mess with. Don't ever do that again!"

I roll my eyes. I know she means well, but I can look after myself. I don't even ask her what she heard in the time I was gone. Frankly,

I don't care. I saw it for myself what kind of guy he is. He can scare others all he can, he's not fooling me.

"Why can't you start running after nice guys?" she mutters to herself.

I grin. "Because nice guys don't need anyone to run after them. And they're also no fun."

She sighs. "I'll be done soon. Wait for me, finish your homework and, for the love of God, stay out of trouble."

"I'm not twelve, Harper."

"Then act like it." She's mad. I didn't really do anything. I just went after a guy because he did something he shouldn't have. What a big deal. A guy that's hot, but it's a shame he's a jerk. The nice-looking ones usually are. And I was never attracted to nice guys.

Harper is quiet on the way to her apartment. I stay at her place a lot. I'm rarely ever at home, so either I'm at school, wandering outside, at the bar or at her place.

But it's not Harper's habit to be quiet.

"Oh, come on! You can't blame me I ran after him. He's hot, Harp. H-o-t."

"That doesn't mean you had to go after him. Especially after he basically told you to fuck off."

I shrug. "I like challenges."

Harper grimaces. "You sound like a guy that doesn't know how to take a no for an answer."

"Well ... I can't take no for an answer, but that does not mean I'm a guy? The last time I checked, I still had a pu–"

"Kadie!" Harper almost yells, looking at me in outrage.

"Am I making you uncomfortable?"

"You're making everyone uncomfortable with your language. You need to stop that."

"I'm not really doing anything. This is just called talking. It's not my fault you all decide to limit yourselves with what you say just because someone said it's unacceptable. Fuck them. I'll say whatever the hell I want. Freedom of speech, bitches!"

Harper sighs, rubbing her eyebrow. "I hear you," she mutters in a dead tone.

Harper is a more reserved one. Her family is nice to her – it has always been. Parents are kids' very first role models and I can say we both had different role models growing up. I don't see my parents as role models anymore, but Harper still does and she values their opinion. Maybe that's why we're so different.

Growing up, I had no one to tell me what's good and what's bad. What's right and what's wrong. Those lines get blurry with me sometimes. I've seen some shit and I've experienced some shit that it was normal to me, but I later found out that it's not normal. Not even close. Because other kids don't hear what I heard. And they don't get to do the things I had to do.

Harper understands me, but she doesn't usually like the things that I do and say and she most certainly doesn't agree with them. She usually says something, but otherwise, she lets me be. Because I don't listen. I know I'm not doing anything bad. I might say bad things and things other people normally wouldn't. But I would never do anything that would put me in trouble or that would be morally wrong. I'm not my parents.

"You had to at least admit I have a good taste."

"In looks, yes. In personality? Not so much, I'm afraid," Harper answers seriously. I know she's scared I'll find myself a guy that will be all kinds of wrong for me just because it's something I'm used to. She makes some valid points sometimes, but she concerns herself with unimportant things. Being mistreated by the people who should've loved me taught me that I will never, ever let anyone treat me badly.

That's probably why I try to be so no-nonsense person. I might say bad things such as swear words (since people like to think this is a bad thing), but that does not necessarily make me a bad person. I fight for justice where I can. This is precisely why I went after that guy before. He might be scary to some, but he didn't fool me.

I didn't go after him to get answers, either. I didn't care if he told me the reasons, I just wanted him to think about it. And I wanted to make sure it was in a way he couldn't not think about it.

"Harp, you're afraid I will find myself a wild guy, as you put it. But I'm afraid that you will find yourself a boring lawyer or a doctor. You will have two point five children and you'll engage in polite sex at thirty. He will open the doors for you and he will pull the chair out for you. But you know what he won't do? He won't make your heart race."

Harper is quiet for a second. "What is wrong with lawyers and doctors? They do good things for this world."

"That just makes them a little boring, don't you think?"

"Not really? Some people don't want spontaneous adventures their whole lives, Kadie. Some people want a peaceful life with a boring doctor."

I squeeze my lips together. That's what your parents convinced you, Harper, dear. I have my own theory. We think we want normal and peacefulness because we love to have a routine. A routine is safe. You wake up and do the same thing you do every day. And then you go to sleep. This is a safe choice. And it's an unwritten rule; school, job, marriage, kids. Maybe not in that order. And then we die.

But I think we crave some spontaneity in our lives. Something unpredictable once and here. Something that makes our hearts race. That makes our blood flow. Something that still makes us remember we're humans and we're not only living to die at the end. No matter how much someone tells themselves they're happy with their boring life, deep down, they know that's not really it.

I know Harper is going to go with a safe choice. She's going to be a good girl who'll marry a good guy and they'll live their (boring) fairytale. This is why she's disapproving my choices. Because I won't go for safe. I'll go for that heart-racing choice.

"You were literally drooling all over him before, Harp. Are you jealous? Because you can have him. Although I'd never say you'd go for his type."

Harper parks the car in front of her house, but she doesn't get out. "Josh knows the guy, Kadie. Well, he knows of the guy. People are talking and he knows a lot of people. He's not a good guy. He probably wouldn't even tell me anything so he wouldn't scare me, but when he saw you go after him, he got worried. He thought you're interested because, well, he knows what kind of guys you're into. But he's really bad, Kadie. Even worse than you're into."

"You don't know him, Harper, you just heard some things and now you're acting as if he ever threatened to kill you."

"Why the hell won't you ever try to listen when people only want good for you? Fucking hell, Kadie!"

"I do hear you. I just refuse to believe some story I heard about someone I barely know. He didn't seem much worse than any other guy. Right now, I don't really have any reason to stay away from him and judge him. Except for the douchey thing I saw with my own pair of eyes he did."

"That mindset of your is going to get you into so much trouble one day, Kadie. Remember my words."

I smile. "I've been kissing trouble on its lips my whole life, Harp. Trouble loves me. And I love it right back."

Chapter 3

I had a feeling I'd see him again.

I have never seen him in the bar before, but I had a feeling he'll be back. Just an intuition.

And I was right.

It took him a week and a half to show up again. I'm at my usual spot and I doubt I'd even see him if he hadn't sat down next to me. It's not like I was waiting for him to come.

I eye him, but I don't give him my full attention just right away. I wait a few seconds before I speak because I see it won't be him who'll start a conversation. "My hero on a white horse. Who spiked my drink this time? Who are you getting thrown out today?"

His mouth lifts into a half-grin. I see Harper is already giving me warning glances. "I don't see any potential candidates right now. Have anyone you want out?"

I lift my eyebrow. "Yeah, you."

"Ouch, princess. You've been sharpening your claws, huh?" He shakes his head. He's amused.

Harper comes to us, stopping right in front of him and giving him a full-on glare. "Order or go away," she snaps. I have to squeeze my lips together so I don't burst out laughing. My cousin learned a few things from me, I see.

The guy looks at her in surprise. He looks her up and down and then his eyes are on me again for a few moments. He looks back at Harper, now serious as ever. "Jack, then. With extra ice."

Harper narrows her eyes first at him and then at me. He doesn't speak until the drink is in front of him. He pays for it immediately. I notice Harper looking at his tattooed hands as he gives her the money. "Keep the change," he says with a raspy, I'm-so-fucking-sexy-you-can't-resist-me voice.

I pretend to give my notebook my full attention.

"It seems like you know about me, but I know nothing about you."

I huff. "Don't flatter yourself, buddy. I don't even know your name." I don't look at him.

"I'm Fai," he says flatly.

"Cool. I didn't ask," I match his enthusiasm.

He's suddenly right beside me. And I mean right beside me. "I just wanted to let you know for later when you're going to moan it in pleasure."

I look up from the notebook, looking right ahead of me. Seriously? Seriously? Can anything else make a guy more unattractive? I turn to him, giving him my sweetest smile. I pat his knee with one hand, putting my other one on his cheek, leaning into him so my lips are close to his ear. "Fai, baby, assholes like you don't make me spread my legs for them."

I lean back, removing my hands from him. That doesn't shock him enough, apparently, because he gets brave, putting his hand high on my thigh. "I might be a bad guy, but I save the good for bed."

I slap his hand away from my thigh. "If you have to say that, you most certainly aren't good in bed. And you haven't even offered to buy me a drink first before trying to get me in bed." I shake my head. "Try better the next time. Maybe with someone else, too."

"Oh, wow." He seems stunned. "You're actually going to play hard to get today? Maybe I should've taken you up for your offer that time when you were all over my dick outside to take you home."

He stands up from the chair.

"You completely misinterpreted me and now you're mad at me for rejecting you. So I stand correct. Your ego is more fragile than glass."

He rolls his bottom lip into his mouth, playing with his lip ring for a second. He doesn't say anything. He stares at me for a few moments and I take a moment to admire his unusual eyes, before he turns on his heel and just walks away. I shake my head to myself. What a disappointment.

Harper suddenly appears in front of me, slapping her hands hard down on the counter. I give her a boring look. "What the hell is wrong with you?"

"What the hell isn't, Harp?"

She just rolls her eyes at me. "Your self-destructive behaviour isn't something to be proud of. If you need to talk to a specialist, just say so. Please, Kadie, don't do stupid things just because you think they'll make you look cool. You worry everyone."

"No, Harper, I worry you. No one else gives a shit about what I do." I slam the notebook shut and stand up. "I need five minutes out in the fresh air. I won't go anywhere and I won't do anything, don't worry."

I know she's worried about me, but I'm such a bitter person when it comes to that. I'm not used to people expressing their feelings around me, especially when it comes to me. I've always been good on my own, but Harper is desperately trying to change that for me.

I've been into a few situations where I had to defend myself. I know how to do that. I'm literally not afraid of anyone because no one can hurt me more than I've already been hurt. They can't even come close. And I know that if I was able to survive that and get out of that mess, I can get through anything.

I take in some fresh air, walking on the abandoned, all too familiar street. This street would've been probably creepy to any other person. It creeps the hell out of Harper, especially at night. There's not a single person around. And that's precisely why I like it so much.

It's not that long and I usually take this route when I need to calm down before I come onto more busy streets where there are all kinds of people walking past me now. To be honest, this creeps me out more than walking on the lonely street. You never know who passes you on the street.

When I turn into a little less busy street to go back to the bar, I hear the sound of motorcycles behind me. I sigh to myself. I hope it's not who I think it is. I mean; what are the chances?

There are five of them, flying past me as fast as they can, it seems. I put the jacket tighter around me when the strong wind hits me, caused by them. Four of them continue forward, while one of them stops. That causes the other four to stop as well.

The one who stopped first turns around and slowly starts riding towards me.

I look up into the dark sky, annoyed. "Why the hell can't I just live in peace for ten fucking minutes without someone disturbing me?" I mutter to no one particular.

"Going somewhere?" Fai asks.

I look at him like he has twelve heads. Yes, twelve. "Yeah, preferably somewhere where there are not assholes around. Full offence."

Fai chuckles. "Wouldn't expect anything else from you, Kadience Myers."

My eyebrows rise on their own. "Wow, really? I didn't know you were so interested in me that you went and asked about me around. Sweetheart! You could just ask me instead."

"I did, but you're not willing to give answers. But other people are." He makes it sound like a threat. But I'm a long way away from getting scared of threats. I classify them as empty promises.

"Then I won't stop you from finding out about my business from them." I shrug and walk forward. I don't like people disturbing my time. This is the time I like to take to myself to just calm down and breathe some fresh air. I don't know why some people just want to pollute it.

Fai has the nerve to turn his motorcycle off and step off it, walking after me. I sharply turn around because I already sense what he's going to do, and that is confirmed when I see his stretched arm, waiting for his hand to grab me. "Touch me and I'm going to break your fingers one by one."

His head tilts to the side. "The fuck's your problem?"

I let out a sarcastic laugh. "Boy, I've got a lot of problems, but you're not my psychotherapist so you're not hearing about not even one of them." I give him a wink. "Look, babe, I think you mistook me trying to be nice and make a conversation for something that's not and I'm sorry to let you down, but I'm really not interested in you. Or any of you. You just don't do it for me, you know?" I scrunch my nose up at him, giving him a fake cute smile.

Fai gives me a half-smirk. The street light is illuminating his face so I can see his expressions clearly. "Princess, I'm not here to ask you out, alright?" He chuckles, shaking his head.

"Then what the hell do you want?" I become serious now.

"Your cousin – Harper, right?"

I instantly straighten up, my eyes narrowing. "What about her?" I ask him in a tone that says he should be careful at how he proceeds.

"I heard she's been asking around about me. And – now, I usually don't mind when hotties like her do it, but she's doing it for all the wrong reasons. She's looking for trouble and she may not even know it, you know?"

I step closer to him. "It's one thing threatening me, but threatening her?" I shake my head. "I don't think so. Stay the hell away from her. Do you hear me?" I'm so angry right now. I feel the temperature in my body rising by just the thought of anything happening to Harper because of him. And partly because of me because I can't keep my mouth in check.

"I wasn't talking about me, tigress. But she might stumble upon people who aren't exactly my friends and they might get a wrong inside idea in their heads. Do you get me now?"

"No worries, Fai. We're not interested enough to ask about you anymore. You're good if you were scared that we would find anything bad."

Fai laughs, closing his eyes. "Princess. I'm not even trying to hide my bad from anyone."

"Mmm. I can see that," I say, forcing a smile again.

Fai flicks my nose with his pointer. "You're hot, too."

I want to roll my eyes so hard they'd fall out. He's so cringe-y that it's hard to believe these lines would work on any girl. Or maybe he's just picking the dumb ones; the ones more like him. "Yeah, boo, I know."

Fai's eyebrows raise. "O-kay then?" he says, unsure of what to say further.

I lick my lips. "Look, Fai, sweetheart. I know how I look. I see myself in the mirror every day. The thing about looks is - I can't change it. That's genes; I got it from my parents and that's it. But when you're able to look inside me and tell me I'm pretty – then we're going to talk." I'm not trying to sound full of myself. I'm far from that. But my looks isn't something I'm proud of and I don't accept compliments about it. That's just about it. I'm tired of hearing things about my appearance. "This is just a heads up if you ever mature enough to realise that hot isn't the thing that's going to be there for you through life. You know what I'm saying?" I sugar-coat my voice.

I think I made him speechless because he really doesn't know what to say back. Mission accomplished. I salute him in farewell. "Take care, buddy." I manage to successfully walk away this time.

I still have a few minutes to calm down before I reach the bar. This guy really is something else. I've dealt with men like him. Worse than him, actually. And if he thinks he's scaring me with his wanna-be dangerous vibe he's trying to give off, he's wrong. Dangerous people don't have to try hard to be dangerous. Dangerous people don't show they're dangerous. You won't know how dangerous they are until you let them get close to you, see your vulnerable side and then strike.

This is the real danger. The emotional one. The threats of physically hurting me don't really phase me. I experienced that. The bruises and scars on my body healed. But it's the mind that really needed a band-aid. And no one offers you help with that.

When I sit in my usual place in the bar, Harper rushes towards me. "I'm getting really tired of you worrying me!"

"I don't worry you, you worry yourself because of me. I'm fine. But, Harp, this time it's actually you I'm starting to get worried about."

Harper pauses for a second. She looks confused and then a little scared. "Why?" She knows I don't worry about a lot of things. I hardly ever worry about anything.

"You need to stop asking around about that guy. People will start to notice and you'll get yourself into a mess. You already figured he's dangerous. Let it rest."

"Did he threaten you?"

Smart girl.

"Not me, you. He knows you've been snooping around. And I swear to God, Harp, I don't want to know any information about him anymore. You don't have to worry, I won't associate myself with him."

I see fear settling into Harper. Good. This will really make her reconsider. I want her to be scared. Because if she is, then she'll be more careful. And I want her to be more careful.

"That guy is really messed up," she tells me. As if I didn't know.

"We all are, Harp. We all are." Well, maybe not as much as him, but we're all on different levels.

Chapter 4

I have a secret.

Well, I have many secrets, but I want to only talk about this one this time.

No one knows about it and no one can know about it, especially not Harper.

I'm working at a strip club.

I'm not a dancer, I only serve drinks there. I'm always dressed, even though if you go topless, it brings you better tips.

I work nights, sneaking out so no one can see me and come back before Harper wakes up. I'm not ashamed of my job, but if Harper found out, she'd have a heart attack.

But she doesn't understand. I'd do anything to get the hell out of this town. This is why I need to save. And I need a good job for this. I'm finishing high school this year and I'm going to college. Hopefully far away from here. And I need money for that.

Also, I really like the people there. I know other people see this as something wrong. I don't. I met girls there who are stripping on the stage to get money for college. They're all very bright and smart, they just have to get money to get a degree. There are single mothers who are doing this for their kids.

But people are so goddamn quick to put a label on them if they know where they're working.

People who come there aren't that bad, either. It's a high-budget strip-club. Not anyone can get into it. You have to have some privileges, you have to fit into some categories and, most importantly, you have to be rich.

This is why I'm not worried that someone may recognise me there. And I'm telling you, working in the environment when people don't know people is so refreshing. You don't have to tell anyone shit. You can lie about who you are if you want to. Most of us do, of course. Because we don't want to be recognised outside of the club. We can be anyone we want to in there. No one will ever know if you're telling the truth or not.

I've been keeping this secret for three years now. I was a minor when I got a job there, which is illegal, but did anyone know that? No. Because I could lie. And so did my employer.

I work at nights, sleep to 3-4 hours and then go to school. I take naps sometimes in the afternoon to fulfil my basic need for sleeping so I survive.

That's the secret I'm hiding from everyone. I'm a person full of secrets. I'm a complicated person if I put it simply. I realise I don't do the things people my age do, but then again, I'm not people my age. I'm different from them in so many ways and I wouldn't even know how to fit in if I tried. So I don't. I'm my own person – have been my whole life and I won't say I'm proud of who I am, but at least I know who I am and I know I'm not trying to be someone else.

This is why I like working here. We're all the same here. No one is better than someone else. You don't hold any kind of power on someone else, no matter the age, religion or gender. No one cares who you are.

I did meet some good women here, although I'm not the one to chit-chat and we're not really people who love to share stories about our lives – well, most of us. I use the breaks to go outside, sit, light a cigarette and just be by myself, staring at nothing but darkness.

Being alone is something I learned to enjoy at a very young age. I love the simplicity of it. I love silence. The calmness that it brings. I prefer this than having to pretend to be nice to people or be careful what you say around them so they don't take it the wrong way or you don't end up being the weird one in their mind. That's exhausting. I don't get why people create what's right and what's wrong in their minds and you have to reach then they judge you whether you reach the certain standards in their minds or not.

I always wondered how exhausting it must be to constantly judge people based on what they think it's socially and morally acceptable or not. These must be such sad people. They don't know how to be themselves. They're afraid to be themselves so they show their anger at those who have the balls to express themselves by pointing fingers and saying that's not okay.

If you constantly live your life in fear of what other people think, you're not living your life for yourself. You're living it for them. You live to please the world and people around you, but you never please yourself. And I never wanted to be that person. I don't like to be around people like that, either.

When my break is over, I put the cigarette out and throw it into the trash. I make sure I make my face look pleasant and nice before going back inside. I have to wear this mask to get money. Because I need this money. I'm willing to pretend to be someone and something I'm not for it if I have to.

Harper doesn't suspect a thing.

I'm glad she's hard to wake up, although I make sure I'm as quiet as I can be. I didn't always have the chance to stay at her place so I don't want to mess it up or make it seem like I'm taking this for granted. I hate staying at my house. I rarely do. Harper understands it and she's trying to help me out as much as she can.

Harper doesn't know my whole story. She only knows the parts of it because even though she's the person I trust the most in the world, I still don't trust her enough to not tell anyone. She could tell her parents – my aunt and my uncle and then things wouldn't be pretty. People are unpredictable and I'm a person who doesn't trust easily, even those the closest to me. I have my guard up so high that probably no one can climb it.

A part of me feels guilty sometimes that I keep this from Harper, but I know she wouldn't understand. She'd try to make me quit the job and I can't do that. I don't like keeping things from her (well, some are acceptable to keep from her), but it's for the best. I know what I'm doing so I don't want to worry her even more since she worries about every little thing all the time.

I come to the bar in the evening as usual. I have a history book with me today. Not the one that's required in school. I've always liked history, it has always interested me. Especially the people, all the leaders and their motives.

Harper chats with me when she has time, asking me how was in school – like she always does. She asks me how I am a lot of times during the day and I know that she's afraid that I'm actually depressed or just deeply sad and thinking about harming myself. I know that because she admitted to me once when she got drunk, which never happens.

I'm not depressed. I'm not even sad. Truthfully, I don't know what I am. I just am. It's so hard to explain, but I always try to reassure her that I'm good and I'm fine and everything is okay and that I'll tell her if I ever have any kind of problems. She's a sweetheart, really. But that's the problem. She's just too sweet. And it's not me who she should be worried about, it's herself. That's part of the reason I come to the bar so often – Harper is too soft to deal with jackasses the way they should be dealt with.

And that's when I step in.

And speaking about jackasses ... "Hey, could you please move just a little bit, you're blocking the light," I say to the man that's leaning over the bar counter right next to me and preventing the light to illuminate my book so I can continue reading.

The man looks at me and then at my book, a distaste appearing on his face. Oh, here we go. "How about you go find yourself a library then, nerd." He turns his attention back to Harper, waiting for her to notice him while he doesn't even move an inch. "Can a man get a fucking beer in here or what."

Now, I usually don't care if people call me a nerd. I call myself a nerd because, heck yeah, I love learning and I love reading. Why should I feel ashamed of that? Why do other people even feel the need to shame others for that?

"Maybe she should get you a book about manners instead of a beer. It seems like you've already had enough of the latter, but you're lacking former."

Now I get his attention. He turns his whole body towards me. He reeks of alcohol. "The fuck did you just say?"

"You heard me, old man."

Harper loudly places the beer bottle on the bar counter, giving me a stare. "Behave," she mouths. I just roll my eyes at her. The man leaves right after he gets his beer and I eye him as he walks away. He looks at me a few times, too, wearing a dark expression. Such a sad soul you are.

I go back to reading my book, but a few pages after, I'm yet again disturbed. Well, not me directly, but Harper. But by someone I now recognise just by hearing his voice. Sadly. Fai the jackass appeared again. I see this is already going to be a good night.

He's standing on my right, his tall frame preventing me to see his face. He's dressed in all black again, which is not that surprising.

Harper is in front of him immediately, probably in fear that I'm going to try to engage in a conversation with him. Rest easy, dear, I don't want to talk to him.

I try to go back to reading, but the question he asks Harper makes me sharply turn my head to him. "Are you single?"

"Are you fucking serious?" I burst out, turning my whole body towards him. Is he dumb? Is he desperate? Or he's just wanting to play some stupid perversive games. "I told you to find someone else who'll sleep with you and she won't do it, either. Just walk away, dude, before I start feeling sorry for you."

Fai leans his elbow on the counter, facing me. "Kadie, sweetheart, there's no reason to be jealous." I scowl, making a face that must be full of disgust. He turns back to Harper. "Actually, my friend was wondering. He just thinks you're hot."

I stare at him for exactly three seconds before I burst out laughing. "In that case, you can tell him that she's not dating cowards."

Fai arches his eyebrow. "A coward? He's far from that. You know, it's really not nice to judge a person you don't even know."

"He doesn't even have the balls to come here and ask her for his number himself. That's cowardly. Make sure you deliver your message with the drinks." I smile.

I see Harper is trying to give me a stare and grab my attention, but I'm just enjoying myself.

"Maybe he was just scared of the rottweiler guarding her, a.k.a you." He chuckles.

"Let me spell it out for you since you clearly didn't understand it the first time: c-o-w-a-r-d."

"Fuck, can you just chill? He's not trying to date her, it's just a question. For fuck's sake, you're so difficult." He rakes his hand through his hair.

I'm not even affected by his words. They make me laugh, actually. "You already received the answer to your stupid question. Don't get mad now because it wasn't something you wanted." I pout a little, mocking him.

Harper slaps her hand down on the bar counter, but neither of us gives her the attention she's calling for. "Princess, I heard no answer coming from the person I asked that question. Now hide your claws because she can speak for herself."

"Seriously, can you just fuck off already and leave us alone? I get that you're trying to be cool and edgy with that macho show you're putting on, but it makes me cringe so badly, you have no idea. Just stay the fuck away from both of us."

Fai has the decency to chuckle that, completely disregarding my comment that wasn't funny at all. I meant every word I said. I just want him to stay the hell away from me and Harper and just mind his own damn business. I'm leaving him alone, as he wished, yet he's now being the one who's coming back here.

"Maybe I'll send my friend over here instead so you can bite some of his nerves off, too. I don't have many left anymore."

I roll my eyes. "Yeah, you're lacking some brain cells as well, check that too when you're at it."

Fai chuckles, shaking his head. "Man," he mutters to himself and just walks off, still smiling. I stare after him, killing him with just my stare. Harper interrupts me by slamming her hands down on the counter once again. "Kadience Rose Myers! What the hell is wrong with you?!"

"What?" I ask. "It's not my fault he manages to get on my very last nerve, okay? He's annoying."

"That doesn't mean you have to deal with him! Please, just – leave him alone, yeah? Just – leave him alone!" Harper is so frustrated she's turning red.

My face scrunches up. "So, what, did you want to give him your number or what's the deal now?"

"No!" Harper exclaims. "But I didn't want you to go into a full debate, either! Just don't do that. I told you people are talking about him and I don't want them to associate you with him, Kadie. Please. Talk to anyone else, just not him."

I shrug. "Yeah, alright. Whatever," I mutter, not having any energy to deal with people anymore tonight.

I feel Harper staring at me, but I just ignore her and go back to reading the book. I get that she's worried, but maybe she's overreacting. I haven't heard about him from anyone and even if I did, what is he going to do? He can bark all he wants if he doesn't know how to bite.

He's just trying to come off as intimidating and all macho, but he's really not fooling me and I'm not letting him get under Harper's skin. I don't care if he tries to play games with me, but Harper is a big no and I'm not letting him do that.

I have to reread the page I just read because I lost my focus and because I'm still fuming. And the night is still young, so who knows what else is going to happen.

Chapter 5

Although the night started out pretty badly and wasn't looking promising, no one bothers me anymore and I get to read my book in peace. Well, my definition of peace since the bar is loud with music and people.

I don't see Fai and his group of friends anymore, either. They most likely left, which makes me all too happy so I don't have to deal with him anymore tonight. It's weird because I don't think I've seen him come here before. At least he never came to the bar counter to order drinks before, yet now I somehow have a feeling that I'll see more of him and that makes me anxious, not because of me, but because I don't want him and his business anywhere near Harper.

Harper is too innocent for the bullshit. She wouldn't know how to stand up against him and I am not thinking this in a rude way. Harper is just a good person and believes in resolving things nicely or just avoiding to make it happen in the first place. I don't want her to deal with these losers. She shouldn't have to.

Harper knocks on the counter next to my book, making me look at her. "Come on, you bookworm. I'm done, let's get the hell out of here."

I put the bookmark in the book and close it, jumping from the barstool.

When we come outside, cold air hits me in the face. I close my jacket tighter around me. "You know, Kadie, maybe you could find a job after school since you want to go to college and it's quite expensive."

"Harp, don't worry about that. I'm working on it." I don't look her in the eyes.

She turns her body to fully face me. "Working on it how?" she sounds suspicious.

"Don't worry about it, really. I'm not putting myself in danger and that's all you need to know."

Harper gives me a tired look. I feel bad for not telling her, but she really can't know anything about my job. "I promise!"

Harper only shakes her head, not adding anything more to the conversation.

But outside the bar, we stumble upon a scene that makes both of us stop. Harper even stops breathing beside me, stumbling backwards, while I remain standing in the spot, my eyebrows lifting.

Even though it's mostly dark with a few lights around, I recognise Fai's voice. Unfortunately.

"You know what you owe us, you bitch ass. All the fucking begging you have going on won't help you pay shit!"

I put my palm over my mouth, but a laugh still escapes my mouth and one of the guys turns his head into my direction, immediately heading towards me and Harper. Harper lets out a small shriek, backing up and trying to drag me with her, but I don't move.

"Kadie!" Harper yells in panic and I see how Fai turns his head around to see where the voice came from and the guy who was coming towards us slows down.

"Fuck me. Are you serious? Is this chick out of her mind?" I hear one of them mutter.

"I hear you! I'm perfectly sane, but what the hell is wrong with you?"

"Kadie!" Harper says from somewhere in the back. She sounds angry.

I see Fai say something to the nearest guy to him and then someone else takes his position, holding the poor man by his throat and not letting him move while Fai takes fast strides towards me. "Kadie!" Harper whispers behind me while I'm just waiting for the storm to hit me.

Fai doesn't say a word when he comes near. He grabs my arm and starts dragging me away with full force, making my smile fall off my face. "What are you doing?" I say, trying to sound calm. Fai ignores me and that makes me explode. "What the fuck are you doing? Release my arm or I'm going to stab you." I'm not even kidding.

Harper's voice finds its strength again, it seems, when she runs after us, saying, "She's not joking, she's really going to stab you." Yes, Harper, thank you for clarifying. She sounds more afraid for him and I'm glad she knows I can turn him into a puddle if I want to.

Fai only clenches his jaw. He doesn't stop dragging me with him. He doesn't say anything – he doesn't even look at me. I make a fist and punch him in the forearm as hard as I can. He only glances at me, lifting his eyebrow.

"Can you fucking release me already? What the fuck is wrong with you?!" I scream, trying to punch him again but he grabs my wrist, narrowing his eyes on me.

"Calm down, will you?" he mutters roughly, his tone giving out how annoyed he is. Well, good. Because I'm fuming.

I make a movement to bite him in his arm, but he releases my hand before I can sink my teeth into his skin. "Jesus fucking Christ, you really are a psycho," he says more to himself than me, looking at me like he can't believe what he has to deal with.

I cross my arms over my chest. "You actually dare to call me a psycho? Look at you. Look at all of you!" I look at the other guys. Two of them are watching us while the other two are still saying something to the man.

Fai takes a step towards me, trying to look threatening, but I don't budge. "You can't be here," he tells me. He's speaking quieter than me, which only makes me raise my voice even higher.

"I can't be here? Really? It's you and your messy business who shouldn't be here! Honestly, Fai, I don't give two shits who you are or how dangerous you want to appear in other people's eyes, but if you came here to cause trouble ... you'll get trouble."

The corners of Fai's mouth lift. "What, princess? Are you trying to threaten me? Should I be afraid of you?" He leans his head closer to mine. "Are you going to scratch me with your claws?" he asks, dropping his voice, making fun out of me.

"No, I'm going to stab you with a knife if you don't get the fuck away from me."

Fai chuckles."Come on, now. Maybe it isn't the wisest idea to threaten me."

"I'm not afraid of you," I say. "You don't scare me."

"Maybe I don't want you to be afraid of me, princess," he replies.

"Stop calling me that. It's obnoxious."

"Fai, if you can't deal with the bitch and shut her up, I'll come there and gladly do the work for you!" one of the guys suddenly calls over to us.

Fai turns to look at him, but he doesn't say anything. I don't even see the look he gives him. But me ... boy. "What did you just call me? Do you wanna come here and repeat it, clown face?"

I move forward, but Fai stops me with his arm, only looking up at the sky in annoyance.

"I think you heard me perfectly clear. I don't like repeating myself either."

"Kadie, should I go get the bodyguard?" Harper asks from somewhere behind me. "I'm going to get him," she answers her own question, clearly shaken up by the scene.

Fai's eyes lay on her and he gives her a serious look. "I would advise you against it," he tells her in a low, dark voice that makes me roll my eyes. Stop trying so hard, will you?

I surge forward again, but Fai is holding me in place. I sink my nails into his forearm, trying to get him to release me. "Will you just fucking let me go?" I push against his arm again. I don't usually go for violence, but this guy. This guy makes me want to commit murder right now. "Let me go, goddamn!" I yell.

And then Fai pushes me back against my struggle and his lips are suddenly on me, kissing me so fast it takes me a few too many seconds to react. I push against his chest, a noise coming out of my throat. I bite his bottom lip as hard as I can and he pulls back, releasing me this time. I take a few steps back, away from him, looking at him as if he lost his mind. "What the hell do you think you're doing?" I ask, my voice faint now – completely opposite from my yelling before.

"Shutting you the fuck up. What does it look like? You're annoying me and everyone else here by involving in a business that doesn't concern you. Now that you're listening to me: walk away, princess. This isn't the scene for you."

My hands are shaking and I squeeze them into fists so he doesn't see. I'm not scared of him. I'm more in disbelief of what he just dared to do. "Move your business somewhere else. I don't want to ever see you here again," I tell him, meaning every word. I wipe my mouth with my sleeve, looking him in the eyes while doing so, giving him a look of pure disgust.

I walk to Harper who stands in the corner with wide eyes, not knowing what to do with herself. "Let's go," I tell her. My voice sounds dead. Emotionless.

I don't turn around as I walk away. I don't care if Fai watched me leave or immediately went back to his group, all I know is that I need to get the hell away from here and from him before I do anything crazy. And I'll be damned if I'm going to let him see how much he wrecked me inside with the action he took. He shouldn't have done that. He shouldn't.

I wrap my arms around myself, walking to the car wordlessly. Harper stays wisely quiet – but that's probably from the shock and she's still processing what happened and not because she senses my inner struggle. She doesn't really know much about it so I don't think she knows why exactly Fai shouldn't do what he just did.

When we sit in the car, Harper doesn't start it immediately. She sits there for a few seconds and I look at her. "What?" I speak only to make her look at me. She doesn't say anything. "Harper, what's up?"

I see her swallow. "Kadie ... these guys ..." She shakes her head, letting out a shaky breath. Okay. So she's still processing it. Although I don't even think there's really much to process because we couldn't see much. I ran away like a chicken before I could do something about what was going on there.

"Yeah, they're major jerks. I know."

She shakes her head. "I meant to say they're really dangerous."

I cock my head to the side. "I beg to differ, but okay."

"Kadie, stop this!" Harper snaps. "You're trying to be this fearless badass, acting like you're not afraid of what could happen to you, but what if they did something to you? You should just leave them alone and walk away. Don't go around, playing a superhero and saving people because you're going to end up just like them." I see tears pooling in her eyes and – fuck, it makes me suddenly feel bad, although I only feel bad for what she had to see, not for what I did. Not that I did anything much there.

"Harp, that's the thing. That's why people get hurt. Beaten. Murdered. Because people are afraid to help people. They're afraid to get hurt themselves so they rather run away than save someone. I don't want to be that person. I'm really not afraid of words, Harp and if getting hurt means that I help someone – then so be it." And I mean it. Because I know how it is to be in their skin. I know how it is to be hurting and no one does anything to help you. To reach out to you. Because of fear.

But fear is something I learned to live with. Nothing much makes me afraid and there's no pretence in it. I feel the adrenaline and maybe a little rush, but there's no fear living inside of me. That fear was killed a long, long time ago. Because when you experience some fucked-up shit and survive it, you realise you're a survivor and you can survive a lot of things. Fear is a liar. And fearless people are people we should fear.

"You have such a self-destructive behaviour ... I wish you'd stop being so reckless sometimes. You worry the hell out of me, Kadie. I literally didn't know what to do out there because I was paralysed in fear. I started imagining all sort of things and I literally do not know what I'd do if he hurt you."

"Oh, Harp. I promise to you that I'm not going to put myself in so much trouble I'd get hurt. Especially not by him. I know you think I'm stupid, but I'm smart enough to recognise real danger. And this isn't it. Believe me."

"I don't think you're stupid, Kadie, please," Harper says immediately and she makes me feel bad yet again because she sounds so ... sad and tired. And, most of all, worried.

"I'm sorry, Harp. I'm sorry for what you had to see, but I'm not sorry for stepping up to them and saying what needed to be said. Someone had to."

Harper is quiet for a few seconds. "He kissed you," she says, her voice barely a whisper. She's still grasping her mind around it.

I look away, shifting in my seat and looking out of the window, my insides getting all twisted in an unpleasant way when I think about it again. "Yeah. And it would be way better if he punched me instead."

I feel Harper looking at me, waiting for me to say something – answer everything she wants to ask but she doesn't dare to, but I just close my eyes and block it all out, not wanting to speak about him anymore and think of everything I shouldn't.

Harper turns the car on and we're driving away. Away from the memories. Away from the pain.

Chapter 6

I have a happy place.

And that's the rooftop at Harper's dorm. It's really nothing special, it's just abandoned and dirty rooftop, but that's why I love it so much. No one ever comes up here.

It's windy up here tonight. There's a big, thick concrete wall, but not big enough to hide the view this height has to offer. But the wall isn't my limit. I usually climb up on it, sitting there or standing on it, just looking down at the streets beneath – the cars, the people; everything.

Standing so close to the edge at such height gives me a rush and it fills me with adrenaline. I'm not suicidal and I don't think about throwing myself off, but I could. I could end it all by just taking one step. And that's what brings me a rush. I'm dancing on the edge of death.

I often think what goes through someone's mind when they're standing so close to the edge, minutes away from ending it all. And what goes through their minds in those seconds they're falling. Are they happy? Relieved? Scared? Regretting it?

Do they feel the same rush I do when I'm up here?

I come up here when I need to think. When I need a reminder that life can still be great, no matter how many bad things happen. Looking down and knowing I'm seconds away from dying if I decided to makes me think back on all the good times and makes me appreciate everything nice happening to me. Because when you're used to bad things, you appreciate the nice things a little bit more.

I'm a dreamer. I'm a person with dreams and plans. I'm reminded of it. I want to become someone in life. I'm curious where I'll be years from now. This is why I could never jump. I still have hope. Because I know I can do everything I put my mind to – everyone can. And I'm still too curious about why I was put on this Earth. Everyone has a mission here. Every single person exists for a reason. We're either here to cause good or cause bad. But we're here for a reason.

And if you decide to jump, you'll never find what that reason is. You'll end it all before you could experience the best days of your life.

I light up a cigarette, pull it between my lips, drag a smoke and exhale it, watching the smoke disappear into the night. I know this is a bad habit. I know how unhealthy it is, I've read all about it, but it still doesn't stop me. I'll die anyway, so why not enjoy it while I can? Even though it's bad for me, I love doing it.

If it kills me, then so be it.

I didn't go to the bar for five days straight. I had a lot of studying to do and I prefer to do it in the library when I have everything I need available at the reach of my hand. I don't usually have to learn a lot before tests since I have a good memory and I remember a lot from just listening in class, but I still like to read more on topics that I find interesting and just go an extra mile. Not for the grade, but for myself.

I never cared much about being the best student. I mean, my behaviour is anything but good. I'm a no-bullshit person. I don't tolerate disrespect. If anyone has to say something about me, I make them say to my face. And they quickly think twice about saying their thoughts about me.

I don't care what they talk behind my back. I care what they say to my face. Pussies don't interest me.

Five days after not going to the bar, I finally go back. I have to say I kind of missed it. This became one of my habits, too.

Harper gives me a smile when she sees me. We haven't seen each other much these past days, either, but we talked over the phone.

Josh, the security guy, greets me with, "And we thought you forgot about us already!"

I grin. "Not going to happen," I tell him. I love how welcomed I feel here. Like many other people, but each for different reasons.

It's one of the rare nights I didn't bring any books or notebooks with me as well because I'm planning on leaving early. I agreed to come to work early tonight because we're hosting a special event and it's going to be crowded. Even more crowded than usual. That's why it's one of the rare nights I just sit at the bar and enjoy being where I am.

I don't look around the bar. I don't care who's here.

"Hey, Kadie. Finished with studying already?" Harper asks me.

I give her a knowing smile. "The day I'll stop learning new things is the day I die, Harper, dear."

Harper chuckles. "Dear God, I wish I had your motivation and hunger for learning."

I put my chin on my hand under my chin to support it. "I just like knowing things, Harp. That's it." And that really is it. I just like knowing stuff. "I'm going home earlier tonight," I say.

Harper's face becomes serious. "Home or my place?" Harper asks.

"Home," I lie. I can't really tell her where I'm going and if I said anything else, it'd be suspicious.

"Alright, then," Harper says. Harper got used to me staying at her place most of the time. She didn't ask me many questions as to why I don't like staying at home. She just thinks I don't get along with my parents. And that's the truth, but she doesn't know the real reasons behind it.

I get off the stool. "Are you going already?" Harper asks.

"No, I'm just going out for a cigarette," I say.

Harper's face can't hide the disapproval. "Kadie ..." she starts in a tone that says she's about to give me a lesson on health.

"I know, I know," I brush her off. "Just let me enjoy my life a little. You know I like bad habits." I give her a wink.

She only shakes her head in disapproval.

I manage to get out fairly fast since the crowd isn't that big yet, going to my usual spot outside behind the building in the pure darkness. This place is slightly hidden by the thick wall, although no one could see me anyway since it's pitch black back here. That means no one comes back here and I have peace.

I take out a cigarette and light it, putting it between my lips. I rest my head back against the cold wall, closing my eyes.

But my peace is quickly disturbed.

"You fucked him up real good, man."

"That piece of shit deserved it. He knew it was coming."

"Shiiit. There was a lot of blood."

"We still didn't get any many out of him. You know we have to pay Mav soon or we'll be the ones spitting out blood."

A pause. "I'll handle it. That man better hope the closest to him have some money, or shit's about to get ugly."

Oh, fuck me. I bang my head against the wall, chuckling to myself. Do I have to run into him every time I'm here now? This is just getting on my last nerves now. The voices stop and then just seconds later, a body presses me into the wall, a hand coming to my collar to grab me. A light comes on, directly in my eyes. I shut them closed.

I don't have to look at who attacked me. Not that I only recognise his voice, I realise I recognise his cologne, too. Well, aren't we getting acquainted with each other ...

I sigh in disappointment. "Oh, come on. Don't stop on my behalf, that was entertaining to listen to." I slap his hand away from my collar so he releases me.

I look at him, the flashlight now turned upwards so I can see his face, too. "What did you hear?" he asks, his voice low and angry.

I smirk. "Wouldn't you like to know?" I ask, dragging the cigarette and exhaling the smoke into his face. He doesn't even flinch.

"Stop fucking around, Kadience. I asked you something."

"Aren't you in a good mood this fine evening?"

Fai takes a step closer. I can see his face clearer now. He looks pissed. The different eye colours always throw me off. Not in a bad way, it's just fascinating because he's the first person I've ever seen that on. It's very rare. "Kadie. What. The. Fuck. Did. You. Hear?"

I shrug, twirling a strand of my hair between my fingers. "Enough to figure it out what was going on," I purposefully don't play dumb and don't say what he wants to hear. I won't lie. I don't care if he knows that I heard everything. It's not my fault. I wasn't eavesdropping, I was just here. "So, who did you kill, Fai? You might give me some more information, the cops will appreciate it."

"You're not telling anyone shit about this," Fai warns.

I slowly lift my eyebrow. "I'm not staying quiet just because you said so, either," I challenge.

I see his jaw clench. "What do you want, Kadie? What's it gonna take?"

"Now we're talking." I grin. "It so happens that I'm in a need of a ride home."

Fai is quiet for some seconds, debating my request. "No," he finally answers.

I shrug. "Alright then, pretty boy. Don't say I didn't give you a choice." I pat his cheek and I want to go past him, but he grabs my arm, not letting me leave. He's looking straight forward, gritting his teeth together. "Is that all? A ride home?" he asks.

"I'm not that cheap, babe. But it'll be a good start."

"What a fucking mess," he mutters under his breath, releasing my arm. "Walk," he orders me.

"Sure, whatever you say," I can't help myself but step on his nerves a little bit more.

He only grunts in response.

I quietly chuckle. He has no idea what's going to hit him.

I speed up my pace so I walk next to him, not letting him be in charge of anything. "You have heterochromia iridium, a difference in iris colouration or, simply said, mismatching eye colours."

"Yeah. So?" Fai asks completely disinterestedly.

"Brown eyes are rich in melanin, whereas blue eyes lack high levels of melanin. If your eye colour changes after you're an infant, it's called acquired heterochromia. But it can also be caused by injuries, such as a hit in the eye, or eye diseases such as glaucoma or eye cancer. Or it can simply be genetic."

"Did you swallow an encyclopedia or something? Get to the fucking point already, you freak. I didn't hear half of the things you just said because I can't find myself to give a shit about your scientific research. The fuck, man."

"I was about to get to the point before you rudely interrupted," I say. He doesn't say anything in return. "I was just wondering if you got this genetically, from the injury or disease. It's a rare condition."

Fai stops completely to look at me, his eyebrows furrowing and he's looking at me with his eyes slightly narrowed, showing he's not ecstatic about my question. "Are you for real right now? That's none of your fucking business."

"You're so boring," I mutter.

"And you're so fucking annoying. Now walk with your mouth shut," he grumbles.

I show my tongue out at his back when he once again walks in front of me. When we reach the guys, they immediately shut up when they spot me. "Ah. Look what the cat dragged in," one of them comments.

"She's literally everywhere," Fai says in annoyance.

"Fai, you might've gotten yourself a stalker."

I huff. "Fat chance," I say. "Maybe it's the other way around."

Fai gives me another angry look, willing me to stay quiet. I lift my head up higher in defiance. "Come on, the sooner I get you home, the faster I won't have to deal with you anymore today," Fai says.

The men look at each other. "Taking her home, Fai?"

"Yes. Shut up, I don't want to hear about it."

"On your motorcycle? You know what that means, right?" Another one of them asks.

Fai curses under his breath. "Shut up," he says once again. Wow, some nice comebacks you have there. "Let's go, princess."

"Bye guys, it was nice seeing you!" I call out to them, chuckling when Fai grunts in annoyance again.

I run after him. "What does me riding on your motorcycle mean?" I ask him.

Fai doesn't answer me.

"Okay, I understand now. Thank you for your answer," I say rolling my eyes.

"Just shut up already, will you? Fuck's sake," he mutters, kicking a pebble.

We come to his motorcycle that's parked in the front. It's not hard to see who's the 'leader' of their group. He swings his leg over the motorcycle, putting a helmet on his head. I stand there and just wait. "You getting on or can I leave you here?" he asks.

"Am I not getting a helmet?"

"No," he gives a simple answer.

"What a gentleman. What if I die?"

"That sounds your personal problem, honestly."

He turns the motorcycle on, making sure I can't say anything more to him.

I climb on the motorcycle behind him. "Where am I taking you?"

I'm not dumb enough to tell him my home address, but I tell him an address close to my house. Not close to Harper's place, but my parents' house. I don't care if he ever finds out by himself where the house is located, he can burn it down for all I care. But I'm not giving him the address on a silver plate, either.

Another thing I learn about Fai tonight is that he's fast and dangerous on the motorcycle. I don't know if he's doing this on purpose because I'm with him and he wants to scare me or whatever, but he should know that I love living on the edge. I love everything dangerous.

I hide my head behind his back so the wind isn't slapping me in the face, but I enjoy the speed and the swerving. It doesn't scare me. It excites me.

When we come to the dark, narrow streets close to my house, Fai slowly comes to the stop, putting a leg down and looking around. I jump off the motorcycle, fixing my hair a little that's sticking out in all ways.

Fai takes the helmet off. "You sure we're on the right street? I don't see any mansions here, princess."

"Maybe you'll realise I'm more of a witch than a princess. And witches don't live in castles, Fai, boy." I wink at him. "Thanks for the ride. I might ask you for a ride home more often now since I don't feel like walking that much." I don't walk home, I usually take the bus if I'm not going with Harper.

"Don't count on it," he says, not exactly ecstatic about the idea. "So, we're good?" He takes his hand through his hair.

"Not even close. I don't want to see you at the bar or around there anymore. Then we'll be good," I tell him, being serious as I can.

Fai looks away. "Pick something else, bee, because I can't grant you that wish."

I shrug. "Have it your way then, babe." I wave at him. "Hopefully I won't see you around anymore."

I turn and walk away, smiling. I hear him mutter, "This fucking bitch," behind me. My smile grows.

Chapter 7

When I step into my room, making sure I lock the door, I remember that I told Harper I'm going out for a cigarette and then I never came back.

"Shoot," I mutter to myself, taking my phone out of my pocket and see I already have five missed calls from her and dozens of texts. I immediately call her back.

"Kadie! Where are you?" she asks hurriedly, picking up on the second ring.

"I'm at home. Sorry I disappeared on you, I didn't want to make you worried, but I'm all good."

"You make me want to kill you sometimes, I swear. How did you get home? Did you walk? In the dark?" She never lets me walk around alone in the dark. I mean, she has a point, but I have a knife and good self-defence skills so I'm not that worried for myself.

"No, Harp. Don't worry, I'm fine. Heading to bed now," I lie.

"It's a little early for you," she comments.

"I know. I'm tired," I say. And that's not a lie.

"Okay, I won't keep you up, then. Goodnight," she wishes me.

"Goodnight," I tell her, feeling bad for lying to her. But it's for a good cause, I tell myself. If she knew where I was going, she'd be more worried and she shouldn't be. The less she knows, the better.

I thought I was already tasting victory and having a reason to celebrate when I haven't seen Fai at the bar for five days straight. But my luck is short-lived.

One of his guys comes to me and says, "Walk with me," without any greeting or any explanation.

I slightly turn on the stool so I have a better view of him, placing my arm around the back of the chair. "Oh, he sent his minions today? Tell your king I'm good."

"Kadience, walk," he tells me.

"Sweetie pie, I don't take orders. You can go walk if you want, I'm good where I am."

"Fai is outside. He wants to speak to you."

"And I'm inside. If he wants to speak to me, you can tell him where he can find me. Although I'd prefer if he didn't."

The man sighs, rolling his eyes so hard it must probably hurt. "Now I see why he's on the verge of losing his fucking mind," he mutters. "I'm not gonna deal with your annoying ass," he says, walking straight out of the club.

I shake my head. "Weak," I mutter to myself.

Harper is in front of me in seconds. "Another one?" she asks me, not even slightly happy about me talking with one of them as she refers to them now.

"Nope, I actually don't know what he wanted, but he for sure didn't get it."

"You should've left them alone, Kadie, now they're all after you."

"I think they want to come across as scary, but they're just being annoying." I shrug.

Harper looks behind my shoulder and her eyes widen slightly. A second later, Fai appears by my side, putting his hand on my shoulder so I face him. "Get the fuck outside. Now," he growls harshly, his serious face getting close to mine.

I look around myself. "Sorry, what? Who are you trying to speak to like that?"

Fai's face gets even closer to mine. "Kadience, get the fuck outside. I'm not playing games with you tonight, this is serious."

John, the bodyguard, is immediately by my side. "Troubles, Kadie?" he asks while eyeing Fai.

"No, J, it's all good. He's harmless." I put my hand on Fai's cheek. "As if hearing a puppy barking."

Fai leans his head back, away from my touch. "What the fuck."

I get down from the stool, intentionally slowly. "It's alright, J, I'm just going to see what this drama queen wants tonight and I'll be back. Won't take longer than five minutes, right, Fai?"

"Oh, yeah. I can probably kill you in three, depends on how generous I'm feeling."

John immediately takes a threatening step closer to Fai and I have to chuckle. "I would like to see you try," I tell him, still laughing. "Walk now, I have better things to do than to ruin my evening talking to you."

Fai is walking behind me. I don't give him the chance to lead today simply because I don't want him to feel he has an upper hand. He doesn't.

The second I step outside, a group of his friends surrounds me, making me stop and lift my eyebrows. "Okay, so what crime did I commit?" I ask, completely uninterested.

"Who the fuck did you tell what you heard?" Fai asks me, his face close to mine. I can smell the cigarettes in his breath and it makes me crave one.

I grin, crossing my arms. "Oh, boy. You've been busted already? You aren't as good as you portray yourselves then."

"Kadie, I swear to fucking God, don't make me lose my mind. Who. The. Fuck. Did. You. Open. Your. Mouth. To.?"

"I mean, I don't know ..." I look at my nails. "Maybe it would help me to remember if you asked me just a little bit nicer ..."

Fai steps back from me, putting both of his hands in his hair, turning around so his back is towards me. "Someone help me before I kill her, I'm not kidding," he says with clear exasperation in his voice. He's on the verge of losing it.

I bite down on my lip, smiling. It's so fun playing with his head. He gets frustrated so easily. "Listen here, bitch. If we get in trouble because of you, you're going down, too. You were seen and if any of them recognise your face, you're going down."

"We don't know if they saw her, alright? Fuck! I don't need this on top of everything now," Fai says.

"Yeah? Well, maybe you should've thought about this before and be more careful!" another one speaks up.

Fai is immediately in his face, his hands at his neck, pushing him hard against the wall. "Maybe consider the words and the tone coming out of your mouth before you open it again next time."

"Okay, guys, can I go back inside now? This is clearly not con- cerning me and I'm getting bored with your childish outbursts. You have the wrong person, I didn't tell anyone shit. Maybe go interview someone else you pissed off, I'm sure I'm not the only one."

One of the guys grabs my arm when I try to get inside and I react quickly, trying to hit him in the leg, but he's faster and he decks the move. "Stop trying to play dirty, I'm not afraid to hit a woman."

My nose scrunches in disgust and I look at him up and down. "Yeah, you do look like a fucking scumbag like that."

His nostrils flare and he lifts his hand in preparation to hit me, but the hit never comes because Fai grabs his hand and pulls him away from him. "We're not doing this," he tells him. "You know the rule and you know what happens if you break it."

I wrap my hands around myself, rolling my bottom lip into my mouth. A sudden breeze sends chills down my body and I start shaking. I lower my eyes to the ground and take deep, long breaths. In. Out. In. Out. Slow and steady like I taught myself.

Fai then steps to me, looking calmer than before. "Look, you may or may not be in trouble. And you're in even bigger trouble if you talked shit around so it'd be better to tell what you know."

"Hold up." I hold my hands out. "Who exactly am I in trouble with? And why?" I feel like they're bullshitting and they're trying to scare me just so I talk. Too sad it won't work, but I give them a point for trying.

Fai looks as if he doesn't exactly know how to answer my question. "Can't tell you who, I can only tell you you're gonna have problems."

I chuckle. "Okay. Thanks for the bedtime story."

"No, I'm fucking serious, Kadience. Stop taking this as a joke because it's really not. You have no idea the shit you could get involved with."

"Aww, don't worry about me, babe. I didn't say anything to anyone yet so I think I'm good. But thanks for worrying about me." I pat his chest, directly over his heart. "Looks like you have something in here after all. Who would've thought?"

He grabs my hand and removes it, his jaw ticking. "Don't fucking say I didn't warn you."

I laugh. "Yeah, okay, kids. Have fun with all the dangerous stuff you're doing." I salute them. What he fails to understand is that I crave danger. I've been broken through and through and I need something to make me feel alive. The lines between good and bad are blurred for me and I've chased danger all my life because I can't help myself.

I've dealt with people like Fai before, maybe even worse. Kissed them. Fucked them. Yelled at them. Got yelled at by them - you name it. I like to deliberately put myself in dangerous situations sometimes to feel something. To fight for my life and either come out pumped with adrenaline and happy that I get to live longer or I end up dead. But I need this adrenaline in my life in order to feel alive. Nothing else works for me.

I go back into the bar and Harper is on me the second she sees me. "What was that? What do you have with them, Kadie?"

"Nothing, Harp. Literally nothing. They're just being annoying, that's really it. They thought I'm an easy target but, hopefully, they're seeing they were wrong."

Harper blows the breath out of her mouth, standing in a motherly stance – her hands on her hips, her eyes right on mine. "He kissed you and you're still talking to them. I don't understand. Do you have a thing with him? You'd tell me if you did, right? I know I must come across as non-understanding and I look like I'm forbidding you, but I don't want you to hide things from me. If you have something going on with them, no matter what it is, I'd like to know, even if I don't approve."

"Harp, no. I don't have anything going on with anyone. You would know, okay? I would tell you, but they're just trying to mess with my head and I don't let them which frustrates the shit out of them. Let's not talk about them because they're not important." I don't tell Harper what I saw the other night simply because she'd lose her shit. I hope they're going to get the hell away from this bar and find a new place to hang out.

Harper nods. She knows I tell her more than any other person. She knows she's the only one that I trust and she also knows that some things, I have to keep to myself, but I always tell her what she needs to know. I don't want to worry her, but she loves to do it. She loves beating herself up for things that she can't change – me, for instance.

"Please, Harp, for my sake, try to stay out of trouble. Don't put me in the grave because of worrying at such a young age. I want to experience my life just a little bit more."

I laugh whole-heartedly. "Don't worry, I'm going to be right by your side when you marry some boring doctor."

Harper shows me tongue.

The universe doesn't want me to live my life in peace.

When I come to the bar the next night, Fai is leaning against the door outside. I let out a frustrated sigh, filled with anger and go straight to him. "I thought we had a deal."

Fai is carelessly leaning against the wall, his foot placed on the wall, his arms crossed. He's dressed in all black – black leather jacket, black jeans and black boots. His usual attire. "The deal's off. People are already talking."

"But not because of me. I did my part."

He leans in close to my face. "There's no deal, bee. Accept it."

I huff. "So? When are you going to jail?" I provoke.

Fai chuckles dryly. "I'm not going anywhere, but you're going to have to come with me."

My eyebrow raises in suspicion. "I'm going to have to come with you? I don't think so." I shake my head, trying to move past him, but he grips my arm.

"Go inside and you're dead."

My whole body stills and I daringly look him in the eyes – slowly. "You're not going to kill me, stop bullshitting."

"No, it won't be me. You were recognised, Kadie. There are people in there who want to see you."

"I was recognised where? By whom?" I want to think this is some kind of game where he wants to scare the crap out of me, but something in his voice and the way he's carrying himself makes me believe he's actually telling the truth, although it doesn't really make much sense.

Fai eyes the person that walks out of the bar, pushing me to the side so I'm hidden. I rip my arm out of his hold. "What the fuck is going on with you?" I ask him in anger.

"Listen, bee, I can't tell you much because you have a big mouth, but I'm advising you not to go into the bar because it's a high possibility you'll get in trouble."

"By who?" I ask, having a hard time believing whatever he's trying to say.

Fai grunts. "Can't tell you. You were seen with me and that is not good. Maybe I should just throw you to the wolves and let them eat you alive so I don't ever have to deal with you again, though," he thinks out loud.

"Then why don't you?"

"Good question," he mutters. "I'm kind of responsible for this and I might be an asshole but I'm not that big of an asshole to at least not warn you about it."

"Okay, my hero. So if those dangerous people who saw me with you are in there, that means they're in the same space as Harper. And now, my friend, this is going to be a problem."

"Your friend's fine. The boys are in there having an eye on her."

"Are you fucking serious?" I ask. "I swear to God if you do anything to her, I won't hesitate to murder your ass. I'm not kidding, Fai."

The door opens again and Fai tenses up, looking at whoever walks out. He relaxes when it's not the person he was afraid to see. "Listen, bee, I'd be glad to stay here and listen to your cute threats, but we have to get going."

"Get going where?"

"Away from here."

"That's not an answer," I say, growing annoyed with this whole situation.

"It's the only one you're getting. Get the fuck on the motorcycle now," he grunts, pushing me so I have no choice but to walk.

"I'm not going anywhere with you."

Fai swiftly turns me around so I'm looking at him again. "Listen here and listen carefully. I could let you walk the fuck in that club and let you and your cute little friend in there get completely fucked over – literally. Or I'll be kind enough to warn you and drive you away from here so no one sees you."

"No one's fucking anyone over, there are bodyguards in there."

Fai knocks on my head. "Bee, if you think they'd be stupid enough to do anything tonight ..." He shakes his head. "They're only here to get a good look at how you look. They'll attack some other time."

"You know what, I don't believe a word you're saying. I'm not dumb enough to go anywhere with you. Especially since you believe it was me spreading the word around about whatever the hell happened that other night."

Fai looks somewhere behind me. "Fuck." He forcingly puts a helmet on my head. "No words. Get on the motorcycle."

"Wha–"

"No fucking words, Kadience," he grits out, straddling the motorcycle. I turn around to see a man looking directly at us and when he sees me looking at him, he starts walking towards when Fai and I are standing. I raise an eyebrow under the helmet, watching him with interest. I don't have a clear view of his face, but I see him pulling out a gun.

I sigh to myself. "This is some fucking bullshit," I mutter but climb on the motorcycle behind Fai because maybe he might've been right and someone came here to kill me tonight.

How awesome.

Chapter 8

Fai drives even crazier than the last time I rode with him. It's fast with a lot of swerving and a lot of fast turns. The thrill of it all actually makes me laugh. This is the kind of rush I enjoy in life while many other people fear it. This is what makes me feel alive.

I don't even trust Fai enough to drive with him like that, I especially shouldn't trust him to be driving as recklessly as he's doing, but that doesn't even matter. This makes my blood flow and this makes my heart race.

I don't know where Fai is taking us. To be honest, I don't think I even care. Sometimes I wonder about myself and the things I fear because rarely anything makes me scared in life. The things that make people shake in fear only make my adrenaline run high and those are the things that excite me.

This moment, for example. Someone was pointing a gun at me tonight and now I'm driving on the motorcycle with someone I don't know somewhere I don't know. I don't look behind me if anyone is following us. I know they are. If they weren't Fai wouldn't make all the sudden turns and drive like a maniac.

I watch the world passing by, having no idea where I am. We're driving between cars, driving past them, making people look at us like we're crazy. I laugh in the thrill.

We go up some hill with a lot of turns. We stop when we come up and I realise we're basically in the middle of nowhere. There is a meadow all around us and a great view of the city, which makes me believe we must be somewhere on the border of the city.

I jump off the motorcycle, pulling the helmet off my head and look around. "Oh, great. One man points a gun at me, the other one kidnaps me. My day is ending great."

"Chill, no one is kidnapping your annoying ass."

I give him a dirty look.

Fai gets off his motorcycle and walks to the side of the road, close to where I'm standing. He goes a little further down and sits down on the grass, lighting a cigarette. "What? Are we having a picnic here or something? Take me home."

"Bee, sit down and give me a break from your voice, yeah?" Fai mumbles, not even looking at me.

I stare at him in disbelief. There's not a single soul around, but at least the view is nice. I sit down directly beside him and he looks at me from the corners of his eyes, shifting away just a little. I roll my eyes. "Harper is going to worry about where I am and if she worries, she starts asking questions."

Fai looks at me. "The hell does that have to do with me? Call her or something, tell her you're still breathing, I don't care."

I write her a message and tell her I won't be able to make it to the bar tonight. "Okay, now explain to me what's going on and give me more details than you did."

Fai gives me a are you serious look, staring at me for a few seconds before saying, "Can you go five minutes without talking?"

"No, Fai, I really fucking can't, so I suggest you start explaining what the hell I'm doing here and why someone pointed a fucking gun at me tonight and I advise you do it fast before I really lose it. And you don't want that."

"Or what?" he asks.

"I can throw a mean punch."

Fai chuckles, shaking his head. "I'm not gonna fight you, bee, that's for damn sure."

"Why? Because I'm a girl? I know how to punch someone if I have to."

Fai huffs, dragging another puff of his cigarette. "You're not punching anyone, either."

I decide it's pointless to even argue with him because it seems like I won't get anywhere, even though I can be very stubborn and persuasive when I get something into my head. I don't quit easily. "How about you tell me the mess you brought me into and then I'll decide if there needs to be any punching done."

Fai has his legs bent and he drops his arm over one knee. "What I tell you, you don't tell anyone. Not even your friend."

I lift my chin up. "You don't tell me that. I'll decide what to do with whatever you tell me."

He glares at me. "Do you want to know anything or not?"

"I have the right to know," I correct him.

He sighs pointedly, making sure I know I'm jumping on his last nerve. Serves him right. "I can't believe I have to deal with your annoying ass," he mutters. "Here's the thing. I fucked up when I let you ride on my motorcycle because someone saw us who definitely shouldn't see us. There's a rule that we only let our girls sit on our motorcycle and no one else. I'm not people's favourite and the word spread around so now people think you're my girl and you're in big trouble right now because they're after your head to hurt me."

I stare at him while my brain is processing all this information. "I can't say if you're making all this up or you're playing some childish games, going around about this gangster shit and believe how dangerous you are."

"I'm not making anything up, bee. You really think I'd willingly drive you away from the bar and spend time with you? I'm getting annoyed just hearing your voice."

I roll my eyes. "You were inviting me in your bed to scream your name, you're not fooling anyone here, sugar boy."

Fai doesn't say anything, just looks forward and takes another drag of his cigarette.

"So now, what? I wait until someone shoots me in the head? Can you at least tell me when do you think will happen so I know how many days I have to enjoy my life?"

"No one's shooting you. You're going to avoid the bar until I settle this mess and then you can go around annoying everyone around you again. Just stay low for a few days, that's it."

I can't believe what I'm hearing. "And Harper?"

Fai shrugs. "My boy threw an eye on her. She's going to be fine."

I turn my upper body so I'm fully facing him now. "You all better stay away from her because you're not worthy to even breathe the air she's breathing. You hear me?"

Fai looks at me from the sides of his eyes. "So, what? Are you going to protect her? Come on, princess. You're starting to make me laugh."

I go right into his face, grabbing his leather jacket. "I'm capable of killing for her. Don't fucking try me because it's gonna be your head the gun will be pointed at the next time."

Fai grabs my hand and removes it from his jacket, his face now losing all humour and is replaced with aggravation and anger. His jaw ticks. "Listen here, baby girl, I'm doing you a big fucking favour so maybe think twice about your words before I just say fuck it and let you die."

"Kill me, I don't care. Let others kill me, I don't care either. But make a hair on her head go missing – boy, I know people who know people. And let me tell you; you're going to be dead men walking. All of you."

Fai searches my face for a few seconds. I see my words hit him and settle into him because he leans back a little, visibly calmer than before. "Chill, he's not going to marry her. He knows she's goody two shoes and she's fragile like a fucking butterfly. He's not going to pursue her."

I sit back, immediately more relaxed when hearing this. I can't be sure if he's speaking the truth or just talking bullshit, but something makes me think that him giving me his word in his own way means I should believe him because he's telling the truth. I'm still staying cautious. I need to talk to John as soon as possible so he watches Harper extra carefully. Just in case.

"Can I have a cigarette?" I ask Fai.

"No," he returns immediately, not even looking at me.

We sit in silence for some minutes, just looking at the view this hill offers. It's nice, but I'm starting to feel bored and anxious. I want to go back. I stand up, brushing my pants to get rid of glass. "I'm bored. Can you just take me back?"

Fai looks up at me as if I lost my mind. "You're really not taking my words seriously, huh? You got a death wish or something?"

"No, I heard you. I just have things to do and places to be. I don't have time to hide from people who want to kill me at the moment." I shrug.

"You're really insane," Fai chuckles, shaking his head to himself in disbelief. He presses the tip of his cigarette into the grass to put it out and throws it away.

"You better pick that up," I tell him warningly.

He sighs. "Or fucking what, bee?"

"I get you're an asshole, Fai, you don't have to try so hard. You can be an asshole without harming the nature more than it already is."

"Do you see a wastebin here? No? Do you want to put it in your pocket until you find the nearest one, then?"

I roll my eyes, looking up at the sky. "The Universe really tends to send me people who test my patience," I mutter to myself. I sit back down by his side. "Can I see your tattoos?"

Fai gives me a weird look. "Is this your excuse to see me naked?"

"If I wanted to see you naked, I'd tell you. I want to see the tattoos only."

Fai turns his head back so he's looking in front of him. "Fuck no," is his answer.

"Do you know what chemicals are in your tattoo?"

Fai sighs. "Honestly, I don't give two shits, bee."

"Not even the tattoo artists don't know what chemicals are in the tattoos. Some pigments are sourced from natural ingredients while others can also be sourced from the textile, plastic or automotive industry. The Joint Research Centre's report says the most dangerous ingredients are known as polycyclic aromatic hydrocarbons, which is mostly found in black inks. There are also azo pigments, although safe when they first enter the skin, they can degrade over time into potentially cancer-causing compounds."

Fai stares at me, completely out of words and with complete disbelief. "You done? You can go show off to someone who wants to listen to your rantings from an encyclopedia." He shakes his head. "Man, you're a weird one."

I shrug, not taking his words to heart. "I just wanted to inform you."

"You could just say you're against tattoos and move on instead of giving me that bullshit speech."

"I'm not against tattoos, I'm just saying people are putting on and in their skin something they don't know much about and chemicals that are dangerous to us."

"Yeah, okay. I'm taking your ass back now because I can't deal with this anymore. Holy shit." He stands up.

I stay seated. "I'm not annoying, Fai, you just don't understand me."

His lips curl in annoyance. "I'm not dumb."

I stand up, wiping my pants from any potential grass. "I wasn't even implying on that."

He extends the helmet in my direction. "Get on the motorcycle."

I grab the helmet, but don't take it from his hands. "Oh, wow. You offering me a helmet almost feels like you're flirting with me." He snickers. "Do you even know how to flirt, though?"

"Just because I don't flirt with you, doesn't mean I don't know how to. Now get the fuck up on the motorcycle before I leave you here."

Okay. So no flirting from him. Got it.

I grab the helmet and he immediately jumps on the motorcycle, turning it on. He doesn't give me much time, but I don't want to test him any further so I climb up behind him. I tell him where to drop me off now that I still have the chance because I don't think I'll have one again later.

He's driving more carefully now, not with such a rush as before and not as wild. I don't even care about feeling the rush at the moment. I just sit there, numb. The only thing I feel is the wind in my hair, but that's it.

He parks near the club I work at, putting his leg down when we come to a full stop. I take the helmet off my head and give it to him, shaking my head to get my hair back into place. I catch Fai looking at me, but he quickly looks around him when I look at him. "Are you going clubbing? Are you even 18?" he asks, probably thinking that I'm going to one of the clubs that are around him. The poor guy doesn't even know half of it.

"This is my workplace."

Fai raises an eyebrow. "Which one?" he asks as if I'm going to tell him.

"You're asking too many unimportant questions, sugar." I wink at him. "Thanks for the ride and the company, even though it wasn't the best one."

His eyebrows draw together as he once again looks around. "Are you a stripper?"

I have to laugh. "Wouldn't you just love to see me naked, huh?" I shake my head to myself. "You don't have enough money to make me undress for you, honey." I turn on my heels and move my head on left and right, making my hair swing as I walk. I purposefully make turns so he doesn't know where I'm going until I'm sure I'm out of his sight.

My good mood disappears immediately and the playfulness is replaced with anger. If I really put myself in some kind of danger because of him, that means Harper can be in danger, too.

Fuck.

Chapter 9

Whenever I have to spend the night at my parents' house, I never sleep, not even for a minute. I usually lay in bed with the bedside lamp illuminating the room enough so I can stare up at the ceiling.

My room is small and simple. I don't have any personal items in here. I don't have any pictures on the walls or any posters from favourite bands like most people my age have. I never saw this room as my home, I saw it as an escape, but not always a safe one. I hate this room with passion.

Sometimes, I go out and walk around until morning just so I don't have to spend any time here. I have a book beside me, but I'm too tired to focus on the heavy reading right now, although not nearly tired enough to fall asleep. I download a few games on my phone, but they don't interest me anymore. I'm really not the type for games, it seems. And that's unfortunate, because they could provide me with some sort of entertainment when I'm just waiting for the time to pass – like now.

I regret not going to Harper's place, but I missed the last bus to there and I didn't feel like walking that long, so I took the bus to here, although I'd much rather sleep outside on some bench than be here. I'm happy I came here late and I only have to stay here for a few hours before going to school.

I know what I'm doing isn't healthy. I'm often sleep-deprived and I know about the negative sides of not sleeping, but I'd probably have to drug myself if I wanted to fall asleep here, honestly. I'm not doing this on purpose. I didn't choose a life like this, I just happened to have it and now I'm rolling with it.

Next year, everything will be different. That keeps me going. Next year, I'll be far away from here.

I have a rough day and I have hardly anything to do. I go to Harper's place and watch a documentary, but I fall asleep during it and then I wake up at 7. I'm not working today, which means falling asleep in the afternoon means I won't be able to sleep during the night.

Harper is working and I decide to go to the bar despite the trouble Fai said I'm in. I don't know if I even believe him. Maybe he's just wanting to see if he has any power over me to make me scared. He really doesn't. I put the knife where I usually put it and finish dressing so I can catch the bus.

Harper is suspicious that something is going on with me because of me not going to the bar and me disappearing in the middle of the evening. I don't want to worry her any further and I certainly don't want her to ask me questions I can't answer.

I put the headphones on my head and put the hood over my head, heading to the bus station. I always try to dress unnoticedly when going out late when it's already dark because there are so many creepers everywhere and dressing like a hobo – literally – lessens the chance that they'll annoy me. It still happens, though, especially by drunk guys, but that's why I have headphones on, so I don't reply to their stupid remarks and get myself in the trouble. I have a big mouth, but I know when it's wise to stay quiet. And I'm certainly not looking to get raped or murdered by some psycho because I couldn't shut up.

I get on the bus and sit at the very end of it by the window. I always take the window seat if it's free so I don't have to interact with anyone and I don't have to give everyone a chance to stare at me. I've never been good at getting stared at. Thankfully, the bus is almost empty at this hour.

The bus station is just behind the bar, so I don't have to walk far, but I don't even come to the entrance door when I'm met with the now very familiar group of guys hanging out outside, smoking and drinking and just talking. I don't know who spots me first, but someone immediately says. "Shit. Fai, didn't you warn the chick?"

I didn't spot Fai at first. He's leaning against the wall, partly hidden in the dark. "What chick?" Fai asks. I see he's smoking, too, but his hands are empty of any beer bottles.

The guy that spoke first nods his head in my direction. I can't see the face Fai makes when he first lays his eyes on me, but I get to see his face when he steps away from the wall and walks towards me. He looks furious, his relaxed posture immediately replaced by the tense, angry one. "What the fuck?" he says as a greeting.

I grin. "Ah, my bodyguard is here! How nice," I say, my words full of sarcasm.

"What the fuck?" Fai repeats.

I tilt my head to the side. "I don't know. What the fuck?" I ask, mocking him.

"No, what the fuck is wrong with you? What's your deal?"

I pout. "Why would anything need to be wrong with me? I'm offended."

"You came here when I specifically asked you not to. You're in some deep trouble, yet you just don't want to listen." He shales his head. "Listen, I'm not going to play your knight in shining armour, princess. I warned you, but that's on you to listen."

"What makes you think I need a knight in shining armour? I can be my own."

Fai rolls his eyes, visibly annoyed. "Yeah, okay."

"Listen, sugar, you got me in trouble, so get me out of it."

"Yeah, I was trying to, you just don't wanna listen. I did my part, I don't know why it's so hard to do yours."

I step to him and put my hand on his chest. "Maybe I just wanted to see you." I give him one of the sweetest smiles that I own.

Fai looks at my hand on his chest and raises an eyebrow, looking right through my bullshit. "Right," he says dryly. "You saw me. Go home now."

I pout once again. "Won't you offer me a ride?"

I hear one of the guys "oooo-hing" while another says "Fai, dude." With a warning tone.

Fai shakes his head. "Can't do that and that's because I'm trying to get you out of trouble. You can't be seen on my motorcycle. Ever again."

I sigh. "Then one of your guys can do it." I look past Fai to the group.

"Oh, fuck no," one of them immediately replies.

"No offence, doll, I would, but we have some rules."

"You're really some pussies, all of you," I throw back at them. Maybe my plan isn't going to work. I might as well just go into the bar, then.

Someone says something in Fai's ear and Fai looks at me as if he's thinking about something. He nods and takes the helmet off his motorcycle, giving it to me. I grin, taking it. I know he has something planned and I don't even care. I don't even care if he drives me somewhere and leaves me there, that's how self-destructive I feel today.

Fai shakes his head in annoyance when he sees the happiness on my face. He sits on the motorcycle and turns it on. I sit behind him and wave to the guys watching us. None of them waves back.

I realise it soon that he's not taking me back home. I didn't even expect him to, but I was curious if he would. But he's also not taking me to some old building where he's going to lock me in and keep me there. I recognise this route from the last time. It's up on that hill that offers a nice view.

I'm happy about that, as long as I'm nowhere close to my home.

When we come to a stop, Fai kills the engine, parking the motorcycle, and immediately gets off it. I take the helmet off and he's in front of me, blocking me from getting down. "What the fuck is wrong with you?"

I raise an eyebrow. "This is the second time you asked me this in a matter of thirty minutes. I am starting to get really offended because why would there have to be anything wrong with me?"

He puts his hands on either side of me on the seat, caging me in, leaning closer. "You're purposefully getting yourself in trouble, that's why I'm asking! Do you want to get yourself killed?" he says through gritted teeth. He's really angry.

I put my hand on his chest and give him a sultry smile. "Maybe I just wanted to hang out with you," I say quietly, calmly – completely in contrast with him.

Fai pauses for a second, even his breathing stops, I think. He stares at me with disbelief and surprise ... until it dawns on him and he steps back. "You're fucking with my head." He pushes his hands in his hair and turns around, his back to me. "Fuck," he mutters.

I jump down, leaving the helmet on the seat. "That view is really nice," I comment. Fai stays silent.

"How did you find this place?" I press further.

Fai chuckles in disbelief. "Why are you like this?" he asks.

I cock my head to the side, truthfully not getting what he means. "Like what?"

"Wanting to be so quirky and going out of your way to be different than everyone else. What do you gain from it? Who are you doing this for or because of?"

I have to say I understand where he's coming from. People often mistake you being who you want to be for a crazy person simply because you have the guts to do something they don't.

"Fai, let me tell you a secret. I am not quirky and I am so far from wanting to be different from others. The fact is, I don't really care about what other people do or don't do or find acceptable or don't. I could give a rat's ass about someone's opinion about me – yours comes in here too. But the thing I care about is doing what I like and doing it freely with no wondering if others like it or not. Fuck people, Fai. They never have my back like I have mine so they can't tell me what I can and can not do. I do what I want and how I want it and if that's something that million other people do or no one at all, who really cares?"

Fai's eyebrows scrunch together. "And you count putting yourself in danger something you enjoy? Can you get any weirder?" He shakes his head to himself, crossing his arms over his chest.

I shrug. "Fear is a liar. If I let fear control me, I probably wouldn't even be here right now."

Fai's eyes widen a little and I see I shocked him. "The fuck's that supposed to mean?"

"You interpreted it both correctly and wrongly, but I'm not going into this with you. Fear is not something that stops me. Fear is something that fuels me."

Fai takes out a cigarette and lights it. He takes a few drags of it, none of us saying anything.

I brought my own cigarettes this time and I take one out, too.

"I'm not letting you die on my watch. I'm not carrying that with me, so don't make me kidnap you."

"What kind of a kidnapper would you be, Fai? Kind? Or evil? Would you feed me regularly? Let me shower? Would you hit me if I disobeyed?"

Fai stares at me as if he's standing in front of a crazy person. "I don't know. Want to find out?"

I drag a smoke out of my cigarette. "If you'll treat me nice, I'll go and stay there willingly."

"I wouldn't exactly bring you breakfast in bed, that's for goddamn sure. And I am many things, have done many things, but I don't women, even if they annoy me as you do. "

I look at him for a few seconds then I burst out laughing. "I tried to imagine the scene, but I honestly can't. I know how to make my own damn breakfast so there is no need for anyone to do it for me and bring it to me."

Fai puts the cigarette to his mouth too, inhaling the smoke.

"How old are you?" I ask him.

Fai looks at me. "How old are you? Are you even of age?"

"How old do you think I am?"

"I sure fucking hope you're 18. You're still in high school so you can't be more than 19."

"I am 19. How old are you?"

"23," he answers simply.

We fall in a comfortable silence after that. He's not really the talkative kind of a guy, I notice.

"Just so you know, this is the last time we hang out like this. Stay out of the bar for some time, a week or two maybe and I don't want you to come to me and talk to me. I hope that's clear to you."

I really didn't think he'd have the balls to do this. I don't know why, but I somehow didn't expect him to cut me off. I know we're annoying the hell out of each other, but he's fun to mess with. He's not a pussy like others, but he just doesn't understand me.

I shrug, not even looking at him. "Yeah, whatever."

"That's way too easy for you to give in. I'm being serious here, Kadie."

I look at him with nonchalant. "So am I. I'm not going to force you to hang out with me, I'm not that sad, Fai. We don't even share anything that would be a shame to break, either, so, yeah, dude, I got you."

I stand up, putting the cigarette out completely and put it in a small plastic bag so I don't throw it on the ground. Fai watches me do this with interest. "Take me back now," I say.

"I don't respond to demands," Fai responds, a similar answer that I once gave him.

"You'll quickly learn how to."

I go to his motorcycle and sit on it. I see he left the keys in the ignition. I've never driven the motorcycle, I've never even driven a car or anything else and I'm not about to start now, but it's fun to see Fai jumping up when he hears the keys clutter. "Fuck, get off it, you psycho!"

He carelessly throws the cigarette down, stepping on it to put it out and grabbing me by the arm. "Not responding to demands, huh?" I devilishly grin.

"You're fucking insane," he mutters.

I caress his arm. "Don't be afraid, babe. It's okay," I coo as if he was a child.

He gives me a death stare. "Move back so I can get up. I better not see you ever again after tonight."

I wrap my arms around his waist when he sits in front of me, leaning up to his ear. "And I thought you're going to come to visit me now that you know where I live." I chuckle when I feel him stiffen. "Just take me back and never search for me again," I say, leaning back and falling completely serious.

If this is goodbye, it better be the last one. For both of our sakes.

Chapter 10

<hr>

The next day I come to Harper's place to hang out with her because she's getting suspicious of what's going on with me.

I don't tell her anything about the potential danger I might be in because I don't want her involved. And by not going to the bar, I'm also not risking it to put her in danger. But she doesn't know that. I'm afraid she'd do something stupid if she found out, like ask someone about it and get people talking and then putting herself at risk because they would connect her with me.

We watch a movie before I have to go to work. I act like I have to go to bed early because I have a test in school tomorrow and I want to be well-rested, which is true, so I'm only partly lying, but it's in hopes that she will go to bed early as well so I can go to work with no worries of getting caught.

Harper usually goes to bed early anyway. But this is just so I don't risk it. She has to leave the living room since I sleep on the couch when I stay at her place.

"Okay, but plan on staying up tomorrow and we'll watch the movie to the end because I really want to see the ending."

"We both know she dies at the end."

Harper's face falls a little. "Don't be so cynical. I still want to see how it ends."

"Yes, okay. We'll finish it tomorrow," I say, but I don't promise anything. I'm working tomorrow.

When Harper heads to her room, I busy myself with reading a book until it's time to change my clothes and go. I always put on an oversized hoodie and jeans that are too big on me when I go to work because I don't feel like walking the streets in my work clothes. I change when I get there or I wear clothes under.

Which is a good thing because I was under the false assumption that Harper is already sleeping, but she gets out of her room when I'm putting on shoes. There is no way I can cover my tracks before she notices I'm not on the couch.

"Where are you going?" she asks me, her eyes trained on me.

"Out ... for a walk. I couldn't sleep."

"It's pretty late to go out alone, Kadie."

"Don't worry, I still remember the moves if I need to kick someone in the face," I grin.

Harper doesn't find this funny. She looks at me for some moments. "Okay, then I'm going with you. I need some fresh air, too."

I slowly stand up, looking for an excuse that will sound believable. "Don't take this in a wrong way, but I would really appreciate some alone time. Just to clear my head, you know?"

Harper crosses her arms. She's not buying it. She's not stupid. "Kadie, are you going out this late to see that guy?"

I chuckle. "What guy?"

"You know exactly who I'm talking about," she says, not happy with this conversation at all.

I look at her, wondering what is the thing she would understand and accept more – me working at a strip club or me going out with Fai? "Yes, I'm seeing him. Occasionally." Okay, that isn't a lie. I'm just telling half-truths.

Harper sighs, dropping her arms. She looks disappointed and her face becomes sad. "Why didn't you tell me?" she asks.

I only shrug. Because there was nothing to tell. "You told me you don't approve."

"Kadie, I ..." She seems to be momentarily at loss with words. "I sincerely hope you know what you're doing. But approving or not, from now on, please inform me about things like this. It's for your safety and because I want to know. Please. For my own inner peace."

I nod, not wanting to stretch my lie any further. "There's nothing serious going on between us, I can tell you that for sure."

Harper just looks at me. "Just be safe, Kadie, okay?"

She looks so concerned for me that I have to go to her and hug her for reassurance. I'm not really a hugger, but I know Harper is and if this is something that will make her feel just a little better, then so be it.

She lets me leave her place, but I know she's watching me through the window. I have to be more careful now that she knows something is up with me. I feel so bad for lying to her, but this lie is better than the truth because I know she wouldn't accept it and she'd do anything to make me leave this job and I can not afford that.

I give it one week before I go to the bar. I can't find any more excuses for Harper as to why I don't go there. Even though she said multiple times that she would rather not see me going to that place, she knows something is up if I just stop going there all of a sudden without any explanation. She knew I wouldn't change my mind that easily.

I have a book with me, but I'm not that into it. I constantly watch over my shoulder and around me because Fai planted a seed of paranoia inside of me with his warnings and I really want to be sure that Harper is safe, or in the worst case, who I have to deal with in order to keep her safe.

Harper taps on the bar in front of me to gain my attention. "Why is your boyfriend here with another girl?"

It takes me a second to really get her words because I was so deep in my thoughts. "What?" I turn around, not spotting him at first, but then I see him sitting with his group with a girl on his lap. "He's not my boyfriend. I told you it's not a serious thing, he can still do whatever the fuck he wants. I'm not putting any handcuffs on him."

Harper purses her lips. "Still not cool. I don't like that guy."

That makes two of us, Harp, but I have to pretend for your own good. I just shrug. "You get used to him after some time, I guess."

"Guys are just jerks, especially his type."

"His type?" I ask, raising my eyebrows.

"Yeah, you know. Bad guy, wanna-be tough and dangerous. Girls fall for that nowadays."

"I mean ... let them if they want. After all, they're great in bed so at least it's not all bad you get from them."

Harper makes a face at me. "Gross. You better shut up here."

I chuckle. "Babe, they're just not your type. Just like doctors and lawyers and all those good boys aren't mine. Don't we make quite a pair?"

"Truly," Harper agrees.

"Not relating to me, but have you noticed how guys look cool in their group of friends when they have a random girl rubbing herself all over them at a club, yet they feel like a pussy or some shit when they have to show their girl some love? This is really some messed up shit, I'm telling you."

Harper nods. "I see this stuff every day, Kadie, some of them even having girlfriends. It's disgusting. It makes me really consider if I even ever want to have a man. So, I'm telling you, don't let him treat you bad. I know you and your type of men. It's like you don't even know how much you're worth and you're willing to put up with their shit because you think you deserve it."

I look down at the counter, her words hitting a spot inside of me that triggers some negative emotions. She's good at reading me. Too good. "Harp, there's not a guy on this planet I'll let mistreat me. Trust me. I like myself that much so I don't get to look like a damn fool. When I tell you it's alright, it's alright."

She stubbornly squeezes her lips together. She already formed an opinion about this situation and it seems that she won't change her mind.

"Go back to work, you lazy ass. You just wanted an excuse to talk to me so you don't have to take orders from others," I try to lighten the mood, wanting her to drop this subject already.

"How did you know?" she asks with fake mortification.

I tap the side of my head. "Sixth sense, dear."

I want to go back to reading, but someone interrupts me again by sitting down beside me. "Won't you go wish the birthday boy a happy birthday?" It's one of the guys from Fai's group.

I give him a funny look. I have a good idea he's referring to Fai. "You can go and do it instead of me, he looks busy and I don't want to interrupt. You can give him a kiss for me. On the lips." I wink.

The guy makes a face, shaking his head. "Don't think that's necessary, he already found someone who'll do that."

I shrug. "Oh, well, then. It seems like it's sorted, then."

I go back to reading the book, wanting him to just go away and leave me alone. Fai and I talked about it and I meant it when I told him to leave me alone. That was also meant for his annoying friends. "Before you go and ignore me, could you call your hot friend over here so I could order?"

I look at him again and I look at him well. I narrow my eyes at him. "You're that guy, huh? You took a liking of her." I nod towards Harper.

He grins. "So what if I did?"

I want to punch him straight in the face. My hand forms a fist. "You better leave her away. Don't put her in any danger because you want to be selfish."

He holds his hands up in defence. "Listen, tigress, I'm not forcing anyone into anything, but, hey, if she's willing, I won't turn around, either."

I go close to his face. "She's into doctors. What can you offer her?"

He stays silent. "Yeah. That's what I thought so." I get down from the stool, positive that I made some point here and I hope he listens. I intentionally call the other girl to our side to take his order while I walk out, holding a pack of cigarettes up for Harper to see. She disappointingly squeezes her lips together, but I don't let it get to me.

I lean against the well next to the front door and take out a cigarette, lighting it up. There's a group of drunk people out here, screaming and dancing and just being overall annoying drunks. They probably don't even see me.

I hear the sirens in the distance, the car honks and people yelling from somewhere up the street not that far away. I know that asking for peace would be too much in a place like this, so I'm not even mad about it.

What I get about it is when a guy comes out, looking to the right and left right at me. He closes the door and walks to me, standing right in front of me, just looking. "What?" I ask him.

"Just wanted to get a clear look of you. Pretty. But then, Fai always knew how to pick 'em."

I straighten against the wall, now looking at the guy with a little more interest. He's bulky and dark-haired. I have to say he's attractive and if that's the person Fai warned me from, I'm not even mad I'm in trouble with him. "You got a look now you can go away and let me enjoy my cigarette in peace."

The guy chuckles humourlessly. "Peace? Sweetheart, there won't be any peace for you anymore. You ended that peace for yourself the moment you decided to involve with Fai and I hope he was worth it."

I raise my eyebrow. "Can you go to Fai and talk your problems out with him instead of crying about them to me? I literally have nothing to do with him or you and your problems."

He steps towards me. Too close. He's invading my personal space. He might not look that bad, but I didn't invite him to come this close to me. He wants to put his hand on my cheek, but I stop him immediately, glaring at him. "You better step the fuck away from me and don't you dare to touch me. I know how to break an arm."

The guy chuckles, not taking me seriously. "So, he likes them feisty. So do I," he says, licking his lips. He steps so close to me that he pushes me against the wall with his chest.

"Go play that macho game somewhere else. Jesus Christ, you're all so fucking annoying with this. Just because I'm a woman, doesn't mean you can show your superiority your gender gives you. That doesn't make you look strong and scary. It makes you look like a damn pussy."

I see my words hit him deep. His nostrils flare and he puts his hand on my throat, squeezing lightly.

"Bitch, you have a lot of nerve. You could be dead in two seconds."

I take a drag of my cigarette and exhale the smoke out right in his face. That makes his hand squeeze my throat even tighter.

The door opens and I see Fai coming towards us with a furious expression.

"Ah. The knight coming to the rescue."

I take advantage of the guy paying attention to Fai to take my knife out of my shoe and turn the position so he's now being pressed against the wall, putting my knife up to his throat. "But the question is, which one did he come out to rescue?" I ask the guy with an ever so sweet smile.

He looks shocked.

"You chose the wrong victim to play your mind games with. I'm not scared of you and your empty threats. I know how to hit back."

I step back, putting the half-smoked cigarette out and throwing it into the waste bin. I'm pissed I got interrupted outside when all I wanted was some peace.

When I go past Fai, I stop, putting my hand on his cheek. "Happy birthday, darling," I say sweetly, standing up on my tippy toes and pecking his lips ever so slightly just for the fun of it. "You said we don't talk to each other anymore when we meet out, so I expect you to keep your promise. Tell your friends to do that, too," I tell him quietly before I step back and go back into the bar.

Chapter 11

I knew Fai would come to me afterwards. I just had a feeling because I know he can't stay away. Not after what happened.

It takes him about ten minutes, but he sits down beside me, placing his tattooed arms on the bar counter. He sits there and just stares at me.

I finally lift my head to look at him. "What do you want now?" I ask him. It seems like everyone is going to interrupt me while I'm reading so I might as well just put the book back into my backpack.

"There's a party we're going to. You can come with."

I stare at him, holding back so I don't burst out laughing. "I can come with you? Really?" I ask him. "Geez Louise, with what did I deserve such an honour?"

Fai shrugs. "I always see you reading books and shit, I want to see if you know how to party. Besides, I heard you promised me a kiss."

I lean closer to him, putting a hand on his cheek in a soft manner. The gesture probably looks cute to other people, but I use it mockingly. "Fai, darling, I'm not that easy. You might be used to getting things easily from the girls you choose to hang out with, I don't know, but you're not getting that from me. Yeah?"

"Who said anything about easy?" Fai asks with a smirk.

I shake my head in disbelief. He's acting like that one time and then he doesn't want to see me another time. Like, decide what the hell you want, dude. "What happened to staying away from each other, Fai? Huh?"

He shrugs. "People are already talking. Might as well just give them something to talk about in return."

I see Harper is polishing a glass and giving me and staring at us. She's studying us both intently so I'll get a full report from her later. Fai notices I'm looking at her. "She can go with us, too."

"No," I say immediately. "Does she seem like a partying type?"

Fai looks her up and down and I want to rip his eyes out for just doing so. I squint my eyes at him. "We can make her be one, that's no problem. How would you know if she is the one for parties if you don't let her party? You don't want her to be anything like you and that shit's entertaining to watch."

I shake my head. "She's completely different from me. We've had different lives and she's one of a kind. But you wouldn't know anything about that, would you?"

"Neither do you," Fai throws my words back in my face.

"Cheers to that, motherfucker!" I say.

Fait pats my knee and stands up. "Decide if you want to hit the clubs with us. We leave in around 15 minutes. Don't expect me to wait a second more."

I wave him goodbye, giving him an innocent smile. "15 minutes. Got ya," I say as if I'm actually going to think about it. I won't. I have to go to work, anyway. But I'm intrigued to see the way his group parties. Are they fun? Do they dance? Or do they just drink? I know they smoke, but what exactly do they smoke? Maybe I'll get a chance to see it some other time.

Harper dances towards me, acting all nonchalant and innocent. I look right through her. She's a terrible actress. "Did he apologise? Was she his sister? Please say it was."

I roll my eyes. "Harp, this is not one of the romantic movies you watch so much. Let him be."

"Are you even into him?" she asks me, putting her hands on her hips.

I chuckle. "What?"

"How can you watch him with another girl? Do you like him or not?"

I almost laugh at her innocence, but I don't want to be rude and I don't want to hurt her feelings. Oh, Harp. so naive. "Harper, it's really not that deep, but you wouldn't understand. No offence."

"What's that supposed to mean?"

I take a deep breath. "You have to find the guy appealing and you have to like his character. He has to be the only one for you and you have to be the only one for him. To put it simply, you have to really be into him before you fuck him. I don't. That's the difference and that's why it's so hard to understand for you."

Her eyes bulge out and she looks around, her cheeks getting red. She's uncomfortable. So innocent it's almost making me embarrassed. "You asked, Harp." I shrug.

"I'm already regretting it."

I just give her a big smile, trying to make it innocent, but Harper only shakes her head and goes back to work. I focus on the book again before Fai shows up at my side again. "So? You coming?"

"Nope," I say, not looking up from the book. "It doesn't interest me that much that I would call in sick to work."

Fai only shrugs. "Your loss."

I look up from the book. He's wearing that nonchalant expression that has the effect to piss me off, apparently. "You know what?" I close the book. "I'll go, but I have a condition."

Fai looks up at the ceiling, annoyed. "I invite you to the party and you get to have conditions?"

I place my finger on his chest. "You want me to come," I say lowly.

"Yeah, in more ways than one. Name your conditions and I'll see how much I really want you with us."

"I only have one," I point out. "Pick one tattoo of yours and tell me the meaning behind it."

Fai's face darkens. "My tattoos don't have any meanings."

"Stop bullshitting!" I say, knowing he's lying.

He stares at me and I stare right back. "Either that or you tell how you got heterochromia?"

Fai rolls his shoulders. He doesn't need much time to think about it and I immediately understand which thing he's not willing to talk about. He rolls his sleeve on the left arm up. He points to a date written in Roman numerals. "The date my mother was born. And that's all the meaning behind this one." There are many, many more tattoos. Pictures, words, dates ... I know they all have a meaning and I know he picked the easiest one to explain.

"That's too easy."

"You said one, you got one." He shrugs, rolling the sleeve back down.

"That one doesn't count. I want to know one more. A picture this time."

"You don't get to change the rules of the game to make it to your liking, bee. Take it or leave it."

"One more and I'm coming."

He sighs and lifts his shirt up in the front, showing off more tattooed skin. It's a skyline of a city over his stomach. "Skyline of Dubai. I was born there."

I place my finger on his skin and his muscles clench. He quickly steps back, away from my touch, pulling his shirt back down. His jaw is clenched. "Dubai?" I ask.

"Yeah. So? I'm not going to wait anymore. You got what you wanted."

"I mean, alright, if you insist ..." I did make a deal with him, after all, and I don't back down when I give my word. I'm not like that. People get from me what I promise them, nothing more, nothing less, no fake promises.

I call Harper over. "Hey, Harp. I'm going with Fai and his group."

She looks suspicious. "Where?"

"To some club." I immediately see she doesn't like that. "Don't worry about me, I just want to have some time. Text me when you get home, please."

Harper frowns. "I'll lock the door so you'll have to wake me up when you come to know you're safe."

I make a heart with my hands before I jump down from the stool. "Take this book with you, please," I say. I can't put it anywhere and I'm certainly not going to take my book with me to a club to a party. I'm not a loser like that.

I send a text to my manager that I feel sick and I won't be coming today. This is the first time I've ever done this so I can get away with it pretty easily.

Fai doesn't want to tell me where we're going. He only gives me the helmet, telling me to just climb on the motorcycle because everyone's tired of waiting on me, apparently. I can't tell what the guys think about me going with them. No one says anything and they're all wearing helmets so I can't see their faces. Not that I care anyway.

It's been a minute since I went out to party. The parties have kind of lost their charms, but I used to be pretty heavy on partying and everything that came with it – alcohol and drugs. But then the scene got boring to me because it was repetitive self-destruction and always some drama with everyone that I just didn't want to deal with anymore.

I put on the helmet and climb behind Fai. And we go into the night, leaving the sound of revving machines behind. It doesn't come as a surprise that we go downtown, near the club where I work. There are known clubs around there and there's a club for every taste and for every age.

We go to the club called 6ix and Fai does a handshake with the bodyguard at the door and he lets us in without checking our IDs. Impressive. It might be useful to remember that Fai has connections to get us into the club.

I've never been here before, but the club itself is not special in any kind. It's just a normal club with dim lights and loud music. There are a few people that greet Fai with either a nod or a fist bump, some even with that manly hug that shows just the right amount of affection, but not too much.

We go upstairs to the biggest table with the couch that's reserved and it's for us apparently. There's already drinks and we all start with shots. I don't even think twice about it before drinking three of them, welcoming the burn down my throat that I almost forgot about.

I do notice that Fai chose a beer for himself, though, and he didn't join us with shots. I get closer to him. "Introduce me to your friends," I tell him.

Fai waves his hand nonchalantly. "They know who you are."

I give him an annoyed look. "Yeah, you dummy. But I don't know their names." And I don't want Fai to be the only person that I know here. It's also weird being with a group of people and not knowing their names.

Fai sighs as if I asked him to do the hardest thing in existence. "Bastian. Cruz. Ante. Lev. Jon." He names them how they sit. Lev is the one who has hots for Harper.

I nod. "Which of them is single?"

Fai now gives me his full attention, rotating his body so he's fully looking at me. "You're not getting with any of my friends, bee. They'd kill you before you could get a full sentence out of your mouth."

I raise an eyebrow. "Don't forget one of your friends laid his eyes on my friend so I just might be the one to kill first." I shrug, taking the glass to my lips and down yet another shot.

"Get over it already," Fai says in an exasperated tone. Yes, because he doesn't know what it's like. He's taking all of this as a game, but it isn't. Not with Harper. He can think he's playing with me, but I know the game and I'm willing to play it with him to some extent. Harper isn't.

I roll my shoulders. "I need way more booze if I'll have to deal with you for the whole night," I say. Frankly, he can get on my nerves like no one else.

"You need something heavier, princess?" one of the guys asks suddenly. Ante, I think.

"How heavier."

"Ante, stop this shit," Fai says.

"Fuck off, Fai. Let her decide on herself."

Fai looks annoyed, but doesn't say anything else. He takes the cigarette out and lights it up instead. I shrug at Ante. "Let me see what you have and we'll talk further."

"I only have Molly with me tonight." He shrugs, taking out a full bottle of ecstasy. Shit, they're really not joking.

I do have some experience with drugs from before. Not much, but something. And it's not a bad experience at all, all those times I had a really great time.

I take one pill and put it on my tongue, showing it to Fai just to sort of piss him off a little further. I swallow it and drink a shot on top, scrunching my nose up and laughing it off. "Okay, shit, maybe take it easy a little bit there. I don't want you to kill yourself."

I pat Fai's cheek. "I know what I'm doing."

The guys go for the heroine, thought and Lev settles for marijuana while Fai takes neither. "What? Are you babysitting? Isn't it your birthday or you lied?" I ask him, stealing the cigarette from him and taking a drag.

He glares at me for that. "Not really into drugs."

I shrug, not thinking too much about it.

I start to feel the alcohol already. It's been some time since I drank and maybe I should take it a little easier from now on.

"You know what I really want to do now?" I ask Fai.

He gives me a disinterested look and I grin. "Dance."

"Fuck no," he says, shaking his head. "By yourself maybe."

I look around the club. "I don't think it's going to be by myself, but you're being cute." I stand up and I have to blink a few times to steady myself completely and remember that I still have legs.

I go to the dancefloor, by myself. There aren't many people upstairs so I go down and lose myself in the crowd. I start to feel the pill because I feel lighter. Happier. I don't really see people around me anymore. I'm lost in myself and in the music.

I don't know for how long I dance. It might be 15 minutes or it might be an hour. That's the thing about drugs, you completely lose track of the time. Five minutes can feel like half an hour sometimes. I go back upstairs when I start to get thirsty. A guy tries to stop me on my way up, putting his arm out and blocking my way. "You showed quite the moves there, baby girl. Want to do it again against me?"

I scrunch my face up. "You just totally blew your chance with your weird fucking words." I slap his arm away, shaking my head.

I come upstairs to find the group is incomplete. Jon and Ante are completely missing while Bastian is talking to some girl at the end of the couch. Lev and Fai are the only one at the table. I don't sit down because I'm afraid the alcohol will have an even bigger effect on me.

Fuck, I'm sweating so much.

I take the sweater off and carelessly throwing it next to Fai. I also realise my ponytail got undid and I lost my hairband while dancing. I don't like wearing my hair down and I almost never do. It's too long and it gets in my way, but at this moment, I can't bring myself to care. "Can a girl get something to drink here before she dies from the dehydration? Where is everyone? Left already? Didn't know their bedtime is so early."

Someone places his arm around me from behind, bringing their mouth close to my ear. "Didn't know you'd miss me so fast."

I push Jon away from me, but I laugh. "Someone has to."

Fai stands up, pushing a bottle of water in my direction and sending a glare at Jon. I groan. "Water? Fuck off, Fai, seriously. Give me something fucking stronger."

Ante shakes his bottle of pills into my direction. "Want another one?"

"Stop filling her with the pills, man, what the fuck's your problem?" Fai suddenly bursts out, looking pissed as hell. O-kay.

I throw my arms around him, unable to match his bad mood, but I rather grin. "Come dance with me. You can yell at him later."

"I would rather yell at him n–"

I crash my lips against his, shutting him the hell up. And just because I felt like kissing him. Because I'm happy and everything is good and, right now, there's not any fucked up shit going on in my head.

Chapter 12

Y ou know when you wake up and you don't even open your eyes and you already know something is off? Besides that, I feel like shit, of course.

When I open my eyes, the first thing I notice is an unfamiliar window and view. I lift my head a little and look around the unfamiliar room. It's big and bright because of the morning sun. Then I spot Fai sitting in the chair beside the window, smoking a cigarette and watching me.

"Oh, this is just a nightmare," I say, putting my head down on the pillow and turn away, closing my eyes.

"Bee, I've been waiting for you to wake up so you can get the fuck out of my bed already so I'm afraid you're not dreaming."

I groan and slowly sit up on the bed. I'm used to waking up early and sleeping for a few hours only, but it's been a long time since I drank and last night must've been wild because I don't remember coming here. "Why the hell am I here?"

"That's what I wanted to ask you," Fai says.

I frown and look around the room again. "I don't know. You kidnapped me?"

Fai scoffs. "I knew I should've just let you sleep outside."

I put my hands in my hair and I realise my hair is down instead of in a ponytail or in my usual bun. I quickly roll it around my hand and tuck it into the back of the shirt – shirt that's not mine. I look down at it as some parts of last night come into my mind.

"Drink this," Fai says.

I grin at him and lick my upper lip. "You're so authoritative," I say. "Are you like that in bed, too?" I ask him, running my finger down his cheek and touching the piercing in his lip.

"If you drink this, you'll be able to find that out later."

I shake my head and wrap my arms around his neck. "Dance with me," I say as I step up on my tippy toes and kiss his neck. I feel so hot. So happy. So carefree.

"Kadience, drink this water before I force it down your throat," Fai says, putting his hand on my waist. He wants to push me off him, but I hold him tighter to me.

"Dance with me and then I'll drink the water."

He throws his head up in exasperation. "You think you're in a position to negotiate?"

"You tell me," I say against his jaw, softly grazing it with my teeth before I turn around and wrap his arms around me, throwing my head back against his shoulder and getting completely lost in the music.

"Did you fuck me?" I ask Fai.

He raises his eyebrow. "You were completely wasted and high on drugs and rape doesn't really interest me," he says.

"What a gentleman," I say dryly and get out of the bed. My legs are bare. "Sorry that you didn't get what you wanted."

"Oh, I did. I got plenty of it," he says with a lazy smile, putting his cigarette out and spreading on the chair. He's shirtless and I get the chance to see many tattoos all over his chest and arms. He's tattooed all the way up to his neck.

"What?" I ask, throwing on the jeans that I find on the other chair in the room. I don't see my shirt anywhere, but my jacket is thrown over the same chair and it reeks of alcohol. Ew.

"Catch," Fai says before he throws his phone at me.

He has a video opened. A video of us. He's sitting on the couch and I'm sitting on top of him with my legs on either side of him. We're kissing. We're kissing like crazy. He has his hand in my hair and one on my ass. I move my head and kiss him down his neck, sucking on the skin. Fai looks at the camera, smiling and I hear the guy recording say, "Fuck, man, you're both giving us a show and it's hot."

I lift my head to look at the camera, too, bringing my face close to it. "What? Wanna join?" I lift my eyes up to look at the one who was recording and then the video ends. I don't remember who was recording this.

I look at Fai and shrug. "You can't say we don't look good together. I'm fun to party with, what do you want me to say?"

And then I remember I told Harper I'm going to sleep at her place and I haven't even called her. Shit. "Where's my phone?" I'm panicking, rummaging through my clothes until it falls on the floor.

Harper called me 21 times and sent me 15 messages, asking me where I am, why I'm not picking up, why am I still not at her place and stating that she's going to call the police. "Oh, fuck," I say, calling her.

She picks up almost immediately. "Kadience, where the fuck are you?!" she says it so loudly that I have to close my eyes because it echoes in my head. I know she's really pissed off when she uses swear words because she never swears. Ever.

"I'm at Fai's, Harp. I'm so sorry I didn't call, but I'm fine and I'm coming to your place now."

"Are you out of your mind? I've been waiting all night for you! I thought something happened to you, Kadie. Do you know how scared I was? I didn't know what to do and I didn't know who to call! Don't you ever do that again, do you hear me?!" She's really panicking and I'm afraid she's going to start crying. Shit.

I feel like a complete shit now because I told her I'm coming at her place and of course she was worried when I didn't come. I would lose my shit in her place, too. "You have every right to be mad. I'm sorry, Harp, I'm running now."

Fai is giving me an amused look from the chair, now sitting with his hands on his knees. I give him an angry glare. "Yeah, you better. See you." She's so mad she just hangs out. She might as well just kill me when I get to her place.

"I think your friend could need some loosening up," Fai says, standing up and stretching. I don't know whether he wants to suddenly show off his tattoos or muscles. Or both.

"Fuck off," I say.

"Come on now. That's no way to thank me for taking care of you last night. That really wasn't cool, by the way. I didn't take you with me to get completely fucked up and ruin my night."

I huff. "You wanted me there so you got me there. You ruined your night by yourself, buddy, you could leave me the fuck alone."

Fai grabs my arm, making me look at him. "Show a little more gratitude," he says angrily, his nostrils flaring.

I straighten my spine, looking down at his hand on my arm, squeezing hard before I slowly look him into his say, daringly. "Or what?" I ask him quietly, calmly. I spike a fire in his eyes. "Or what, Fai?" I repeat impatiently.

He releases my arm, stepping back from me and showing me his back so I come face to face with the huge roaring lion he has tattooed all over his back. He takes his hands into his hair, getting his anger under control. My heart is beating fast in my chest from adrenaline.

"Yeah, that's what I fucking thought," I say, grabbing my jacket and throwing it on, leaving Fai's shirt on. "I'm keeping your shirt," I announce just to spike him a little bit further, but he doesn't react in any way.

I shake my head and get out of the bedroom, putting shoes on the way. "Are we going to see each other again?" Fai says suddenly.

I shrug. "Yeah, at the bar most likely since that became your favourite place to hang out, apparently."

"I didn't mean that," he declares.

I turn around and just stare at him trying to figure out if he's fucking with me or if he's actually being serious. Could he be that dumb? I refuse to believe it. "Look, I really had fun last night, but let's not make this complicated, yeah? There's no bad blood between us, but I'm not suddenly your girlfriend now." I would probably kill him in his sleep.

"So, what? You're just going to leave now?" Fai says. He looks confused and like he doesn't really know what to do. I bet he had to throw all the other girls out before me, but I'm walking out freely.

"Yep," I say. "Oh, by the way, you don't happen to have a hairband laying around here somewhere?" I say, looking around the place for the first time. It's not bad. Nothing fancy, but it's an open space and it's quite spacious. He doesn't have a lot of furniture and decorating isn't really his forte.

"No, I don't bother with that, I just let my hair fall down my back freely, you know," he says dryly.

"Funny," I say seriously. "See you around, buddy," I say.

I didn't expect Fai to offer me a ride, but I don't know how the buses here drive and I don't think I even know where the bus station is so I have to use my last percents of battery for searching a bus station on google.

I pull the hood up over my head as I wait with other people and a few kids for the bus. They look at me weirdly, but I got used to getting the weird looks from people who are trying so hard to blend in with everyone and be normal, too scared to stand out. It sucks to be you, losers, yet you're the ones judging me.

The bus is full. It's that hour when the kids are going to school and people are going to work. I hate crowded buses because everyone's pushing you around and you're squeezed between people, plus there's always some weird smell as if they forgot to take a few showers. Disgusting.

My phone dies so I can't even listen to music and therefore I'm forced to listen to other people's conversations. I hang my head, closing my eyes and try to block it all out, but I get a sudden flashback from last night.

Fai is comfortably sitting on the couch, his legs parted while I'm sitting next to him, cross-legged. He's smoking and I'm watching the people dancing and I'm smiling to myself. I feel happy. I feel really good.

I take the cigarette from Fai's mouth and take a drag, letting out smoke right into his face when he turns it to look at me. "Can you not?" he says, taking the cigarette back.

I only shrug.

Ante is sitting across from us and he leans on the table pointing his hand first to Fai and then me. "Are you guys a thing now or ...?" he wants to know.

I chuckle while Fai's face remains indifferent. "Does it look like we're together?" I ask.

His face scrunches up. "Yeah, you're kinda giving that vibe away."

I shake my head to myself, not even wanting to answer that.

Fai looks at me for a second before he huffs, looking away once more. I let out a yawn and I slowly feel all the euphoria slowly dying down and the ecstasy losing its effect. Damn Fai for forcing me to drink so much of that goddamn water.

I stand up, wanting to go to the dancefloor again because I still feel like I have some more energy to get out, but Fai grabs my arms and pulls me down so I sit on his leg. I glare at him. "Stop spoiling all my fun," I mutter.

He takes all my hair in his hand and puts it away, leaning closer to my ear so I can hear him better. "I am your fun."

"No, you're –"

"Kiss me and I'll let you go."

"Oh, for fuck's sake," I say, annoyed by this game.

I place my mouth on his, kissing him for I don't know which time tonight. I feel his piercing against my mouth and it's all kinds of hot, but it's also the kind that needs to end. Here. And tonight.

I move away and stare into his eyes, stroking his hair. "Hope you enjoyed this one because it's the last one you're getting from me. Ever. Your birthday's over, party boy."

I'm happy that I'm at my station and I can get the hell out of the bus. I have a three minute walk towards Harper's place and when I come to her door, I hold my breath and press the bell.

Harper opens the door angrily and looks me up and down as if she wants to make sure I'm still alive. She jumps at me then, throwing her arms around me and almost knocking me off my feet from the force. I awkwardly hug her back.

"Don't you ever do that, Kadie. Ever," Harper almost sobs.

I purse my lips, waiting for her to step back and stop hugging me. I'm really not big on hugs. "I'm sorry, Harp. I really am. It won't happen again."

She steps away from me. She's still in her pyjama and she looks bad. As if she hasn't slept a minute. Now I just feel really bad for making her worry and selfishly thinking only about myself and having fun. I deserve her anger.

Harper shakes her head. "You made me so worried, you have no idea. You know I have a bad feeling about the guy."

I shrug, moving past her into the apartment. I don't want to give anyone a show or have anyone hear us. "He's cool, Harp. You don't have to worry about me when I'm with him. He's harmless."

She just gives me a look that tells me she's disappointed in my choice of men. Disappointed or not, I can't change it. She lives in her own perfect world and doesn't understand how different it is for me. How far away perfection is from me. I like imperfect people while Harper dreams about the perfect ones. And she just can't understand that because she doesn't know life like that. She's looking at it through different eyes.

She takes in what I'm wearing and her shoulders drop. She thinks whatever she wants to think and I'm not going to say anything if she doesn't ask me about it. "Whatever. You better get ready for school because you're already late."

"I'm not going to school," I say over my shoulder, on my way to the bathroom.

"What do you mean you're not going to school?" Harper says disapprovingly.

"I don't feel like going and missing one day won't kill me. I might go shopping later, depends on my mood."

Harper looks at me weakly, knowing that she's defeated and if I made up my mind, she won't be able to change it. I wink at her. "Relax," I mouth to her, even though I kind of feel bad for her.

She lives a life full of worries and I live a life full of things that make her worry.

Chapter 13

Harper has classes late in the morning. I feel bad because she hasn't slept much and now she has to go through hours of forcing herself to concentrate.

I, on the other hand, go shopping. I always shop for clothes at thrift stores, which is not very often. I'm not really into shopping, but I'm into searching and finding new things that I like. I don't really have a style and I don't bother with fashion. When buying things, I don't think through with what I'm going to match it with. I buy something because I like it and then work around with it.

I find a few pieces today that I like. Nothing too drastic or that would stand up. I usually just go for plain clothes with no inscriptions on them and in one colour. That's the main reason why I don't buy brands. If I do buy clothes with inscriptions, it's just plain white or black shirts with some sarcastic sayings.

I like to take time when shopping to look through every piece, feel all of them and try them on. It often happens that a piece doesn't look how I imagined it'd look on me. Even though I don't complicate over these things, I still want to feel comfortable in what I wear and that's the main goal for me.

Afterwards, I wander in the city. I visit a museum by myself and even go to the cinema afterwards, just blindly choosing a movie. I don't have preferences when it comes to movies, I watch it all. Old, new, thrillers, dramas, comedies, horror ... Except for romance, I don't like romantic movies, but I watch them if I come across them just for my own fun. Those sappy happy endings are just ... meh for me. They're just for people to make them feel better about their sad lives and to fill them with the hope that they'll get a happy ending like that one day maybe.

I end up watching a horror movie. Nothing to brag about and nothing that would make me remember the movie, just something to pass time with.

When I get out, I see Harper sent me a text.

Going straight to the bar. Where are you?

She's the responsible one. She sends a text because she doesn't want me to be worried. She tells me everywhere she goes and who she goes with, sometimes even giving me their numbers. Just in case, she says. She's always playing it safe. She doesn't party, she doesn't drink.

There's not often she goes somewhere, and when she does, it's with friends from college to go and study together or grab lunch together. It's not that she doesn't have many friends, it's just that she chooses them wisely. She's a social person, yet she doesn't hang out with just everyone. If you're in her circle, you have to be special and this is why I'm never worried about Harper. She always makes sure she's safe, but I appreciate her telling me about her whereabouts.

Went to the cinema. See you later.

Thankfully, she forgot about that movie she wanted us to watch together. I hate when she picks movies because she's a sucker for romance. Movies, books, series, you name it. And I suffer through them because I love her and I owe her for putting up with me.

I wander around the city some more, exploring it like a tourist and discovering new places before I go back to Harper's place and go straight up to the rooftop. The sun is going to set in a few minutes. I get up on the wall and sit on it, looking down at the cars, people and little stores beneath. This always fascinates me. Not really how much you can see from here and how beautiful the view is, but looking down and just watching people walking, running, driving bicycles, motorcycles, cars ...

I lift my head up, looking at the sky and enjoying the breeze blowing across my face. I close my eyes, living in the moment. Up here, away from everyone and everything, enjoying the peace and aloneness. I'm one of those people who just love to be alone. People exhaust me and I'm not the person to eat their bullshit just to appear nice. I'm not nice, but I'm not rude, either. I'm just something in-between. Truthful, if you may. With no pretence in front of anyone.

I take one last look down and around the city before I jump down from the wall and go back in the building. I don't take a book with me tonight because I don't want to read. I'm too restless for that. I need another escape and I might just know how to get it. Or who's going to give it to me.

I go to the bar with the bus and greet Harper. She's still mad at me, but at least she's not holding a grudge and is talking to me. "Hey, Harp, I'll wait for Fai outside and we'll go to his place. I'll stay there tonight, so you don't have to worry about me. Cool?"

Harper presses her lips together, which means it's not cool with her – at all. But she's not going to say that. She's going to say what I want to hear. To make me happy. Even though it doesn't make her happy. "Yeah, okay. See you in the morning?" she asks.

I nod and salute her before jumping down from the stool. Tomorrow is Saturday so I don't have to go to school. I'm not staying at Fai's tonight, that's just a lie because I know she'll check if I'm home when she gets there and I have to go to work tonight.

I go outside the bar, leaning against the wall beside the front door so I see when he comes. And I know he's coming. Because he can't stay away.

I'm smoking a cigarette and twirling my hair around my finger so the time passes faster while I'm waiting for him to come.

I hear him before I see him. The unmistakable sound of his motorcycle is hard to miss. I put the cigarette out and throw it into the wastebin, smiling to myself because I'm excited I get to annoy him. For no reason at all.

I lean back against the wall, placing my foot against the wall and wait for him to finish talking so he comes to the entrance. He's the first one in the group, but is the last one to notice me. Others are not really happy and impressed to see me. I don't care about them, though. They don't even matter. It's not them that I need. Well, I don't need Fai, either, he's just convenient.

When Fai looks up and sees me, his smile disappears, as well while mine reappears. He slows down, turning to the guys and telling them to go ahead and he'll be in in just a few minutes. He stops in front of me. "Waiting for someone?"

"Yeah, you," I say.

His eyebrow arches. He takes out a cigarette and lights it. "Why?" he asks nonchalantly like he can't be bothered.

"Do I need a reason?"

His eyebrows raise. "Yeah, you do."

I grin. "I'm lucky that I have one, then. Take me to that hill again."

Fai just continues looking at me for a few minutes. "What am I? Your chauffeur?" He scoffs. "No," is his answer before he takes a drag of his cigarette.

"Oh, come on, Fai. You know you want to spend time with me." I want to put my hand on his chest, but he steps back, not letting me touch him. He's not letting me play a game with him tonight, it seems.

"The fuck do I get out of it?"

"My company," I grin.

He shakes his head and drops the cigarette on the floor, stepping on it to put it out. "Stop wasting my time." He wants to go inside, but I step in front of the door, blocking the entrance completely by extending my arms out.

His nostrils flare, our faces now inches apart. "Fai, come on. What do you want? A handjob? A blowjob?"

"Move, Kadie. I'm not playing."

"No," I say defiantly.

"I said I'm not taking you anywhere. Quit being annoying and find someone else to take you."

"My, my. You're being really mean to me tonight. I miss the Fai that begged me to come out to a party with him for his birthday and asking for kisses. Where's he hiding?"

His jaw locks. "Move from the door, Kadience."

"Take me to that hill."

"No," Fai says. "Ask someone else."

"But I want to go with you."

He scowls. "And I don't want to go there now."

I drop my arms from the door, showing my defeat. Partly. I still don't go away from the door and I don't have any intention to do it. "Please," I say quietly.

Fai falls silent. He stares at me, his eyes running over my face, his eyebrows furrowing. "Why?"

I shrug. "I feel like going away from everyone. Take me away, please."

Fai steps away from me, putting space between us. He looks like he doesn't know what to do for some moments. "Get on the motorcycle," he says grumpily.

I bite down on my lip, smiling to myself. That was pretty easy. I happily skip to the motorcycle, getting on behind Fai. I feel the bad mood radiating off him when I sit behind him. It's a weird game we're playing here, telling each other to stay away, but then doing things together, kissing and arguing and laughing and dancing.

I'm smiling the whole way to that hill. I watch the city, looking at it as we disappear from it and away from it. Far, far away from it.

When we get there, I get off the motorcycle first while Fai stays on it a few seconds longer. "I could just leave you here, you know."

I turn around. "You could. But you're not going to." I turn back around and walk to the grass, sitting down and taking in the view. Fai comes behind me, quietly sitting down beside me, as well.

We don't talk for a long time and Fai seems like he's starting to get bored. He stretches his legs out, leaning back on his hands.

I look at him sideways and then, with a small, mischievous smile, I turn and lay down on the grass, putting my head on his legs. Fai looks down at me, confused. I also notice he's scowling.

"So I have a better view at the stars," I explain, giving him an innocent grin.

He doesn't say anything, but he doesn't move away, either. I clasp my hands over my stomach, looking up at the night sky. Fai takes a look at it, but quickly loses interest and looks at the city, but I feel his eyes on me a few times. He doesn't say anything. He's not one of the talkative people and that's the main difference between us. I could talk about anything with anyone.

"You know, we're almost completely made up of empty space. Everything around us is made up of atoms, tiny particles composed of a nucleus orbited by electrons. These tiny particles are filled with energy, but they have quite a bit of empty space; in fact 99,99 percent of all of the matter around us is empty space. This means you've never touched anything in your life. We're actually floating above this grass we're sitting on thanks to incredibly small electromagnetic forces."

I extend my arms up, looking at the sky through my fingers and then looking up at Fai who's staring at me, quietly, but with interest. "Pretty crazy, huh?"

"So if I do this," he says, placing his hand on my cheeks, close to my lips, "I'm not really touching you?"

I shake my head.

He removes his hand. "Bullshit," he says, looking at the city again.

"It's science, really. It's hard to understand, but that's why I love it so much."

I look back up at the sky and we're coated in silence once again. "Do you know how to tell stars and planets apart?"

Fai looks up at the sky and then at me. "Am I getting a lecture about science tonight?"

"Don't you want to learn more about everything around us?"

"No, not really, no."

I ignore him, continuing to look up at the sky. "It's actually impossible to see with the naked eye, but the main difference is shape, of course, which you can only see with the telescope. But if you watch the sky closely, you can differentiate stars from planets just to see which ones twinkle and which ones don't, but even that can be deceiving sometimes, because even planets can twinkle sometimes because when looking towards the horizon, we're looking through more atmosphere than when we're looking straight up which means more light refraction that causes them to twink."

I notice Fai is looking up at the sky, even though he feigned disinterest before. "You seem to really love the science," he says as an observation.

I continue looking at him. "And what about you? What do you love? Who do you love?"

He looks at me with a serious expression and then lets out a sigh. "Love is a pretty strong word," he murmurs.

I shift a little on his legs so I have a better look at him. "It is," I agree. "Have you ever felt it before? The rush, the excitement of seeing another person?"

He just stares at me as if he doesn't know what to really say. "No," he says with a gruff voice.

"But do you think you ever could? Feel something so strong towards another human being?"

His eyebrow slowly raises. "I may be fucked up in the head in many ways, bee, but I am still just a human being and I do feel things, just like every other person in the world. If you're asking me if I'm capable to love someone, yeah, I'm pretty sure I am, but that doesn't mean I should."

I smile, lifting up my hand and touching his jaw. His jaw locks, but he doesn't move his face away from my touch.

"What's the point of these questions? Are you trying to ask me out?"

My smile intensifies. "No, you're going to ask me out. I was just wondering."

He moves his face away from my hand. "I already asked you out. You turned me down."

"You asked me to sleep with you. Not really asked, you just made a comment about it."

"So? That's the same thing."

I shake my head to him. "No, Fai, that's a very different thing. And you'll know it. You'll learn the difference one day, I'm sure."

"When I fall in love?" he asks mockingly, laughing like he finds the idea funny.

I don't say anything back.

His face becomes serious again. "And you? Have you ever loved someone?"

"Not anyone. Not ever," I say truthfully. The only person I've loved is Harper, but that's a different kind of love. I haven't even felt love towards my parents. I don't know how that even feels. "Do you believe in soulmates?" I ask him while looking up at the sky again.

He takes out a pack of cigarette, taking one out and lighting it. "Do you?"

"Well, I don't believe in the theory that everyone is made for someone else. So, no, I don't really believe in soulmates. You can only be made for yourself, too. You can end up being with yourself for the rest of your life and that's okay, too. I think we should all ditch an idea that we have to find someone or else we'll end up alone. I mean, you're not alone if you spend your whole life with yourself and friends. You can be your own soulmate."

Fai takes a drag of a cigarette, looking at me. "And you believe you're your own soulmate? Do you believe you're not made for anyone else?"

I chuckle. "I have no idea, Fai. I have a whole life in front of me. I'm just saying that I would never settle for anything less than I really want just because I'd fear to end up alone. I've never belonged anywhere, to anyone, but maybe I'd like to experience that, even if just for one, short moment. And if I don't have that heart-racing love, then I don't want it. That's all." I sit up, so I'm right beside him, facing him. "What's it gonna be, Fai? Do you think you could give me that?"

Chapter 14

T his is the thing about Kadience Myers – I never know when she's joking and when she's being serious. Is she ever being serious? Except for the times when she's talking about science and all that bullshit?

And when she says shit like this to me, I don't know what the fuck to think. I can't read her because she doesn't show anything she doesn't want to and it's pissing me the hell off because I don't know what to make out of her. That might be one of the reasons I can't really stay away from her. I want to understand her because there must be something way deeper she has inside of her that she doesn't show the world.

I feel like she sees me. She sees me. That bothers me. It bothers me a lot because I don't see her because she doesn't want to show herself. She's hiding behind this mask and she doesn't want to take it off for anyone, not even when she's drunk and high out of her mind. Or maybe that is her. Maybe that's the true her; something so unique that no one will ever truly understand, even though she'll make them all crazy with wanting to get her.

"I can't promise you to give you the whole galaxy, bee," I tell her, looking at her to see what exactly she wants from me. I can never tell with her. One time she wants me close, the next time she doesn't want me anywhere near her.

She chuckles, sitting on the grass cross-legged now. "I'm not really asking you to give me anything you can't give me. Or am I?" her head cocks to the side and a few strands of hair fall over her face.

I avert my eyes, clenching my fists. "Don't ask for something you can't reciprocate, either."

One second she's sitting beside me, the next she's crawling closer to me, putting her leg over me and sitting on my legs. She brings our bodies close together, putting her thumb on my bottom lip, touching my piercing, looking straight into my eyes.

Shit.

"Kiss me," she says quietly.

Double fucking shit.

"Why don't you kiss me?" I taunt her.

Her thumb softly touches my bottom lip. Her touch completely disarms me and that's a dangerous fucking thing. "Because I want you to do it." Her voice is so quiet, she's almost whispering.

"Why?" I ask her, equally as quietly, my lips moving under her finger.

Her lips slowly turn up into a smile. "Because we both want it."

Shit, I feel high. No joke. It's that what-the-fuck-is-happening-to-me moment because this is something I haven't experienced with anyone before and it's weird as hell because my thoughts feel clouded and I just don't know what to think about this situation. She confuses the heck out of me.

I grab the back of her head with my hand, pulling her head closer and she comes willingly, putting her mouth on mine as if that's all that she wanted to do for this evening; as if she was dying to do this.

She's a selfish kisser. She takes and takes and controls it, doing it the way she wants it, but when she gives back, it's the best thing you've ever felt because she makes it unforgettable each time.

I feel her smiling against my mouth, her hands gently cupping my face and I swear it almost makes me feel something. It almost makes me feel. It almost makes me feel something other than the despair and hatred I constantly carry with me.

I break the kiss and she leans back, sighing, keeping her hands clasped behind my neck. She gets off my lap and she lays down on the grass beside me. I look ahead, at the city, at nothing particular, just not at her. Anything but her. "What the hell are we doing, Kadie?"

I feel her looking at me. She's smiling. I don't have to look at her to know that. "We're just having fun, Fai. What else?"

Of course. Of course. What else? What fucking else? I stand up. "Are you ready to head back?"

Kadie sits up, but she doesn't stand. She's looking up at me, her head tilting to the side. She's studying me. I clench my jaw. I hate when she does that. I hate when she's trying to read me like one of her books. I hate that I let her. As if I have any other choice, really.

"You're pissed," she says. "Why are you pissed?"

Fuck. Seriously, fuck. "I'm not pissed," I deny, refusing to look at her.

She muses. "Ok, so you're pissed that I want to have fun. If you don't want to have fun, what do you want to have then, Fai?"

My lips tighten. "Nothing. I don't want to have anything." I turn and go to the motorcycle. "Get on, I'm leaving. Or you can stay here, whatever the fuck you want."

She raises her eyebrow at my attitude. She stands up, grinning to herself and shaking her head. "Or maybe you just don't know how to have fun," she taunts me, taking the helmet and sitting behind me, wrapping her arms around me, putting her head on my shoulder. "Or you're just lying to the both of us," she says quietly, almost whispering.

I rev the engine of my motorcycle in answer.

I have a business I need to take care of tonight. I'm always in a pissy mood when I have to do the dirty work, so I can't blame Kadie for stepping on the wrong nerves tonight. She can't help herself with me as I can't with her, but only when I'm in the mood. I wasn't in the mood tonight.

Jon comes to me, alone. Other guys better know to stay the fuck away when I'm making plans. I can't fuck things up because they depend on me and if there's a hole in my plan, if there's something I don't think through, things can get bad. Very bad. And quickly.

I lift my head to Jon. I was waiting for him. He's late. "Your princess is safe at work."

Safe. At the strip club she works at. She's anything but safe there, but at least I know when she comes and goes from there. Ever since she decided to come into my life and stay, there's one more person I need to look after because she's been in danger ever since she first sat on my motorcycle. A mistake on my part, but there's no going back now.

The moment a person enters my life, their life changes forever. That's why I'm always so careful who I speak with, especially with the opposite gender. I don't trust anyone else than my circle because trusting someone else could be a mistake that could cost me life.

But I wasn't careful, not with her. I let her come into my life, all carefree and badass, like she's invincible, like she's not scared of anything and anyone. She almost convinced me. But she's not invincible. She thinks she's tough, but she isn't. Not really. Not when it comes to the people I deal with.

"Good. Thanks," I keep my answer short.

Jon lingers, hesitating to go. He wants to say something. I only lift my head, looking at him. "It's not my place to say anything, but, man, do you think she's a good idea?"

I hold myself back so I don't snort. "She's as bad as it can get, bro, but what can I do about it now?" I shake my head. "I have a plan for tonight, let's head out," I say, closing that subject because I don't want to discuss it with anyone. They know enough, they don't have to know any more than that.

I know about Kadience Myers, I know some necessary details about her life. I knew where she lived before she told me. I know she lives with her mother and her step-father and that her father died when she was 9 years old. I even know her routine, when she goes to school, when she goes out of it, where she goes after it, I know where her cousin lives and I also know her family enough to know it's harmless.

Does that make me a creeper? Sure. Maybe. But it makes her safe.

The guys are waiting for me outside, ready to go over the plan. And we do. We plan everything in detail, in minutes, in seconds even. Because a second can be a second too long sometimes. We go over everything. We use coded signals with hands, everything different ones because people can quickly learn the moves. Word travels fast here and we have to be faster.

When you're in this as long as we are, you learn the tricks. The tricks save your life at the end. If you don't learn the tricks, you're dead. Immediately.

So we go over the plan, perfecting it to the last detail, check our guns and we're on our way.

We park the motorcycles in the distance of the building we're headed to. They're not expecting us, so making noise is not necessary tonight. We have to be quiet for this.

I look at them all to make sure we all know what to do and to see if they're ready before I go first. The building is guarded. I know about the cameras and the bodyguards. I also know about alarms. We move slowly and quietly, looking around, but it's peaceful. No one knows what's coming.

We stop behind the trees, spotting the first two bodyguards. I look at the guys and give them a nod. We wait three seconds before it all begins. We surge forward, fast and out of nowhere, or so it seems for them. They're not fast enough to pull out the guns, so they're left with only fists.

They're strong and big, but we're fast and know the tricks. I punch my guy in the jaw, making him grunt and lose focus just enough so I can punch and then kick him in the stomach. He gets one punch at my face, just one that I allow, before I push him against the wall with so much force, all the breath leaves him, and kick him in the stomach, my fists coming for his face.

Other guys are behind me and then beside me, taking my place so we don't lose time and I can enter the building.

I shoot at the cameras and at the alarm, disabling it completely. The fucker really isn't as protected as he wanted others to think he is, this is some amateur work we're doing here, yet it's enough to bring him down.

I run forward, knowing exactly where I have to go. Running upstairs, I turn to the right, but someone grabs me from behind, his arm coming around my throat and squeezing. Ah, fuck.

I kick him, trying to pry his arm off but he doesn't budge. Another one of the gorillas. Goddamn. "Where do you think you're going?" he growls angrily.

I have my hands free so I make a fist and blindly aim for his face. I hit him directly in the nose. "Fuck," he grunts, his hold loosening just a little. Just enough so I can twist around and lose his hold on me completely. He takes a gun out immediately, aiming it at me.

"Wow, easy," I say, slowing down, not making any hasty movements. I know Lev is right behind me. I extend my arms out, so if he looks upstairs, he'll see it as a sign.

"Don't you fucking move if you don't want me to paint the wall behind you with your brains."

My eyebrow twitches and I desperately want to give him a piece of my mind. I chew the inside of my cheek, acting sombre and defeated, making the guy think he really got me. Jesus Christ, does he think I'm this easy to get down?

So I sight to myself, slumping my shoulders, counting the seconds in my head. 5 ... 4 ... 3 ... 2 ... 1. The gun goes off and the big boy in front of me falls to the floor with a loud thump. I grin at Lev before I dart back to where I wanted to go before I was so rudely interrupted.

I break into the office of the fucker I want to see. He's trying to get out through the window, but we both know he won't have any luck. He wasn't prepared for us. He didn't think through it.

He looks back at me, clear fear shining from his eyes. I stop in the middle of the room, cocking my head to the side. "Are you headed somewhere?" I ask him calmly as if I came here for a casual talk.

I did come for a casual talk, one too many times. This time, it won't be just talk anymore.

The man knows he's dead, either if he jumps from the window and risks getting his neck broken, or he gets killed by me. I'll be kind and let him choose his death.

"Please," he pleads.

I tsk. "I think you owe me something and I came to collect it."

The man is shaking his head. "I'll get it to you in two weeks, I promise. Just two weeks."

I roll my head back, already getting annoyed. I take my gun out and look at it with interest, caressing it with my hand as if I'm trying to clean it. The man starts shaking. "No. Please. I'll get you the money. Come on, I promise."

"You know what I'm so fucking tired of? You're all brave at the beginning, brave and full of money. You think you have it all and that you're so protected nothing can get to you. But in the end? You're all weak as fuck, begging, crying, fucking praying. Where's all the braveness now, tough man? Huh?"

As if my words did something for him, he straightens up and faces me fully. He's at least 25 years older than me, yet he's scared shitless of me. "I know about her, your new hot, blonde thing that's making you pant after her. And, really, I can't blame you." He sounds so confident saying this.

Fuck. If he knows it, others know it by now too. Fucking hell. This is not the time to think about her, either.

I plaster a smile on my face and raise my eyebrows. "And I know about your daughter. Sweet, young girl. Can't wait to fuck her, to be honest."

His face pales. "You leave my family alone, you hear me? This is between us?"

I chuckle. "Is it? You started dragging others in this. The thing is; you may think you know something, but I always know more. Also, you're not really in a position to make demands here, don't you think?"

"I hope you'll rot in hell!"

I merely shrug. "I'll see you there, then."

I lift the gun, aim and pull the trigger.

Chapter 15

T hose surprise tests we randomly get at school bore the shit out of me because they give us the easiest questions that I always finish early and then forbid us to leave the classroom, because the lesson will continue after we're done writing.

It's always the same shit. I usually do the questions in approximately 7 minutes and I have 23 minutes left to do ... nothing.

In times like this, I either plop my elbow on the table, support my head with my hand and just stare through the window. Other times, like today, I draw. I like to draw when I have time and when imagination strikes me.

I draw a lion today, the one I saw on Fai's back, but drawing it by memory is quite hard because I don't remember all the details, so I only draw what I remember I saw, even if just for a few seconds. I have to draw it on the test paper because I'm not allowed to use anything else right now, but I'll get it back, anyway, so it's all good. I have to make it small, though.

When I look at it, I smile. It's not quite right because I know some of the details are missing, but I swear I'll have him show me his tattoos one day because his body is a work of art and I could get a lot of inspiration from it.

When the teacher comes to collect the tests, he stops by my table, looking at the drawing. She shakes her head to herself, not commenting anything, but I know she's impressed. They don't know how I do, probably because there's no one else like me. And I'm not sucking my own tits, but I'm just seeing it how it is.

The rest of the class, I sort of just stare out of the window, twirling the pen in my hand and wait until the bell rings so I can get the hell out of here for today.

When I'm out in the hallway, I'm approached by Mandy, my class-mate and also the bitch of this school. She's not even a bad bitch, she's just a bitch thinking she's bad because her daddy's rich and she can wear designer clothes, thinking that'll make up for her shitty personality.

But she's someone other people want to be on good terms with, if not even friends with her. Guys want to fuck her, girls want to befriend her. To be completely honest, I've never given two shits about her. I don't give two shits about anyone at this school and she's not an exception. She tried things with me a few times, but that never went well for her, so she just left me alone.

"Hey, Kadience," she says sweetly, doing her infamous hair flip with her long, black, shiny hair.

I just raise my eyebrows at her, not even bothering to say anything back to her.

She straightens her posture, trying to look intimidating. My eye-brows lift even higher. "Can I ask you a personal question?"

"Just shoot it out and get moving, I'm in a hurry here," I tell her, not in the mood to eat any of her shit today.

"Are you dating Fai Mills?"

If it'd be possible, my eyebrows would raise to the moon right now. Ah, so the word is spreading fast around here. People are already making assumptions, and she's one to believe them. Of course she is. She's actually someone who makes assumptions about people and spreads them around like she's spreading her legs, if she's right or not, she doesn't care, as long as she has shit coming out her mouth, she's content. And others are too, because they're eating everything she gives them.

"What's it to you?" I ask her in annoyance. If I don't like something, it's people spreading rumours. I don't care about them, but I don't like them.

"So you are?" she asks, her own eyebrows shooting up in surprise. She loses some of her confidence she approached me with, I see.

I smile to her, stepping closer to her as if I'm going to tell her a secret. "None of your goddamn business. Maybe focus a little more on the history book the next time because I saw you struggling in there today instead of things that don't have to do anything with you." I give her a wink before I push past her, my shoulder brushing hers.

I didn't think people in this school knew who he was, but I know there are people from here who go to the bar frequently and it's no surprise they're talking, although it makes me so fed up to listen to assumptions about me and about other people. I don't care if they're correct or incorrect, but it's annoying as hell and that's why I'm always careful I never tell anyone anything more than they deserve to know; which is nothing.

Fai doesn't come to the bar that night. He doesn't come the night after that, either. He actually shows up on the fourth night when I'm not even expecting him to show up anymore. And it's messed up that I was kind of looking forward to seeing him because it's exciting and we have some fun together, but it's whatever.

I've been drawing these past three nights at the bar. I put the lion from his back on A4 format, but it's still making me mad that I can't get the details right, so the whole drawing is off as a result.

Fai is a head-turner and that's a fact. It's hard not to notice him when he goes somewhere because everyone looks. He has something that makes you want to look. Besides a hell of a good looking face, that is. I have to look over my shoulder to see him. He doesn't look at me, at all. They sit at their regular table and Fai lazily scans the bar.

I look away before he can look at me. And I know he will, he's just trying to play it cool. Harper is trying not to look, too, but she's not succeeding. I just wait for him to come to me.

I feel him standing behind me just minutes later, looking at the drawing I don't even try to hide from him. I don't care if he sees it. He watches it for some moments, inspecting it.

"That looks very familiar," comes his familiar gruff voice.

My lips turn up at the corners. "I'd be disappointed if it didn't."

Fai sits beside me and I turn my head to look at him, my smile freezing on my face slightly. His face is bruised. His lip is cut and he has a bruise that turned purple on his temple. "Oh, wow. You gave yourself a make-over to suit your bad boy persona going on, huh?"

He gives me a half-smile. "Wanna kiss it all better?"

My eyebrow raises. "I'm good, thanks."

Fai glances at my sketch once more before he stands up. "Come on, let's go," he suddenly says.

I give him a weird look. "Excuse me, what?"

"I said come on, let's go."

I have to chuckle. "Go where, Fai? Where was the question in this?"

He rolls his eyes. "You can stay here for all I care, bee. You know where I'm going. I'll wait outside, if you're not out in three minutes, I'm going without you."

I stare at him as he walks out, biting the inside of my lip and smiling like a goddamn fool. Okay, then. I look at Harper and catch her watching with raised eyebrows. I close my sketchbook and jump down from the stool, giving her a wave. I think Harper started warming up to the idea of me hanging out with Fai.

She was always so afraid of me ending up with someone destructive that would ruin my life with his dangerous ways of living, but she might've finally started seeing that I'm, in fact, a big girl that has her own head to think with. Fai is not a threat. He's not going to do anything.

I walk out, making him exactly for three minutes. He's smoking a cigarette, leaning against his motorcycle with a helmet in his hand. He notices me walking towards him, but he shows indifference. He's not surprised I came. We both play this game around each other.

Fai puts a cigarette out, throwing it into the wastebin this time, handing me the helmet. "Put it on."

I stare at the helmet in his hand. "Order me to do something one more time if you dare."

He only raises his eyebrows, obviously not taking me seriously. "Put it on," he repeats his order.

"No, fuck you. You put it on."

Fai stares at me, his amusement quickly disappearing from his face. "For fuck's sake, if you got paid for being annoying, you'd be a fucking millionaire. Jesus Christ," he mutters, stepping to me and putting the helmet on my head. He rests his hands on top of it, keeping my head in place and looking into my eyes. "There's a time and place for your defiance, bee. This is not it."

I make a mocking face at him, although, inside, I'm gloating at the way he knows how to handle me and doesn't back down when I get up against him. Hot damn.

He gets up on the motorcycle and, with no further words, I sit behind him, wrapping my arms around his waist.

I don't know what's riding with him, but it's addicting. I feel so free, so safe. It's almost unhealthy, but it brings a smile on my face. This is all fun and games. I know Fai and I have no future together. We're not going to get married and have kids running around. This is not us. This is Harper, but this is not me. I don't get to have that kind of future.

I've always liked to live on the more dangerous and adventurous side. If that gets me down at the end, I'll go down happy. In some way, at least. Or content.

I think this is becoming my new happy place. I have to share it with Fai, though, but it's no problem. It's because of him that I discovered this place. It's so peaceful up here, especially here on the hill, in the middle of the meadow, away from the road, away from the city, away from everything, everyone. Just us. In the middle of nothing and with a hell of a pretty view.

I turn to Fai, looking at his face, inspecting his bruise. I lightly press my fingertips against it, barely touching it. He sharply turns his head into my direction. "What are you doing?" he asks abruptly.

"Do you know why bruises change colour?" Fai groans, but I don't let this discourage me. "Bruised capillaries release fresh blood that's coloured red by hemoglobin; a protein that transports oxygen throughout your body. The oxygen-rich blood causes the injury to appear read at first and then after one or two days without circulation, the hemoglobin begins to break down, coloring the bruise blue, purple or black.

"A week-old bruise becomes olive green because the iron in hemoglobin that's used to make new blood cells, for example, is gone. And at the final stage, your bruise turns yellow or light brown. The color comes from bilirubin, a byproduct of hemoglobin breakdown.

"And about the bruise changing shapes, that's –"

Fai's mouth is suddenly on mine, shutting me up, his hand in my hair, gripping my head so it stays where he wants it to while he mercilessly attacks my lips. He kisses me fast and hard at first, his movements strong and desperate, but then the kiss softens and he becomes more gentle, his tongue coming out to search for my own that happily greets his.

A soft, barely there groan leaves his mouth and he lays me down on the grass, climbing on top of me, keeping his lips on mine. I put my hand on his neck, open my legs to make room for him and he settles between them, his hard-on pressed right against my center. He pushes against me, getting a moan out of me.

Oh my God, this guy knows how to kiss. He takes my other hand that's free and laces it with his own, bringing it over my head and moving his mouth down my jaw to my neck where he softly sucks the skin, all the while his hips are expertly moving against me. It feels like he's fucking me without really fucking me.

But then my phone starts ringing with Harper's ringtone. "Oh, fuuuck," I say in disappointment. Fai backs off and the spell between us is immediately broken. My mind feels a little hazy for a few moments.

I answer with a breathless, "Yeah?"

"Kadie, where are you?" Harper's panicked voice makes me immediately sit up and put me on alert. "Something happened. I'm still at the bar, I can't get out. Some guy ... I don't know, it was scary. He was looking for you and Fai."

"Stay right where you are, I'm coming to get you." I'm already on my feet and Fai is looking up at me, standing up too. We look at each other and by my expression, he immediately notices something's wrong. He threads his hand through his hair, impatiently waiting for me to finish the call.

"No. Don't come here, Kadie. I don't know if he's still here. He'll hurt you. Don't come here," Harper repeats, but she's so scared, her voice is shaking and she's on the verge of tears.

"Just stay where you are, Harper," I say, trying to sound calm and reassuring.

I end the call without breaking the gaze with Fai. "We have to go back. Something happened at the bar. Some guy was looking for us."

Understanding dawns over Fai's face. "Let's go," he says, spurring into action.

Chapter 16

Fai drives us to my home and before he can even come to a full stop, I say, "No."

He puts his feet down, but I don't do the same. "God help me, Fai, if you don't take me to that goddamn bar right at this moment." I'm angry as hell. Angry because Harper was in danger tonight. Angry that she's alone there, alone and afraid, not knowing what's going on. I'll be damned if anyone's keeping me away.

"I'll make sure Harper gets home safe," Fai says with a calm voice.

I punch him in the shoulder. "No, I'll make sure she gets home safe. She's my family, I'm looking out for her!"

Fai turns to look at me, giving me an angry glare. "And who's going to look out for you?" he asks with a bitter tone.

I don't dwell on his comment too much. "Me!" I reply. "I can take a taxi there. Or bus. But you're not keeping me away, you hear me? I'm involved in this and I'm fighting back."

Fai groans to himself, now pissed, too. "Can you just get the hell off and stop causing problems for me? The longer we're arguing here, the more things could happen to you cousin."

And don't I know that. "Drive, Fai. I have a knife I'm not afraid to use; even on you if it means getting what I want."

He lets out one last frustrated growl and afterwards, we're on our way to the bar.

It's not that far from here and when we reach it, Fai doesn't even come to a full stop and I'm already jumping down, pulling the helmet off my head and running straight towards the bar. "Kadie, wait! Goddamn it," I hear Fai behind me, but I don't stop.

He grabs my arm, stalling me and I give him an exasperated, annoyed look. "Stop playing my goddamn hero, Fai," I say, more pissed at the situation than at him.

He clenches jaw, but he doesn't bother saying anything back, yet he doesn't go of my arm either, walking one step in before me, which pisses me off, but his hold only tightens when I want him to release me and I just stop bothering because I have enough of everything today.

Stepping into the bar, we both stop. It's a mess. The workers, the police, everyone is here, inspecting the mess and cleaning it up. Or at least trying to. I look at all the faces in here, at each one of them, but I don't find Harper's.

She said she's in the back and I manage to lose Fai's grip on me, taking advantage of people not looking and slipping back where I want Harper sitting on the floor with her legs extended, her head laid against the wall, her eyes closed, with a phone in her hand.

"Harp," I say softly, crouching down beside her. Her eyes fly open. "You okay?"

She hesitates before nodding her head once. "Are you?" she asks.

"Yes. I was with Fai. What the hell happened?"

Harper shudders. "A planned attack, apparently. Guns and everything. It was messy, Kadie. I thought we were all going to die. You could smell fear in the air. But they were looking for someone. Fai, I think. Someone mentioned you but I'm not sure because I was hiding behind the bar." She shakes her head, obviously shaken up.

Well, shit. This evening is really going to shit. "Come on, let's go home."

I make Harper a hot chocolate when we get home because it's her favourite thing and she always makes it for me when she thinks I'm feeling down, although it was never really my favourite thing, but I appreciate her thoughtfulness, so I never told her that.

She's sitting on the couch, mindlessly staring out of the window. Something's on her mind, but she isn't speaking about it. She will, when she'll want to. I know that by now.

I sit down next to her, giving her the mug with the hot chocolate. She takes it, looking down at it. "Can I tell you something?" she says all of the sudden, still looking down at the cup.

I sit with my legs beneath me. "Anything," I promise her.

She looks at me, deep in the eyes then. "Today, when I felt I was for sure going to die with everyone else, I was so scared. Scared of dying and not living my life, not really. Scared that I'll die without knowing the true meaning of life. Without experiencing love. Heartbreak. All that stuff."

My chest seizes up because, holy fuck, Harper could die tonight and I'd probably lose my goddamn head if it happened. Harper's really the only person in my life that I trust and doesn't get on my last nerve. If something happened to her, I'd just die with her because she's the only one that actually kept me alive and she doesn't even know that.

"You're going to experience that and so much more, Harp," I say with reassurance, truly believing that. Of course she's going to. She's hot as fuck and twice as smart.

"When you're with Fai, what do you feel?"

Her question confuses me for a moment. I know what she wants to know. "Free. Most of all, I feel free because I am who I am with him and he just ... lets me. But what Fai and I isn't love, Harp. It's just two young people having lots of fun and living recklessly."

Harper smiles a sad smile. "What is love if not reckless? I always watched you from a distance. Always envied you a little because you're so nonchalant, not giving shit about people and anything, just doing your own thing and doing it proudly. You live, Kadie. You're out here living your life and I'm ... not."

"You are," I tell her, putting my hands on top of hers. "You just do it differently, but you are living it. You're going to be successful and you're going to marry someone who's going to be good to you and you're going to have children, a big house and a nice car, all that. That's what your living for."

Harper thinks for just a few seconds. "I don't ... think I care about all that stuff because at the end of the day, they don't mean any-thing. I want something real. Someone who's going to give me a real thing. Maybe a little reckless and spontaneous. Someone that will make my heart race. I don't want to settle for a shitty sex, either."

"Harper, there's going to be someone crazy about you – because how could he not? – but it doesn't have to be someone like Fai, either. It doesn't matter who he is and what he does, you'll know it when it's right."

Harper is thoughtful for some moments. "And what if it is some-one like Fai?" When she sees my confused look, she shakes her head. "Never mind. I just need to rest."

When Harper gets read for bed, she asks me if I could stay with her until she falls asleep because she doesn't want to be alone right now. I go with her to her room, sitting on the bed while she lays down. We're in complete darkness, neither of us saying anything.

What if it is someone like Fai? Yes, what if it is? I always thought Harper's type are people that aren't like me and Fai, I always thought she'd want someone stable, someone she'd know what to expect from.

But we don't always choose who we fall in love with and her question makes me scared for her. Harper isn't for this. She's pure and honest and innocent. This life would ruin her.

I stare forward into the dark space when my phone starts vibrating in my pocket. I take it out and when I see a number I don't recognise, I just put it on silent so it stops vibrating and ignore the call. Seconds later, it starts vibrating again. I frown and silence it once again.

Then a text comes through.

It's Fai. Pick up your phone.

My frown is replaced with the incredulous look.

I don't remember giving you my number, I type.

He calls me again and I walk out of Harper's bedroom so I don't wake her up. I answer him while walking outside of the apartment. "Where did you get my number?"

I walk up the stairs to the rooftop. "That's not important," Fai says. "How's your friend?" he asks.

"Shaken up but she's going to be okay," I say with assurance.

"Good," Fai says as I step out on the rooftop. "And how are you?"

"What do you think? Pissed as fuck. She could get hurt tonight."

Fai is silent for a few seconds. "She wouldn't. My guys were there."

"That's not the point. She had to see this, had to be a part of this because of me."

"Technically because of me, but yeah," Fai corrects me.

I lean on the concrete wall and just enjoy the view for a view seconds, feeling calmer already.

"You can't go to the bar for some time now, you know that, yeah?" Fai reminds me. I know it. Of course I do. It was because of me and Fai they were there. Both of us.

"That's not an option, though. Harper isn't safe there alone."

Fai lets out a long exhale. "My guys will make sure she's safe."

"Yes, sure. But your guys don't love her like I do. I'd die for her if that meant she'd stay safe."

Fai is silent for a heartbeat. "Good thing Lev has hots for her, then, huh?" he says it lightly but he's not joking.

I smile to myself. I think Lev is a good guy from what I saw. Hot, too. He's not for Harper, but he could fight if he needed to and I think he needs to do that. A lot. "And what about you? Are you going to stay away from the bar, too?" I ask Fai, resting my head on my hand, looking into the distance, not focusing on anything particular.

"Yeah. I'm staying on the low for now, just in case."

My forehead scrunches. "And what if I want to see you?"

Fai is quiet for some moments now, obviously debating if I'm serious or not. "Then you'll see me," he tells me with a confirming tone.

I grin, biting down on my lip. Hanging out with Fai is becoming addicting. It's exciting. It makes me feel carefree. Free. He takes my mind off of the shitty things that go through it.

"I'll go now. Bye, Fai. Message me some time now that you have my number." I make a kissing sound and Fai's laugh rings in my ear.

"Yeah, bee," he says gruffly.

We disconnect and I place the phone on the concrete wall. I lean forward a little, looking down on the street. I close my eyes, trying to envision the fall – like I always do. Trying to envision how it feels like. How fast would I reach the bottom? But this time, it turns out, I don't want to imagine the fall.

Just the view from the top stays behind my closed eyes. No fall tonight.

I'm trying to convince Harper to find a different job, but she doesn't even want to hear about it and that budges me. She saw how dangerous that place got and, yes, it might be because I was stubborn and kept hanging out with Fai, stupidly thinking that Harper wouldn't get involved, but now that they know about me, they'll know about her, too, and I'm scared shitless for her.

She, on the other hand, doesn't seem to worry about it, not even a bit. Which is weird. Because Harper is always the panicked one, about everything. She gets scared quickly.

It seems that the accident she saw truly moved something inside of her and she's fighting against herself.

I haven't gone to the bar in three days. I haven't seen Fai, not even talked to him since that night, either. But I'm getting bored. If I have to stay at home, forcingly watching some boring movie and worrying about Harper, I'm going to go nuts.

I think about inviting Fai here. When Harper's not home, of course, but I don't even mention that to her because I don't really know what her reaction would be. She warmed up to the guy, but she still has some restrictions and limits if I know her well. And I do know her very well.

After school, I go to the library, but I don't find anything new that would be interest me enough so I'd read it.

I cave in and shoot Fai a text.

Meet me tonight?

I put the earbuds in and play some music on my phone, taking the bus to Harper's place, my hood over my head.

I see Fai texted me back when I'm exiting the bus.

Wanna come to my place?

I shake my head with a grin. I was wondering how long he'd last without asking that question. He lasted pretty damn long for someone like him, so I give him props.

I think he deserves a little award for that.

Yep. Pick me up around 6, have to go to work later.

Fai's text comes in seconds. I guess he was waiting for my answer.

I got ya.

You don't. But you will soon, it seems.

I put the phone back into my pocket, whistling to myself the rest of the way.

Chapter 17

"You look happy," Harper notices.

I look up from my sketchbook, letting the smile I didn't even know I had on my face die down. Happy? No. Smiley? Yeah. Sure. But far, far from happy. I only shrug. "I'm seeing Fai tonight."

That grabs Harper's interest. "At the bar?" she asks.

I shake my head. "I'm going to his place."

Harper stays quiet and when I lift my head again to look at her, I see she's mulling this over in her head, her mouth twisting. "Have you two like ... slept together already?"

I have to smile at the modest phrasing Harper uses. "Nope," I say.

"But you're going to? Tonight?" she asks.

I tilt my head to the side, looking at her. "Yeah. Most definitely."

Harper nods, looking away. I see how her hand is playing with a thread on the couch's hand rest. I close the sketchbook, giving her full attention. "Okay, what's up?"

She turns her surprised eyes my way, but I only lift my eyebrows. "What would be up?" she asks me ever so innocently.

I lean forward, my sketchbook now dangling from my hands. "Harp," I say, giving her a pointed look. I'm reading right through her. She can't even hold my gaze.

"I like someone," Harper blurts out suddenly, looking anywhere but at me.

I blink a few times. "Wow, hello! Yes, finally some juicy news from you! Who is it?" I wiggle my eyebrows at her and she blushes.

"It's ..." She shakes her head. "It's not even important because we can't happen."

I frown. "Sure you can. Why wouldn't you be able to?"

Harper just looks at me and sighs. "Because he's ... way more different than I am and ..." She shakes her head. "Forget it. It's just a stupid crush that'll probably pass soon."

I frown. Knowing Harper, she doesn't just get a crush that passes. If she likes someone, she likes them. It's not for nothing. I narrow my eyes at her. "But you'll tell me if it gets serious? I want to know about your love life," I sing the last part out happily. I wish nothing more but happiness for her and a man who'll deserve her.

Harper smiles and only nods.

I go to Fai's place a little earlier because I don't have anything else to do now that Harper's gone. I don't even make sure he's home, I just go there, unannounced. I remember well where he lives so I can take the bus there.

He actually lives in a good neighbourhood, just a little out of the town centre and the apartment he's in must not be cheap. I still don't know what he does. Not really. I have my assumptions, but nothing that would confirm or deny them, so that's why I keep them just that – assumptions. Because I hate them and I try not to assume things about other people, too, until they tell me how it really is.

I go upstairs to his apartment. He lives somewhere in the middle at the very end of the hall. I rub my lips together and knock, pushing my hood off my head.

I don't hear him inside, but if he's in there, I know he'll be checking his peep-hole and I make sure I look into it and give a big grin. The door opens soon after and Fai leans against the doorframe. "Hi?" he asks. "It's not 6 yet."

I shrug. "Decided to came earlier and give us more time for, you know, more rounds." I give him a wink and go to him, stepping up on my tiptoes, leaning up and press a kiss against his mouth, then I push him away and enter his apartment."

I hear voices from the inside and I turn to him. "Am I interrupting something?" I ask while walking in the direction of the voices. And there they are, his group, sitting around the table, each with a beer, obviously discussing something important. They all shut up when they see me.

I give them all a grin. "Hi, guys!" I say in an obviously fake cheer voice.

Fai comes in behind me. Bastian scowls, his gaze swinging from me to Fai. "Shit, Fai. Seriously?" he asks in disbelief.

Fai slips past me, just shaking his head at his friends. "It's good. She's cool" Fai tells them and I give them all a satisfied grin.

I sit down on the couch next to the table, but Fai doesn't join me. He sits with the guys instead. I know they have some unfinished business, but no one wants to continue their conversation, probably not trusting me with it.

"I suggest we wrap it up early today since you two have plans already," Lev suggests to Fai, looking between us.

"You can finish what you started. I'll pretend I'm not even here."

The guys just look at Fai, who only sighs. "Yeah, let's just wrap it up."

I'm kind of disappointed because I thought this would be my chance to finally learn what he's really doing. I have a feeling it's nothing good, but I just want to see how bad it really is. I think Fai sees right through me. Maybe he doesn't trust me all that much with it, either.

They stand up and start putting the papers on the table together. They look like plans for something. I narrow my eyes, but I can't see anything useful.

"Bye, Kadience." I lift my eyes to Jon and give him a wave.

Ante slaps Fai's back. "Have fun, man."

Fai doesn't say anything in return. He's the only one that keeps seated, not even bothering to see them out. We look at each other until they all leave, leaving us alone.

"Why did you come here early?" Fai asks.

His tone indicates that he thinks he knows why. "I was bored. Thought we could have more time."

He doesn't believe me. What? Does he think I came here because I knew he'd be with the guys discussing whatever they were discussing? I lift my eyebrow at him in a challenge to see if he'll go and say what he thinks.

I stand up and slowly walk to where he's sitting. I push the chair back a little with my foot and lean against the table so I stand right in front of him. I cross my arms over my chest. "Say what you wanna say."

"It's not cool to come here without saying anything first and announcing yourself."

"Got ya," I say with a sly smile. I uncross my arms and go forward, sitting on his lap. "Want me to apologize?"

His hands automatically fall on my legs. "Yeah. Yeah, I want you to. And make it good," he says, a lazy smile forming on his face.

I place my lips on top of his. Our kiss isn't romantic. It isn't soft, either. It's just a kiss, full of passion and need for each other and yearning for what we've both wanted from the start.

His hands fall on my ass, pushing me closer to him, making me grind against him. He groans into my mouth and it might be the sexiest sound I've ever heard. I smile against his mouth, kissing him deeper.

Fai stands up and I wrap my legs around his waist, not once breaking our kiss. He walks us to his bedroom where he throws me on the bed, not gently at all, climbing on top of me. He grabs my hands and pushes them down against the bed, preventing me to move.

My body tenses up at the movement and I stop kissing him, staying still.

Fai leans back, looking down at me. "What?" he asks.

I smirk at him, trying to still my breathing. "I love being in charge." I wiggle my hands so he knows what I mean.

He raises his eyebrows, slowly releasing my hands and sits up. "Of course you do," he mutters.

He climbs off me and lays on the bed beside me. I roll on him, straddling him. "Don't worry. I'll make it good for you," I tell him, pushing my hands under his shirt and lightly drag my nails over his skin. I feel him twitch underneath me and my smile widens. I push his shirt upwards, exposing the skin and I slide downwards, placing a kiss over his stomach – a light one and then softly grazing it with my teeth.

I look at him from under my eyelashes and see him looking at me with hooded eyes. I smirk, my lips hovering just above the waist of his jeans. I make him pull the shirt over his head and he obliges in seconds. I can't help but smirk at his eagerness.

I open the button of his jeans, letting my breath hit his skin. I see his fist clenching at his sides. I let my chin brush against his erection and he hisses. "No," he grits out. He pulls me up by my forearms, sliding my body against his, and puts his hand at the back of my head, pushing me down and kissing me.

My eyebrows shoot up, but I only grin in return, surprised and excited about his boldness. "What? No blowjob?" I question.

Fai shakes his head. "Not today," he says, his voice low, almost growling. I put my finger to the corner of his mouth, softly touching him, running it across his bottom lip with a light, feather-like touch. He becomes serious, his eyes intently watching me and my every move. I grind my hips against him.

"Condoms?" I ask him.

He only nods towards the nightstand. I climb off him and crawl to the end of the bed so I can reach the driver. "Clothes. Off," I order him.

"Of course, madam. Whatever you wish for," he replies, but he obliges.

I smirk, taking a box of condoms out of a drawer and crawl back to him, sitting on top of him once again, now topless. I lean down so close that our noses touch. "I wish for a lot of things," I whisper.

I get down closer and kiss him on the centre of his chest before my hands go towards the waist of his pants and unbuckling them, then taking it off of him, leaving him completely naked while I'm still fully dressed.

"You can't fuck me with your clothes on," Fai points out, forever the smartass.

I give him a smirk, taking my hair out of a ponytail and shake it. Fai looks in fascination. I take my shirt off first and my pants follow quickly. There's nothing slow or romantic in this, I'm not even trying to be sexy and hot. I just want to give us what we both want without wrapping it into some shiny paper. There is no need for that. There is no pretence with us.

I take a condom out of a box, take it out and roll it onto his cock, touching him for the first time. He lets out a moan, his eyes closing just for a second.

I position him at my entrance and lower down on him, his hands coming to my hips immediately. "Holy fuck," he grits out through his teeth.

I flip my hair once more so it gets out of my face. Fai is gripping my hips so tightly and firmly that I am unable to move. I roll my hips, erupting another moan from him and his hold loosens.

I place my hands on his chest for support and start moving up and down on him, doing it fast and doing it hard.

I'm biting down on my bottom lip in pleasure while Fai's hands are freely roaming all over my body; my ass, my thighs, my hips, my stomach, my breasts, curling around my neck, touching my mouth...

This is pure fucking, just pleasure and nothing else. This is just us chasing our passion and we're unapologetic and unrelenting about it.

Fai pushes his heels into the bed, fucking me upwards. "Fuck. Fuck, I'm close."

I smile, my head falling forward and I take his mouth with mine, sucking on his tongue, our teeth clinking together.

"Kadie, shit," Fai grits out, grabbing my hips tighter. And then he stills and I feel him pulsing, his arms coming around me so he can hold me to him while he rides the waves of pleasure.

I wait for him to come down from the high, my arms going around his neck and just breathing hard.

His head leans back and he looks at me, his eyebrows knit together. "You didn't come," he observes.

I climb off him, standing from the bed. "I never do," I say and walk to the bathroom to clean myself up and to also escape the questions that are definitely going to follow. They always do, every time it happens. Some like to pretend it didn't happen, others want to make me come with mouth and fingers because his ego wouldn't allow him otherwise, but there's no point. I'm a broken machine and I already accepted that.

Fai comes and stands at the bathroom door in nothing but boxers while I'm still fully naked, putting my hair up into a bun. He crosses his arms and I just look at him in the mirror. "What?"

"Are you for real?" he asks.

I raise my eyebrows, dropping my arms when I'm satisfied with my bun. "About?" I ask nonchalantly.

"Fucking hell, Kadie, you're one of the smartest people I know. Don't act dumb."

I lean against the sink. "Okay, ask. I know it's coming, anyway, so shoot, Fai. You won't be the first one."

He frowns. "You can't ... orgasm?"

I shrug. "Nope."

"With no one? Not even yourself?"

"Look, I experience and treat sex a little differently. You'll have to be ok with this explanation because I'm not explaining further." The thing is, I can't explain it because people just don't understand. And this is not something you just casually talk about with just anyone. Not even Harper knows about this.

"When did you figure it out?" Fai asks.

"The first time I had sex? I don't know. Like I said, sex for me is just … not what it's like for others. I enjoy it, sure, kind of, but it's not a necessity."

Fai doesn't understand and he shows it fully, but I don't expect him to. I walk past him, saying, "I'll give you some privacy to clean up." In the bedroom, I find one of his shirts and put it on.

I check my phone just in case Harper texted me. She knows where I am so I'm not surprised there are no new texts from her, although I can never be too sure when it comes to her.

I go to Fai's kitchen, searching for some food. I notice he's a clean guy with a full fridge, too. And he lives in a nice apartment, which makes me wonder how the hell he can afford all this. What is it that he truly does?

I take orange juice out of the fridge and mix it with water in the glass, enjoying the coldness when it goes down my throat.

I look around his the kitchen. I noticed he's not big on decorations. He doesn't have any pictures hung up on the walls. He doesn't have any plants or excessive furniture. He's very basic and it's hard to feel cosy or at home.

Fai walks to the kitchen with sweatpants on this time. "I see you made yourself at home," he notes.

"I had to since I got no help from you." I watch him going to the fridge and take out orange juice as well. "So what does someone have to do to afford an apartment in this area?" I ask vaguely.

Fai doesn't even look at me. "Work hard and smart."

I knew he wouldn't make it easy for me. "Okay, Fai, what do you really do? How do you earn money?"

He gives me a look that says he isn't exactly happy with my question. "What's with the questions, bee? Why are you so concerned about where my money comes from?"

"I'm just trying to get to know you. Calm your balls, Jesus."

A slow smile slowly spreads across his face. "Tit for tat, babe. Where do you work?"

I look away from him, signalling that I'm over this conversation.

Chapter 18

Kadie leaves for work. She didn't even want me to take her and I don't know whether she's mad at me or ashamed, but I don't know what reason she'd have to be either.

I still don't know what the deal with her is and that bothers me way more than it should.

Jon calls me when I'm sitting at the table with one of the sketches I've been working on for a few days now. "Yeah?" I answer.

"Is Kadience with you?"

I stop drawing. "Why?"

"I think they're planning something tonight."

"Fuck." I rub my eyes. "How do you know?"

"Ante overheard something. Look, I don't know what's going on with you two, I just thought you'd like to know about it."

"Yeah, thanks. She left for work before. I don't think they'll try anything there."

"Not while she's working and not with all the people around. But what about when she finishes?"

Goddamn it all. "Do you think they know where she works?" That might be a stupid question. I know where she works and not because she told me.

"It's not that hard to find out, is it? I mean ... I found it out for you in just a day."

I rub my face again, standing up. "Alright, you're right. Don't worry, I got this."

"Need someone to come with you?" Jon asks.

"Nah. I'll call if I'll need a backup. I have to check out the scene first."

"Alright. Stay safe."

I grin. "Don't I always?"

She needs a long time to notice me. And in that time, I get a chance to watch her work. I don't like what I see. I mean, the outfit is a turn on, of course. And she looks like she can act nice when she gets paid for it so that's good to know.

I don't care about being noticed about her, either. I checked the place. It has good security and there's a lot of people here, so I don't think they'll be stupid enough to try something here. But I can never be too sure with them. They tend to get too brave sometimes.

When Kadie approaches me, she's not happy. In fact, she looks taken off guard. She looks around and then walks to me. "What? Are you stalking me now?"

I grin at her, looking her up and down. "Nah. Just came here for a lap dance. So, when are you free so I can take you to a private room?"

She frowns, not amused. "You're out of luck, buddy. You'll have to ask someone else for that. You can only tell me what you want to drink and I'll get it for you."

I rub my pointer across my bottom lip, still grinning at her. "Oh, come on now. Don't I get special treatment?"

She raises her eyebrows in that challenging way that could make any man fall to his knees and apologise. Most men, at least. I know her tactics by now. "You're not special enough to get special treatment."

My eyebrows raise in surprise. I spread my legs, turning my body so I'm facing her full. "Right to my heart, bee. Could be a little more careful with your words, or I'm not leaving you any tip," I taut her.

"Oh, fuck you, Fai," she grits out in annoyance, wanting to storm out, but I stop her with my hand on her arm.

"When do you finish?"

Before she could even say another smartass remark, a bodyguard is by my side, his hand on my shoulder. "Sir, I'll have to ask you to remove your hand. You can look, but you can't touch."

I look at him and then at Kadie. She looks back with a challenge in her eyes. "You heard him ... sir."

My nostrils flare, but I release her. "It's okay. I'm not looking for trouble."

"You better not or your ass will be out in the street before you know what happened."

I give the bodyguard a dirty look. Yeah, I'd really like to see you try.

Kadie walks away and I just let her because I have a bodyguard on my ass now and I don't want to piss him off and draw any attention to me.

Someone else walks to me to serve me. I keep an eye on Kadie for the majority of the night and she doesn't even look at me once. Well, if she does, it's completely by accident. And it's pissing me off.

I don't get a chance to talk to her, so I have to sit here and wait until the club gets closed so I can take her home safely.

The good news is that I haven't noticed anyone that would look problematic to me. There's a lot of middle-aged men here, a lot of them wearing rings on their fingers. And I'm not saying I'm a saint myself, but I do have a few morals left.

"I decided to be generous and I'll give you two minutes to explain why you're here."

I swing my head to see Kadie standing beside me, her arms crossed over her chest. I give her a lazy grin. "I just wanted the promised rounds. You only gave me one."

She rolls her eyes. "Cut the bullshit, Fai. How did you know I work here? Did you follow me or did one of your guys do the dirty work for you?"

"Why does it matter? I'm here. Doesn't matter how I got here."

She's not happy with my answer. "Your two minutes are almost up."

I narrow my eyes. "I have some business to take care of here. When do you finish? I'll take you home."

"Like hell you will," she protests immediately. "I know how to come home by myself, thank you." I feel like she said that thank you a little sarcastically, but what do I know?

Leave it to me to find the most difficult woman to deal with and decide to go after her. "Listen, you should be a little more grateful that I'm here, dealing with your ass when I could just be at home sleeping."

She gives me such a dirty look that it makes me shudder a little. "As if I asked you to come here? What the fuck, Fai. Just go home." She sounds annoyed.

"You know what? Since I'm already here, I might as well just enjoy my evening. You can be kind enough to bring me another glass, though, babe," I tell her, extending my arm out and giving her my empty glass.

She looks at the glass and then at me. She takes it from my hand, harder than she'd need to. "I'm already regretting fucking you," she mutters to herself and goes away.

Someone else brings me another drink and Kadie goes back to avoiding me. My night isn't going like I thought it would, but I knew I was too optimistic thinking she'd just give in easily.

I might as well just enjoy my evening since there's no danger in the sight. I mean, I have almost fully naked girls dancing in front of me and God knows when I'll get another opportunity like this again.

Kadie and I both successfully ignore each other until the end of her shift. She didn't come to tell me when she was done. I had to find it out from one of the girls here.

I couldn't go into the back where the changing rooms were so I had to go outside and wait for her there. I checked the front entrance and the back one just in case. There was no one there.

Kadie comes out of the back entrance and she catches me smoking a cigarette by the door. She stops when she spots me. "What the hell do you want, Fai?" she sounds tired.

"Why are you in such a bad mood?" I ask her.

"Because you can't seem to leave me the fuck alone!"

I roll my eyes, throwing the half-finished cigarette on the ground and stepping on it. Just then a shot is heard from the front. My body freezes and I swing my head into Kadie's direction. I push her against the wall.

"Don't fucking move from here. You hear me?" I say harshly, hoping she won't fucking move even an inch.

I take the gun that I hid outside before because they wouldn't let me into the club in the other case. I walk to the end of the building right by the wall. I heard a few screams so I suppose people are gathering around. I look back to see Kadie is where I left her, lighting a cigarette.

I peek around the corner and see people running towards the girl that's laying on the ground. "Fuck," I mutter, looking around.

I know by now that they're gone. I go closer to the scene. I see the girl lying on the floor and people are around, frantically calling 911 and trying her breathing and heartbeat.

I go back to where Kadie is. "So? What happened?" she asks nonchalantly, smoking a cigarette, not looking scared or shocked at all.

"Someone was shot. Look, we have to go. I can't be found here. You shouldn't be associated with it, either."

She tilts her head to the side, not taking the situation seriously. "Is it one of the girls?" she asks me.

"Yeah. We gotta go," I tell her, hearing the sirens.

"That should've been me, right? That's why you're here tonight." She snickers to herself.

"That should be no one," I say pointedly. "Start walking, Kadience, before I drag you to the motorcycle. I'm not kidding, we need to leave. Now."

"Yeah, fine," she grumbles. She takes the cigarette out and throws it away.

We get on the motorcycle and before I drive away, I cast a look towards the scene, now with police and paramedics there.

I take Kadie to my place. She gives me shit about it the second I kill the engine. "I'm not staying with you just so you can play my fucking bodyguard."

"Give me a fucking break," I mutter, stepping off the motorcycle and pull the helmet off, ruffling my hair. I take my phone out and call Jon while walking upstairs, not even waiting to see if Kadie is following. If she's smart and knows what's good for her, she'll come.

When Jon picks up, I go straight to business. "They attacked tonight, outside the club, right after the girls finished. One of them got hurt, I can't say how badly, but it wasn't nice. Call a meeting for the afternoon."

"Shit. So they aren't kidding. Is your girl fine?"

I look back to see Kadie following me quietly. She gives me an angry glare. "She's good," I say, turning back around and twirling the keys in my hand. I unlock the door and let us in. "We'll go over everything in the meeting. Good night."

"Bye, Fai."

I lock the door and throw the keys and the phone on the kitchen table. I go to the bedroom, taking a cigarette out on the way and plopping down on the chair by the window. I open it to let in some fresh, crispy night air.

Kadie sits on the still unmade bed from before. I didn't bother tidying up. She crossed her arms over her chest. "Now what?" she asks in one of her moods.

I just look at her, wishing she, for once, wouldn't give me a headache.

"I'm not staying somewhere between four walls and be scared shitless and you know that, so I hope you have some other plan."

I know pretty well that I couldn't force her to stay at home even if I chained her to the bed. "You're in luck because you might just have to spend some more time with me now since I can't lock you in some room."

"Oh, so you're going to play my bodyguard for real? Fantastic. All I've ever wanted, really," she says with heavy sarcasm, even rolling her eyes for good measure.

I put my elbows on my knees and lean forward. "Yeah, I'm not exactly shitting rainbows about this situation, either, bee, so ... suck it up."

I take a drag of cigarette and Kadie falls back on the bed with a sigh, looking up at the ceiling. "You know how to use a gun?" I ask her.

She looks at me. "Sure."

"You have one?"

"If I had one, you'd be already dead."

"Good to know," I say with a dead tone. I stand up and unlock my safe, pulling out one of my guns and throwing it on the bed next to her. "Use it if you need to. Just not on me."

She sits up and takes the gun in her hands, looking at it with interest. "You're giving me a gun? What a thoughtful gift."

"I'm lending you my gun."

She extends her arm and points the gun right at my head. I notice she has a good aim. She closes one eye, her tongue playfully coming out. I don't even flinch. She chuckles and drops her arms.

She looks at me, her head dropping to the side slightly. "Have you ever killed someone, Fai?" she asks me.

I take a drag of a cigarette. "What's the point of this question?"

She shrugs and looks at the gun. "I think I'd understand if you did. Because there was once someone I'd kill if I had a chance."

I don't say anything for a few seconds. "They still alive?" I ask.

She smiles at the gun. "One yes. One no." She lifts her head. "He did it himself and, sometimes, I'm angry he did it because I was fantasising about the ways I would end his life, only for him to take away this pleasure from me and do it himself."

I shake my head. "And here I thought I was fucked up."

Kadience only smiles as if she hasn't just revealed something so dark about her.

Chapter 19

I wake up with a headache and to a sound of someone cursing.

I open my eyes and just groan, staring up at the ceiling. I hear a few more curse words coming from the kitchen.

I get out of the bed and put on one of Fai's jackets that I find in his closet. "What the hell is up your ass this morning?" I ask him, going to the fridge and taking out the orange juice.

Fai just looks at me. It seems like I'm not getting any good morning from him. "You're finally up. You need to go."

I bring the glass with the juice to my lips and raise my eyebrows. "Where?" I ask after taking a sip.

He scowls at me, tapping his knuckles against the table. "Home."

I lick my lips. "Why? Do you have to be somewhere?" I ask him, looking him up and down, noticing he's fully dressed. "What time is it?"

"Ten," He says courtly. "Get dressed. We're going in five minutes."

"So much for the hospitality," I mutter when I walk past him. I get dressed but I take longer than five minutes just to piss him off even more. I redo my ponytail a few times just to pass my time. I make sure I have no messages from Harp which is kind of suspicious at this time.

Fai isn't the one to knock on the door, he just barges in. "The hell's taking you so long?"

I'm in the middle of taking a selfie and I make a kissing face and look at him, snapping a photo. "Wanna take a selfie with me?"

He grimaces. "No, I wanna go."

"Fuck, you're grumpy in the morning," I state. He just gives me a glare. I grin in return and dance towards him, giving him a kiss on the cheek.

He drops me off at Harper's place and drives off. When I get to Harper's apartment, I immediately hear the music blasting. And a love song out of all! It's not even 11 am.

I reluctantly step in, the door unlocked. I cautiously go forward, finding Harper in the living room laying on the couch, her eyes closed.

I turn the volume down and Harper's eyes snap open. "Hello? I came to kidnap you. Not that you'd hear."

"Oh. Hi. You aren't in school?" Harper asks, not even moving.

"No. Overslept. The fuck's wrong with you listening to this shit in the morning?"

Harper shrugs. "I just like it."

I raise my eyebrow. "Since when?"

Harper closes her eyes again. "Since yesterday."

What. The. Fuck.

I go to the couch, standing over her, putting my hands on my hips, looking down on her. "Are you alright?"

She smiles but she doesn't open her eyes. "Yes. Just stressed out because of college. This is my way of relaxing."

Huh. "Okay," I say, happy that she didn't go crazy. "I'll grab a shower and something to eat before going to school."

"You're late already."

"I can still catch three classes. Can't fuck up with my attendance too much."

I get a text from Fai when I'm in the middle of the class, finishing a drawing of the lion on his back.

Are you at home?

I think about lying to him, but then I remember this will piss him off even further.

At school. Thinking about me?

He types,

Yeah, my sixth sense told me you did something stupid. I'm picking you up when you'll finish.

My eyebrows raise.

Not even asking when I'm done?

Fai replies immediately.

No need. I already know.

Of course he does. This is starting to get a little creepy.

Stalker.

He doesn't respond this time.

"Miss Myers, put your phone away. First and last warning."

I look at the professor. I grab my bag and hold eye contact with her, smiling as I put it in. "Done, professor." I want to wink so badly, but I hold myself back since I don't have time for detention.

Fai is waiting for me outside school, parked right in the front and leaning against his motorcycle, wearing shades and looking all badass. I can't lie he doesn't make a great sight because he is hot.

I walk to him, leaning up and peck his lips. "Take me somewhere to eat."

He takes the shades off so I can see the disbelief on his face. "Hello to you, too. Who do you think I am?"

"Who do you want to be?" I wink.

I take the helmet and put it on. I notice Fai is looking somewhere in the distance and as I turn around, I see Mandy the bitch looking at us. "Ah. Long lost lovers," I taunt.

Fai doesn't comment. "Just get on the bike."

I climb behind him and just because I feel like proving a point to Mandy, who thinks she rules the goddamn school and is so pretty she could have anyone, I wrap my arms all around Fai's torso and lean my head on his back. If I wasn't wearing a helmet, she'd see me smirking.

"So, what's the deal with you and Mandy?" I slurp the coke. Fai decided he's too cool to eat with me while I had no trouble ordering a cheeseburger, big French fries and a Coca-Cola while also eyeing ice-cream to order for dessert.

He's sitting across me, one arm extended on the seat, the other supporting his head as he's looking at me. "Don't have a deal with no one."

"Oh, come on. You two clearly know each other, so it must be something."

"What do you want me to say? She wants me to fuck her. I don't. That's it."

I'm eating a french fry, my eyes narrowing. "Mandy wants you to screw her and you're saying you don't want to? Yeah, right." I roll my eyes.

He taps his hand against the seat, looking all relaxed there, almost half laying. "The fuck did you want me to tell you? She's not my type." He grimaces.

"Who are you trying to fool here? She's every guy's wet dream. Please."

He gives me an annoyed look. "Clearly not every."

"Huh," I say to myself, smiling. Someone who sees her for who she really is and not just who she's trying to fool everyone she is. She might be hot but she's brainless. And I'm not the one to judge people but she deserves my judgment.

"Will you be done soon? I have to be somewhere."

"Seems like you're a very busy guy," I note. I take my half-finished cheeseburger and take it to his mouth. "Want a bite? I was thinking about getting an ice-cream."

Fai scowls and I push the cheeseburger closer to his mouth before he could voice his protest. He takes a large bite of the food.

"Good, huh?" I ask him while popping another french fry into my mouth.

He moves his head away when I want to feed him another fry. "Stop this shit," he mutters, looking around. I rub my lips together, trying not to smile.

"Will you buy me ice cream?" I ask him.

He tilts his head to the side, giving me an incredulous look. "I'm not buying you shit. We're going."

I grimace. "You're such a party breaker, Jesus Christ." I have to pay for my food and leave the restaurant because I'm pretty sure he'd leave me here otherwise, the fucker. He's by his motorcycle, smoking a cigarette. "Give me one," I demand. If I couldn't get ice cream because of him, I can at least have a cigarette.

He actually holds out the box for me to take out a cigarette without any objections. "Hurry up. I have somewhere to be." He takes out his phone and texts someone.

"You're in a really bad mood," I notice.

Fai doesn't say anything.

I smoke the rest of the cigarette quietly, not bothering with him anymore.

Fai doesn't take me home. He takes me to some abandoned building that's God knows where. "You could at least tell me you were kidnapping me. I had plans for the day."

"I'm not kidnapping you," Fai mutters, walking towards the entrance. I notice other motorcycles parked outside and I soon figure out what's going on. Are they planning something? Or is this their meet-up point?

I hear the laughter before we even come inside. I have no idea why he took me here. Maybe he'll try to kill me. They all will. That'd be fun to watch.

I walk in beside Fai, my hands in the back pockets of my jeans, my posture relaxed and confident. "Hey, guys!" I greet them cheerfully. Fai gives me a look that tells me to shut up, but I enjoy too much wiping the guys' smiles off their faces.

"Dude. What the fuck?" Ante asks.

"No. Why the fuck?" Cruz chimes in, sitting up on the couch he was previously laying on. I go and plop down on the couch next to him and he just gives me a weird look.

"Because why the fuck not? Right, Fai?" I look at him and give him a wink.

Fai walks to me with his jaw clenched. He leans down, grabbing my chin. "Stay here. Don't move and, for God's sake, stop talking."

I put my hand on his wrist and give him a seductive look, licking my upper lip. "Make me."

His hold on my jaw tightens, but he's not hurting me. I don't know what he's afraid of. He looks at my eyes for long moments before he leans back and releases me.

"Hey, maybe you should bring your cousin with you the next time. Just to lighten up our Jon here a little bit," Ante calls and Bastian whistled and then chuckles with him.

"Yeah, bring Jon's crush next time so he won't be so stuck up anymore."

I don't think of Jon as a stuck up. He's more mature than these idiots around him and of course that makes them think he's uptight.

"Are you going to bring your asses here and get your head straight or you want to continue acting like you need a babysitter?" Fai snaps at them.

"Jesus fuck," Cruz mutters. "Maybe suck his dick the next time so he'll chill out." Fai glares at him.

"Doesn't help. I tried. It just might be his personality." I shrug. I'm the one that gets a glare next. I give Fai an innocent smile and make a heart with my hands. He just sighs.

"Can we get to business or what?" Fai snaps.

They all scatter around the big table that's standing almost in the centre of the room. There are no chairs around so they stand. They talk quietly, mostly Fai, I notice, but I don't bother to listen to what they're saying. I'm not the one to eavesdrop.

I look around the big room. It's chill in here. It has no windows, but the trees and the bushes around prevent from anyone to see in and us seeing out. And the room we're in is pretty empty, aside from the big table, a few old chairs by the wall, the small couch I'm sitting on and another table, a smaller one.

I quickly get bored and get off the couch and walk around the room, just looking out the windows. I wouldn't even notice the guys giving me wary looks if Fai didn't just say, "Ignore her," to the boys and, "Kadie, can you please sit the fuck down and chill?" to me.

I scowl at him. "I am chilling."

He hits the table with his hand, giving me a hard look. "Stop being childish."

I show him my tongue just to annoy him even further, but I go sit down on the other table in the room because I have nothing else to do anyway. We're literally in the middle of nowhere. When I take my phone out, I see I don't even have any signal here.

But what I do have is some music on my phone. I put some on, turning the volume up. I don't even have to look to know they're all giving me some death stares right now.

I don't see Fai until he snatches the phone from my hands. He stands so close to me that his thighs touch my knees. I have to lean back a little, my head falling back so I can look at him.

"Can you, for the love of God, please just stop and let us work? I'll take you home afterwards straight away, but you really have to let us finish."

A smirk falls on my face. I lock my feet behind his legs, pulling him even closer to me. "Kiss me," I tell him.

He leans back so he can get a full look of my face.

I wrap my arms around his neck. "Kiss me," I repeat.

"What the hell is your problem?"

"Do it," I tell him. "Kiss me." A challenge appears in his eyes. I'm not challenging him. I'm simply telling him. I don't push his head down, either, when I could simply do it. Or I could kiss him myself. But I want him to do it.

And he does. It's supposed to be a peck or a slow kiss from his side, but I want more. I always want everything or nothing. The full deal. I kiss him like I wanted him to kiss me; with no restraint, losing himself completely and forgetting about the world for just a minute.

I pull back first and I smile at him. "That's all I really wanted. I'll leave you all alone to finish and go outside. You can give me my phone back later." I don't ask for a phone back because I simply want to show him that, somehow, I trust him and I'm not calling anyone and rat them out.

I lightly push him away so I can jump down from the table. I turn around to look back when I'm at the old door only to find him still standing there and looking at me in confusion and, well, lust.

I wink at him and go outside.

I don't know for how long I walk around. I don't hear any cars, so I know the road isn't anywhere near. And all around me is forest, so I don't want to get a chance to get lost by going inside. I only walk around, in all ways of the building. I find an apple tree and there are still some good apples left on it, among most of them lying on the floor.

I pick one and play with it when I go back inside. All heads turn upon my arrival and I salute them. "What are you planning for so long, a goddamn war?" I mutter and sit on the same table I was sitting on before.

"You know, we could wrap it up," Cruz says, stretching. Fai lifts an eyebrow at him, but Jon jumps in before he could say something to him.

"He's right. We have it all covered, man."

"Yeah, you better do," Fai says seriously, looking each of them in the eyes.

Ante is the first to walk away and he comes straight to where I'm sitting, minding my own business and wiping the apple in my shirt. "Quite a show you made before," He says, leaning against the table.

"You can join the next time," I say mockingly and end another glare from Fai. He's putting together the papers on the table while chatting with Jon.

Ante makes a face beside me. "No offence, but neither of you two are my type. I like 'em quiet."

"Mmm," I murmur. "I bet you do. That's also the difference between you and Fai. He knows how to make them quiet."

"He sure doesn't with you because he could put tape over your mouth and you'd still be running it."

I put my hand over my chest. "My, oh my. You know me so well."

I notice Fai wraps it up and is ready to leave. He doesn't say anything, he automatically assumed I'll just follow him. The ego of this man!

"I don't, which is why you should better stay away from Fai before you get his head up in the clouds where it absolutely shouldn't be and serve us his dick on a plate."

I grimace. "Classy. I love your imagination and your dark fantasies. Keep it up, maybe they become real one day." I take a bite into the apple. "What Fai and I have is none of your goddamn business. Mind your own, yeah?" I chew the piece of apple I took and push the bitten apple into his chest so he has to take it before I jump down and run after Fai, putting my hair out from under my jacket so it falls down my back, not bothered to put it up.

When I reach him, I grab his hand in mine. He doesn't react in any way, just squeezes my hand and out we go.

Chapter 20

Fai drops me off at Harper's. When I get down from the motorcycle and pull the helmet off, shaking my head, Fai kills the engine. "So, when am I seeing you?" he asks, taking the helmet for me.

I put my hand on his jaw and kiss him. "Whenever you want," I tell him against his lips, opening my eyes to look at his.

I give him a wink before retreating.

He grabs my arms before I can go anywhere. "Kadie, this thing going on between you and me ... what is it?"

"Relax. We're just having some fun, babe." I pull my arm from his grip. "I'll call you," I tell him. I wave at him and send him a kiss before I disappear into the building, running to the apartment.

Harper isn't home yet. The place is idly quiet and I take a moment to throw myself down on the couch with a shit-eating smile on my face.

I get up to make some lunch for Harp when she comes back. And then I settle on the couch with a science book in my hands. I get a message from Fai not that much later.

You still can't go to the bar.

I think this overprotectiveness is absurd and, usually, I'd never let anyone tell me where I can and can't go, but it's different in this case. I kind of like that he cares so much that he takes the effort to keep me safe.

Can you take me to our place then?

I started referring to that place he first took me as our place. I still don't know exactly the address of it or where exactly that is.

Can't tonight, he replies.

Tomorrow then. We can go back to your place afterwards ...

I realise Fai is a quick texter. His response comes in just seconds.

You're working?

Nope.

To which he only replies, Ok.

I text back, It's a date simply because I don't want to let him have the last word. He doesn't respond to this one.

When Harper comes home and sees me sitting on the couch, she stops. "Oh. You're here." She nervously tucks a hair strand behind her ear.

I give her a weird look. "Where else would I be?"

"I don't know. With Fai?" she asks, walking to the kitchen. "And you cooked! God, I'm starving."

I close the book and follow her to the kitchen. I sit down, just watching her. "Did you eat yet?" she asks.

I nod. "Went on a burger with Fai."

Harper looks at me. "He took you out to eat?"

"Something like that. Nothing as romantic as you're picturing in your head right now."

"Oh," she replies. "But still. That's nice." She sits down. "So I take it you two are serious now?"

I shrug. "Eh," I say. I sort through the mail that's on the table.

"What? That's not an answer."

I look at her. "I don't know what else to tell you. We're just fooling around a little, nothing too serious."

"But do you have any feelings for him?"

Feelings? I've never had feelings for anyone. Ever. "No. I like him, that's all."

"I don't really believe that." When I just tilt my head to the side, Harper elaborates. "You're happier now. You smile more. I don't know, you're just different."

I put my feet on the chair and lean back, putting my hair up in a ponytail. I understand what's getting through her mind. It's true that she never met any guy I was fucking, and I never fucked anyone for long enough for her to meet him anyway, but her idea of love is a little different than mine.

"What can I say? He gets me. The real me. And I like that. And I like that I can talk to him about all kind of shit. You know?"

Harper puts her head on her hand, forgetting about food. She's also smiling. "I'm happy for you, Kadie. I don't even care that he's not a good guy, if he's good to you and makes you happy, then you have my blessing."

I raise my eyebrow. "Why are you team Fai all of a sudden? And why are you trying to convince me of something here?" I don't love the guy, although Harper, apparently, thinks I do.

"I'm not team anyone. I'm telling you this because I don't want you to hide things from me. I want to hear about you two."

I make a weird face. "Harper, darling, you need to find yourself a boyfriend. Pronto."

She rolls her eyes and goes back to her food. "As if I have time for anything else or anyone else right now."

I just grin as I stand up from the table. "You have to make time." I give her a wink. "Going back to the book now," I tell her.

Fai is late the next night and I make sure he sees my annoyance because I had to wait for him outside.

"Oh, shut up," he says before I even say anything.

He puts his hand on my chin and kisses me before he gives me the helmet. "Get on," he says.

I jump on behind him and he drives off. I was really looking forward to this today because I started looking at this as a getaway from everything. A quiet place in this loud world. I started to enjoy riding with him. I get the excitement and the thrill now. It's awesome. It feels like you're flying.

When we get to our place I just lay down on the grass and close my eyes. I love the serenity around me. Fai is quiet beside me and I opened my eyes just to look at him. He's looking at the city, too.

I slowly sit up. "How did you find this place?" I ask him, remembering that I asked him this once already, but he left the question unanswered.

He shrugs. "On one of the rides."

"Mmm," I say in acknowledgement. "Do you go on those often? Alone or only with the guys?"

"Yeah. Alone, mostly." He looks at me.

"You can take me with you the next time you go."

He chuckles and shakes his head. "You know, about what you said the other day, about us just having some fun. I don't do fun, Kadie. You're either in or you're out. There's no being halfway in this shit."

I lean my head on my arm. "I think we both know I'm in this shit already."

He looks at me. "Are you really?" I catch the double meaning. I know what he wants to know.

"Yeah, Fai. Really."

"I hope you know what you're agreeing to," he says.

And I just look at him. "Actually, Fai, I don't. I don't know what it is that you do."

He raises his eyebrows. "You're smart. I'm pretty sure you figured it out."

I shake my head. "No, I can only assume. And I hate assuming things. So unless I hear you say it to me, I don't know shit."

He gives me a long stare, probably just trying to figure out if I'm telling the truth. I think he's also debating if he can trust me. "Drugs," he finally says.

I cock my head to the side. "Drugs what? You do them? Sell them? What?"

He rolls his eyes. "I don't do them. Obviously." I just shrug. "Sell. And I collect money. It's not a pretty business."

I roll my bottom lip into my mouth as I process this information. No, I believe it's not a pretty business. I know about it. I didn't sell drugs and I wasn't particularly into drugs, but I experienced it, nonetheless. "And in future? What do you see yourself doing in the future?"

"What's the point of thinking about the future when we still have today to live?"

"Sure you have dreams. Everybody does."

"What are yours?" he asks me.

That's an easy one. "I want to become a lawyer."

He raises his eyebrows. "A lawyer?" he asks as if this is the last thing he expected.

"Yes, a lawyer, Fai. What's so surprising about it?"

He purses his lips. "Nothing. You're smart. You'll be a good one. I just thought you'd wanted to be something ... I don't know, less boring?"

I have to laugh. "I can do boring if I want to," I tell him. "Your turn," I tell him.

"I have my own tattoo shop and I want to continue with that."

My mouth falls open. "How did I not know that? That's so cool. So drugs aren't your only business."

One side of his mouth pulls up. "You have to have something clean going on if you want to hide the dirty stuff."

We're silent for some moments, just looking at the lights. "When will it be safe to go back to the bar? I can't keep stuff from Harper for much longer and she'll completely lose it if I tell her I'm in some sort of danger. She only just started liking you."

Fai raises his eyebrows. "Good to know I'm starting to have a fan club. You can go when I'll be there. It'll be safer that way. And I'll take you home."

I throw myself at him, wrapping my arms around his neck and just laugh. "Thanks, baby," I say with a high-pitched voice.

"You'll thank me later," he says this with a smirk.

I know what he means by that. I turn against him and he lets me reposition myself so I'm still sitting on him, close to his chest, and now watching the city before me.

And I can't help but think how nice this is. How different. Fai started opening up more to me. He started talking to me more and sharing things. We have a connection, but we both know this can't be anything more than just a little fling. I leave in a few months, anyway, and he'll just be a really nice memory then.

Fai is a good kisser. Especially when we're about to get naked. He's possessive and dominating and he devours my whole mouth as soon as we come to his place. I help him get rid of his jacket and he throws it somewhere on the floor. He presses me against the kitchen wall, pushing my jacket off.

I'm pulling his shirt up and he has to detach his lips from mine to take it off. In a hurry, I take mine off as well and I hear him growl before his mouth takes mine again.

I take my hands down his bare chest, coming to his jeans and cup him over them. He's already hard and I feel him pulse against my hand. A smile forms on my lips, but I don't stop kissing him.

He suddenly turns me around, my front pressing against the wall. "Really?" I say hazily as I try not to panic for losing that little control he let me have.

He presses against me from behind, his mouth coming to my neck. "Yeah. Really," he says softly. "Undress," he orders me as I hear him do just that.

I take my pants off and I look over my shoulder to see him taking a condom out, completely naked. I want to turn around, but he stands back up, pressing against me again. "Nu-uh."

"But I want to see you," I say. It's not a lie. But I also want just a little bit of control, too.

"Nuh-uh," he says again. I feel his hand coming to my stomach and then downwards, his other hand coming to lightly wrap around my neck. I tilt my head back, almost meeting his shoulder when he touches me right between my legs. He splays his fingers, his pinky finger touching my lips and I bite down on it.

He pushes his index finger in me and curses. "Fuck, you're already wet, Kadie."

I smile and I take his finger into my mouth, sucking on it. He lets out a shaky breath and I love how much I affect him. "Fuck me," I breathe as a plea, not hiding how desperate I am. I push my hips backwards, closing my eyes. Make me forget. Replace the memories, Fai ...

He takes his finger out and when I think he'll replace it with his cock, he starts rubbing my clit instead. "I want to make you come," he says against my ear.

My eyes snap open. I shake my head. "No. Fai, please, just fuck me," I groan.

He doesn't say anything and I push my hips against him harder, rubbing against his cock. I pry his hand away with both of my hands and put it over my breast instead.

As if Fai wants to punish me, he suddenly pushes inside of me. Fast and without a warning and so hard, he pushes me even harder against the wall, making me let out a squeak and then we both moan at the sensation of him finally being inside me.

I press my cheek against the wall as Fai seems to hate-fuck me. I think he's angry because I didn't let him play with me. I'm not sorry about that. I like it rough, anyway. I like it any way he's going to give it to me.

He lets my hair out of a ponytail just so he can wrap it around his hand and tilt my head back. His mouth is on me in a rough kiss. He bites my bottom lip and I bite his tongue. He fucks me even harder for that and I just groan into his mouth.

His hand comes to my throat again, the other playing with my breast until he puts it over my stomach and then to my hip, squeezing it. He detaches his lips from mine, kissing me down my neck until he comes to my shoulder where he bites into my skin and I arch my back against him.

Holy fuck, is he intense or what!

"Can't believe how fucking good you feel," he mutters.

"So do you, Fai. Fuck," I say, probably wishing for the first time that I could come just to experience the relief that I never can.

But I don't. And when Fai comes, I enjoy it just the same because there's something satisfying hearing a man come while inside you, feeling his cock pulse and hearing him groan next to my ear. It's sexy as hell.

He takes a moment to calm his breath down before he steps back, pulling himself out of me. I suddenly feel lazy and tired and just well-fucked, even though I can never feel fully relaxed after sex because I'm still worked-up and I can't get off.

Fai takes care of a condom and I go pour myself a glass of water since I'm in the kitchen. We didn't even get to the bedroom.

I take our clothes and bring them to the bedroom, sitting on the chair by the window and grabbing a pack of cigarettes, taking one out and lighting it up. I put my feet on the window ledge, still completely naked and that's how Fai finds me.

I hear him go to the kitchen but he comes back right away and gets on the bed, still completely naked.

He checks his phone and then puts it down, turning his eyes on me. We don't say anything to each other. He's just watching me smoke the cigarette and I enjoy him watching me smoking it.

"Why don't you come here?" he asks me when I finish it.

I raise an eyebrow at him. "I'm not really a fan of cuddling after sex."

He takes his already hard cock in his hand, slowly dragging it up and down while watching me with a dirty gleam in his eyes. "Who said anything about cuddling?"

Chapter 21

As I lie awake in the middle of the night in complete darkness and silence, tracing Fai's chest, drawing circles on the skin, I think about what he told me. And I think about telling him my truth and my secrets. I know I could tell him. He'd understand, probably.

He's sleeping next to me, but I have trouble sleeping at night since I stay awake for so many because of my work. And I'm forced to lie here and think about things that I don't want to think about.

I place my head on Fai's chest, my cheek making contact with his warm skin. I hear his heartbeat under my ear and there's something comforting in this. Some intimacy. I close my eyes with a soft smile. Just for a moment here, life is beautiful. And all is okay.

I wake up because of my alarm clock, notifying me that it's time for school. Fai lets out a deep groan of displeasure, shifting. I'm still laying with my head on top of his chest so I feel his every movement which wakes me up even faster. "No the one for cuddling, huh?" he mutters. "Turn that thing off before I throw it out the window."

Fai is not a morning person, I notice. I have to roll off him and turn the alarm off. "Thank you for volunteering to take me to school. I'll be ready in minutes," I say over my shoulder as I step out of the bed. Fai puts a pillow over his face.

I don't have anything here, so I have to take a quick shower and put on my clothes from the previous night. I have to use my finger to brush my teeth.

I put my hair up into a bun and when I get out of the bathroom, Fai is still on the bed. I crawl on the bed and sit on top of him. "Leave me alone," he mutters.

I smile to myself. "Take me to school," I say, leaning down and start kissing him on the jaw. He shifts in bed.

"Can't you take the bus?"

"I want you to take me. Pleaseee," I say close to his ear.

He sighs and finally caves in. He pushes me off and gets out of the bad, granting me a view of his fine, naked body. "This is bullshit," he murmurs to himself as he goes to the bathroom and loudly shuts the door. I just grin.

"What kind of coffee do you drink?" I call after him.

"Black," he calls out.

"Figures," I say to myself.

I go to the kitchen, making myself at home completely. I make myself breakfast, noticing that Fai has a well-stocked kitchen. I wonder if he knows how to cook. I decide on tuna with eggs in a tortilla. It's quick and easy and it's also delicious.

When Fai walks into the kitchen, now fully dressed, I'm wrapping the tortilla and he looks down at it. "That for me?" he asks, nodding at my food.

"Nope," I say and give him his coffee instead. "That's for you."

He rolls his eyes. "Good to see you made breakfast for yourself and not me."

I shrug. "I didn't know what you'd like."

He looks at my food. "What you're eating is fine." But he doesn't make the same for himself. He makes himself oatmeal and I have to hide my grimace because that is something I just don't like. And there isn't much I don't like to eat.

"Do you cook?" I ask him when he sits down beside me.

"Yeah," he says absently as he puts his iPad on the table with a pen in one hand, a spoon in the other and I see he's working on what must be a design for a tattoo.

"That is an amazing design."

"Thanks," he says absently.

"Did you design all the tattoos you have?"

"Not all. Most of them." When he starts drawing lines, I notice he's left handed. Another new thing to learn about him.

"Will you show me your designs? I'd love to get a tattoo."

That gets his attention enough so he lifts his head. "What kind of tattoo?"

I shrug. "I don't know. I'm still looking for ideas. I'd like it here." I point at the spot above my ribs on the side.

"Small one?"

"Here, yes. I'd maybe get a bigger one on my back if I found anything I'd want."

"Huh," Fai says thoughtfully and goes back to drawing.

"Would you tattoo me?"

He shrugs. "The line is pretty long. It'd take a while I'd be able to take you."

I raise my eyebrows. "I'm sure you could free some of your time for VIP people."

"You're not special enough to be my VIP client."

I chuckle. "Ouch, baby. If I had a heart, you'd just hurt it."

He just gives me a lazy look. I stop bothering him and eat my breakfast. I stand up to clean the dishes, but my foot tangles around leg chair and I drop the plate and the cup while trying to catch my balance. The sound of something breaking is defeating and it makes me freeze.

I stare down at the floor at the pieces laying on the floor and I want to pick them up and I immediately drop down on the floor and hastily start picking the pieces together.

"Leave it," I hear from above me and I wince.

"I'm sorry. I'm sorry. I'm sorry ..." I'm mumbling.

"Kadie, leave it. You'll cut yourself. What the hell are you doing?"

I shake my head. "I'm sorry. I'll clean it up, I promise. I'm sorry."

I see blood on my hands, but I don't stop.

Fai grabs my arms and pulls me back up on my legs with force. My hands are shaking and my whole body is trembling. I know it's coming. I know it.

I close my eyes and wait. Everything is so still around me. So quiet. So peaceful.

"Kadience!" I feel Fai shaking me softly but I only squeeze my eyes tighter.

Please, just do it. Get it over with. Please do it.

"Oh, what the fuck." Fai wraps his arms around me and pulls me tightly to his body. "I'm not mad. I'm not going to hurt you."

I don't cry. I never cry. But my body keeps trembling and I can't do anything about that.

"Kadie," Fai says softly. He puts his hand on the back of my head, cradling it just like my mom used to do to calm me down.

It helps calm me down. And when I come back to my senses, I realise I'm standing limply while Fai is having his arms around me still. When he notices I calmed down, he pulls back, keeping his hands on my arms and his eyes on mine.

"Sorry about that," I say and when I bring my hand up to place it on my forehead, Fai stops me, his hand quickly grabbing my wrist. I freeze and look at him.

"You're bleeding," he states, pointing at my hand in his hold. He's frowning.

"Oh," I say, looking at the hand as well.

"Come. Let's clean this up."

I give one last glance at the mess on the floor before I let Fai drag me into the bathroom.

I sit on the washing machine while Fai looks for pads and disinfectant. I extend my hand when he comes to me and he carefully and gently cleans my hand.

"You're good at this," I comment.

His mouth pulls up at the corners. "I've had a lot of practice."

My ankles cross and I tilt my head, watching his tattooed hands cleaning up my hand. I move my eyes to his face then, noticing his messy dark hair, his dark eyebrows that are pulled together in concentration. His lips are pressed together.

"You're making me nervous," Fai says with a smile. He knows I'm watching him.

"Can't help myself," I say.

"You're going to make me blush, bee." Then he lifts his eyes and runs them all over my face. He doesn't ask me any questions. He doesn't say anything. He only sighs, puts a band-aid where I cut myself and we're done. "Let's go now."

"I have to clean–"

"Leave it," he says with a final tone, no room for objections. ns. My shoulders hunch, but I leave the mess where it is.

Fai takes me to school on the motorcycle. He has to make a stop at Harper's place so I can get my stuff,

When he drops me off at school, I see Mandy standing by the entrance, chatting with other barbies from her group, and watching us. I can't help but roll my eyes. Is she seriously waiting for us to come? "Look. Your fan number one is there, waiting to get a glimpse of you," I tell Fai as I take the helmet off and give it back to him. I shake my hair and redo my ponytail.

Fai looks towards where Mandy is standing and back at me, not reacting in any way. I grin. "Must be awful, huh? I mean look at her and then look at me. You could have her, but you ended up stuck with me."

Fai takes the helmet from my hands, but he doesn't even glance at Mandy. "Have fun," he says, not commenting on my words. He places a quick kiss on my lips and drives away. I puff the air through my mouth, turning towards the building and groaning before I drag myself in the building. Just a few more months.

I drag Harper to a kickboxing practice with me. This is her first time while I go when I can. I used to go a few times a week, but now I only go a few times a month. I can still kick a mean ass, which puts me in a good mood afterwards, while Harper is groaning and moaning. "I'm going to be so sore tomorrow. This is really not for me."

"That's because you're afraid to hit."

She gives me a look. "I know how to hit. If I have to."

"Uh-huh," I say unconvincingly. "But a little practice still wouldn't hurt."

She only shrugs. I can't even believe I convinced her to come. And it didn't even take long. Harper is usually against everything violent, so this is a big change for her. "I need a shower," she grunts. I let her take the shower first because she has to go to work soon and I have nothing, so I have time.

I make us a late lunch, noticing one of us should go grocery shopping. I wait for Harper to get out of the shower and leave her with the food so I can shower, too and then we can eat.

When she gets ready to go, I clean the dishes and then plop down on the couch, sighing.

"I'm going. Be good," Harper says, rushing past me, but not quick enough so I wouldn't notice she's wearing a dress.

My eyes narrow. "Who did you pretty yourself up for?"

"No one. Bye!" She's out before I can ask another question. Well, isn't that interesting.

I don't know what to do with myself in the now silent apartment, so I go to the roof to catch the sun setting. I sit up on the wall and light a cigarette as. I look down and then close my eyes, just enjoying this moment.

I notice the bandage on my hand and I'm reminded of this morning again. And everything else ...

I wince, taking a long drag of the cigarette to divert my thoughts. I am so not thinking about the past when I'm up here. That's a dangerous thing.

When I finish the cigarette, I go back down because I don't feel good on the roof today, even though that's supposed to be my happy place.

I still have a few hours to spare so I actually decide to go to the bar, even though I'm technically forbidden to go. I throw on my oversized hoodie and my washed-off jeans, taking my headphones with me.

I take the notebook with me and draw the whole way on the bus.

When I get to the bar, I realise I missed this. I missed it.

I greet John with a big smile. "It's been a long time since I saw you. We all missed you!"

I give him a wink. "I missed this, too."

The first weird thing I see when I get to the bar is Harper and Jon. He's sitting at the bar, alone, and Harper is laughing at something he's saying. I walk straight to him. Harper is the first one to see me and her smile immediately turns to shock.

I wrap an arm around Jon's waist from behind, making him jump up. I lean close to his ear and whisper, "If you don't stop flirting with my cousin, I'm chopping your balls off."

"Oh fuck," he says, backing away. "The bulldog's back."

I only smirk. "Back away."

He looks at Harper. "Talk to you later," he tells her.

I raise an eyebrow. "Or never."

"Yeah, we'll see about that," he says, bumping into me as he gets off the stool. I watch him go with my eyes narrowed.

And then I look at Harper. "What the fuck?"

Her shoulders drop. "Nothing," she says defensively. "We were just talking, Kadie. Besides, did you and Fai break up or something?"

I pull back a little. "Why?"

Harper looks elsewhere and when I follow the direction, I see Fai. I see him, alright. With another girl sitting on his lap.

Chapter 22

I put my hands on the bar and look at Harper. "See? This is what happens when you hook up with assholes like him," I tell her, mostly because I don't know what hell she's thinking, talking to Jon. It's a good thing she sees the kind of men they are. "I need a cigarette," I tell her, pushing myself back from the bar and go out again.

I can't say I'm mad. I guessed he's the kind of man who can't be just with one girl. Maybe I'm just mad that I was right. And maybe I'm a little bit mad about him telling me I'm either in or out when he has the option to be somewhere in the middle.

I lean against the wall, crossing my arms. Before I can take the first inhale, the door opens. I don't even have to look who just came out. I can feel his presence, which makes me even more pissed off. "Ah. So you saw me."

Fai chuckles incredulously. "I sure did." He stands in front of me. "What the fuck are you doing here?"

"Same thing you are. Enjoying myself," I daringly look at him, wondering if he'll grab the vibe.

"After I explicitly told you to not come here?" he grits out.

I chuckle. "Do you really think you could keep me from doing something just because you said so?" I ask him. I put my finger on his cheek and drag it down to his mouth, staring at it. "You'd have to tie me up," I say quietly.

"Don't tempt me," Fai says, his eyes flaring, the muscle in his jaw ticking.

I drop my finger and step back. "I wonder if you wanted me away so you can be with other girls? Because that was really not necessary. I don't mind."

He raises his eyebrows. "If I wanted to hide something, I wouldn't come to the place where your cousin works."

I shrug, taking another drag of my cigarette. "Just don't tell me you were kissing or fucking someone before you did it to me because I just might throw up. I at least hope you're not that disgusting."

"You just said you don't care, so what does it matter?"

I cock my head to the side. "Well, I hope you like the taste of another man's cock in your mouth when I'll suck him off and then kiss you."

He recoils, horror and shock on his face. "I'm only fucking you. I'd hope it was the same case for you, otherwise this won't work."

I shrug. "Tit for tat, Fai. Do it to me how you want me to do it to you."

He nods once. "That's fair." He looks somewhere in the distance. "I gave you a choice, you know. You said you're in and I had you for someone who keeps her word."

"I just told you, Fai. Treat me like you want to be treated. If you want a slut, you can get one. No problem."

"Shut up," he says with anger. "Just ... shut up."

I roll my lips together.

He looks around. "Let's go somewhere else," he offers.

I click my tongue, shaking my head. "Nope. I came here to have fun. Just like you did."

Fai stares at me in pure disbelief. I just smile at him.

"You shouldn't let your company hanging." I point my head towards the building, hinting on the girl I saw him sitting on his lap.

"Jealousy doesn't suit you, Kadie."

I shrug, taking the last drag of my cigarette before I put it out and throw it away. "What's the deal with Jon and Harp, by the way?"

Fai's eyebrows draw together. "No idea. I don't put my nose in other people's business. Maybe you should try this sometime."

I only cock my head to the side.

Fai takes his hand through his hair and looks around. "Let's just get away from here, ok?"

"Why? Are you nervous that I'm here?"

Fai sighs. "Yeah, actually. I am."

"Alright, then. Take me away from here."

I shoot Harper a text on the way to Fai's motorcycle. He takes us to our place, as I predicted he would. As we sit down on the grass, I notice he's tense and that he's nervous about something.

I playfully nudge him. "What's up?"

"Can I talk to you about something? You really think my life is a joke and this situation is something you can test, but it's so much more than that." At the seriousness of his tone, I sit up a little bit.

"Tell me," I say.

He stares at me for some long seconds before he sighs and looks forward. "My mother comes from Dubai. She met my father there when he went on a trip and they ... got involved. They weren't in love, but they got married because my mother got pregnant and her family insisted. We lived in Dubai until I was 7, and then my father insisted we move to America. So my mother moved here, even though her family was against it. My father was ... he was great for some time until he suddenly wasn't.

"He got involved in a gang and he started doing awful things. Things I'm doing now. He got a lot of money out of it. I don't remember much of him as a kid. He usually came home in the middle of the night from his missions and I remember hearing them argue a lot. I didn't know anything about it as a kid and I didn't question it.

"But then, when I was 13, I hid in his car when he went on one of his missions. I was just trying to be a rebel. I saw him kill a man that night. And I saw him get killed by another man. I don't remember what it was about, but I saw my father die in front of my eyes that night. From then on, all hell broke loose. They started coming for my family because of my father's unfinished business. I have a sister, you know. She's younger than me. My mother was scared to death because she wasn't safe. And then I escaped home at 15.

"I searched for them in the darkest of the streets and when I found them, I told them I'm going to finish my father's work if they leave my family alone. I wrote my mother a letter that she has to go back to Dubai and stay there. I haven't heard from her since and I haven't seen her. We don't have any contact anymore.

"And, Kadie, this is the life I live. I'm not fucking around with you and trying to scare you. This is some real shit and it's not fucking funny. If you want to be involved with me, you have to follow my orders when I try to protect you and not go against me just to defy me because you're putting yourself and everyone else in danger, too."

I knew Fai was hiding a story from me. But I didn't think it went that deep. I really just thought he was doing this to be a rebel or just because he got into some shit himself when he was young. But cleaning up his father's mess? "What mess exactly are you cleaning up here, Fai? For how long will this shit go on?"

"No longer than two more years if everything goes according to the plan. Look, this is just a dirty job and you can't get out that easily, but I made a pact with them. And even when this shit blows out, I'll still have blood on my hands."

"I don't care about all that. As long as you're good to me and Harp, I don't have a problem. Your flaws are just that to me: flaws. Besides, we all have our own war to battle in, just different ways of doing it."

"I have no reason not to be good to you and your cousin. But my flaws, Kadie, are real big, you know."

I just shrug. "Just because you do bad things, doesn't mean you're not a good person."

Fai chuckles incredulously. "You really believe that shit?"

"In some cases, yes. Not in all. I don't see you as a bad person. I know bad and you're not it."

He puts his chin on his hand. "You have a story to tell, too," he tells me.

I look away. "Don't we all?" I ask distantly.

"No."

I chuckle. I move and sit on his lap, my legs on either side of him. I put my hands on his face and pecking his lips. "Thank you for sharing this with me. I'll tell you my story. Just not tonight."

Fai nods courtly and wants to look away, but I keep my hands firmly pressed on his face. "You care about me," I say.

He runs his eyes all over my face. "Yeah," he says.

And I smile. I smile so big. I kiss him and he kisses me back. He puts his hand on the back of my head and I feel it in his kiss. I feel the respect. The tenderness. I've never felt this from anyone. I never had this in my life. No one has really cared for me. Except Harper, but that's different.

When I pull back, I'm still smiling and Fai is staring at my lips. "This is why I don't fuck girls like Mandy. They wouldn't get it." His eyes move up to mine.

I lightly trace my thumb against his lips. "You keep me safe, I'll keep you wild," I whisper.

A smile form's on his lips and I tighten my hold on his face. "But if I ever see another girl sitting on your lap, you won't hear from me anymore. You get me? I'll disappear without a word to you."

His smile disappears. "I get you."

"Good." I release my hold on him, dropping my hands to his neck. "You showed me your happy place. Now I want to show you mine."

Compared to the place he showed me, mine is nothing extraordinary. Just a normal rooftop for everyone else, but it has a special place in my heart. This is where I leave all my thoughts. I empty my head up here.

"A rooftop?" Fai asks when I lead him upstairs. It's fully dark out now and the view is magnificent. When I look up at the stars, I feel closer to them up here – which I basically am.

"Yeah," I say, climbing on the granite wall that's there for protection, but it doesn't have much meaning for me. Fai looks at my movements. "Come here. The view will leave you breathless."

He places his hands on the wall and leans forward to look down at the city below. "Fuck, that's high."

I grin. "What are you scared of? There are no limits up here. You had to leave all your worries and fears by the door."

He states at me for some moments before he climbs up, refusing to look down until he's firmly seated. "This is what makes you happy?" he asks, his face pale.

"Immensely. You're scared of the heights," I notice, saying it as an observation.

"No," he says. "But it makes me a little nervous being this high with nothing to protect me."

I smile and close my eyes, welcoming the soft breeze that caresses my face. "You can be anyone up here. You can go anywhere in your thoughts. It's up to you."

"I'd much rather get back down on the ground," Fai mutters.

"You're creating limits for yourself. It's a shame." I open my eyes but keep my gaze forward. A few locks of hair escaped my ponytail and are now dancing around my face. "We are all free as birds when we're born. And then they build a cage around us and we just accept it, not even trying to open it and fly back out."

Fai looks at me. "Are you in a cage?"

"Not right now. But I'll have to fly back into it and that doesn't make me entirely free, does it?" I look at him back.

"What is being free, anyway?"

"Not belonging to anyone. Not belonging anywhere, but everywhere."

I hear him let out a breath and he casts his gaze forward. "In that case, I don't like the idea of being free."

I chuckle because I'd like to think I know exactly what he's thinking. "Don't interpret my words incorrectly. You can love someone and you can be with them, but you don't have to belong to them. And you can live in a city, build a house there, and not belong to it, as well. Free as a bird, Fai. It means having the option to go anywhere at any given moment and then come back. Or maybe not."

"That's some way to put it ..." He's silent for a few moments. "So when you go to college and leave the city, what is it going to be? Will you return?"

I let out a bitter chuckle, looking down at the cars in the far distance. "Fai, if I leave this goddamn city, I fear I'm never going to come back."

Chapter 23

A nte comes to the club I work at. I don't see him at first, but when I do, my mood completely shifts and I become annoyed. I walk to him and lean against the table, raising my eyebrows. "Let me guess. Fai couldn't come and he sent you."

Ante lazily shifts his head from the naked dancer on the stage and looks at me, swirling the almost empty glass around. "Hello to you, too," he drawls.

I just raise my brows.

Ante looks at me with interest. "What Fai sees in you is beyond me. He could have anyone, yet I have to sit here and save your ass while trying to not get bit by you."

"Nice thinking." I nod. "You're not going to offend me that easily, by the way, so you can save your nasty words for someone else." I hold my head up higher. "And if Fai wants to fuck me, you'll have to suck it up and just deal with it already."

Ante takes a sip of his drink. "Mmm," he says. "Fair point." He sits back in the chair, a small smile curving his lips. "You're not really that bad, actually. He's had way worse before."

"Why are you telling me this?" I ask him, not in the mood to listen about Fai's past experiences. This is not Ante's story to tell. If Fai wants me to know, I want to hear it from his own mouth.

Ante shrugs. "I'm just saying. Just don't go and fuck it all up because he hates people who go behind his back. And more than those he hates cowards."

I tilt my head to the side. "I'm only here to collect drink orders. I don't get paid enough to listen to your life advice you think I might need."

Ante lets out an easy chuckle. "Alright, cupcake."

I shudder at his pet name. "Why are you here? Is there really any danger or this is some fucked up way to have me under control."

Ante shrugs, taking another sip of the drink. He turns his head towards the stage and lets me know he's not going to answer my question. I sigh in frustration and march away from him.

I take a bathroom break just so I can write Fai a message.

Can you call your watchdog off? This is ridiculous.

I'm angry. He should know how much I'll hate this. It's like a prison. A cage. I don't like being in a cage and he knows it because I told him so just hours ago.

He answers with a simple answer.

No.

I almost hit the wall in frustration.

I'll stop by later. We need to talk.

I don't care if it's in the middle of the night. I'm not doing this with him if we're not on the same page.

I don't wait for his answer. I turn my phone off and leave it in my locker before going back out and finish my damn shift.

"You can drive me to Fai's. He's expecting me."

Ante glances at his motorcycle and then at me. "You know I can't do that."

I grunt. Of course. Their stupid rule. "Well, you didn't really think this through, did you? Bye then. I have to go catch the bus."

Ante seems like he doesn't know what to do. "You're going to Fai's?" he asks.

"Yep," I shout over my shoulder.

He's unsure of what to do. I stop in my tracks and grin. "What are you afraid of, sugar? Nothing will happen to me on the way to his place. And he's expecting me, anyway."

Ante finally shrugs. "Fine. You're his problem now. I did him a favor, but I'm off duty. Have a great night."

I wave at him and walk to the bus station, pulling my hood up and put my headphones on. When I turn my phone on, I see Fai sent me a text not that long ago.

Will be waiting.

I'm the only one on the bus, which is expected because you don't see many people walking around at this hour. I lean my head against the window, looking at the lights passing by. We get to Fai's street fast because there's not much traffic at this hour.

I have a few minute walk from the station to his building. I look around when I step off the bus because Fai created some sort of paranoia inside of me that someone's really after me and I should never be too sure.

I roll my shoulders and laugh to myself. I'm kind of sick of one man trying to come off as a danger to me and the other one trying to save me.

I take in a deep breath, calming myself down before I face Fai.

As he told me in the message, he's waiting for me. He opens the door shirtless and only in sweatpants and I see he's been working on drawings in the kitchen. I put my stuff on the kitchen chair and face him, crossing my arms over my chest.

Fai just sighs. "What?"

"Stop."

His eyebrows shoot up in genuine confusion. "Stop what?"

"Stop trying to control me. Stop coming after me when I don't ask you to come. Stop sending your guys to look after me. I don't want that Fai and if we can't agree on that, we're ending everything in this moment. I will never, ever let anyone control me. Do you hear me? Especially not your goddamn friends."

"That's why you're mad? Because I want to protect you? Are you fucking serious, Kadie? This has nothing to do with me controlling you. I don't give a fuck what you do when we're not together. But you still don't get it even after I told you what's going on in my life."

I don't stop glaring at him. "Alright. And you could've just told me. Hell, Fai, we have bodyguards there. Do you really think anyone would try something?"

Fai takes a threatening step towards me, his face coming down, close to mine. "They shot someone because they thought it was you, Kadie. Stop treating this as a joke because it's not. You're too late to go out now."

I let out an angry breath through my nose. "So what? I get to be followed every day by you or one of your friends? You might as well just lock me in a room, then."

Fai goes through his hair in frustration, his nostrils flaring. "You're so goddamn thick-headed, I can't believe this. Kadience, you're smart. I know you are. But you're acting so stupid right now." He shakes his head. "Why?" he asks suddenly. "Why do you want to be reckless so badly?"

His question throws me off a little. "I'm not trying to be reckless," I mutter.

"Then what?" he asks in frustration.

I shrug. "I just don't want to feel like being in some sort of drama you're watching for your entertainment."

Fai steps back a little and looks at me. "It's about you feeling like you don't have the freedom, isn't it?" I bite the inside of my cheek. "This is not about me wanting to know what you're doing at all times. It's not about watching you, but watching others who are trying to hurt you." He rubs his face and I take notice for the first time how tired he must be. He takes his hand to his neck, trying to loosen the tight muscles. "You're right. This is not going to work."

I purse my lips, staying quiet. My stomach sinks just a little, but I don't show it. I don't show him my weakness. I never do. "Alright. Then having any further discussion is completely pointless if we both agree on that."

I take another step back, putting more distance between us. "I'll be going then."

"Just like that?" Fai asks.

"Yep. Just like that. It was fun while it lasted, but this whole thing is suffocating me. I need my space and my freedom back. I can't have that with you."

I see his jaw clench. I take my backpack from the chair. "Take care," I tell him and get the hell out of there as fast as I can because I already feel like I'm going to get a panic attack and I definitely don't want to get it in front of him. Goddamn it to all.

As I walk down the stairs, I can't help but think how awfully easy this was for him. How easy was it to just end it all.

I rub my eyebrow in frustration. I was tired before, but I'm suddenly feeling wide awake. I take a deep breath, looking left and right before stepping out of the building. It's really dark outside and there's no one around.

I decide not to go to Harper's place. I know I won't be able to sleep now and before I'd get there, it'd be already too late because I have to go to school in a few hours.

So I wander around.

It's dead silent with minimal traffic. I wonder what the people in the cars that are passing by must think of me, walking around with my hood up and a backpack on my back. I turn my phone off. Harper will think I stayed at Fai's place.

The Westside of Atlanta is not categorised as the safest place on the Earth, but when living here your whole life, you get used to the city and the people. I don't live in a rich area and I can hardly say it's a nice city. There's graffiti everywhere, criminals at every corner. It's full of drug dealers, there's a lot of theft, but this is just how it is.

These things become completely normal.

I sit down on the bench I find, putting my feet up. I hear shouting in the distance, coming from a few men. There must be a fight going on. I sigh to myself, hugging my knees and close my eyes because I know what's coming.

It gets louder for a few seconds before the sound of a gunshot rips through the air, piercing my ears. And there's a complete silence after that. I exhale, realising I made fists with my hands and I'm pushing nails into the skin.

I'm starting to get cold when I sit for too long, but I see the sun is going to start rising soon because it's getting lighter out. I wonder if Fai is sleeping right now. If he's sleeping at the safeness of his home, after the talk we just had.

This is why I don't do any kind of relationships. I prefer raw sex over getting to know someone and getting our emotions involved. Because it's shit in the end. It always ends shitty and you have to deal with all these stupid emotions on your own.

I don't think what Fai and I had was love. It was something, yeah and it happened in a short time. We got close and he opened up to me. But that's still not the definition of love.

I am sad it had to end that way. I am sad it had to end because I thought I finally found someone who gets me and someone I can maybe trust. This clearly wasn't the case here.

But if something doesn't serve me anymore, I let it go and find something better. I came too far to have someone standing in my way of being and doing what I want.

I turn my phone on again so I type Harper a message that I'm going to school earlier today because I have to study for a test so she doesn't worry when I don't come to pick my things up. One look in my room would tell her I'm lying because my school bag is still there and I didn't take any of the school stuff with me.

I think maybe I should go somewhere where it's warmer because I'm starting not to feel my fingers anymore.

I put my headphones back on my head and put on some music again, distancing myself from the world completely.

As I'm walking, I feel the prickle against my neck. My heart starts beating faster all of a sudden. I want to take my headphones off and look around, but when I put my hands up to take them off, I'm stopped by someone.

I don't think, I don't freeze, I just react. I try to wriggle out of their hold, stepping onto his food and trying to kick him. I know it's a man because he's way stronger and taller than me. I bite down onto his arm, but his hand covers my mouth with a cloth and someone else appears in front of me, putting a bag over my head so I don't see anything.

Fuck. I try not to breathe in because I know I'll pass out and fight around. I'm strong, but the man wraps his leg around my ankles from behind so I can't kick anymore and his grip on my wrists tightens.

I'm starting to suffocate because I refuse to breathe and give in, but I can't fight on for much longer. It only takes a few breaths that my eyes start closing. I fight against it, moving my head side to side, but he pushes his hand onto my mouth so tightly he could knock my teeth out from the force.

I can't fight on.

I feel my head limply falling forward and my eyes close.

Chapter 24

I don't have to open my eyes to know that something is terribly wrong.

I'm very uncomfortable. My shoulders are hurting and I can't feel my arms. When I try to move out of the position, I realise I can't.

I have a hard time opening my eyes. I have a terrible headache and I feel weak. When the room comes into a full view, I sigh to myself. My head falls back in exasperation, seeing I'm tied to a bed with my arms up and over my head and in a standing position, my feet touching the bare mattress.

I'm in the centre of an old building with no windows and no doors in a view. "Oh, fuck me," I mutter to myself and sigh. This is so fucked up.

I try my wrists, but they're tightly tied together. If I move them, it only hurts more. I hold my body up by standing on my feet because my shoulders are starting to hurt like hell from having to have my arms up.

I lick my dry lips, groaning because of the pounding in my head. They had to put a lot of chloroform on the cloth. The stupid assholes could've killed me.

I hear a loud sound of a door opening and closing somewhere and my head lifts up, my body becoming alert. I hear footsteps getting closer to me and I wait in anticipation.

I don't recognise the man that keeps walking towards me. He turns his head to the side, looking at me with interest. "So you've finally gotten enough rest and decided to wake up," he comments.

"I'm used to much more comfort than this."

He smiles. "I bet you are." The man has to be over thirty. When he gets nearer, I get a chance to look at his face even closer. His head is shaved and I see multiple tattoos on his neck that go up to his head.

"Do we know each other?"

He tilts his head to the side, looking at me with complete interest while I have to fight the disgust appearing on my face. "I'm not sure. Did your boyfriend ever tell you about me?"

So it is about Fai. I should've known. I scrunch my face up, blinking at him. "And who, exactly, is my boyfriend?"

The man chuckles. "Let's not play games."

"Sir, you might have the wrong person here."

He clicks his tongue. "Does Fai Mills ring a bell?"

In this moment, I truly wish it didn't. I laugh. "He's far from a boyfriend. I'm Kadience, by the way. I could say it's nice to meet you, but I'm cutting down my lies, so ..."

He sits down on the bed, near my feet. "I know who you are."

"But I don't know who you are," I tell him, looking down at him. I try not to make any sudden movements or show him any of my fear.

"Stefan. I'm glad I have the chance to finally meet you."

The way he's looking at me makes me want to throw up. And I just might if he tries something. "So, how long do you think you will keep me here? I really can't afford to miss much more classes in school." I sigh dramatically.

"Let the school be your last concern. It all depends on how smart your boy is to figure out where you are and to come after you."

I pout. "But I can already figure out you are not the smartest. Fai isn't coming after anyone because we're not even a thing anymore. Damn, now I'm going to fail this year just because of you."

Stefan's nostrils flare and he grabs my ankle. My hands make fists, my body tensing at the sudden move. "I have many, many ways to either shout your mouth or make you scream one thing – my name."

I raise my eyebrows in a mocking interest. "Oh, for real? I wouldn't be too sure about that."

His hand travels higher up my leg. My jaw tenses as he tsks. "Want to bet I can make you come harder than Fai?"

Oh, so it is a competition now. This man, who's way older than Fai, is acting like he's 15 and he's in some action movie or something. "Eh. Fai was pretty useless in that department so it's easy to be better than him. I think I'm more into girls."

His eyes shine disgustingly at my words. "He is pretty useless if he made you start to turn your head into the other direction. But, hey, I'm all for clearing his mess up."

He stands up and when he puts his hand under my sweater, my eyes narrow. "If you like what he had previously put his mouth on, then go ahead. I'm not going anywhere," I say calmly, acting like I'm bored out of my mind.

He takes a knife, putting it in front of my face so I see it. I just look at him in boredom. He grips the sweater and tears it open with his knife in one sudden move, making me sharply take in a huge breath. Oh, fuck.

"Not my mouth, don't worry. But I have the other part of my body who can enjoy a whole lot of you."

He looks at my chest, licking his lips. I have to look away. I'm still breathing calmly. "Okay. But you should hurry, I'm getting tired again." I let out a long, fake, loud yawn, blinking my eyes a few times as they get blurry.

He grabs my jaw in his hand, forcing me to look at him as he brings his face close to mine. "For every time you piss me off or get too brave, you lose a piece of clothing."

A small smile spreads over my face. "Bring it on, you motherfucker. I love playing games."

He steps back with a cruel smile on his lips. "We'll see about that, darling."

When I wake up again, I have a weird taste in my mouth. I feel pain in my wrists from having them tied so tightly together. My arms start to feel numb and my neck hurts like hell when I lift my head.

There's someone standing by the end of the bed, looking at me. When my gaze clears, I see it's the guy that tried to attack me in front of the bar one night. My lips pull up into a snarl. "So we meet again," I say. My voice is groggy because I haven't had anything to drink in God knows how much time.

I don't know how long I've been here. There are no windows to tell the time.

The man steps closer to me and I see he's holding a tray with food and water. I'm fucking starving. I lick my lips and look into his eyes. "Are you going to untie me or are you going to feed me?"

His lips pull up into a sardonic smile. "Who said the food is for you?"

I roll my eyes, groaning. "Fuck, just kill me already or whatever you want to do to me."

"Shut up and stop crying. Here, I'll feed you." He doesn't sound happy about it. I'm not happy to have him this close to me when I'm only in bra and my pants.

"This is starting to feel like a hotel," I grin. "I'd give you two stars, though, because the comfort isn't the best."

He shows a fork of unflavored rice into my mouth to shut me up. I grimace. "Yeah, and the food isn't anything to trip over, either."

"Be happy you even get anything, you ungrateful bitch."

I know I shouldn't, but I hope that Fai, by some miracle, finds out or figures on his own what happened and comes here to rip these misogynistic assholes apart.

I eat the food silently because I have no energy to fight on. I know it's useless. And as long as they all leave me alone, it's good. I'm not scared about what they'll do to me. I know I'm not any use to them, I'm just here to get to Fai. And if they kill me in the end, that's okay. I hope they'll make it painless, at least.

And if they keep me alive and let me go ... I'll probably kill them for daring to fuck with me. "Are you going to keep me tied here?"

The man feeds me again, shrugging. "Probably."

"How original," I say dryly. "What's your name?"

When he looks at me, I notice a scar just above his eyebrow. "Peter," he says.

I can't say anything else because he puts a spoon of tasteless food into my mouth again. "Can you give me some water?"

He does as I say. This is really degrading. I want to punch him every time he gets too near to me, but I can't. If he tries anything ... my legs still work because they're not tied.

I hear a door closing loudly somewhere and Peter doesn't let it disturb him and he calmly continues feeding me. I eye the man from before – Stefan. My blood turns cold just at the sight of him.

He stands at the foot of the bed, his hands in his pockets and looking at us. Me, precisely. Fuck. "Leave us," he tells Peter and he immediately backs away and goes out. What a pussy.

I keep my gaze on Stefan as he walks to the side of my bed. He starts taking the dress shirt off, starting at the buttons on his wrists and continuing from his neck down. Fucking hell.

I keep calm, watching him with a bored look. "So you came back now when I'm well-rested. How thoughtful of you."

Stefan's lips only curl up in the corners. He takes the shirt off, letting it fall down on the floor. He's nicely built, but nothing I couldn't take on. He has tattoos everywhere as well and his nipples are pierced. I raise my eyebrows at that.

He gets on the bed, stepping up and coming face to face to me. I stare at him with a daring look.

"Let's leave Fai a little gift, shall we?"

"Or just kill me and deliver my body at his doorstep."

Stefan chuckles, running his finger down my neck. I move my head to the side, slowly blinking to show him how tired I am of everything he's doing. "Where would be the fun in that?" He leans his head closer to my neck, wanting to place a kiss there, but before he can do that, I wrap my foot around his and, with all the force I can muster, push him backwards. He doesn't move far, but it's enough so I can't extend my leg and kick him into his stomach.

He grabs my foot and twists it painfully. I don't let out a sound. He looks at me with stormy eyes, but I don't react in any way. When he gets near me, I spit right into his face. And, despite everything I can only imagine is coming to me, this is such a good feeling that I have to chuckle. The look on his face is priceless.

I see a vein in his neck throbbing. He gets to me, leaning against my body and slapping me across my face. Hard. It turns my head to the side from the force and I immediately feel my cheek stinging. I close my eyes, but he harshly grabs my jaw and turns my head so I look at him. My emotionless eyes stare right into his stormy, angry ones.

"You fucking whore. That was a stupid, stupid move."

His hand goes to my neck and he squeezes it tightly, choking me. I just blankly stare at him, a small smile spreading across my lips. I hope he understands what my eyes are telling him.

Do it, you motherfucking pussy bitch. Get it over with.

I passed out. That's what I find out when I come to my consciousness again.

When my eyes open, the first thing I feel is stinging on my cheek and then, right after that, the cold. When I look down, I see the asshole took my pants off, too.

The positive thing is that I'm wearing nice underwear, at least.

I know sad people like him. I thought Fai was like this when I first met him. I'm glad he isn't.

I don't know if Stefan has some sort of a sensor or if he's filming me that he knows exactly when to come back into the room.

He wears a curious look and my first thought is that he'd make a terrible poker player because he can't control his thoughts from showing on his face. "The princess awakes again."

"Why didn't you just kill me?" I ask him.

He knocks his chuckle against the bedpost. "That would be far too easy. But I'm losing patience, rest assure. With you especially. I'll give it two days, maximum. Either Fai is really stupid or he really doesn't care about you ... and if he doesn't? You're completely useless to me."

Chapter 25

"**Y**ou fucking useless piece of fucking shit!" I yell, hitting the smoothie maker in anger and frustration because it just stopped working. Just like that. "Fuck," I groan. It's safe to say I didn't wake up in a good mood today.

My phone rings. I don't even check who it is and when I answer I bark, "What!" I keep it on the kitchen counter, putting the person on speaker.

"Bad timing?" Jon asks.

I take a deep breath, taking my hand through my hair and put my hands on the counter, leaning on them. "What do you want?" I ask, completely fed up with this day already.

"Flyn sent us money."

My ears perk up at this. I take my phone in my hand and turn around, leaning against the counter with my hip. "How much?"

"Ten grand."

"That's not enough."

Jon sighs on the other side. "I know, but –"

"Jon," I cut him off with a warning. "We had a deal. He knows what's coming."

Jon's silent for a few moments. "Tonight?" he asks.

"Tonight," I confirm.

"Okay," he agrees as if he has any other option. He knows better than to go against me, even if he doesn't agree with everything I say or do. "By the way, Harper asked if you could let Kadie know to return at least one of her calls since you've apparently locked her in your apartment." Jon chuckles.

I frown, standing up straighter. "I haven't seen Kadie in three days."

I can just hear the laughter die on his lips. "What? Are you sure?"

"Fucking hell!" I say, now really hitting the goddamn smoothie maker.

"I'm calling everyone now. We'll be there in half an hour the latest."

"Make it twenty minutes," I say seriously and hanging up.

"How the fuck is that possible? How the fuck did it happen?"

Ante is looking as if I'm going to explode and strangle him any minute. "Fai, I don't know. I was there with her the whole time at the club. She went on the bus to your place. I followed her so I know she came here." He's looking at me with wide eyes.

She came here, alright. But she left soon after that. I didn't even think that her not contacting me or answering my texts was anything unusual. I wanted to give her some more time to cool off before trying to have a reasonable conversation with her.

It seems like this won't be necessary.

"Are we sure they took her?" Bastian asks.

I just give him a look that makes him shut the hell up and just nod.

"Where could they take her?" Cruz asks next with a toothpick hanging from his mouth.

"Fuck knows," I snap in irritation. I feel like we've already wasted too much time and now we're wasting it even more. I'm going to kill those motherfuckers. Every single one of them. I'll make it so slow and painful, they'll beg me to end their lives. The stupid fuckers. He really thinks this is a game.

I look down at the papers spread on the table that are showing all his hidden places that we know of. If Kadie wasn't in one of them, I'd put them all on fire.

"Let's break it down so we can find her in which building it is and then make a plan for how to enter." Ante leans over the desk in the same way I'm doing and looks at the plans of different buildings in different locations. He puts his finger on the first one that's in the middle of the forest.

I immediately shake my head. "Too obvious." Ante makes a red x over the building. He points to the next one. I stare down at the paper so hard I'm afraid I'll make a hole through it. "We're wasting too much time here. Fuck, we can't waste any more time." I hit the table with my fist and turn around from everyone to cool down, taking my hand to the back of my neck, my head hanging forward.

Knowing Stefan, he won't give her much time, even though nothing of this is her fault and she shouldn't be in this mess. My mess.

Looking back at the guys, I notice they are looking at me warily. "We're going to find her, man," Lev says.

"We're going to have to split up," I say suddenly.

That makes Cruz stand up to his full height, his face full of disapproval. "Fai, man," he says as if he has to talk slowly and carefully to put some sense into me. "That is not really a good idea."

I just give him a cold, sombre look. "What else do you suggest?" I ask him in an obvious mockery. "We can stay here and chat, okay. And while we're here in the comfort of safety, she's fuck knows where getting tormented, if she's not already dead. Because of me. So spare me the fucking preaching, because I know the danger and I'm telling you we split up because I expect you all to go into this as if she was your girl you had to save."

I look each of them at their stunned eyes. "Now, move your fucking asses because we don't have a second more to spare."

"What about tonight's mission with Flyn?" Ante asks, completely nonchalantly, although all of the guys are wary because they're not used to me losing my shit because of a girl.

"Does it look like I'm in the mood to deal with Flyn right now? He can fuck off for now, he's the least of my worries."

And then some sort of realization suddenly hits me. "The phone," I say. Everyone just stares at me blankly. "We can track her by her phone. If it's still turned on."

Cruz spurs into action. He's the man for stuff like that. "Shit, man, why didn't you say you haven't done this already sooner. Give me her number," he says impatiently, taking my laptop.

I let him do his thing while I march around the room. Every second that passes makes me realize Kadie is one second away from dying. "Did you tell her cousin anything? Harper?" my question is directed at Jon. I don't know what's going on between these two, but it's something.

"No, I haven't. That's why we need to bring her back alive, Fai."

I go through my hair again. I'm going to be bald by the end of this day.

"So, what? You're seeing her now? For real?" Ante asks Jon, his lips up in a curl.

Ante had hots for Harper first, but I doubt it was anything serious. He probably just wanted to fuck the innocence out of her and Kadience would most likely shoot him if he came near him. And then she'd shoot me.

I start sweating at the thought of shooting because I just hope she wasn't the one getting shot. Fucking hell.

"Got her," Cruz says. Her phone is off but I'm sending the location to your phones where it was last detected. Hopefully it's off just because her battery died."

I shoot him a look for that unnecessary remark and he just shrugs, half-apologetically.

I look at the location and then at the map on the table with Stefan's buildings. That motherfucker. He literally took her in the middle of nowhere.

"Someone has to go with a car, others are going with motorcycles to get there faster. We don't know what we're going to find there." I get a weird taste in my mouth just for saying it.

"How the fuck do we even get there? There seems to be no road," Bastian says.

I'm already putting on my jacket and taking the gun out, making sure it's fully loaded. "We don't have time for questions anymore. We'll have to make a plan on the spot when we get there."

It turns out that there is a road to the building, it's just not shown in the maps. The fucker thinks he's smart for this.

We go right to the door, not even caring if he'll hear us. Instead, I hope he does. I want this fight to be fair so I hope he gets ready for what's coming.

I'm surprised there isn't anyone waiting for us already in front of the building. It's quiet. I feel chills running down my body in an uncomfortable way that tells me something is wrong. Something is very wrong.

I'm not trying to be careful, I'm trying to be fast. This building has no visible windows. It has one hidden door that we open up with difficulty. It takes all three of us to break in this godforsaken building.

It's cold in here. Cold and dark. I run forward with the guys running right after me. I come to a full stop because I have to take in a scene. She's the first thing I see, tied up to a bed in only her underwear while Peter, one of Stefan's bastards, stands by her bed.

Kadie lazily lifts her head and looks at me with no emotion. Fuck. Her face is full of bruises. When my eyes move downwards, I see her body is bruised, too. Fucking hell. Looking at her, I slowly lift my gun and point it right at Peter's head completely cold-blooded.

"I really wouldn't do that." He lifts his hand up and shows me a little black device in his hand. "With just a press of my finger, this building is going to explode. And then we all go to hell." His lips turn up into a demonic smile. My blood temperature rises.

I look sideways to see Jon standing completely still. I tighten the grip on the gun.

"If we have to die, we can all die together, right?" Kadie says in a complete monotone voice. "Just fucking kill us all and stop toying with us. I'm getting real fed up of these boring games."

I give Kadie a sharp look to just be quiet, but she's not even looking at me. She's looking at nothing in particular.

"Aw. You'd let your boyfriend die just after days of waiting for him to come and save you?"

She gives him a cold look. "I wasn't waiting for anyone, you were. So maybe you should go to him for hugs and kisses because you were more excited to see him than me."

I don't know if Kadie is just pretending and lying or she's serious. I never know with her. I would've thought she'd be happy to see me so I can save her from this hell.

Peter's jaw ticks. She struck a nerve. "I don't know you can deal with this bitch," Peter says to me. "She's literally asking to get slapped." My blood is boiling.

"Let her go and she's not going to be your problem anymore," I say, trying to keep my voice calm and collected, but clear and loud.

Peter chuckles humorlessly. "It's not going to be that easy. How much are you prepared to give for her?"

I scowl at him. "How much am I prepared to give? What is this, a garage sale? And why are you doing Stefan's dirty work? He too much of a pussy to face me?"

Peter just shrugs. "Just following orders."

"Yeah because that's all you really know how to do, anyway."

He moves his head to the side. "Careful there. I also know how to press this button right here. Especially if you don't lower your gun. Now."

I take out a deep breath, slowly lowering the gun while not taking my eyes off him. "What the fuck have you done to her?" I ask him, dead serious.

"Ah, this? Just rewards for talking back."

My nostrils flare.

"Don't worry. He couldn't make me come, either," Kadie suddenly says sarcastically.

I hear Lev coughing to hide the sudden laugh. I ignore him."And what the fuck do you want from me?" I'm losing my patience now.

"We have unfinished business, Fai. I want you to finish it."

"No," I say automatically.

Peter shrugs. "As you wish." He suddenly lifts a gun and points it at Kadience.

I hear the surprised intake of breaths behind me of the guys.

"Wait," I say, subconsciously taking a step forward. He gives me a warning look. "Let's make a deal," I say.

"You finish the unfinished and you get your girl back. That's the only deal."

I narrow my eyes at him. "You let her go first and then we can talk business."

I hear shooting outside. My whole body tightens and I see Peter's does, too. "What the fuck is that? Are you fucking with me, Fai? Because I'll shoot her right now."

I shake my head. "I don't know what's going on. Maybe you should check it out? It sounds serious."

He just gives me a dirty look and I shrug. But I notice he looks nervous. He doesn't know what's going on. I'm not worried. Cruz and Bastian know what's up and they're dealing with it. I'm surprised Stefan didn't make sure to think this through more. This was stupid of him.

I hear my phone vibrate in my pocket. Once. Twice. I tilt my head to the side and smile. The horror starts to rise on Peter's face. He knows something's up. "Ah, my dear Peter. We didn't come here without a plan."

He only raises his eyebrows, but he's terrified. "You can let her go and let us leave or this might just turn ugly. And I'm pretty sure you know what ugly means when it comes to me."

"Am I the only one getting turned on right now?" Kadie suddenly asks.

"Definitely the only one," Lev says. I don't look away from Peter.

"What the hell did you do, Mills?"

"Great things."

Cruz and Bastian have no trouble walking in. They're both wearing a smile of triumph on their faces and I can't help but grin. "Now, if you don't mind, I'd like my girlfriend back. I'll gladly forget about this little incident and the disrespect if you let her go. Otherwise, I'll show you hell."

Peter is indecisive. He doesn't know what to do because he hasn't planned that far. Stefan has some really bright people on his side I see ...

"I'm afraid I can't do that."

"No? Are you willing to die for your boss, Peter? Does your life really mean so little to you?"

He hesitates with the answer. He grips that useless black thing in his hands tighter. "How much does your life mean to you? And your girlfriend's? Huh?" His finger hovers over the button and I'm tired of thinking he got us and that he has any kind of power over us.

"This was so very stupid of you." I shoot up once as an indication, but Peter reacts too slow. Before he even gets to aim his gun again, I shot him in the knee and he falls on the floor with a loud scream, his gun flying over the floor. I see he's pressing on the button on the black device in his hand, but ... nothing happens.

I go to Kadie and cut the rope with a knife. Her hands were tied so tightly together that she has red, deep marks all over her wrists. She leans against me until I free her ankles. I take my jacket off and wrap it over her body.

I jump down from the bed and when I want to take her in my arms, she refuses. "I can walk," she snaps. I just lift my hands up and let her walk, but I still wrap my arm around her shoulders. I know she's trying to act tough, but I feel she's trembling.

I let the guys deal with Peter. Stefan is happy he's not here because I'd rip his head off with my own hands tonight.

Chapter 26

I put a blanket over Kadie's body that I find in Cruz's car that's already waiting for us. She sits in the passenger seat and I get behind the wheel. My jaw is starting to hurt from gritting my teeth together so hard.

I look at Kadie, but she's just staring forward. I start the car and drive the hell away from this place. Neither of us speaks and the silence in the car is making me uneasy because I'm not used to it when it comes to her.

"You're very quiet," I say as a simple observation.

I see Kadie puts the blanket around her even tighter. "Is this your car?" she asks.

"No, it's Cruz's."

She nods and falls silent again.

"I'm sorry," I say softly. I'm worried that this is our breaking point and we have nowhere to go from here.

"For?" Kadie asks. Her tone is clipped.

"For everything they did to you."

"You didn't do anything you have to be sorry about."

"This is all my fault," I say, gripping the steering wheel tighter. If it wasn't for me, Kadie wouldn't go through what she went through. And I'm not sure if I want to know what they did to her.

"Stop," she says. "You didn't kidnap me. You didn't tie me to the bed and beat me. You didn't do any of this. I don't want to hear you apologize for this because it's not you that has to apologize for anything."

Her voice is harsh and leaves no room for contradicting. It's weird how she's still so feisty and strong. I know many would cry if they were in her position. But not her. She's still spitting fire, although I know she's hurt. I saw the bruises.

"What did they do to you?" I ask.

"Nothing that hasn't already been done to me before."

My face twists and I swiftly look at her. "Kadie ..." I say softly.

She doesn't look at me. "Please don't pity me," she says. "They didn't do much. The bruises are external."

My shoulders relax, but just a little. I know my guys will make sure Peter pays for this, but Stefan will go untouched and that doesn't sit well with me. I want to see him suffer twice as much as he made Kadie suffer.

We ride to my place in silence and when we get there, I run a bath for Kadie while she's waiting on my bed, still wrapped in the blanket and staring into nothing. It's so weird seeing her like this. I feel like I have to tiptoe on eggshells around her now because I don't know what's going on in her mind.

"You can take a bath," I say softly when the water's ready.

She nods and stands up. She stops in front of me in the bathroom, looking me in the eyes. "Stop acting like I'm a bomb that's going to explain. Stop holding yourself back. Don't look at me differently now, Fai. I've survived much worse."

She puts her hand on my cheek and drops it quickly, turning and walking towards the bath where she drops the towel. I walk around to give her some privacy while she undresses and goes into the water.

"You don't have to leave," she says. She's giving me a choice. I think this means a lot to her. I think she needs me to act normal in order for her to feel normal.

I clear my throat and turn around, but I don't step any closer to her because I want her to feel comfortable and safe. She's laying with her head on the edge, her hair spilling over, reaching the floor, her eyes closed. She looks calm and peaceful.

She suddenly pinches her nose together with her fingers and slides down until her head is underwater. Seconds pass and she stays down, completely still. "Jesus. Kadie!" I say loudly, rushing to her, but before I can reach her and pull her out, she comes up to the surface, breathing hard, but she's smiling at me. I take a step back, shaking my head.

She puts her head back again and looks up at the ceiling. "I was 6 years old when my father raped me for the first time."

My whole body freezes.

Kadie extends her arm and slowly lets her other hand run across her skin, focusing on it. "He came into my room late in the evening. I was already sleeping. You know, when you're a kid, you trust your parents to do the right thing with you and protect you because they're your parents. And you trust them. Period. He told me that what he was about to do was completely normal and I should relax and be quiet so I don't wake up my mother. He said it's going to hurt just a little but he's going to be careful."

I want to throw up.

"I didn't know what was going on, but it didn't feel right. I didn't want it. But he just put his hand over my mouth and ... did whatever he wanted to do. It was going on for three years. My mother thought I was making up stories in my head. She told me he sleeps by her every night and there's no way I'm telling the truth. When I was 9, he committed suicide. I remember his funeral. I didn't cry and people thought I was in shock. But I stared at the hole dug in the ground and I was content. Happy that he was gone. Because if that's what having a father meant, I didn't want one.

"My mother started drinking and doing heavy drugs after. I didn't see much of her because she worked a lot and I was in school. I was also often spending time at my aunt's place with Harper. When I was 10, she met a guy who also liked to drink and he also liked to hit things and people. Me, mostly. If he ever hit my mother, I didn't notice. He got angry quickly and I was convenient for him because I was small and I couldn't fight back. I think he was angry because my mother had a daughter and he didn't get all of her attention, even though she was drunk and drugged so hard she couldn't see straight most of the time.

"He was careful not to touch my face. He would often tell me it's too beautiful to ruin it. When I was 14, I stabbed him when he slept on the couch. He didn't die, unfortunately, but it was a warning. Soon after that, he was killed. I don't know by whom or why. I don't care. I didn't go to the funeral. My mother now has a new man who I've seen just a few times because I spend most of my time at Harper's place."

She moves her head to the side, looking at me. "You wanted to hear my story, Fai. Here it is. Here I am."

I'm so angry. I'm so angry I allowed this to happen to her. That she had to go through this again. Because of me. I don't know what to say to her because I'm so shocked by what she just told me. My whole body is shaking in shock and violence because I want to kill someone.

When I turn around, I see myself in the mirror and with the urge to hit something or someone, I punch the mirror with the full force, causing the glass to shatter all around me. I put my hands on the sink, ignoring the pain in my chuckles and the blood that's appearing on my skin.

I remember it then. When Kadie dropped the glass in my kitchen and it shattered. She reacted in such a weird, closed to having a panic attack.

When I look over my shoulder, she has her knees up to her chest, her arms wrapped around them and her head leaned down, her face hidden. I see her shoulders shaking. She's scared. I take a careful step towards her and I see how her muscles tense up. "Kadie," I say softly.

She shakes her head and I realize she's scared I'm going to hurt her. She doesn't react well to violence, especially not right now. "Kadie, I'm not ..." I swallow the bile in my throat. Fuck. "I'm not going to hurt you. I'm sorry."

I take slow steps towards her and crouch down in front of the bath. "I'm not going to hurt you," I repeat. I slowly lift my hand and place it on top of her head. She freezes at first, but then leans into my touch, relaxing. Her head falls to the side, towards me and I hear her sob.

Shit. "Come here," I say softly, putting my arms around her and pulling her out of the bath. I wince when I see her bruises and I try to be careful. I dry her off with a towel and then take her in my bedroom, wrapping a blanket around her to warm her up because she's shivering.

I sit on the bed and put her on my chest. She puts her face into my neck, seeking comfort and I tightly wrap my arms around her. "I got you," I whisper. "I got you. You're safe now."

I don't know what else to do other than hold her while she cries and whisper that everything's alright, even though I know it's not.

Kadie fell asleep on top of me and that means I can't move. She's restless and I think she's having a nightmare. I run my hands over her back, trying to calm her down. Her hair is already dry now and I can't help but run my hand through it, enjoying the soft feel. It's very rare that she has her hair down and maybe now I understand a little more clearly why she's trying to hide her beauty and isn't moved by the compliments.

I get a text from Jon that they dealt with Peter accordingly and it's all taken care of. I exhale, relaxing a little bit, although my body has been in a cramp ever since Kadience told me that horrible stuff that happened to her.

When she stirs awake, I notice she's disoriented. She looks around and then at me. Her body immediately calms down. "Sorry," she mutters, although I don't know what she's apologizing for. She gets off me and lays on the bed next to me, wrapping the blanket around her even tighter.

"Are you hungry?" I ask her.

She shakes her head. "Does Harp know?"

"I don't think so."

She nods her head. "Please don't tell her. They took my phone away, so I'll call her with yours. Later," she says, closing her eyes.

My arm automatically wraps around her. She looks so small and so vulnerable at the moment ... it disarms me completely because I'm not used to seeing her like this. She nuzzles her head into my side, seeking – comfort, warmth – hell, I don't know. Whatever it is, I want her to find it with me.

"Thank you, Fai. For coming after me and taking me away. I was hoping you would, although I was scared you wouldn't after how we left things that night."

I squeeze my eyes shut. She was hoping I would save her. "Get some rest. We'll talk later," I say with my lips against her hair.

Her body soon relaxes again and I realize she fell asleep again while it takes a lot more time for me to end those racing thoughts and before sleep takes me, too.

When I wake up, the spot where Kadie laid before is empty. I sit up quickly, hearing happy whistling coming from the kitchen. I get up from the bed and walk there with a frown, finding Kadie with earphones in her ears, wearing one of my shirts and dancing around the kitchen, her hair up into a messy bun.

I stand at the doorway, feeling as if the previous events were only a dream. I rub my eyes, confused as to what's going on.

When Kadie turns around and sees me, she freezes for a moment and then a wide smile spreads across her face. She takes her earbuds out. "I hope you woke up hungry because I'm making dinner."

I feel disoriented, looking around the kitchen. When I look at Kadie's bare legs, I see the bruises which prove that, no, it wasn't just a dream and it happened.

I take a deep breath. "Kadie ..." I start slowly, but I don't know how to continue. I rake my hand through my hair and Kadie gasps. I freeze.

"God, Fai! Your hand! Why didn't you take care of that before?" she says, coming to me and grabbing my hand – the one that's not bruised. She drags me to the bathroom and she winces at the shattered glass. She freezes momentarily.

"I'll take care of it," I mutter, side-stepping her.

"No," she says with a definitive tone.

"I'll grab things and take them to the kitchen, then," I tell her, softly pushing her backwards so she doesn't step on any of the sharp pieces. She's barefoot, for God's sake,

She stands at the doorway and watches me grab the pads and the disinfectant. I shut the door when I come out so she can't see the mess anymore.

Her face is pale and so serious all of a sudden. "What's going through your head?" I ask her gently because I see she's internally panicking.

Her shoulders sag. "That I'm acting like a weak fuck," she mutters as if she's angry with herself.

My muscles tighten in awareness. "Kadience," I chastity softly. I'm shaking my head at her. "You're not weak. At all," I assure her, my lips pressed tightly together. "You're the strongest person I've ever known," I admit gruffly.

"How did you know what happened?" she asks. "How did you know they took me?"

"Jon said something about you not calling Harper back because she thought you're with me. That was three days after you came here that ... night," I finish.

"I knew my only chance was you. And I thought you wouldn't come because you didn't know or didn't want to. In that case, I hoped they'd make it fast and painless. Killing me, I mean."

My chest squeezes tightly at her admission. "Kadience, I told you. You can't go out just because you disagree with me. When you told me you're in, that meant you're in with no option of going out."

She presses her lips together. "Which means I basically can't just end things with you."

My mouth lifts in a corner. "You can try, but I won't take you seriously."

"It still took you three days," she shoots back.

"Because I wanted to give you some time to cool off. And give you some days to start missing me." I shrug.

She chuckles, but it quickly dies on her lips. "I actually did miss you," she admits. This is one of the rare moments she's wearing her heart on the sleeve. She's completely, disarmingly honest about her feelings. "I'd rather be tied and held prisoner by you, you know. You could make it a little more fun, I have a feeling."

A groan erupts from my chest and I can't help but go and wrap my arms around her. "No one's going to tie you up and keep you a prisoner. Ever," I promise venomously.

I feel her relax against my body. "Let's go clean your hand up before we both turn into pussies." But she holds onto me for a few seconds longer.

Chapter 27

I call Harper from Fai's phone, sitting on his bed while he's drawing in the kitchen. I don't know if she'll answer when she'll see the unknown number.

I wait, letting it ring and, staring at the dark TV screen until I hear her reluctant voice. "Hello?" she asks carefully.

"Harp, it's me," I say.

There's a pause. And then, "Kadie?" she sounds hopeful. "What happened? Where are you? I've been trying to reach you for days!"

I grimace. I don't want to tell her, but she has to know. Especially if she decided to have this life, too. With Jon. "I don't know how to say this any differently, but I was kidnapped. For three days. Fai saved me and I'm here now."

I hear a gasp. "Kidnapped," she repeats, her voice faint. "Oh, my God. Kadie. Oh, my God," she panics.

"I'm okay, Harp. I'm all good now. I wasn't careful and they just wanted to get to Fai through me, but they didn't do anything."

"You got kidnapped and I didn't even know! I thought ... I thought you weren't answering your phone because you were with Fai. I should've known something happened."

I sit up on the bed. "Harp, shut up. This is not your fault, really. I promise I'm alright. I'll stay with Fai for a few days just to be safe and to keep you safe, okay?" It's mostly because I don't want her to accidentally see my bruises.

"Kadie," she says weakly and I know she's struggling to find words to say to me. I also know she wants to say something I won't like to hear, so I cut her off.

"I know what I'm doing. Just take care of yourself and I'll see you in a few days. Oh, and save this number, I'll call you from Fai's phone until I get myself a new one."

"I have so many questions, you can't just leave me hanging!" Harper says and I hear her sniff. Oh, boy. She's probably also scared that something will happen to her, too.

"Harp, this is for both of our safety. I could be watched right now and I don't want to risk anything. You shouldn't, either," I say softly, hoping she knows what I'm getting at.

She exhales slowly. "Okay. Be safe. Please call so I know you're okay," she says.

"Yes, will do. Take care, Harper."

I squeeze my eyes shut when I end the call, taking a deep breath. Well, that went well.

I go to the kitchen, quietly sitting across Fai and twirl his phone around absently, watching him work. He senses I'm waiting for him to give me some attention, apparently, because he lifts his head.

"Where does Jon stand with Harper?"

"Don't know. Don't care," he says.

I huff. "You guys talk. Does he ever talk about her?"

Fai's eyebrows slowly raise up. "When we get together we don't talk about who is fucking who, that's for damn sure. I know he spends time with her. That's it." He goes back to drawing.

It seems like I'll have to take the matters into my own hands. I pick Fai's phone up again and go through the last messages. I don't read them, this is just an easier way to find Jon in his phone.

I call him and he picks up immediately. "Yes?" he says.

"Hi, Jon," I say sweetly. Fai's head shoots up in interest. "First things first. Fuck up Harper and I fuck you up. And, for your own good, I hope you know what you're doing. Don't come on my shit list."

"Okay. Anything else?" I can hear he's not taking me seriously.

"Go to her. If you're dragging her into this mess it's on you to protect her and she needs someone right now."

A pause. Then, "Okay. I'll go." His voice now sounds softer.

"She'll pack a bag for me with everything I need. Bring it to Fai's. I'm staying here."

"Yes, speaking of which - is he there with you right now?"

"Sitting right across me." I grin at Fai. "Want me to tell him you said hi?" Without waiting for an answer, I move the phone so I'm not speaking directly into it, but I don't bother covering the receiver with my hand. "Jon is sending you kisses," I say to Fai.

He scowls.

"Hanging up now. Glad to see you're doing okay, though," Jon says and, surprisingly, he doesn't say this with sarcasm.

"Thanks," I say meaningfully. I hope he catches that I mean that for everything he did. Before we hang up, I add, "Fai is sending you kisses back."

My grin gets wider when Fai gives me a grim look. I hear Jon chuckling before hanging up.

I text Harper to prepare me a bag and tell her that Jon is coming to pick it up. I don't know if I did the right thing, sending Jon over there, but I can only hope that he's not going to fuck her over. Harper isn't like me. I don't think she'd want this life. I don't think she would even be able to go through it.

I put the phone down and sit cross-legged on the chair, watching Fai draw. "I have a proposition," I say after minutes.

"I'm all ears," he says, not lifting his head.

"I want a tattoo and I want you to draw it. I'll draw one for you in return."

He lifts his head now, interested. "What if I don't want a new tattoo?" he says.

I shrug. "That's okay. You don't have to get it. I won't be mad."

His eyes narrow. "You want me to draw you a tat and tattoo you? But you only get to draw me one?"

I shrug. "Yeah, pretty much."

He chuckles. "Alright. Want to go through my drawings?"

I immediately shake my head. "No," I say fiercely. "I want something unique. Something that reminds you of me."

He raises his eyebrows and he looks at me thoughtfully. "Right," he says slowly. I grin. "I do want payment if I'll do your tattoo, though."

My grin disappears. "Oh, fuck you. How much do you even charge?"

"Not talking about money, princess."

I raise my eyebrows. "What then? Sex?" My grin appears again. "Now you're talking my language!" I wiggle my eyebrows.

He darts his tongue out, making a way across his bottom lip with it. "I want to make you come."

I let out a huff. "How about I make you come? That sounds fair to me."

"Nah," he says, dismissing the idea. "You know what I'm talking about."

"And you know that's not possible because I told you already. I'd rather just give you money. How much will you cost me? So I'm prepared."

"That's my deal. Take it or leave it." He crosses his arms.

"Fai," I say, looking him in the eyes, silently letting him know he's being absurd. "You can try, sure. So you'll get that smug look off your face when you won't succeed. Your ego will shrink as well. Are you willing to take the risk?"

"A challenge," he says, grinning. "Yeah, I'm pretty sure I know all the risks."

I just roll my eyes. "That was way too easy. Maybe I should make deals like that more often. I'd save so much money!"

Fai's smile disappears and a dark look crosses his face. And speaking about money ... I have to call my manager about my job. "Lose that scowl," I say to Fai. "I'm only joking. I'm all yours." I send him a kiss and grab his phone. "And you'll be a sweetheart and lend me the phone because I need to save my job."

It turns out I'm an amazing actress. I didn't go into details why I missed days of work, but I told him it was a family emergency and that I've also lost my phone so I'm contacting him from someone else's to let them know I'm still alive and ready to go back to work.

Fai is scowling when I come back. "Aren't you a grumpy one?" I ask him, plopping back down on the chair.

"You were kidnapped and you're talking about going back to that place and work. Did you lose your fucking mind?"

"Why? You'll be looking out for me." I blink innocently.

He puts his iPad down on the desk and stands up, putting his fists on the table and leaning over it, looking me deep in the eyes. "You are purposefully putting yourself in danger which puts me and everyone else in the danger. You know that, Kadie? Or you only think about yourself and your stupid fucking stunts you want to pull all the goddamn time so we have to come and save your ass out of the shit you put yourself in?" He doesn't raise his voice, but he speaks the words with venom.

Oh, he's pissed. "I need the money," I say calmly.

"I will give you the fucking money if you need it that bad," he growls.

"The hell you will!" I say, standing up, too. Now we're both pissed.

"You can't go to work!" I see the vein appearing on his neck from the anger.

"Watch me," I say sweetly.

He growls, sidestepping the table until he's right in front of me. "You fucking watch me if you decide to go."

I step closer to him so we're nose to nose, glaring at him. "What are you going to do, then? Huh, Fai? Hit me?"

He steps back as if I punched him and I see his shoulders drop. "Why would you - fuck no. I'd never hit you. What the fuck."

This is not the first time I said this to him. I think, deep down, I know he wouldn't because he's not like that - at least not around me. But I've also been betrayed by many men in my life. What is one more?

"You're not going to work until all this comes down. And that's final. Just try and fight me and I will lock you into this apartment." He glares at me to make me know he's completely serious.

"Oh, fuck you," I say, sitting back down, feeling defeated. He's right, of course, although I loved pushing his buttons to see just how much he really cares. There's a big part of me that will always be wary, I think. I can never fully believe a person, especially not men. I always wait for their hit. Maybe that's why I love dating assholes. I at least know what to expect with them.

"Good," Fai says as if I just told him I agree with him completely. Which I think I did, but in my own way. "Jon's here," he says.

"What?" I ask, confused.

He's already walking to the door. I walk behind him to the door and when he opens it, I peek over his shoulder. "Hey, Jon! You and Fai really have such a strong connection that you don't even have to knock because he just feels when you come." I give Fai a pat on the shoulder. "I didn't know that. Cute." I kiss him on the cheek.

Jon just stands there, dumbfounded. "Yeah. Don't even ask, man," Fai says, aggravated.

I lean closer to Jon. "If I suddenly go missing or if you find my dead body, it was Fai," I tell him quietly, yet loud enough so Fai can still hear me.

He puts his hand on the back of my neck and pulls me back with a grunt. "See you, Jon," Fai says and closes the door, turning to me.

I beam. "I really need a cigarette," I say looking around. I know that I don't have any here and Harper definitely didn't pack them for me.

"What you need to do is sit your ass down and talk," Fai growls.

I raise my eyebrows at his tone. "I'm not your bitch. If you want someone to order around, get a dog maybe."

"Kadience, stop testing my fucking patience. Stop pretending nothing happened."

I cock my head to the side. "Why? Are you suddenly interested in becoming my psychiatrist? Boy." I shake my head.

"No, I want to hear what happened so it doesn't happen again. I want to hear what they did and how they did it."

I roll my lips into my mouth. "Can't tell you exactly what and how. They came to me in the dark, there were many of them so I couldn't fight them. They drugged me and when I woke up, I was tied to the bed." I shrug as if that's the most normal thing in the world.

"Naked?" he wants to know and I hear how sharp his voice got.

"I lost a piece of clothing for every time I made him mad."

"Stefan? That motherfucker." Fai curses, turning away from me. To calm down, I assume.

"He didn't really touch me, though. He's too much of a pussy and he doesn't know what to do with one." I don't tell him about the hickey he wanted to give me. He didn't succeed, so there's no point. "You know what I want to do? I want to go to a party."

He gives me an incredulous look. "You're in house arrest. You can't leave this fucking place so you better stop wanting to do things that involve the outside world."

I put my hand over my chest. "Wow, dad. Okay. whatever you say, sir!" I salute him and he gives me such a grim look that I chuckle. "Why not have a party here, then? Lots of booze, lots of drugs, lots of fun. And lots of fucking afterwards. Hey, we can even have a groupie."

His eyes widen slightly. "How about we not?"

I pout. "You're clearly no fun."

"And you're clearly fucking with me," he says, letting out an exasperated sigh.

I send him a kiss.

Chapter 28

Going back to school after just being lazy the whole weekend with Fai in bed sucks balls. Fai tried to convince me to stay at his place, but I couldn't. I've already missed too much school already and I could be facing detention. Or they would be calling my parents. Who wouldn't show up, anyway.

And then I see Many the bitch and my day gets even worse. She gets in my way when I try to get to my locker. I look at her, cocking my head to the side. "Pardon, bitch. Trying to pass."

She snarls down at me. I saw her before, bullying a girl. Because she's that kind of lowlife. She's yet to get a piece of mind for that. One day, I'll just drag her through school by her hair and dump her in the trash outside – where she belongs.

"Then move," she says simply, making her clones behind her snicker.

I go up to her face. "I am not one of your brainless twats you could order around. Think again before speaking to me like that again."

She just chuckles, her tongue running over the roof of her mouth. She looks to the side with a self-observed look like she owns this school. And she does, in some kind of way. Because her daddy has money and she's not afraid to run her mouth. But me? I'm known as the weird one. Mostly quiet, but I'm not big on running my mouth. I'm big on action.

I also know I'm rubbing her in the wrong way because I'm with Fai. I saw her, looking at us when he dropped me at school. She's so fucking obsessed it's pathetic. "You think you can be brave just because of who you're dating? You poor little thing."

A slow, ruthless smile spreads on my face. "Oh, Fai? The one who fucks me every night, all night?" I see the fire in her eyes when I mention him. "I pity you, baby girl. I understand why Fai didn't want to put his dick in you. And he probably never will. You're so pathetic, you're not even good for that." I shrug. "You can have your money and your fucking bitchy attitude. At the end of the day, you're nothing but just a sad little girl, crying about the guy that doesn't want her."

I pretend to wipe a tear from under my eye, pouting. She surges forward, trying to hit me, but I push her back so hard that one of her clones has to step behind her back to stop her from falling on your ass. "Think again," I say spitefully. "And, by the way, bullying other people for no fuckin' reason is a big turn off for the boy you're masturbating to. Just so you know." I wink at her and just walk past her.

I've tried to stay out of her business and out of everyone's business. But I've never supported bullying and whenever I saw it, I tried to step in because no one is getting treated wrongly on my watch. Especially not by Mandy.

I don't think my day can get any better after spitting into Mandy's face. Not literally, of course, but I would love to get a chance to do that. I don't do well with people who try to get into my business. And everyone knows it because when I walk away from the queen of bitches herself, no one dares to say anything to me because they know I'd kick their asses. If I were someone else, they would all come to Queen B's rescue immediately. Not because they all love her – everyone hates her. They just have to pretend they love her so she doesn't turn against them and their life would be ruined.

What a start to the day!

I go to the class, putting my headphones on because I'm early and I don't want to be bothered. I pull out a book about disease processes, evidence-based clinical pharmacology and optimal drug regimes. It's something I borrowed for Harper and she pleaded me to give her a review so I'm even making some notes while reading the book.

I get a text from Fai two minutes before the classes start. Fai got me a phone I can use until I get a new one. The classroom has gotten pretty full now, but I don't take the headphones off because I don't want to hear the noise of other people talking.

I open the text from Fai, reading it twice to make sure I read it correctly the first time.

Could you not make scenes, especially with Mands?

Mands? Is he fucking kidding me?

So your little girlfriend already cried to you about it?

That bothers me. That bothers me a hell of a lot. If he's in contact with Mandy, or Mands, that's not okay. I didn't know they were keeping in touch.

He doesn't answer and that makes me fuming. This is exactly the reason I never did relationships with anyone. It's too complicated and too messy.

I look over to Mandy and she's smiling. I want to punch her so hard, it would send all her teeth out.

This day is probably the worst ever. I was sent to the principal where I was questioned about my absence. I felt like I was being questioned by the police, Jesus Christ.

And then, in PE, Mandy was trying her best to hit me with a volleyball ball in the head. She didn't succeed and I didn't give her the satisfaction to lose my mind. I know what she was trying to do and, looking back, I'm proud of myself for keeping my cool. I just kept smiling at her, giving her a boring look and taunting her if that's all she has to give.

Sad, really.

When I'm done with the classes, Fai is waiting outside. I kind of forgot he was picking me up and it's like a sucker punch to the stomach. I'm mad again. This day really sucks.

I walk towards him. He's leaning against the motorcycle, his sunglasses on, his phone in his hand. He looks hot as fuck. "I hope you're here for your Mrs Bitch because if you're waiting for me, you're waiting for nothing."

I can't see his look because his eyes are covered with shades, but I see he's frowning.

I keep walking past him.

"Are you fucking serious?"

I keep walking.

He grabs my arm and spins me around, his hand gripping me hard. "What's your problem now?"

"You. Obviously."

I slap his hand away and step back from him, crossing my arms. When he steps towards me, I stop him. "Touch me again and I'm making a scene."

He's full-on scowling now. "What's with the goddamn attitude, bee?"

I shrug. "I don't know why you're even here, bothering to talk to me. Go save your princess there." I nod my head towards where I know Many is standing. I don't even have to look. She's so obsessed she's in the same place every day, waiting to get just a glimpse of Fai. I can't imagine being that sad and pathetic.

"Wow, that was petty," Fai says with a shake of his head.

"I don't care."

"What's gotten into you? Seriously."

"How did you know so fast about what happened?"

I know the answer before he even says anything. Just by looking at his face, I know what he's going to say.

"She told me. So what?" He sounds bothered.

"I didn't know you two were friends." Maybe because she's friends with hardly anyone. You have to be really fucked up to be her friend, though.

"God, can you drop it? It's literally nothing. Are you really throwing a jealous fit right now? Over a goddamned text?"

I raise my eyebrows. "Give me Stefan's number, then. Let me become all buddy-buddy with him."

"How is that even the same thing? Stop acting so childish, Kadience." I feel like he's losing his patience with me.

I lift my head up higher, knowing that Mandy is watching us, probably rooting to just keep fighting.

"You know, I have a theory. You and Mandy - or Mands ..." I wink at him, wanting to gag when I say it, "You wanted to fuck her. Or still do. But she's this rich girl that runs her mouth and her daddy could cause problems for you if you did her dirty. How wrong am I?"

His lips curl up. "Completely. I'm not scared of no one's daddy, princess."

"You didn't deny you want to screw her."

"My fucking God, just shoot me," he mutters to himself, looking up at the sky. "Kadience, once and for all, if I wanted to fuck her – or anyone else – I would do it, rich daddies or not. I'm not fucking their dads, bee."

I look towards where Mandy was standing, but I don't find here there anymore. She probably got her show and left. She ruined my whole day today by just existing. I'm acting sad all of a sudden with this ugly attitude. Since when did I turn into a whining girl who's panting after a guy?

"Why are you even in contact with her?"

He clenches his jaw. "She texts me here and there."

"What the fuck for?"

Fai shrugs. "I truly don't give a shit, Kadie."

"You clearly did this morning," I mutter.

"Stop," he says, putting his hands on my cheeks, looking deep into my eyes. "I'm with you. Not her. I don't want her to cause problems for us."

"I despise the kind of person she is, Fai. if you're friends with those kinds of people ..." I shake my head.

"I'm not," he reassures me. "She's really not important."

I put my hands over his, step on tiptoes and kiss him. I like that Madame Bitch isn't standing there and watching us because I do this simply because I want to and not because I want her to see.

He keeps his forehead against mine, his eyes closing. "It's you and me against the world now, bee," he says quietly.

"Hey, can we watch a movie?" I ask Fai, mindlessly flicking through TV channels while laying on the bed while he's sitting at the chair by the window, drawing again, holding a pen in one hand and a cigarette in the next one.

His eyes flick to me and then the TV. "What do you want to watch?"

"Something romantic. The Notebook? Do you have it?"

He just stares at me, horrified. "Does it look like I watch it in my free time? No, I don't have it. If you wanna watch that, you're watching it alone." He makes a face.

I give him a charming smile. "Are you working on my tattoo?"

"Nope," he says.

"You know, you can go out and do whatever you normally do. I would hate to keep you from your obligations."

He puts his foot on his knee, arching an eyebrow at me. He inhales the cigarette and then slowly exhales the smoke out while watching me the whole time. I have to say that's hot as hell. "I would have to tie you to something and lock you in and you still wouldn't stay in here."

I huff. "I just love how much you trust me, baby."

He shrugs.

I give up on trying to find a movie to watch and take my own book of writings, which is a literal classic notebook instead of a fancy iPad Fai is using for his sketches.

I twirl my pen around, looking at Fai through narrowed eyes. "Can you take your shirt off?"

He snorts - actually snorts. "What the hell for?"

"For motivation."

He sighs, but he complies, taking his shirt off. I grin, whistling.

He just shakes his head. "The things I do," he mutters.

I actually know what kind of tattoo I want on him and where. "Hey, can I decide on the tattoo placement as well?" I ask him with a pen in my mouth.

He looks up, thinking about it. "You can suggest it, I guess."

"Cool," I say back.

I see a small grin on his face before I focus on my drawing.

"By the way, I got you a new phone. With the same number."

My head lifts immediately. "Did you really?" I still have to take care of replacing my ID and everything else since I had my wallet with me when they took me and I didn't get it back. Thank God I never carry any money in it.

Fai throws a box on the bed. "Thank you. I'll pay you back," I tell him, taking the phone out of the box.

"No need," Fai says dismissively.

"I will pay you back, Fai. Every goddamn cent," I say fiercely. He just lifts his shoulder, most likely not even hearing what I said. I let out a long breath. I hate being indebted to anyone. Although the job is kind of a joke right now because I had to take some time off. It wasn't safe to go to work.

I unlock the phone and see that Fai set some things up for me already. I have to take a double-take at my new background. "Your selfie? Really?"

"It's a good thing you like looking at me," he murmurs, so deeply focused on his drawing that I'm surprised he even heard me.

I grin, looking down. I see I have a few new texts from Harper.

Hey! Jon told me you got a new phone so I can text you again.

I have something important to tell you. Please call me ASAP.

I don't know if I should write this in the text, but Jon and I did it ...

My mouth falls open. "The hell you did!"

Fai shoots his head up to look at me, his forehead staying crunched together, but I'm already walking out of the room, dialling her number.

I guess that means Harper lost her V-card. And to Jon out of all people in the whole wide world.

Chapter 29

- -

"**H**arp! What the fuck!"

She giggles on the other side of the phone.

"You and Jon? For real?" I ask her, still having a hard time wrapping my head around the fact because I never thought Harper would go for someone like him. Honestly, I thought Harper might just stay virgin until she's married because she was old-fashioned like that sometimes.

"Shhhh," she says, still laughing.

"Is he there?"

"No, he left like an hour ago. He had some things to do."

I narrow my eyes, not really liking that. They had sex and he just left? "Okay, but you and Jon, Harp? How the hell did that even happen? And when?"

"Uh, I don't even know. We just connected. He came to the bar a lot and we talked. He's not like others think he is, you know. He's nice and he treats me nicely."

Yeah, he better. "Okay, and the V-card?"

I already know she's blushing. Harper is usually reserved about stuff like this and doesn't really talk about guys or anything that's related to them. "It just happened. I don't know, it felt natural. And he was really gentle and nice, even afterwards."

Well, damn. "You know what? It's actually super cool you found someone that made you feel like that. I was afraid you were going to die a virgin or something."

She gasps. "Kadie! Seriously."

I chuckle. "I'm just playing around, chill. Jon better watch out because if he does you wrong, I'm not afraid of cutting his balls off."

Harper huffs. "Yeah, I think he knows that. He said that he admires Fai for knowing how to put up with you because he'd go crazy in a day in his place."

A laugh erupts from me. "It's a good thing Fai knows how to handle me just fine." I pause for a moment, getting serious again. "You know, I feel like Jon's a good guy. In his own kind of way, of course." I don't know how much Harper knows or if he told her anything about his life and what he does. This is weird for me because I've never wanted Harper to have this kind of life where you always have to look over your shoulder.

This is not a joke. What happened to me isn't a joke and it shouldn't be taken lightly. I'm just scared it could happen to her if we're not careful and I definitely know that Harper isn't like me. She wouldn't take these things so lightly.

"He is," Harper reassures me. "At least to me. And for me. I don't know, I didn't want to get involved at first, you know? I'm not you and I thought I'd always end up with someone ... different. But, sometimes, life doesn't want that for you and you just have to go for it, you know?"

This sounds like a completely different Harper. This isn't the organised, having her life all planned out Harper. The Harper that wants to finish school, marry at 27 and have a child at 29 the latest.

"Harp, you can still have a boring life later if you want. But you can live a little now. Enjoy having good, wild sex and have lots of it just in case you'll have to be in a missionary position for the rest of your life later."

"Kadience, I swear you have literally no filter," she says. I hear how embarrassed she is.

I just chuckle. "Live it up, baby! But be careful, okay? Jon might not be the guy you think he is, so never look at him through rose-coloured glasses. These guys are no princes."

"Princes are good and all, but, sometimes, the villains are more fun to be with."

I snort. "Okay, yeah. You're definitely smitten," I reply. "You know, I'm really happy for you, Harp. Just be careful, yeah? Tell me if he doesn't act right and I'll sort him out."

Harper lets out a heart-warming laugh. "Yeah, okay. I think I can manage him just fine for now, though, so I'm good. But I'll keep it in mind."

"Okay! Have fun, but not too much fun. And, Jesus Christ, please be safe and use protection."

"Okay, hanging up now! Bye, Kadie. Stay good and don't run on Fai's nerves too much."

"Can't promise that."

Harper laughs and. When I walk back to the bedroom, I'm still wearing a smile. Fai lifts his head when he hears me coming in, arching an eyebrow in silent question.

I tilt my head to the side, knowing I should guard Harper's secret with my own life. "I guess Harper and Jon are getting pretty serious."

Fai just shrugs, disinterested. He looks back at his tablet and I sigh. I'm bored out of my mind because I'm not used to doing nothing. "Could you take me to the library?"

"Right now?" he asks without lifting his head.

"Yeah." I'm standing by the bed, continuing looking at him. "I'm bored out of my fucking mind here, Fai," I say in aggravation.

He sighs, putting his iPad away. "I'm sorry. We can watch a movie if you want and I'll take you to the library tomorrow."

"The Notebook?" I ask him, biting down on my lip.

He grimaces and then quickly schools his expression back to normal. "You can choose whatever you want."

He sits on the bed and logs into his Netflix account then lets me search through it to find something for us to watch. "Oh, look at this. A documentary about Hitler. We can watch this."

Fai gives me a pained look. "The Notebook doesn't sound such a terrible idea, after all."

I burst out laughing at his expression. I put my hand on his thigh. "Don't worry. This will be fun, too."

"Your definition of fun is weird."

"Stop hating. Do you have a popcorn? Chips?" I jump up on my feet, going towards the kitchen.

"Both, probably. Grab me a beer since you're there, will you?" he calls out.

I feel a soft caress against my cheek. A finger against my lips, barely slipping inside my mouth. I stirr awake, my eyes opening into nothing but darkness.

Someone is standing beside the bed. The hand goes into my hair and I move my head away from the touch, feeling my heart race.

The hand moves the cover away from my body and by the way my body suddenly cools, I realise I'm completely naked. A hand touches my hip and I try to move away from it, but I can't. I can't move.

The hand moves between my legs, forcefully parting them open, and I feel fingers touching me right there.

I want to get away, run away, scream ... I can't do anything but just lay there. Why can't I move? Why can't I talk? I feel like I'm suffocating.

"Shhh, my beautiful little girl. I'll make you feel really good."

No. No. I recognise that voice. Go away. Go away from me! I can't move. I feel tears streaming down my face. His finger enters me slowly. No. I don't want this. Please. I don't want this.

His other hand comes to my throat. Up to my mouth. A finger slips inside my mouth and I want to bite down on it. I can't. I can't do anything. Please, stop.

A second finger comes inside me and I feel him shudder. I want to throw up. "So tight and soft. So tender. My cock is going to feel very good inside, won't it?"

I scream. "Get away from me, you fucking monster!" I move and roll with such a force that I fall down on the floor from the bed, tangled in the sheets. I'm scrambling away, trying to detangle myself. I hit something with my hand. I don't care. I don't even feel the pain. I just want to go away.

"Kadience! Stop." A light comes on and Fai is standing by the door.

I immediately become still and stop moving. The panic inside me completely paralyses me. I give Fai a helpless look. "I'm going to throw up," I tell him with a faint voice.

He reacts immediately, coming to me and lifting me up, untangling me from the sheet and walking to the bathroom where he puts me before the toilet and I limply fall down, emptying my stomach.

I feel him moving my hair away from my face. "Go away," I choke out when I'm done. He really doesn't need to see this.

He doesn't say anything, but he doesn't move, either. I flush the toilet, staying on the floor, feeling defeated, weak and sick. So sick.

I close the toilet seat and Fai sits on it, looking at me, but I can't look at him. I lay my cheek against his thigh, closing my eyes. It's been a long time since I had a nightmare, so long that I forgot how draining they are.

"What do you need?" Fai asks me.

I shake my head, my eyes opening again. His hand comes to my cheek. "Come on up, don't be on the floor," he says softly.

"I have to brush my teeth," I say, grimacing at the disgusting taste in my mouth.

I get up and go to the sink. I avoid looking in the mirror because I can't bear to see my own face right now. Fai sits on the closed toilet seat, watching me. "I'm going back to bed. Are you coming?" I ask over my shoulder after thoroughly cleaning my teeth.

"Yeah," Fai mumbles, standing up. I grab the sheet that's now laying in the middle of the bedroom and put it back on the bed. Fai turns the light off and it's pure darkness again.

He climbs in the bed after I do and I rest my head on his chest. Neither of us speaks.

I know I'm not going to be able to fall asleep so I don't even bother.

"Does this happen often? The nightmares?" Fai asks after long minutes of nothing but silence between us.

"They used to be a regular thing when I was younger, but not anymore. I work most nights and, therefore, I don't sleep in the nights, but rather during the day after school when I'm already too exhausted to even dream about anything. I'm also not really used to sleeping with someone in bed with me."

"Should I go sleep on the couch?" he asks me. I feel his muscles are all tensed up.

"I said I'm not used to sleeping with someone, not that I don't like it."

He relaxes, but only slightly.

I place a kiss on the centre of his chest. "Thank you for helping me fight my demons," I thank him quietly. I feel vulnerable right now, but I'm not afraid for him to see me like this. I trust him and I feel safe with him. For the first time ever.

"You fight mine, too. It's the least I can do," he admits.

"Do I really? How?" I wonder, tracing my fingers on his naked chest.

"Just by being here with me," he murmurs.

I smile sadly. I'm too awake to try and fall asleep, the adrenaline still too present in my body. Besides, I'm scared that if I fall asleep, the dream will repeat itself. So I talk. "You know, when we first met I was fighting with you every chance I got and Harper thought I was out of my mind. She was scared for me, but I wasn't. I'm not. Not of you, not of anyone else.

"I've been fucked over by the people closest to me and you can imagine my childhood and teenage years were ruined. I promised to myself that I'm going to be fearless because I've gotten the worst things imaginable done to me. I'm never bowing down in front of anyone because the worst they can do is to kill me and, fuck, did I sometimes wish someone would just do it sometimes."

Fai's body tenses up again. "Don't say that, Kadie. Don't ever fucking say that." He sounds serious. Mad even.

"It's the truth, though. I did wish someone would end it because I am too much of a coward to do it. I don't wish for that now, though. Although I don't fear death and I love dancing on the edge sometimes."

"And that's supposed to make me feel better?" Fai asks tightly.

"The truth rarely ever makes you feel better, Fai," I say softly, my fingers still tracing his skin.

I hear him let out a long, ragged breath. "Does Harper know about what happened to you?"

"Nope. She thinks we're just a dysfunctional family and that my mom had – has troubles with alcohol and drugs."

"Why didn't you tell her? Or anyone?"

I smile sardonically. "When your parents break your faith in love at such a young age, you learn to trust no one. You learn to love no one, not even yourself. I was on a path of self-destruction as a teenager and others thought it was normal because I was a teenager and I was going through a phase. I was healing myself in the only way I knew because I had no one who could help me. I had no one but myself, Fai, and it's always going to be that way."

His arm tightens around my body. "Not really true. You have Harper. You have me."

My eyes close and a soft smile appears on my face. Yes, it seems like I have him; in the darkest times, too. "And you have me," I whisper. "You and me against the world, Fai," I tell him the same words he said to me today.

Because the words I love you just don't want to exit my mouth, even though they're dancing on the tip of my tongue.

Chapter 30

F ai wakes up with his cock deep in my mouth. "Oh, fuck," he curses, his hips thrusting upwards, his head hitting the back of my throat, making my eyes water a little.

I smile up at him, taking him deeper and his head falls backwards, his eyes closing. "Love your fucking mouth," he grits out through his teeth.

"You love fucking my mouth," I correct him, placing teasing kisses down his length.

He's looking at me now, his eyes tired, sleepy and hooded from the pleasure. I place one last kiss on the tip and climb up his body, positioning him at my entrance. My hair falls forwards when I lean my head down and his hands come to my hips.

"Condom," he says tightly as I tease both of us, circling his head right at my entrance.

"I'm on the pill and you should be safe because you better not be putting your dick anywhere else."

He lets out a rough laugh and stops immediately, cursing when I slam down on him. My head falls back as he fills me completely, stretching me so wide that I have to pause for a few seconds to get used to him inside. "Fucking hell, Kadie," Fai mutters and then his mouth is on my nipple and he's sucking and circling it with his tongue while I ride him fast and hard.

I tug his head back by his hair so I can kiss him, our kiss hot and needy. "Just so you know, this is me thanking you for driving me to school afterwards."

Fai chuckles groggily, kissing down my neck, his teeth nibbling my skin. "You can thank me like this every morning, bee."

I know Fai is trying to prolong his release. He's gritting his teeth together, trying to help me get off by hitting that sweet spot inside, but it's only making me more frustrated because I'm on the verge, but I can't let go.

"Kadie," he says breathlessly.

I shake my head, my teeth latching down onto my bottom lip. "Please, let go. I can't. I can't, Fai." I drop my forehead to his, closing my eyes so he doesn't see the tears of frustration that appeared there. I don't want him to see my weakness.

"Fuck," he says in aggravation, but he can't hold back much longer and he lets go of his restraint, coming in me.

I stay there, pressed against him until I get myself under control and catch my breath again. I kiss the corner of his mouth and slowly get off him, feeling him drip down my thigh. "You still have some time before you need to get up," I tell him.

Fai puts his arm over his eyes, coming down from his high. "It's early," he grunts.

"I'm sorry. Is that complaining I hear?" I ask him over my shoulder, still buck naked.

Fai drops his arm and puts it under his head, the other one causally laying on his stomach. "Not from me." He grins; a grin of pure male satisfaction. But then his smile drops suddenly. "One of these days, I'm going to make you scream so hard when you're going to come that the neighbours are going to call the police because they'll think someone's getting murdered in here."

I let out a chuckle, but it has a sad note to it. "I'd like to see you try, big boy."

He gives me a cheeky wink and I walk to the bathroom to shower with ice-cold water. Because, even though I like knowing I can make a man come so hard he sees stars and becomes completely weak, that also means I get no release and my body hates me from that.

Fai wakes up and comes to the kitchen when I'm already finished with breakfast, playing a game on my phone with my feet on the table.

He scowls at me, pushing my feet down. "I eat here, Kadience. I don't want your dirty feet on here."

I give him a charming smile. "Don't worry, they're clean."

When he goes past me to the stove, he, completely nonchalantly, places a soft kiss on top of my head. It throws me off guard so hard that I lose focus on the game and die. "Son of a bitch," I mutter to myself.

"You have a test today?" he asks, taking a notice of two maths notebooks, laid on the table in front of me.

"Yep," I say, focusing hard on the game. I hear him making a coffee.

"Studying hard, I see," Fai muses.

"I knew this stuff by heart four years ago already."

He snorts.

When I lose the game again, I put the phone down on the table, watching him sip his coffee. "You should wait to drink coffee for at least an hour after you wake up so it kicks in properly."

He pauses mid-sip, looking at me. "Been doing this for years and it's kicking in just fine."

I shrug. "Suit yourself, but you're doing more bad than good to your body. You can Google it if you don't believe me."

He sighs, putting the cup down and starting to make breakfast. My lips pull up.

Something's changed between us. I feel it. There's this new deep connection with us, some kind of new understanding and even more fondness. I've told him things I've never told anyone before and instead of being disgusted with me, or even thinking I'm crazy just like everyone else, he understands me and is still here by my side.

He eats breakfast and drinks coffee and I continue playing the mindless game on my phone just because I have nothing better to do.

I wait for him to take me to school. Fai makes sure I always get there on time which is really thoughtful of him but he knows I'd probably give him hell if he didn't.

When we get there, I jump down and give him the helmet back. He takes it from me and then I kiss him goodbye. He deepens the kiss, holding onto me for a few more seconds and I push him away, laughing. "Is your friend watching?" I ask, my lips curling upside.

I watch Fa's eyes, but he doesn't look. "Don't give a fuck and neither should you."

I nod. "Good answer. Now I want you to keep it in the head when she texts you again because I'll break your fingers if you continue having little secretive chats between you two, you hear me? I am not competing with anyone, Fai, especially not with that A grade bitch."

"My fucking God," he mutters. "Never had you for a jealous type, bee," he says.

"Never had you for a guy that loves stupid girls who love to put other people down, but we're both learning new things about each other every day, right?" The beauty of having a relationship with someone ...

"Whoa, back the fuck off there, princess. Just because we exchange a few words, doesn't mean I'm in love with her, yeah? You have nothing to worry about. You're the centre of my universe." I know he's joking when he says it but when he places a kiss on my forehead, I have to look down because my chest is suddenly painfully squeezing and my stomach feels like it's in knots.

"Ah, yes. The all-time favourite couple."

The moment between us passes and I step away from Fai, glaring at the queen of bitches over my shoulder. "Mands. Don't," Fai says and when I look at him, I see his jaw tick.

"Don't what? I just came to say hi."

"Hi," I grit out. "Now get the fuck out of my face."

She cocks her head to the side. "Not to you," she says softly as if she's talking to someone who's not able to understand English.

I give her a sarcastic smile. "He's not going to fuck you. I promise you he's not."

Mandy just smiles. "Could you be so sweet and give us a minute then?" Her voice is dripping with honey.

"Of course. That's all you'll ever get, right? A minute." I chuckle. "Ciao," I call over my shoulder to Fai who has a grim look on his face, looking at me. I send him a kiss, mostly to piss Mandy off even more and then walk towards the class, leaving them alone. I'm not letting her ruin my day.

I don't even come to the class when I get Fai's message.

Are you mad at me?

I chuckle.

Do I have a reason to be? I type back, walking in the classroom and sitting down.

My phone vibrates. Definitely not.

I purse my lips, still smiling. I believe him because I trust him. I've never trusted anyone like I trust him, but I somehow know I have to mean more to him than some meaningless fuck, otherwise he wouldn't deal with my annoying ass.

Then I'm not. Don't text and drive, baby. See you later x

I purposefully call him with endearing and I'm not doing that to poke fun, either. Things have definitely changed between us and I really like it.

One week later, things get back to normal. Well, slightly. I'm allowed to go back to work, but Fai still keeps an eye on me and I still stay at his place. But I convinced him to throw a small party for everyone because I'm bored out of my mind just staying there and not having anything to do.

Fai doesn't agree to a party, but he agrees to a get-together, which actually turns into a small party because his guys bring the beer and drugs. Harper comes, too and this is the first time I see her in two weeks.

We have both missed each other so much and there are so many things to talk about with her.

I thought it would be weird for Harp to be here and see the things going on with these guys, but she has her eyes for Jon only and he's not drinking or taking drugs.

"Hey, Kadie! Want something to mix that with?" Ante asks, nodding at the drink in my head.

Fai turns to look at me. He's drinking but he's not taking anything, either. "Not today," I turn him down.

"Boo-hoo," he says, but turns back to Bastian. I wink at Fai and the corners of his mouth pull up before he looks away.

Harper is looking between me and him with interest. She's standing to my side with Jon's arm wrapped around her shoulders. "Things have changed between you two," Harper observes.

"What do you mean?" I ask her, taking a sip of my drink, welcoming the strong burn.

"It's just different. It seems like you two have some kind of connection that no one in this room has."

"No one but you and Jon you want to say?" I ask her with raised eyebrows and her eyes automatically go to him and she blushes.

"Let's sit down and talk," I tell her, nodding towards the couch where we'll have more privacy. Not that any of the guys are listening, anyway.

She turns to Jon and whispers something into his ear. He leans his head down to hear more clearly and then nods, turning his head and placing his mouth against hers.

I smile, looking away and start walking towards the couch, but Fai grips my arm and looks at me in question. "Just going to the couch to talk with Harp. Don't worry, I'm not going to get lost." I chuckle, leaning up and pressing a kiss to his chin. "Don't miss me too much," I say. Maybe we will need to have a talk about this sudden protectiveness. I'm at his place, for God's sake.

Harper is already sitting on the couch and I plop myself down next to her. "So. What's up with you and Jon?"

Harper shrugs, looking down at her hands. "We're just ... spending time together."

"Just spending time together my ass. He wants to eat you," I say, catching him looking at her again. Who would've thought.

Harper blushes even further, but then gives me a look that says she's over the moon. "You know, when we talked about you and Fai and you said that he gets you? It's like that. It feels like that. Jon gets me. And it's so easy with him, it's just ... I don't know, my heart beats faster whenever he walks to the room and he makes me feel good." At my smile, Harper hurries, "And not just in bed."

I nod because I know that. I know exactly what she's talking about because it's like that with Fai and me, too. We always understood each other, no judgment, and we knew what the other person needs.

I know I'm not an easy person to be around sometimes, but he makes it look so easy and that makes me so scared sometimes because there's no future for us and I already feel way too much than I should, even though I promised myself I wouldn't and this is just having fun.

"And, you know, Jon and I are very different and I sometimes think I don't get him, but he assures me that I get the most important parts about him and that everything else is just irrelevant," Harper continues.

My eyes fly to Fai. because I get it. I get exactly what Harper is talking about. You don't have to understand someone wholly, you just have to understand their most important parts.

Chapter 31

I don't think I have ever imagined myself being in a relationship with someone and what it would be like, but if I did, I'm pretty sure I wouldn't see this. And I don't even mean it in a bad way, it's just something completely unexpected. And Kadie staying with me means it never gets boring.

We have to go on a mission today. We're behind because of what happened to Kadience and I refused to leave her unsupervised. I can't know when the next hit will happen and I know for sure it will happen. I also didn't trust Kadie that she will stay put and won't go anywhere because she has a mind of her own and can be a pretty hard nut to crack sometimes.

I didn't tell her about having to go out tonight so she won't think ahead and make some plans by herself. As far as she goes, she's still on a house arrest and will be until I tell her otherwise. She knows it, she also knows the danger, she just likes to taste the waters sometimes. And my temper.

I know I won't be able to just snuck out because Kadie is a light sleeper and there's no way I can get past her, so I won't even try that.

I sigh to myself as I watch her read a book and make notes; probably some heavy scientific shit she can't live without. "I have to go out tonight," I announce.

She lifts her head and looks at me. "Where to?"

"Have some business to do." I tie my boots.

I hear her closing her book and when I look up, I see I successfully gained her interest. Fuck no. "Can I go with you?"

I immediately straighten up in the chair. "Absolutely not."

"Why not? I can fight like hell."

I shake my head. "You're better here when I come back, Kadie. I'm serious."

She sighs miserably, laying on the bed and spreading all fours. "Well, where else would I be? You locked me here. I feel like a fucking rapunzel."

"It's either that or you end up dead. I think I gave you an easy choice, bee."

She rolls her eyes. "Yeah, whatever."

I shoot her a look. "Don't be difficult. Not about this. It's about you."

"Yeah, yeah," she dismisses me.

I walk to her and lean down, putting my fingers under her chin to make her look me in the eyes. "Stay out of trouble," I tell her seriously.

"I can stay out of trouble, but the trouble won't stay out of me." Her mouth pulls up and she puts her hand over mine. "Now kiss me and get the hell out of here because I'm going to sleep."

I oblige her, dropping my head and giving her a kiss, but then I look at the clock. "You never go to sleep this early," I say suspiciously. It's half past nine.

"I need my beauty sleep. I sleep better when I'm alone."

I look at her with doubt. She has the beauty already, but I know she needs to sleep because she spends a lot of nights just laying awake because she can't sleep or a nightmare wakes her up. She refuses my offer to sleep on the couch, though and it infuriates me because she's intentionally suffering.

"Alright. Goodnight, then."

She waves at me. "Bye. Be quiet when you come back," she murmurs, nuzzling her head into the pillow.

"Yeah, yeah," I mutter. I go and take my gun out of my safe, making sure it's loaded before I put it in the waist of my pants.

I put the lights out and go out, making sure I lock the door. The guys texted me they're already here, waiting for me. As I walk down the stairs, I shake the awful feeling off me. Lately, I've been feeling a lot more under pressure about these things. I just want to be done with this once and for all.

The ride there takes us around thirty minutes. We park in the nearest parking lot, walking towards the house. It's coated in darkness, except for one room. We did our homework and we know our target is home alone. I take a deep breath, biting inside my cheek to calm down my nerves. I look at the guys. "Ready?" I ask them.

"Born ready," Ante says, pumped with adrenaline.

We easily get into the house because it has no alarm system. We checked. We walk around in the house and Bastian walks to the kitchen, opening the fridge. "Fucking wanker has nothing good to eat." He slams the door shut and I raise my eyebrows. "What? I'm starving."

I shake my head. We go upstairs, pausing in front of the door where we can see the light coming from underneath them. His office. I knock and loudly open the door, startling the man sitting behind his big desk. "Wha – Who are you? How did you come in here?" he scrambles on his feet, looking at all of us with fright.

"We came to collect what you owe us," I say, circling the room and looking at the office. A lot of boring books. Some prizes on the walls. Nothing too personal.

"Wh– what do you mean?" he staggers.

"Money, Rosewick. You owe a shit load of money. Now, do you have it or not?"

"I –" His eyes roam around the room, looking at all of us. "Not right now, but I'll get it in a few weeks." He looks down, nervously moving the papers around his desk. He's a terrible liar.

I cock my head to the side, standing behind the chair and casually leaning on it. "We don't have weeks to wait again. Your time is up. You know the consequences."

The man looks like he's going to piss himself. "I can give you a quarter now and I'll get everything else, just give me a little more time. Please."

Another one of those who don't know what to do with the money when they have it. Shame, really. "This has been going on and off for months now. You give us money now or you stay without your head. You knew the deal. Did you think we weren't being serious?"

I casually take my gun out, twirling it in my hand and walking to the window, looking out.

"Pl-please. I have a family. A wife and a daughter. Don't do this."

My fist clenches around the gun handle. I hate when they're begging. I hate seeing people realising they're living the last minutes of their lives. Why can't they think about this sooner? Why don't they take things more seriously?

I turn around, pointing the gun directly at his head. He lifts his arms and I see he's shaking. "We're here to do our job. We have an option. We either come back with money ... or a body." We actually don't have an option. Our only option is to come back with a body, with money or not. But he has to die. Tonight.

"Oh, God," he says. "I'll get the money. I swear I'll get it," he says, his eyes wide with horror.

"You've been getting money for quite some time now. We're done waiting."

"Please," he begs.

"Goodbye. Have fun in hell."

I used to feel some kind of a rush when I pulled the trigger and the deafening sound was heard, followed by a thud of a body and then ... nothing. A complete silence. But now I only feel sick to my stomach. Especially when I catch a picture on the desk. A family photo; his daughter and his wife. The daughter is young. Probably around 10 years.

I clench my jaw and turn around while the guys search the house. I have to get out of here. Another job done. Another step towards my freedom.

When I get out, I light up a cigarette, rubbing my eyebrow with my thumb. I lean against the trailing outside, my muscles all tensed up. A hand clasps my shoulder. I look to the side, seeing it's Jon. "Just a few more, man. Just a little bit more and we're done."

He understands me. He wants out just as much as I do. Jon's always been one of the better guys, one with the best heart out of all of us and I understand he's longing to get out now more than ever because he has a girl who doesn't understand the things we're into.

"I can't fucking wait to be done with this shit," I admit because it's heavy on my chest and I need to get it off. "Shit's been hard lately. Probably because I'm so close to freedom I can taste it. And it tastes damn sweet, I can tell you."

Jon chuckles, putting his hands in his jeans pockets. "Yeah, dude. You don't say. I'm counting the days until I get to say goodbye to this."

He rubs my shoulder.

"Found something. Not much, but they can't say we came back with empty hands," Ante comes out, carrying an envelope with money.

I nod. "Let's get out of here before the police comes," I say, putting the cigarette out and throwing it away on the street so I don't leave any traces behind. Not that it'd matter, the guy deserved what he got and police should be happy we did their dirty work for them.

We have to make a stop on our way back home; a spot where we agreed to leave the money and the Big Guy will come and fetch it. We never deliver it to him personally. I only met the guy once and I don't ever want to see him again. We drop the money off and then we're on our ways. After every mission, things get heavy sometimes and we don't bullshit with the whole goodbye, see you soon. We just go.

When I come back home, I try to be as quiet as I can. I don't turn on any lights and just blindly go to the bedroom, which my minimalistic decorations allow easily. When I enter the bedroom, I expect to see Kadie's sleeping form illuminated by the moonlight. What I see is an empty bed. My blood immediately turns cold, my body tensing up.

"Where have you been this long?"

I turn around when I hear a voice behind. "Fuck, Kadie!" I say.

"What?" she asks innocently.

"I thought you weren't here. Don't ever creep behind my back like that ever again. I could hurt you."

"I could hurt you," she mimics me. "Yada, yada." She yawns, crawling on the bed.

"Couldn't sleep?" I ask her. It wouldn't surprise me. She has bad nightmares often.

She stares at me when I start undressing. "You know, it's a funny thing. I had a hard time sleeping with you in the same bed and now I have a hard time sleeping without you in the bed. Huh," she says thoughtfully, making my hands pause.

My lips lift up. "Well, well. It seems like I'm starting to grow on you, eh, bee?"

"Grow on my nerves, yeah," she mutters.

I don't respond to her, but I go to the bathroom with a big smile on my face. I put all the clothes in the laundry basket and hop under the shower because I can't touch my girlfriend with blood still on my hands.

My stomach rolls in dread as I remember what happened just hours ago and I'm now here, going to lay beside her and have a good night's sleep. I rub my body until it's red and burning and then let the water fall down on my body for a long time. I lean against the wall, my head hanging as I breathe hard.

I'm counting the days until I get rid of you looming over me, motherfucker. I want my life back and I want it to be my own.

I turn the water off, drying myself off and going to the bed. Kadie is sitting on the bed, looking up at the wall and twirling her thumbs. "You good?" I ask her.

"Yes. Tried to get myself off with you in my thoughts, but it still didn't happen."

My whole body reacts to her words, my muscles clenching. Leave it to her to say the most random stuff in the middle of the night. After I just came home after killing someone. "I don't know how I feel about this. Want me to try?" I ask her, completely seriously.

She slides down on the bed and turns on her side, facing me, putting her hands under her head. "Maybe tomorrow. So, did you kill any bad guys tonight?" she asks nonchalantly, making my eyes widen.

I put my fingers on her cheek, feeling her soft, delicate skin underneath my rough one. "And if I said I did?" I whisper.

"I'd tell you you did the right thing," she whispers back as if we're just casually sharing some secrets in bed.

"But then I would have to disagree with you."

"Why?" she asks me, shifting into a better position.

I remove my hand from her cheek. "Doesn't killing bad guys make me a bad guy, too? Technically?"

She chuckles. "Don't expect me to feel about people who enjoy doing bad things, Fai. They deserve what comes their way."

Of course she thinks that. Because she had an experience with bad guys early in her life, but other people don't always think like that, especially when we have people in high positions who are doing the same things as those bastards and surely they don't think they're in the wrong.

But if Kadie doesn't question me about it and puts her trust and faith into me, then I'll shut up and accept what I get. And, fuck, if I could get a better match for myself than this girl.

I put my hand on her hip, leaning forward and kissing her on the lips. "Who sent you in my life?" I murmur against her lips, sighing.

Her hand comes to my neck as she lightly touches it with her fingers. "The devil himself, baby," she whispers into the darkness.

Chapter 32

"I think you kept me in this prison for long enough now. Can we go to a party or just do something exciting?" I ask Fai, laying on the bed with my head hanging off the edge, close to the floor. I'm bored out of my mind while Fai is working.

"I'm working on your tattoo," he says as if that's what I asked.

"Cool. I'm still bored."

He lets out a deep sigh, turning off his iPad. "Where do you wanna go?"

I sit up on the bed immediately. "To some club to have fun and wild out." I'm going back to work tomorrow, so there'll at least be something to keep me occupied. I don't think I've ever wanted to go to work this badly and I don't think I've ever missed my job before.

"Suppose we could go. But there'll be ground rules." He levels me with his look.

I roll onto my stomach and put my hands under my head, letting my legs dangle in the air. "Are you going to bring your gun with you?" I ask, biting my bottom lip, my lips pulling up into a smile.

He raises his eyebrow. "It goes where I go, so yeah."

"Nice," I say with a low voice, making his gaze drop before he quickly looks away.

Ah. How easily I learned to distract him. I get up from the bed, going to my phone. "I'll call Harp."

"When did you change your mind about her? You were all about how she's not this kind of girl and these things aren't her thing. You were basically like a mother hen."

I glare at his direction. "I miss her. Bite me, will you?"

He smirks, standing up, too. "I actually might," he says, winking.

I cock my head to the side. "Promises, promises ..." I trail off with a wink of my own.

I clap my hands together in excitement. "Finally something exciting happening!" I exclaim, already writing a text for Harp. Instead of texting me back, Harper actually calls me. "Hello, hello!"

"Kadie, you know I'm working. I can't go," she says as a way of greeting.

"Wait, really? Can you come later?"

"I don't know ..." she trails off.

"Jon's coming, too," I say. I might be a little mean for playing on these cards, but I know her weak spot and I'm starting to learn how to use it.

Harper is silent for a few seconds. "I'll think about it."

"Are you two okay?" I ask her.

"Yes. Why?"

I plop myself on the bed. "Just making sure. I'll swing by to pick an outfit. I might just take something of yours if I don't find anything appropriate in my closet."

"And how appropriate do you plan on dressing?" I can hear the smile in her tone.

"You'll see if you come." I make a kissing sound. "See you later, maybe."

"Yes, maybe. Bye, Kadie."

"Ciaooo," I sing-sang.

When I hang up, I look at Fai. "We have to stop at Harp's place. I need some clothes."

He looks me up and down and sighs. "Yeah, fine," he grumbles with a tone that indicates he doesn't want to do it, but he knows he doesn't really have a choice.

"Okay, then. Let's go, darling," I drawl, standing up from the bed.

"Now?" he asks.

I give him a questioning look. "I need an hour to get ready, Fai."

"Oh, for fuck's sake," he mutters. "Let me get changed then."

I got ready in twenty-five minutes and I used the extra forty-five minutes making Fai happy. And it included a bed and no clothes. It certainly seemed to put him in a whole better mood.

I'm wearing jeans and a shirt under a jacket because I'm simply not a girl for dresses and Fai and I are going there with a motorcycle, so a dress or a skirt couldn't even be an option.

We're the first one at the club and we reserve a table for everyone. I decided I'm drinking tonight because I can and because I just want to get loose. Fai doesn't because he's driving and he's also a guy that doesn't want his head clouded with alcohol because he always likes to think straight. His words, not mine. In my words, he just likes to be lame.

I go to the bathroom, checking my phone just in case Harper texted or called and I missed it. She didn't. I don't know whether she's coming or not. Jon isn't here, either, so they're either spending the night together or they had a fight because I don't think Jon's the man to prioritize Harper over Fai. I might be wrong about that, though.

When I get back to the table after I refresh my face and put eye drops in my eyes because, God, I look stoned, I notice two things. Harper is here and she's not in a good mood. And a waitress is chatting up Fai. I decide I want to deal with the exciting part first, the corners of my lips tipping up when I see her starting to scribble her number on a napkin.

"If you want to have a good time ... here's the number to call," I catch her saying when I get back.

I take the number from her hand. "I'll take that, honey." I look her up and down. "I assure you, when he wants to have fun, he's going to have it with me. But I might take you up on your offer. It looks like I could maybe teach you a few things." I wink at her.

She straightens up and I see she's embarrassed. Now, I know she saw me with him, so I don't even feel bad about putting her on the spot like that. I'll never understand girls like that. Why go after men that are taken? Sure, they look good, but so does their girl with them probably.

Fai chuckles to himself, muttering, "Goddamn tigress," under his breath.

"Damn right I am," I say.

I turn to face Harper next, laser-focusing on her. She looks away from me because she knows what's coming, playing with the metal straw in her drink. I see the distance she put between her and Jon. Does she think she's fooling anyone at this table? Maybe Ante who's too high to even know where he is at the moment.

I lean forward. "Uh-huh, missy. Let's go and have a little talk."

Harper turns her big, innocent eyes my way. "Whatever would we talk about?"

I narrow my eyes. "Don't bullshit me. Come with me." I nod upwards. I turn to Fai who's sitting on the couch in a relaxed posture, his arms spread wide, looking like he has no care in the world. But he better cares about what I'll tell him now. "And if I see another girl chatting you up when I come back this time, I'm borrowing your gun."

His eyebrow shoots up. "What am I supposed to do if they come to me?" he asks teasingly.

"You have a wild imagination, baby. Use it." I playfully flick his nose, winking at him and standing up then, seeing Harper is still sitting. "Harp. Start walking and talking."

She sighs. "You're so bossy, I don't know how I put up with you sometimes."

Jon focuses on Harper when she stands up and when he sees me waiting on her, his eyes widen. "What? You're seriously going to tell your pitbull about me so she'll come barking at me?"

"I'll even let her bite you," Harper shoots at him, walking away. My eyes widen a little. Oh, this boy really fucked up.

Harper and I walk to the restroom where I expectantly look at her. She nervously looks at all the closed doors and I roll my eyes. "Relax. No one knows who you are," I reassure her.

Harper takes a huge breath, her eyes running all over the place, unable to stay on the same spot. I know what she's about to tell me must be a huge deal for her, so I cross my arms and wait. "Okay, here goes. I, uh ... When Jon and I were, you know ... doing it," she says the last part quietly, her eyes going to the doors again and I raise my eyebrows, expecting some juicy details about him not being able to get it up or some shit, but she continues and it's not something to laugh at. "And when he was, ah, finishing he ... said another girl's name."

"Oh, for fuck's sake," I say, banging my head against the wall. This is exactly why I wanted him to stay away. Jon was my favourite in the group, true (besides Fai, of course), but that didn't mean he was a good guy. He was still bad and still does bad things, he's just slightly more pulled-together. Or so I thought.

"Please don't tell me I should break up with him," Harper blurts out, twisting her hands.

I give her a weird look. "What?"

"I'm not breaking up with him," she says.

"Okay, then don't?" I can already see Harper has fallen in deep with him and that I was most afraid of. She can't help herself. She falls in love easily and people could take that for granted. I just know that if Fai did that to me, I'd twist his balls, cut them off and feed it to him for dinner. But Harper is not me.

Harper slumps against the wall, looking defeated. "I don't know what to do. He said it doesn't mean anything, that it's just an ex from a while ago, but it still sucks."

My eyebrows shoot up. Yeah. Yeah, I bet it sucks. I think about how to go about this softly and not lay it out harshly on her. "Look, Harp. Jon is not a saint. He might be the second best one in the group, second best looking, too, but these guys do things that are straight out bad. If you want to be with him, you have to know these things and know what you're heading into, otherwise you'll be disappointed big time."

"So, what? Do you think he's playing me? Do you think this is just him having fun with someone like me so he can brag that he could get me?"

I shake my head. "That's between you and him. I don't know him well enough to answer that. I don't know what else to tell you other than you're way too good for him and he was bound to fuck up at some point."

Harper sighs. One of the doors opens and a girl walks out. Harper avoids her eyes, pursing her lips because she wants to say something, but now she can't. We wait for her to walk out and only then Harper turns back to me. "You know, it's just my luck that I finally like someone and this happens."

I know what Harper wants to hear from me, but I can't tell her that. I also can't just say that she should break up with him. I love Harper more than I love myself, but this is not my fight to fight and she has to do this on her own. "Okay, Harp. I can just say that this was an asshole thing to do, intentional or not, but I think you have to trust your gut in this. It could be just a slip of tongue on his part, but I can't tell you what you expect me to tell you. I'm here to listen, but I'm the last person to give relationship advice. Trust me."

Harper lets out a groan. "Maybe I'll just moan another guy's name the next time," she mutters to herself.

I grin. "Let him taste what he cooked." I wink at her. "Are you good to go back now?"

She shrugs. "I think I'll just go ahead and go home. You know, call a taxi and sneak out. I don't feel like being here tonight. I came here, thinking I'd feel better, but I just feel worse and I don't want to be around him right now."

I don't have a heart to ask her to stay because it's understandable she wouldn't want to. "It's all good, Harp. I'm surprised you even came. I'll wait with you."

When we step outside, Harper turns to me. "You and Fai are good, I suppose?"

I grin at her. "Oh, yes. I have big plans with him tonight. I'm feeling rather ... spontaneous."

Harper grimaced, lifting her hand up. "Don't proceed. I don't want to know."

I just grin. "Don't worry, I'll ruin Jon's night, too."

"No, don't. Just ... leave it. I'll sort it out."

I shrug, seeing the taxi approaching. "As you wish. You can call me if you change your mind."

She smiles. "Nope." She nudges me. "I'll just see you around? When is this mess going to end, by the way?"

"I feel like it's ending, but Fai's overprotective ass still doesn't believe it's all ended."

"That sucks," she mutters and then comes to me and wraps her arms around me. "Take care of yourself. Don't do anything stupid."

"Okay, mother."

She chuckles and I wave her goodbye when she sits in the car.

When I come back to the table, all eyes come to me. Except Jon's. He's looking past my shoulder. "Where's she?" he straight-out asks.

I shrug. "On her way home," I say nonchalantly and sit down beside Fai.

Jon stands up immediately. "You must be fucking kidding me," he growls.

I stand up again and walk to him so we're face to face. "Piece of advice, Hulk. When you're fucking someone, make sure you moan the right name of the girl you're fucking. Harp's not looking forward to being a rebound and if that's what you want for her, just sit down and don't bother."

I see a vein in his neck appearing. He's holding back his anger. "A piece of advice to you, too; stay out of other people's business that has nothing to do with you."

He brushes past me, bumping his shoulder against mine and walks straight to the door. My lips lift. He better be doing the right thing.

I sit back down, taking Fai's drink from his hand and taking a sip. He turns his head, looking at me. "Causing fire?"

I lick my bottom lip. "Just making sure they're aware something's burning." I give him his drink back, non-alcoholic, of course, and lean up to his ear. "Have you ever made out in a club full of people?" I ask against his ear.

His arm goes behind me on the back rest again. I see he's grinning. "I'm not 10 anymore. Sure I have, princess."

I put my hand on his chest and grip his shirt a little. "But have you ever had sex in a club full of people?"

He turns his head and gives me a serious look. "Pretty sure I'd get arrested if I did that, bee."

"What fun is it if you're not willing to walk on the edge here and there?" I say quietly. "Come after me. Up the stairs. You have just about five minutes, starting now."

I stand up, take Jon's unfinished drink he left behind and drink it all. I put the glass down and wink at Fai before I walk away, grinning all the way upstairs.

Chapter 33

Fai doesn't disappoint me by keeping me waiting. He shows up even earlier than I told him to and smiles the whole time walking up the stairs, too. He looks like a man who's going to get fucked soon. And well.

"Finally giving me a private show in one of these rooms?" he asks with a raise of his eyebrows.

I give him a secretive smile that means I'm having a secret only he'll know. "Oh, we're not going to any of the rooms."

Fai gives a narrow-eyed look. "Don't fucking tell me we came up here to talk or some shit," he says, annoyance heard in his voice.

I chuckle, putting my hand on his stomach, grabbing the waist of his pants. "Maybe if you kiss me, you'll figure it out quicker what we're doing here," I say suggestively.

Fai glances down to make sure no one is watching, but they'd have to look really hard and long and exactly to where we're standing if they wanted to see us here because we're far away enough and it's also dark up here.

I put my hand on the back of his neck, pressing his head close to mine, his lips just a whisper away from mine. "Kiss me," I say again, craving his touch as if he didn't touch me just hours ago.

"You're insane," he says back, equally as quietly as if we're exchanging secrets.

About you, I think, but can't say because he complies and presses his lips on mine. My lips pull up into a smile against his and he softly grazes my bottom lip with his teeth in response. I feel his piercing every time we kiss and it's insanely hot.

My hand that went to the waist of his pants before now goes under his shirt, my nails scratching the skin on his stomach, feeling how his muscles clench beneath my touch. I graze his stomach, my hands travelling downwards until I come to his belt and I start unbuckling it.

He chuckles into my mouth. "We're really doing it right here?" he asks, obviously still thinking I'm just trying to mess with him.

My hand slips in his pants and I grip him through his pants, showing him that I mean business. "Oh, fuck," he mutters and I graze his neck with my teeth when his head slightly tilts backwards.

His hand goes to the back of my neck, under my hair, and he pushes my head back, tilting it slightly so he can put his lips against mine in a scorching kiss that makes my toes tingle. His hand goes into my paints, his fingers grazing my already wet centre. I let out a soft groan, but I don't stop kissing him.

"We have to be quick, Fai," I say, my lips moving against his mouth.

Fai retreats back, giving me a full look. "I can do quick. And dirty," he says with a naughty grin.

"Show me," I say, my grin matching his.

He pushes my pants down, just enough to expose my panties, yet he doesn't take those off. He swiftly turns me around, pushing me against the wall, pulling my hair to the side. I feel his hot breath against the back of my neck and I turn my head to the side, looking down the stairs if anyone noticed us already. They haven't.

He pushes my panties to the side, his fingers going between my folds to see how wet I already am. I arch my back, pushing my ass out, trying to get him to push his fingers inside. He doesn't.

He teases me at first, but not for long. Two of his fingers enter me and I have to bite down on my lip to keep a moan inside me.

Fai presses his front against my back and I can feel how hard he is. He takes his fingers out and the next thing I hear is the zipper going down. But then he pauses suddenly and curses. "I don't have any condoms on me right now. Shit."

I look at him over my shoulder. "You don't need one for my sake and you've better not been sticking it in any other holes."

Fai grimaces. "Way to be romantic, bee."

I chuckle. "But we're not doing any romance, so hurry up." I wiggle my ass, seeing how his eyes go down on it and he suddenly smacks it. I gasp, pausing my movements but Fai leaves his hand on my ass, lifting his eyes to look at me, his eyebrow going upwards in a challenge.

My eyes narrow, but he doesn't give me a chance to tell him off because he pushes inside in one sudden, swift move. He plants both of his hands on either side of me, his front against my back.

I groan, a smile appearing on my mouth for getting exactly what I asked for. Fai wraps my hair around his hand and fucks me. It's fast, yet it's not any less hot.

We try to be quiet, although no one from the downstairs can hear us, but there are rooms on the floor we're on and I'm not sure they're completely empty. I'm supporting myself with my hands on the wall because Fai pushes me against it with every harsh thrust of his hips.

I'm biting down onto my lip so hard, I start tasting blood in my mouth. I feel the pressure inside of me building, but I know it's for nothing because the satisfaction won't come and it'll just make me feel even more frustrated and drained.

When Fai is close to coming, he squeezes my hips, his head pressing against my neck. "One day, I'll make you come, even if I have to eat you out for hours," he groans his promise.

I squeeze my eyes shut. That sounds like torture for me, actually. Hours of building up pressure, only to be left empty-handed at the end. All because of one man who took it away from me.

He pulls out when he comes and he comes all over my ass. I stand there against the wall, squeezing my legs together, waiting for the pulse to stop. I can feel the satisfaction I failed to reach and it's making all my muscles tighten and clench.

"Sorry about the mess," Fai says.

I exhale, willing my body to relax and letting my mind clear the haze that appeared in it. Just like every time. "Just bring me something to clean myself," I say, raking my hand through the hair and smooth it down.

"Yeah, sure," Fai says, putting his clothes back in the place and trying to make himself presentable. "Wait here," he orders.

He goes downstairs to the men's toilet. I wait up there because I don't have anywhere else to go, anyway. Not like that, at least. Now that the adrenaline is wearing off, I think about what I just did. I subconsciously went back to my old ways. I used to be like that.

For years, I detested sex and I couldn't even let anyone touch me without wanting to rip their arms off. But then, I changed the game, and I started using sex against me. Finding men who were willing wasn't a problem, so I started doing it to erase the ugly memories my father created. I wanted to erase his touch with others.

It did kind of help in a way, but a part of him always stayed with me. I could never reach orgasm. Not since him, that is, but I was too inexperienced then and I couldn't control that. It was a natural reaction and I hated myself for it every time. I felt disgusted.

That part of me stayed imprinted in my mind and I couldn't change it, no matter how many times I've tried and with how many different people.

I was broken. And while I had control over everything else; stopping my fear of touch and stopped being disgusted by sex, there was still one thing he owned and I couldn't take it away from him.

Fai comes back with paper towels and he helps me clean up. When I make myself presentable, we go downstairs, both of us silent. I think he knows I'm swimming in my own thoughts and he just lets me. "I have to go to the bathroom. I'll meet you back there," I tell him.

Fai grabs my arm before I go, making me look at him. He has his eyebrows knitted together, trying to figure out my mood. "We're good?"

I plant a smile on my face before I put a quick kiss on his lips. "Better than anytime," I say sincerely. Because he's not at fault for my demons. He's just there while I fight them on my own. And he's doing more than he knows.

When Fai and I are ready to go home, I tell him to drop me off at Harper's place.

He's not too happy about it. "What the fuck for?" he asks in annoyance.

We're outside by his motorcycle and I stop, looking at him. "I'm sorry?" I ask him with a tone that lets him know he should watch his tone. "Because I said so."

"You know what, with that attitude, you can go and walk there."

"Yeah? Well, I might just go and do that, then!" I say in anger.

Fai stares at me. "So, what? You're going to pick a fight with me just because I asked a simple question? Stop fucking living in your head so damn much, Kadie."

I clench my fists at the sides. "It's not any of your goddamn business!" I don't know why I'm so prickly about this right now, but this hasn't been my evening and Fai knows exactly what buttons to push when he wants to.

He steps so close to me, our noses touch and our breaths mix together. "Yeah, princess. It is my business. You're my fucking business. Now hop on and text me the reason later. And if I don't get that text, I'm coming to haul your ass and you're coming back with me. That clear?"

I grit my teeth together, pushing him away from me, but he doesn't budge, yet I don't step away, either. "Fai, it's really not your fucking business so shut the fuck up with your mancave threats because it's not hot."

He steps back. "I'm not taking back what I said. You have a target on your back and I'll need your trust here, even if I have to force it out of you. Now get the fuck on." He straddles the motorcycle, holding out a helmet for me to put on.

I'm still standing there, raging. I know what he's doing. He's pissing me off and talking to me like that because he knows that he's not going to get anywhere with me if he'll plead and beg with a soft voice. There are other times for that. And I know that he's trying to force me to realise that I have him and he's not going anywhere, no matter how hard I push. He's always going to push back harder.

I bite the inside of my cheek, taking the helmet from his hand and get on behind him. He doesn't say anything but I can feel how tight his muscles are when I wrap my arms around him.

I pissed him off. I could see that from a mile. Hell, I pissed myself off. But what can I do? This is my defence mechanism and I can't go against it. I've been wired like that my whole life. Trust no one because everyone betrays you at the end, especially the ones closest to you. And it hurts like a motherfucker when that happens. And it does happen. Every time.

The higher your love, the higher you fall from when it ends.

Fai drops me off at Harper's without any complaints, but I see he's in a bad mood from before. When I get off the motorcycle and pull the helmet off, I hesitate, shifting on my feet a little, wondering if I should say something to him or just leave things as they are.

"Drive safe," I finally say, giving him the helmet back.

Fai nods, but doesn't say anything back. Well, fuck you, too then.

I turn on my feet and go inside the building without another word. I march up the stairs, putting my hands in the pockets of my hoodie.

I enter the apartment with my key so I don't wake Harper up. I slip off my shoes and tiptoe to her room. When I get near the bed, I hear her shift and realise she's not asleep. It's early, close to the morning already.

I slip under the covers. "You good?" I ask her.

"No," she croaks out. She's been crying. I can hear it in her voice.

"I'm sorry," I say. Because, truthfully, I really am. I tried to warn her about him and about what kind of men these are, but it's her lesson to learn now and I can't do anything about it. I can't just sit by her and comfort her.

"He came here right after I got home," she says.

"Yeah, he left immediately after he realised you were gone. I figured he'd come here."

"I didn't talk to him. He was at the door for hours, I think. It's just ... he was my first and I'm not used to guys like him, but I don't want to be just another girl to him. I'm afraid he doesn't feel the same about this. About us."

This is what I was scared of. Harper is the one that falls too fast, too deep. And I was scared it would happen with Jon because he's not someone you go into this too fast. I sigh, grabbing her hand under the covers. "Harper, Jon is going to fuck things up. Regularly. And you have to know that because you won't be able to change him for the better. Men like him don't change, Harp. You can either accept it or ... not."

She sniffs again, but doesn't answer me. I stay with her because I know she needs some comfort right now.

She manages to fall asleep pretty quickly this time. I, however, don't. But this is not surprising. Because I'm haunted by demons and they love to come out at night to play.

I grab my phone and write Fai a text now that I calmed down.

I asked you to drop me at Harp's because your friend is an asshole who already hurt her. Not that it's any of your concern. See you.

This is my way of apologising. He better take it because he's not getting anything else from me.

And I guess the only response I'll get in return is silence because the jackass left the message on read.

Chapter 34

I go to school with the bus the next morning. It almost feels weird doing it because I got used to Fai taking me every day. But now he's not speaking to me, apparently, so fuck him.

The air feels chilly today, not usual spring weather. The sky is grey, showing signs it's going to most likely rain today. It seems like today's weather decided to match my mood.

The bus is late, which means I'm late. I don't know what expression I'm wearing today, but everyone leaves me the fuck alone – even the teacher.

I pull the earbuds out of my ears as I sit down and stare out the window, not even bothering to take notes. I know this stuff already and I know that most of it is useless because I'll never need it in the real world.

My phone vibrates in my pocket. I smile to myself because I already know who the text is from.

You in school? Fai decided to break the silence and get his head out of his ass.

I consider not responding to him, but I also can't help but be a little petty about it.

Yeah. Can say hi to your good friend Mands if you want.

I deliberately use the nickname he used for her once. It makes me want to throw up just thinking about them. No, she makes me want to throw up and I still hope that one day she'll get what she deserves for every bad thing she's ever done to others. She's just a bully with a rich daddy, nothing else. If anything, I feel sorry for her because, deep down, she's just a sad little girl that wants attention.

She can fool others, but she won't fool me.

Fai reads the message, but he doesn't respond. I throw the phone on the trouble in anger and it creates a loud thud. The teacher stops talking and turns towards me. "Mademoiselle Myers, arrêtez d'interrompre la classe."

I make the most innocent expression I can muster. "Je suis désolé. Cela ne se reproduira plus." Basically me pointing a middle finger at mademoiselle Green's face because she hates my guts and I hate French, even though I can speak it well enough for her to shut the hell up every time she decides to speak because I kill her with kindness. In French. Every time.

Mandy throws a bitchy smile over her shoulder, clearly thinking she knows more than she does. I cross my legs under my table, staring at her, basically telling her to mind her own fucking business for once.

God, I'll throttle this bitch one day, I swear. Just not today. I don't feel like dealing with her stupid, self-centred ass today.

When the classes are over, I almost miss Fai waiting for me outside the school because I wasn't expecting him. I don't know what made me slow down and look to my left. Probably a reflexive thing.

And there he was, leaning against his motorcycle with shades on, his arms crossed, looking all badass. He's also wearing a scowl like jewellery.

"You here for Mands? I saw her in the hallway, she'll be out soon." I'm being bitchy to him on purpose because he pissed me off with him ignoring my texts.

This is why I avoided getting involved with someone. I absolutely hate being needy and dependent on someone and Fai's making me all those things.

His scowl deepens. "Don't be ridiculous, Kadie. Hop on," he says as if everything's back to normal again.

"Oh! So now you're actually speaking to me. Good to know," I snicker, detangling the earbuds in my hands.

Fai lets out a deep breath and I can just see him trying to calm down. "What exactly is your problem again, Kadience?"

"My problem? My problem? You threw a whole goddamn fit yesterday because I spent the night with my cousin and refused to talk to me. And you ask me what my goddamn problem is? What is yours?" I get into his face, feeling all kinds of angry and frustrated with him. I'm making a scene in front of the entire school, but I can't bring myself to care.

"Are you really going to do this now? Here?"

I bite the inside of my lip. Hard. I stare at him and then just shake my head. "You know what? No. No, I'm not doing this. At all. Have a nice day." I angrily shove the earbuds in my ears and leave it like that, not playing any music because I'm curious what he's going to do next.

He doesn't disappoint. He rounds me, stepping in front of me, stopping me. I raise my chin up and he takes the sunglasses off so I can see his glare, yet I refuse to be intimidated by it.

"Park your ass on the motorcycle and let's finish what's bothering you at my place. Preferably in bed."

I huff. "I'm not going anywhere with you. You made your point."

"I did not make anything, bee," he growls. "Now walk to the motorcycle and get on or I'll put you on there myself. You have ten seconds to decide. The clock's ticking, babe." He gives me a devious grin. He's totally serious.

We get into a staredown match, the seconds passing by. I groan loudly, grinding my teeth together. "You're so fucking annoying, holy shit," I mutter, but I walk to the motorcycle and get on, ripping the earbuds out of my ears.

Fai is fighting his grin when he walks towards me and it makes me even angrier. He takes the helmet and puts it over my head. I refuse to help him and make it any easier for him. I'm acting childish and petty and I actually hate it, but I also absolutely hate being ignored on purpose, so I want to serve him the dish he cooked.

We go to his place and I try to ignore him as much as I can, letting him know that I'm actually really mad about the way he acted for absolutely no reason, but he refuses to let me be mad and instead just pokes me with amused looks. God, I want to punch his handsome face so much sometimes.

I don't make myself home this time. I let Fai know that I don't have any plans to stay here. "You better start explaining yourself some time today. I don't have the whole day to stand here."

Fai raises his eyebrow, dropping his keys on the table, putting the jacket off. "Explain what, exactly?"

I roll my eyes. "You acting like a child because I didn't do what you wanted."

Fai shakes his head. "You actually got it all wrong in your head. It wasn't about you spending the night at Harper's, it's about you not trusting me and refusing to open up to me."

I gape at him. Actually gape because I can't believe what he just said. "I'm sorry? I'm fucking sorry, what? I don't open up to you? I?" my voice gets louder and more hysterical. "I told you about things not even Harper knows about, Fai. And you? You didn't tell me shit. You couldn't even tell me about the shit you're in and the things you're doing when you go on your missions."

Fai slams his fist against the table. "I can't talk to you about that! I can't tell you."

"Can't or won't?"

"Can't," he stresses the word, gritting it through his teeth.

"Well, tough shit, Fai! Because I got kidnapped and almost raped the last time because you thought it's better I don't know anything about it. So, tell me, who's it better for? Because it doesn't make any sense that I'm safer if I don't know anything. I have absolutely zero ideas the danger I'm in."

He walks closer to me and he raises his hand to touch me, but I step back, not allowing it. "You can't know things because people can get to you just because of that. They'll use you for information. Don't you get it?"

I tilt my head to the side. "No. But it seems like I don't get a lot of things."

Fai sits down suddenly, pulling his hair in frustration. "Fuck," he murmurs with a tight voice, his hand trailing down to the back of his head.

"What happened to your eye?" I ask him. I reckon I asked him this once, but he didn't answer.

He sits back in the chair, his tongue playing with his lip piercing, his fingers tapping on the table. I see he considers what he's going to answer. I cross my arms over the chest and tilt my head slightly, showing him I mean business.

"I was not much of a fighter before my father died. When I learned about the business he left behind, it was a little too late to get experience. The first fight I got into – or more like a hit they did on me – was so bad I ended up in the hospital. My face felt like it was broken. My eye lost the color because of all the blows it received, but I still see normally. Any more questions?"

I sit down, too, feeling a little calmer now. "What the hell do you do? In those missions? And why? What's the point of it?"

Fai grabs a pack of cigarettes and takes one out. He offers me one, but I decline, yet I patiently wait for him to light it. "I can't go into the details with you," he says.

"Just tell me the basics then."

He rubs his forehead with the hand he's holding a cigarette with and then takes a long drag of smoke, tilting his head backwards, exhaling it out slowly. I cross my legs and while I appreciate the sight before me, I'm trying to learn things and I'm not giving it a rest until I get answers. "I haven't seen my mother and my sister or even heard from them for 9 years. My mother doesn't know if I'm alive or not. I don't know how she's doing either. She knew things, not much, but enough that she understood she married a monster and that her son has to finish what the bastard started. You see where I'm going with this? I had to say goodbye to my family when I was 15 and I haven't seen them since."

I kind of knew about this already because he told me some of this stuff, but it doesn't make my heart break any less hearing it for the second time. We're both so fucked up in our own ways, both so broken in different parts ... I think that's our thing. We understand how it is.

We understand how it is to wander around this world all alone. We understand each other's pain and that brings us closer.

"So, yeah, Kadie. Trust me, the less you know, the better. I know what I'm doing because I've been in this shit for years while you've been only in it for weeks. It can get pretty ugly if it blows up."

"At least tell me some things ... Just to fill me in. Like, what do you do when you go out on those missions? What are you involved in exactly?"

Fai looks down at the table and stares at it for a hot minute. "The deals I do ... it's mostly drugs and collecting money – or more like paying visits to those who did not pay and won't pay and just ... do what I have to do."

"You kill them," I say, feeling the chills run down my body.

"Yeah," Fai says. "I do. I kill all of them, no matter who they are. I kill them, even though they have their own lives and families because if I don't kill them, they kill me and everyone else. It's a whole goddamn pyramid system." He finally lifts his eyes to look at me. "Can you take that? Can you be with a murderer?"

I shake my head, wrapping my head around it. I knew it. I mean, I assumed most of it, but I didn't want to assume too much unless I heard it from him directly. "I told you I don't have a problem with that."

Fai chuckles darkly. "You don't have a problem with someone killing people?"

"I don't have any problems with people killing bad people."

Fai raises his eyebrow lazily, taking a long inhale from the cigarette. "But doesn't that make them a bad person?"

I chuckle. "Honestly, Fai, everyone has different definitions of wanting to have a good world to live and everyone does different things to make that happen. I'm here for it. Criminals, murderers, rapists ... in my opinion, they deserve an instant death. But, sadly, we live in a world where justice won't help us with that so we have to take matters into our own hands."

"And you want to actually become a lawyer with that mindset?" Fai asks me.

I shrug, crossing arms over my body. "I want bad people locked up and I want them to suffer. I have my own ways to make that happen, you have your own."

Fai leans forward, a small smirk on his face. "You know you could easily throw my ass in jail for all the things I've done and will do, yeah?"

A mischievous smile forms on my face. "Yeah, darling. I know that and I'm glad you do, too, so you better not get on my shit list." I wink.

He runs his tongue over his upper lip, smiling a little. His phone goes off then and he takes it out of his pocket with no hurry at all, sighing. He turns the screen around to show me the caller. "Wanna take this?"

It's Jon calling and I narrow my eyes at the screen. "He's currently on my shit list, so no."

Fai chuckles, leaning back in the chair with an easy, relaxed smile, keeping his eyes on me when he answers. "Yeah?" His smile falters a little. "Hold up." He moves the phone down to his shoulder. "Have you heard from Harper today?" Fai asks me.

"No. She's supposed to have classes," I say, looking at the clock and then back at Fai's face, trying to guess what's going on.

"Fuck," Fai curses, putting the cigarette out on the table. Just one word. Just one word that makes my stomach drop. "You're sure of it?" Another pause. "Alright. See you in a few."

He hangs up and I stare at him, waiting for an explanation, already on the verge of my chair.

"Harper went missing."

Chapter 35

I have enough fingers on my one hand to count how many times in life I've been scared to death. Definitely that time my father came to my room for the first time. And then, one time, when I thought my mother stopped breathing. That was a time I still loved her. And then when my stepfather hit me.

That's it. Ever since then, I've been looking fear dead in the eyes and showing it my middle finger. Sometimes, we were even friends. Sometimes, we liked to make out.

But not right now.

I immediately started freaking out as soon as Fai delivers that punch. "How do you know that she's missing?"

"Jon's keeping an eye on here and she's nowhere to be found."

Fai is already standing up, getting ready to go out. I stand up with him. "She's supposed to be at classes. Are you sure she's not there?"

Fai gives me a pointed look. "Yeah, Kadie. He's sure she's not there. She never made it there, in fact."

I feel chills run down my body in shock when he says that. "How's that even possible? You said he's keeping an eye on her!" That shouldn't have happened. She shouldn't be involved in any of this.

"Yeah, but you stayed with her at night and he'd thought you two would be alright."

I put my hands in my hair, gripping it hard. "I had to go to school. Her classes started later than mine."

"This is not your fault," Fai says calmly.

I take my phone and dial her number. Her phone is turned off, which makes it all too real because she never does that. She's too paranoid for that and she always tries to keep safe.

When he grabs his gun, making sure it's loaded before he tucks it in the waist of his paints, I really start losing it. "So, do you think they just took her like they took me? Did they watch her? Wait for her to be alone? Oh, my God. What if they already did something to her?"

Fai is in front of me in seconds, clasping his hand around my wrists to keep my hands from flailing out like crazy, coming into my personal space. "I'm sure she's fine and they just want to scare us, but we can't know until we find her. I'm always prepared for the worst scenario and so should be you. That comes with my life."

I try to punch him in the chest, but it doesn't work. "That's your way of trying to calm me down?!" I yell. "We have to go and find her!"

Fai shakes his head. "No, that's me telling you how it is. I'll inform you as soon as we find anything new." He puts a jacket on, grabbing his keys and a helmet.

"What? No. I'm going with you," I say, grabbing my jacket hastily.

Fai just shakes his head and walks towards the door. "You're staying here."

"No way. There's no way. It's Harper."

I think he heard the panic and desperation in my voice because he swiftly turns around to face me. "Yes, and you're you. We'll make sure she's okay and I have to make sure you're okay. You're staying here."

He doesn't raise his voice at me, although he says the words fiercely to prove a point. "No, Fai. I don't care about me, I'm going with you. You're not going to stop me."

"Watch me," he says, dangling the keys of his apartment in front of my eyes.

I'm really desperate here and it's obvious. I mean, it's Harper. I want to go with them and help them. It's not that I don't trust them, it's just that I'd only feel too helpless if I stayed here and waited. "Please," I beg him. And I never beg.

Fai keeps walking. He's not going to budge on this. I go after him, grabbing the sleeve of his jacket to stop him. "Just ... She doesn't know. About any of the stuff you guys do."

Fai looks at me and just gives me one court nod. I think he already knew that, but I just wanted to remind him that Harper is not like me. Far from it.

When he closes the door and I hear him turning the key, the frustration only grows. "I could just jump out of the window."

"I don't advise you to do that. You won't do us any good if you're dead."

I put my forehead against the door. "Fai?"

"Yeah?" His voice is already distant. He's walking away. "Be safe."

"Yeah," he calls back.

"And, please ... find her."

The answer comes, although hesitantly this time. "Yeah." And then he's gone.

The pacing starts then because I don't know what to do with myself. I'm gripping my hair, biting my nails, chewing on my lip ... Overall, just going insane with worry.

I'm scared because I knew this would happen, yet I still allowed her to get involved with Jon. And look at the mess now. He turned out to be an asshole and now she's also in danger. But I also stayed at her place tonight and I have a target on my back, so they could easily kidnap her just to get to all of us.

I wish there's some other explanation because I can't even begin to think that she's facing the same fate as I did. She's not cut for this. She can't go through what I did because I know she's not going to fight back.

I sit down, placing my chin on my hands. And then stand up because I can't sit still. I check the phone. I look out of the window.

It's only been 15 minutes since Fai left and I know this could take hours, even days. I don't know what to do with myself right now. I know that if I just sit and wait, I'm going to go crazy with worry. I start walking around Fai's apartment and start cleaning up, although there's not much to clean. The guy lives a pretty clean life (at least when it comes to tidiness), which is admirable.

I still scrub the bathroom clean. Wash the dishes in the kitchen. Change the bed sheets in the bedroom. I even go so far that I start organizing things, just going through his stuff. Is he going to be mad about that? Absolutely. But he'll get over it, especially if I give him a blowjob. He always falls for that.

I occupy my mind with Fai instead of Harper and her disappearance because it would drive me crazy otherwise that I can't do anything to help finding her. So, yeah. Fai. I've been avoiding these thoughts about him at all cost because I'm scared to dive too deep with him, although I'm sure it's already too late for that.

He and I started our thing with a plan to make things simple and easy. We both know we have a timestamp when this is all going to be over and we'll go our own paths. I'm not delusional. A guy like him won't wait for me to finish college and do long-distance. And I don't want that, either. At least I didn't from the beginning, but now I'm starting to realise it's going to be really hard to say goodbye to him. He's already way too deep under my skin to just get him out as easily as I thought I would.

When my phone rings, it almost slips from my hands because of how fast I try to answer the call. "Yes?" I ask eagerly.

"We got her," Fai says.

I sit down on the couch putting my head on my hands, closing my eyes as the relief washes over me. "Thank you," I say, my voice hoarse with gratitude.

I know Fai catches it because there's a long pause. "See you soon," he says.

I grip the phone in my hands, sagged like an empty bag on the couch. I let out a long breath that I've been holding probably since Fai left, feeling my body relax finally. A small smile appears on my lips because I'm happy it turned out okay and I'm happy she's okay. At least I hope that she is.

I wait for all of them, curled up on the couch just staring out the window. I have to go to work in a few hours and just the thought of that makes me want to groan out loud.

When I hear the key turn in the door, I immediately jump on my feet. Fai is the first one to walk in, followed by the boys. Harper comes in last with Jon's arm around her shoulders. She's huddled against his chest, physically looking okay.

I immediately attack her with a bear hug, making her stumble back a little and causing Jon's arm to fall down. "Oh, Christ," Harper says and chuckles. "I'm alright. Nothing happened to me."

I lean backwards, looking her over, trying to see if she's hurt. "What happened?"

"False alarm," Fai says. I hear he's irritated. "She was just out, roaming the streets, deliberately turning her phone off because someone," he glances at Jon, "wouldn't stop bugging her."

"Fuck off, man," Jon mutters.

I give Harper a stern, disbelieving look and she turns embarrassed. She looks remorseful as if she did something bad. Which she did. "Harp." I level her with a stare. "What the fuck?"

"I just needed some break and to clear my head. I didn't know I wasn't allowed to do that," she mutters like a small child.

I give her a serious look. "But you realize how serious this is, Harp? You can't just wander the streets alone anymore."

She looks down at her feet. "I know, I ... Kind of forgot about it a little," she murmurs. What she means is that she's not used to this. She's used to a simple life, no limitations, other than the ones she created for herself.

"It's alright, Harper. Just, please. Be careful. This is serious."

She lifts her eyes, looking at me from under her lashes. "Is it always going to be like this? Will we always have to look over our shoulders?" Harper whispers, not wanting to be heard by the others.

I give her a tight smile. I don't know the answer to that myself. "Hopefully not," I say. It's not okay for me to see her hurting like this when it's partly my fault I brought us in this mess. "Let's just be careful and trust these guys for now."

A small smile stretches her lips. "I hope you don't mind me saying this, but Fai looked so hot when he went all badass."

I let out a laugh and peek in Fai's direction. "I know, right? Hot, but annoying," I say it with a grin. But then I get serious when I notice her staring at Jon. "And you and Jon?"

"We're going to figure things out." Harper nods confidently. I kind of knew that because there's no way for two people looking at each other like that and not figure things out. "But slowly and at my pace."

I grin at her. "Make him work for it." I wink at her.

Fai walks to the kitchen and I follow him with my eyes. "I'll be right back," I tell Harper.

She nods and watches me go after him with a grin on her face before she turns and walks towards Jon who immediately, as if it's a completely subconscious move, wraps his arm around her shoulders, pulling her to his side, and kissing her temple.

I look away from them, walking to the kitchen. I sit on the counter right next to where Fai is and he lifts his head, looking at me. "What's up?" he asks casually, pouring some drinks.

"Come here," I say.

"I am here."

I part my legs. "Here," I say, patting the counter between my legs.

Fai's eyebrow lifts. "We can't have sex with people around."

I just shake my head. He sees I'm actually serious and he must see the look on my face because he puts the bottle on the counter and steps between my legs. "What?" he asks, his eyebrows pulling together.

I wrap my arms around his neck, pulling his head a little lower. I place my lips on his jaw, kissing him tenderly. "Thank you," I whisper.

I feel him shudder a little. He doesn't ask what I'm thanking him for. He knows.

In this moment, in my state of vulnerability, I want to say so much more. I want to say so many things to him. I love you. You're only the second person in my life that I've ever loved. Thank you. Thank you for choosing to be gentle with me when everyone else only ever chose to be rough and harsh. Thank you for showing me the world can be kind and gentle when I used to wander around, all lost and tired, thinking this world is nothing but ugly. Thank you for coming into my life at the exact right moment. Thank you for saving me from myself. Thank you for painting my world in colors after it's been black and white for so long.

I don't say any of those words. I can't. Because our thing has an end date and we're getting closer to it every day. I know I shouldn't start anything with him. Deep down, I knew it was going to be my ruin. That he was going to be the one person I'll willingly give my heart to, even though it's full of scars from everyone that hurt it before.

I tighten my arms around him and hold him just a little closer, just a little longer, hoping he can feel what I can't say.

Chapter 36

When everyone finally leaves, it's just us again. I don't mind company, but I'm happy I get to spend some time alone with just Fai before I have to go to work. I'm so not in the mood to go there today, but I know I have to do what I have to do. It's for my future.

"I'm going with you tonight," Fai says when I come to the bedroom from the kitchen after washing the dishes.

"Oh?" I ask casually. Internally, I'm thankful it's him and not one of his friends.

"Yeah," he replies, putting his phone away and sitting on the bed. "What do you want to do until then? Because I have a few ideas," he says suggestively.

I grin. "Do you? Let's hear them."

His palm connects with my thigh and he looks at it in thought, starting to trace patterns with his finger. "I want to make you come."

I give him a funny look. "You can't do that."

He gives me a challenging look back. "Can't I?" he asks lazily, still drawing patterns on my thigh, going higher now. He shifts closer to me, climbing on top of me, plastering his lips on mine.

I kiss him back with a surprised groan, burying my hands in his hair. His hand goes under my shirt, pausing my stomach before going upwards to cup my breast in his hand. He squeezes it, hard, twisting the hardened nipple. My hips buck upwards and I let out a sigh.

"You're going to just tease me. Bringing me towards the edge and leaving me there."

Fai kisses down my jaw. "No," he states.

I want to believe him. So badly, but I just know how it's going to end. "Don't torture me," I beg him, tilting my head back to give him for space when he starts trailing kisses down my neck.

He ignores me, sucking on the skin on my neck. He pushes my shirt up and I help him take it off and then he pushes my bra down, just enough to attack my nipples with my mouth. I let out a loud moan of pleasure, my eyes closing. My breathing is getting heavier now. He softly grazes my nipple with his teeth and then twirls his tongue around it.

I become a writhing mess under him and it's already getting too much to take. I let him continue, though, because I'm curious to see what he has in mind, even though it's going to be painful for me in the end when I'll be unsatisfied. Again.

He takes his shirt off, but leaves his pants on and busies himself with putting my pants down my legs until I'm only in my underwear and he pushes that aside, too.

When he goes lower on my body, I tense up. "What are you doing?" I ask him. No one has ever gone down on me. And I literally mean no one.

"Making you feel good," Fai replies, placing a kiss on my inner thigh, awfully close to my center.

My legs are all tensed up as are my stomach muscles because I'm holding in a breath, suddenly all nervous.

He puts his mouth on me – finally, and I have to grip the sheets, my eyes rolling back in my head. "Oh, God," I groan out because sweet Jesus!

I can feel his piercing move against me when he sucks and licks and circles and it's sending shocks of pleasure down my body. I'm starting to sweat and I'm panting like I'm running a marathon, only this is more pleasurable.

When he pushes first one, then two fingers inside, I place my arm over my eyes, just chanting, "Please, please, please ..." Although I'm not really sure what I'm begging for.

I can't fully relax. Even though I want to because Fai's doing wonderful things to me that are making me a screaming mess, but my legs are still tense and when I have my eyes closed, I still see him. And I want to throw up.

"Look at me, Kadie. Fucking look at me and don't you dare to look away," Fai growls suddenly, his hands tensing on my outer thighs, gripping me more firmly.

He noticed he was losing me.

I drop my arm and look at him, biting down on my lip. "I can't do it," I say brokenly. "Please stop." I'm almost sobbing now.

I see the frustration on Fai's face, but there's also a hint of determination. He sits up and starts unbuckling his pants, pulling them off. I almost whimper from the loss of him, but I'm also relieved, even though this is pure torture to me. Wanting to come so badly, but not being able to ... it's hell.

He lays down on the bed next to me, saying, "Get on top."

When I want to sit on him, he stops me. "Turn around. Suck me."

"Can I at least get a please?" I mumble under my breath, sitting on top of him as he requested.

"You're also not going to talk back," he says, slapping my ass before he puts his hands on my hips and drags me back, putting his mouth back on me.

"Jesus," I say with a sigh, my head dropping.

Fai lifts his hips up, a silent request to wrap my lips around him. I grip him in my hand, putting my lips against the head and tease him at first, but then he pushes his tongue inside me and I let out a long moan that he silences by pushing his hips up and his cock in my mouth.

I let my hair fall down like a curtain when I start moving up and down because I forgot to put it in a ponytail before.

"Feels good, doesn't it?" Fai murmurs, pushing his hips up to meet my movements.

I just moan in response. He occupies my head with him. Because he's everywhere. On me, against me, in me ... My thoughts have no space to think about anything or anyone else and I only get to focus on the pleasure he's giving me and the pleasure I'm giving him back.

No one has ever done this to me before, but I feel the pressure inside of me building and it almost makes me start crying in frustration.

I suck him harder. He licks me faster. His fingers are inside me, and his mouth and tongue are playing with my clit.

I'm digging my nails into his thighs when he suddenly pulls his fingers out and presses them against my butt. I tense up again, but he keeps licking me and pressing his finger slowly, slowly inside the tight hole where no one has ever been before.

"Fai," I warn, but he sucks on my clit and I let out a moan right afterwards.

My chest is heaving and I'm panting and it feels so good.

And then, all of a sudden, he slips his finger fully inside me and I feel it. I feel how my inner muscles clench and I feel something so strong and powerful I've never felt before in my life.

I'm gasping for air, crying out his name in pure pleasure. I'm coming and coming and it's so good, I feel tears run down my cheeks.

Fai is caressing my backside, keeping his mouth on me. I'm almost sobbing now, placing my forehead against his thigh to calm myself down. "Oh, my God," I whisper when I'm starting to regain my focus. "Oh, my God," I say again. My body is still shaking.

Fai pulls his finger out of me and slips from underneath me, then grabs me and pulls me to him, wrapping his arms around me to calm me down because I'm still too shaken up to speak.

"I told you I'm going to do it. And now you're mine. Completely."

He didn't come yet. He doesn't ask me to finish him off, either. Not this time. He lets me have my moment.

I'm walking to my next class after my lunch break the next day when my phone starts vibrating in my pocket. I take it out with a groan, seeing it's a number I don't have saved in my phone. I consider not even answering it, but I never know who's calling me and for what reason.

"Yes?" I answer. Not cautiously and not reservedly as some people do when answering unknown numbers, just a normal who the hell are you and what do you want yes.

"Kadie. Kadie, is it you?"

My spine stiffens and I stop in the hallway. Someone runs into me from the back and I hear them shout, "Can you fucking move?!"

I'm too shocked to even show them my middle finger.

"Who's this?"

"Kadie. Oh, it's your mom."

I taste bitterness in my mouth when I hear her say that. "Sorry, wrong number," I say, hanging up. I go to the bathroom to take a few deep breaths, but it's not empty. I don't care.

My phone starts vibrating again and I consider just turning it off. "What?" I bark into the receiver. "What do you want?" I get a few curious looks and I even hear a snicker.

"Kadie, please, I need your help." My mom's voice is tired and she's begging. Is she crying?

I scrunch my nose up, turning to the wall so the other girls can't see my face. "I don't have time."

"Please, it's important. I – Stephen left. He – he's not coming back and it's really bad. I just need a little bit of money. I can't pay all these bills by myself."

I close my eyes, feeling vulnerable and weak. And guilty. Although I have nothing to be guilty about. "Go get a fucking job then. Don't call me again because I'm not going to help you."

I end the call before I'd break down and help her. I turn it off, too, so she doesn't call again. And then I just stand there, facing the wall, all the voices around me disappearing.

I shouldn't feel obligated to help her. She didn't give me anything. Everything I have in my life is because of me because no one ever gave me shit. I'm not going to help her just like she didn't help me when I was a kid and I went to her for help and she called me a liar. And just like she didn't help me when she got another man that was abusing me and she just turned blind because it was suiting her. She didn't care about me as long as she was okay and living well. Meaning she had the money for alcohol and probably drugs.

She's not my mother. She gave me birth, but that's all she ever gave me. Besides pain and mystery, that is.

And I'm especially not giving her money because that money is for my future and no one is touching it. I have to work at a strip club to afford to be alive for fuck's sake.

I pull my shoulders back and lift my head up.

I am not going to be her daughter when it's convenient for her just because she couldn't be a mother when I truly needed it before.

Tit for tat, mom. Tit for fucking tat.

When Fai comes and picks me up after school, he immediately notices something is off about me. I don't know how, but it only takes him a few seconds and one good look at me to see that something happened. I used to believe I'm very good at hiding my emotions, but it appears that I'm not.

"Something happened?" he asks me, sitting on his motorcycle, looking all cool and hot.

"Life happened," I answer vaguely. "Can we stop at the library? I need a few books."

"Sure," he says, his eyes still roaming all over my face.

I don't want to talk about my mother right now and I don't even want to think about her, so I sit behind him so he can't see my face anymore and read too much into it because he was making me feel nervous. And I never get nervous.

We drive through the streets towards the city's library. It's the largest and I love going there because I always find what I'm looking for because the library at our school just sucks. I'm plastered against his back, enjoying the ride there.

Fai waits outside for me, lighting up a cigarette. I promise him I'll be quick because I know what I'm looking for.

But then things get a little complicated when they can't find a book that I'm looking for and it says it should be in the library. And when they finally find it, there's a big line.

Fai has called me twice already and I had to shoot him a quick text that it'll take a little longer but it's not my fault. I'm already having a shitty day, so this just adds to my platter, and I come back out in an even worse mood than I was in before.

Fai is visibly frustrated and irritated because he had to wait so long. "Let's just go," I tell him, placing the books in my bag and sitting on the motorcycle again. I think he hears the tone of my voice that tells him I'm not in the brightest mood, too, so he wordlessly takes us to his place.

I go straight for his bedroom, getting on his bed with one of the books I brought home with me.

Fai appears at the door literally minutes later, his arms crossed over his chest. "What's the deal with you today? Did something happen?"

I flick my eyes to his. "No," I say, dropping my eyes back to the book.

"Really? What is it then?"

"Why does it have to be something?" I mumble, not even looking at him.

"Because it's you. And if you don't tell me one of your witty or sarcastic remarks the moment you see me or at least after spending an hour with me, then something is clearly wrong."

I close my book with a loud snap, glaring at him. "Alright. Do you want something witty and sarcastic from me? You have a small cock. There you go."

He makes a weird face. "That's not sarcastic, that's a straight up lie and you can do better than that."

He's taunting me and I'm punishing him when this is none of his fault. I fall back down on the bed, staring up at the ceiling, the book resting on my stomach. I'll have to get used to the idea that he's just someone who cares about me, besides Harper. That I have someone else besides her who I can talk to and trust now because he's already saved my ass so many times by now.

"My mom called today," I say.

He knows my story and he knows why that's not a usual thing for her to do. "What did she want?"

"Money," I say casually. "Her husband left and she has no one to finance her alcohol and drug addiction anymore."

"I hope you told her to go straight to hell," Fai says with venom and anger.

A smile rises on my face. "Not like that, but maybe I should."

"And what? Are you going to help her?" Fai asks after a few beats of silence between us, his voice merely curious.

I sit up on the bed so I can look at him now. "She's not getting a penny from me. She brought me to this world to ruin my life. I'm not going to save her ass and do good by her. But that doesn't mean it doesn't make me feel a little shitty, you know? And how fucking sad is that?"

Fai carefully sits on the edge of the bed. "Not as sad as you think it is. You're just a good person, despite having to deal with bad people all your life and that's not sad; it's brave. But like you said, just because she gave birth to you, it does not mean you're obligated to do anything. She wasn't there when you needed her. Let her deal with her own problems like she left you – as a child – to live with your own, looking the other way."

I crawl over to him, pushing his hands away from his lap and laying my head on his thighs, needing to be close to him because my soul is too heavy with emotions right now and I can't carry them on my own. And it's different now, laying down in bed. It's different because my demons used to lie down with me, filling all the space, but now I'm so full of him that the demons have no space to live inside me anymore.

Chapter 37

F ai insists on going with me to the work. Sometimes he stays, sometimes he just drops me off and goes back home and comes to pick me up.

I told him all of this is unnecessary, but he doesn't even let me argue about this. He says he chooses to do this because he'd rather be over-protective than getting me hurt again.

But all of this is slightly making me paranoid, as well. I'm constantly looking over my shoulder. I constantly have a feeling as if someone's there. I know there's no one. But what if they are, though?

And so I can't do anything but accept that he cares too much about me to wander around in the night, even if it means that he doesn't get enough sleep and it's showing, although he never once complains.

I'm grateful for that and it makes me happy knowing that I have someone like him. I feel safer. I know he'd protect me, no matter what.

Things have changed a little between us. Our gazes became longer and filled with longing, our touches became sweeter, yet still desperate for each other and I think there are more kisses now. And a hell of a lot more making out when we have time for it.

There's not that much with my school and his job and we often just take a nap in the afternoon because, otherwise, we wouldn't function normally.

Tonight's a rowdy night. Which means there are a lot of customers and I already have my eyes on a few of them. I know that allowing men to touch you and tell you all kind of inappropriate stuff gives you more tips and I know that kind of behavior is appreciated, in some cases even expected, from the girls, but I don't allow it.

I can put on one hell of an act of sweetness and seductiveness, but I can also throw a mean punch. It wouldn't be the first time.

And one of the guys is really walking by the thread, standing out to me in particular. He's getting drunker and he's getting bolder every time I walk past or to their table. But I'm not concerned about it or him.

Fai, however, is a different story.

When I come to his table to check on him and see if he needs a refill and just to get another look of him, I notice he's clenching his jaw and seizing the guy that's acting out a little up. He doesn't even see me approach.

I lightly put my hand on his arm and he slowly movies his head, locking his eyes with mine. "Do you need anything?"

"Yeah. Another drink and for that man to stop fucking trying to touch you. That's all."

I blink. "You better relax, Fai. This is my job. Don't even think about causing a scene."

Fai arches his eyebrow. "A scene? I'll put a bullet right through his skull if he doesn't stop."

I give him a bored look. "No, Fai. You won't," I say gently, patiently. "Because you can't. We have bodyguards for that. Don't play a personal one. Not tonight."

I find it quite hot that he's so blatantly jealous. He's not even trying to hide it, he's just straight-out, shamelessly showing it.

I pat his shoulder as I walk away with his empty glass. I try not to touch him too much in front of the others so as to not give any of the men in the room any ideas that they could touch me, too because I let someone do it. They don't know who Fai is to me and I have a feeling they don't wouldn't want to.

I try to avoid their table as much as I possibly can in the next hour because, not only do I not want a scene from Fai, but they also annoy me and I'm afraid it'll be me causing the scene any minute now.

And Fai is fuming. He's getting more and more furious every time I walk up to him to check on him.

And at one point, thinking that it's going to make things better, I sit down on his lap, wrap my arms around his neck and kiss him. In front of everyone. He doesn't hold back, either, his hand coming to my jaw, the other one caressing my outer thigh.

I did this mostly to calm down the chaos I'm sure he's experiencing in his mind, but also to show them I'm very much taken.

It was a stupid idea.

I learn that when I hear hoots around us and when I pull back, all the pigs are now grinning at me with their sleazy smiles, thinking they're going to be next. I almost throw up in my mouth just thinking about it.

I get off his lap, straightening my clothes.

And then things get progressively worse with the guys that have been causing trouble all night. Not only them, but others join them now, too.

Fai has murder in his eyes and I'm on the verge of breaking a glass – or a bottle of an expensive champagne – on someone's head. This might be one of the worst shifts I've had and, usually, guys like this didn't annoy or bother me that much. I'd ignore it or sort them out, either myself or I'd call the security.

But now, it bothers me. Much more than it used to and I think that has to do a lot with actually having a guy in my life now. The only guy I let touch me. Everyone else is just repulsive to me now.

And at one point, when someone actually grabs me (which is forbidden, anyway) and forcibly pulls me on their lap, I've had enough. Fai has, too, but I'm quicker than him, although he's approaching at a fast pace, but I know self-defence, and the guy isn't ready for me to fight back.

I elbow him in the chin and he immediately loosens his hold on me in reflex, so I am able to stand up. I do what I've been wanting to do and throw the expensive champagne in his face. I'd do much worse if I were somewhere else, but there are people and they're watching.

I also have to put my hand on Fai's chest to stop him before he'd attack him because it seems like he either doesn't notice people around anymore or he just doesn't care and he's ready to kill in plain sight.

"Get the fuck out. All of you," I say, feeling myself getting worked up.

"Now, wait a damn minute, baby girl. What did we do that others didn't?" One of the men asks.

My eyes flick downwards involuntarily, spotting the ring on his left hand. Figures. That's been my hobby here, looking at the men's hands, seeing if they're wearing rings. Most of them are. Some of them aren't because they're hiding it in their pockets – for whatever reason. We also get a lot of bachelor parties held here and all kinds of disgusting things happen for the grooms-to-be.

"Get the fuck out before I –" I put my hand over Fai's mouth, not letting him finish the sentence. He can't say anything that might put him in trouble because things could quickly get out of hand. This is a place where threats are not welcomed and you could get thrown out immediately.

"Before you what, boy?" one of the men chuckles.

I catch an eye of a security guy that's been waiting for my signal, watching the scene unfold. "These guys giving you trouble?" Rodrick asks me.

"Please be kind enough to escort them out," I say.

"Gladly," Rodrick smiles that sadistic smiles that tells me he wouldn't like to do anything more than that right now. "Boys, either you walk willingly on your own legs, or I make sure you'll never be able to walk again."

Yeah, Rodrick is a scary guy, but he's on my side and I love that for me. I wouldn't want him as an opponent.

The men around the table look at each other, gauging how serious this situation is and if it's worth the fight. They mutually agree with no words spoken that they're going to walk out peacefully, although I can see their ego took a big hit because all of them eye me devilly as they walk past me as if they're trying to memorize my face.

I shake my head. Fuckers.

I swivel around to face Fai. "Well. That was fun," I say dryly. Fai doesn't say anything to that. "You can go back to your seat now. I'll be done soon, anyway," I say, feeling drained all of a sudden. I don't want to be here and that's obvious. Not just today, but lately, I've been starting to despise this place more and more. I mean, who would want this kind of job? It pays good, sure, but it's like you're in hell.

Just a few more months. And then I'm gone. Forever.

The next day, I am allowed to visit Harper at the club she works at. With Fai right next to my side, of course.

I feel almost nostalgic stepping inside it because it's been quite a while. John, the bodyguard working there, is surprised and happy to see me. "Look at who came tonight. It's been some time, huh?" he asks me with one of his tight-lipped grins.

"Yeah. Way too long," I say in agreement.

I go to the bar, finding Jon sitting there already, his eyes trained on Harper. If he's anything, he's persistent. And I guess he really meant when he said he'd be looking over her. He's with her just like Fai's with me and I appreciate him for that, even though he's probably going to mess up one million times with Harper because it's just who he is.

Harper almost drops the glass she's holding when she spots me sitting at the bar, her eyes wide in surprise. "Oh, my God!" she squeals happily and I wince a little, but keep a grin on my face.

"I'm happy to see you too," I say.

She immediately rushes towards me. "It's been so long ... I think the whole club missed seeing you here."

I'm sure they did. "That's surprisingly good to hear," I say. "Hey, Jon," I offer to my left side. He just nods in acknowledgment. I also notice he has a glass of water in front of him, which makes me relax even more because Harper's in good hands here, I can't deny that. At least if we're talking about safety.

Fai quietly sits down next to me, greeting Jon with a nod, no words spoken. I look around myself, realizing I've missed this place. It holds a lot of memories.

I put my hand on Fai's thigh to grab his attention. "Remember the first time we've met?"

Fai eyes me. "I remember you being bold and annoying the hell out of me, yeah."

I bite down on my lip to suppress a chuckle. "I remember you almost begging me to sleep with you."

Fai snorts. "Must be some other guy because that wasn't me, princess."

I nod my head with a click of my tongue. "Oh, it was definitely you," I say, squeezing his thigh.

Fai pushes his tongue against the cheek, his eyes smoldering a little. "Now I don't have to beg anymore, do I?" he says quietly, intimately.

"Definitely not," I agree. "We've come a long way from there, haven't we?" I ask, still lost in the memories.

Fai breaks our eye connection, his eyes settling on the glass in front of him that Harper put there. "We sure have," he responds, looking like he's miles away, too.

Harper puts her hands on the bar, turning our attention towards her. "So, are you officially out of prison yet?" she asks and I know she means it lightly and she says it as a joke, but both men sitting on either side of me tense up.

"Not completely, but my bodyguard now allows me to take walks, so that's a progress." I nudge Fai a little and he purses his lips, making my eyes fall down to them.

"One walk here and there only. Otherwise, the princess is still locked in the tower."

He purposefully doesn't use the term prison. And, truthfully, I don't look at my situation that harshly, either. It is what it is. If it makes Fai sleep better at night, I'll do what I can because he's already doing so much for me and that's only fair of me to not cause him even more trouble. I know he's dealing with a lot of things on his own, too.

"How romantic," Harper says with a small smile.

When I give her a long, studying look, I notice a few things. She's definitely changed. She's smiling more, she's more energetic and bubbly whereas before, she was usually closed-off and sheltered.

Things with Jon must be going in the right direction, then.

Someone sits on our left, ordering a shot of whisky. I don't know what it is about the person, but that voice makes all of our heads turn into the direction it just came from.

And I immediately recoil.

I'm met with the pair of eyes that aren't unfamiliar, yet I wish they were.

The guy looks at us – at me – with a self-satisfied smile. "Evening," he says easily. Like he didn't kidnap and almost raped me once.

Chapter 38

K adie completely loses it.

I have to wrap my arm around her waist and pull her towards me because she was ready to attack him right here in the bar.

"You fucker!" she screams. "How dare you ever show your face in front of me again? You fucking psycho."

Stefan gives Kadie a dirty look. "Maybe you should control your little bitch, Mills. You have your leash on way too long."

Kadie bounces forward so fast and hard that I have to get off the stool I'm sitting on and pull her back even tighter. "Don't cause a scene," I say into her ear while I keep my eyes on the bastard in front of me.

"I'm going to fucking kill him," Kadie says, thrashing against me.

"Kadie," I warn.

"And I'm going to kill you, too if you don't let me go right now," she says with venom in her voice.

I just let out a sigh and keep holding onto her so she doesn't latch out. "You have some nerve showing your face here Stefan," I say with a low voice, giving him a seriously angry look. My whole body is ready to fight him at any given second. Just pull the gun out and shoot him.

Stefan smiles and leisurely and slowly – like he has all the time in the world – takes a swig of his drink. He puts it down and moves it with his hand until it's where he wants it. "Just like the old times, wouldn't you say?" Stefan grins. He's baiting me.

I clench my jaw, but I don't grab the bait. "Just get the fuck out of here," I say through gritted teeth.

"Why? I have as much right to be here as you do."

"I'm going to kill him," Kadie mutters again, trying to get out of my hold again, but I don't let her.

Stefan slowly moves his gaze to Harper and I see how she flinches when their eyes connect. She quickly looks away, trying to look busy by wiping the surface. I see she's shaking a little.

"Bill, please," Stefan says, still looking at her.

I see how Jon goes into a bear-mode, ready to attack at any given second. Just one wrong move and all hell will break loose.

Fuck, it's killing me that I have him so close to me and I can't do anything. I want to blow his little brains out, but I can't. Not here, at least.

Harper quickly gets him the bill and Stefan pays. We all watch as his hand lingers a little when Harper wants to grab the money. He doesn't let go and their hands touch. Jon stands up, going up to Stefan.

"No," I say sternly, not letting him ruin this.

Harper quickly pulls her hand away and goes to the register, away from us.

Stefan slowly gets off the chair, nodding at us. "Always a pleasure to see you."

Before we could see what's coming, Stefan extends his arm and touches Kadie's cheek. Before any of us could interact, she quickly slaps his arm away and spits in his face.

Stefan's eyes widen, his smile vanishing, clearly not expecting that. "We'll meet again, you little bitch," he says.

"Yeah, in hell after I'll be done with you," Kadie shoots and I have to tighten my hold so much that I'm sure she probably has trouble breathing because I'm squeezing her stomach so tight.

Stefan just gives her an ugly grin, wiping his face off and leaves. We all watch him in silence, all of our bodies tense.

When I feel Kadie sag a little against me, I slowly release my hold. "You okay?"

She looks at me and then looks at Harper and at Jon. And then at me again. "Harper is in danger, isn't she?"

Jon and I catch each other's looks. I don't have to give Kadie any verbal answer.

"Fuck," she says. "Fuck!" comes again, more fiercely this time.

"I'm keeping an eye on her 24/7. She's safe with me," Jon reassures her. Harper doesn't say anything.

"This shouldn't have happened," Kadie says.

"It shouldn't have," I agree. "But we're handling the situation now. You're both safe as long as you cooperate," I put the emphasis on the word cooperate because Kadie can be strong-minded sometimes and has her own ideas. And what she forgets sometimes is that I have the best intentions for her because it's my mess and I know how to deal with it more than she does. I don't particularly like it when I have to cut her freedom short, but it's what I have to do.

Kadie gives me an accusing look. I don't know what for. "We have things we'll talk about when we get home. Right now, I'm spending some quality time with my cousin."

Her tone isn't implying she's looking for any answer from me or, God forbid, reluctance. But I give it to her anyway. "Do we really? I didn't know anything about that."

Kadie just gives me a look. She doesn't need to say that she wants me to shut the hell up. And I grin at her because I understand it all too well, but I also love taunting her. When she gets pissed? Yeah, she's a sight to see. A hot sight.

I put my arm around her shoulders and bring her to my side. "If you wanna fight, bee, you're going to fight with yourself," I say into her ear.

Kadie slightly turns her head. "It depends on what your answers will be, Fai," she says back.

That earns her a surprised and amused look from me, but I drop it and leave the subject for later. I place a kiss on her temple and in that moment, I spot Jon staring at me as if he's never seen me before. I release Kadie and give him a questioning look.

He just shakes his head and looks down, but I catch his smile before he can hide it. Ah, hell.

I look away, my jaw clenching. I know what he thinks. I've never been like that with any girl before. But there has never been a girl like Kadie before. She's ... I can't compare her to anyone because she's her own person completely. Fearless, smart as hell and hot-headed. And completely fucking gorgeous, of course. So, she's a threat to everyone. Because I know that everyone that'll meet her, they won't ever forget her.

Neither will I. But our time together is limited, although I've already started thinking about some other options. Do we really have to end? I could go with her for the time when she'll be away at college. Long-distance is neither of our thing, I'm sure, but if everything goes right, I'll be done with the last mission soon enough and it'll be behind me. Nothing else will tie me to this place anymore.

I look at Kadie. She's talking to Harper. Smiling. Laughing, even. That's quite a rare sight. She really loves her cousin.

And looking at her, being this happy ... it hits me that she's going to forever stay with me. Parts of her, at least. That I'll never be able to forget her. And I probably won't be able to let her go when the time comes, either.

When I come out of the bathroom, fresh out of the shower, I catch Kadie drawing by the window with a cigarette in her hand. "What are you working on?"

She inhales. And exhales. Looking at me. Not answering.

I flick my eyes to the paper, not knowing what I'm looking at first. It's a caterpillar, I quickly discover.

"Caterpillars don't know they're going to become a butterfly one day. They don't know they'll get wings to fly anywhere they'll want to. That they'll be able to explore the world freely."

"That's ... nice?" I'm not really sure how to answer her.

She puts her sketchbook aside and gives me a serious look. It makes me shift a little on my feet. "Harper wasn't just wandering around with her phone turned-off, did she? Something happened. And none of you wanted to tell me."

Fuck. I close my eyes briefly. I should've known she'd figure it out. She's too smart for bullshit. "Look –" I start, but I get nowhere.

"No, you look." She stands up, puts the cigarette out and slowly walks towards me, standing so close that only a few inches are between us. She's smaller than me and she has to look up at my face, but she's no less intimidating than some of the men I've dealt with in my life. "If you ever lie to me – not just about something this big and not just when it comes to Harper – but, in general, Fai, if you ever tell me a lie, no matter how small, we're done. Do you understand what I'm saying? I'll walk away so quietly you won't even know. And you'll never see me again. Yeah?"

I swallow thickly. "Yeah," I say with a gruff voice.

She smiles, lovingly putting her hand on my cheek then. "Now, babe. Why don't you start by telling me why you decided to lie to me and then tell me exactly what happened, yes?"

Her hand on my cheek is not a loving gesture. It's a threat. "Nothing happened. We were at the right place at the right time."

Kadie shakes her head, clicking her tongue. "No. I said you start with why you decided to lie to me. Not with excuses. Keep those to yourself."

I place my hand on top of her on my cheek, but her expression stays unchanged. She's waiting for me to speak. To tell her. To tell her what she already knows, but she still wants to hear it because she's punishing me.

"Because it was safer you didn't know," I say with an exhale.

"Safer for who, exactly?"

"You, of course." Always you. "It was Harper's idea, by the way. She said you might do something stupid if you knew something happened to her and that it's better you don't know because it might be a trap to get to you. And she had a point, but I didn't agree with her."

"Yet you still got along with her plan." Her hand presses harder against my cheek.

"Yeah, because she had a great point, Kadie. You're like a mama bear when it comes to her, but you're not safe, either. And my concern is, primarily, you. So, I'm sorry I lied, but it was for your own good."

She softly shakes her head. "No. It was for your own good, Fai. You were scared. Scared that I'll cause a riot and cause trouble, but you're forgetting that, before you came into my life, I was doing just fine and I ate assholes like Stefan for dinner if I needed to."

I step away from her. "You still don't understand, Kadie. This is not something to fuck around in your free time. These guys are murderers and damn good ones. Just fucking trust me and work with me, can you?"

"I am working with you. I was, at least, until you started working against me. You see how it goes?"

"Don't. Just don't start. I lied, yes, and I'm damn sorry I did it because I know I shouldn't."

Kadie nods. "And why shouldn't you?" she prompts.

I wait for a few heartbeats. One. Two. Three. Four. "Because if someone lied to me like that about you, I'd cut their throats without thinking twice about it," I admit.

Kadie grins, nodding. "Exactly. Now we're getting somewhere." She speaks with a softer, gentler voice now. I don't even know what she's going to do next and that makes me nervous. She crosses her arms over the chest, inspecting me closely. I only arch my eyebrows in return because I don't know what she's planning on doing.

"When you think you're doing me any favors – don't. Because you most likely aren't. And I don't like being a charity case." I want to protest, but she doesn't let me say anything, shushing me. I blink at her in disbelief. "I'm talking now," she says. "And do not keep things from me. Especially things that concern me. Just because you're involved in my life now, doesn't mean you can make decisions for me."

"I already said I'm sorry. What else do you want me to say?"

Kadie cocks her head to the side, but I don't get an answer because someone rings the bell.

My head snaps in the direction of the front door. It's really late and I'm not expecting anyone. I take the gun out of the waist of my pants and turn to Kadie. "Stay here and don't even move an inch."

I go to the door, pressing my ear against it, but I don't hear anything, of course. I have my gun ready when I open it just an inch. And then another.

And I frown. "Who are you?" I ask through the small crack.

"Oh. Fai. It's really you. Hi. Hello." The stranger that turns out isn't really a stranger stumbles on her words.

All the color disappears from my face and I feel my body went completely limp. "Mom. What the hell are you doing here?!"

I briefly hear Kadie walking out of the bedroom, coming towards me. She fully opens the door with a big smile on her face. "Laila, come on in. I'm so happy I get to finally meet you!"

I look at her with a confused look and before she lets my mom in, she turns to me and whispers, "You're not the only one going behind people's backs, babe."

Chapter 39

When I invite Laila inside and guide her to the kitchen, I show her to sit down at the table and ask her what she'd like to drink or eat. Fai is still standing by the door with his mouth and eyes wide open.

"Fai, won't you join us?" I ask him sweetly.

I see his mother is nervous. She's glancing between us unsurely, twisting her hands.

I didn't really picture Fai's mom before, but as I see her for the first time now, it's hard to miss she's absolutely gorgeous. She looks way younger than she is and I can spot a few similarities between her and Fai – for instance, they have the same smile and Fai's one brown eye is the exact same shade as hers and he definitely got her hair color.

Fai slowly walks into the kitchen as if he's in a daze. His mother watches him as I put a glass of orange juice down in front of her.

"What the fuck?" Fai asks.

I join his mother in looking at him. "Huh?" I ask innocently, sweetly, batting my eyelashes.

"What the fuck?" he repeats, still standing there in the middle of the kitchen, staring at us as if we're ghosts.

"I – maybe this wasn't a good idea?" Laila directs the question to me.

I put a reassuring hand on her shoulder. "Nonsense! We're both very happy to see you."

Fai clenches his jaw. Then unclenches it. Then he clenches his hands in fists and unclenches then. He repeats this a few times. "How did this happen?" he asks when he gets himself under control, it seems.

"It's a long story, honey. Maybe you should sit down and we'll both tell you the story." I take out a chair for him to sit down, giving him my sweet smile. This will teach you, darling. You don't mess with me without getting something in return.

He sits down, looking like he's in a daze. I turn to the stove and put on water for tea. "Do you want some tea, too, honey?" I call sweetly.

I'm waiting for some long seconds for the response. "No," he finally says.

I make some tea for me and his mom and none of us speaks until I set the cups down and sit down, too. "So! How was your trip? I hope everything was well."

"It was. Thank you, Kadience." She turns to Fai then. "You have a lovely girlfriend, Fai."

"Lovely," he repeats incredulously, his eyes settling on me again.

I just support my head on my hand and give him a smile.

If I hate anything, I hate liars. Fai knows that.

I knew he was lying that day. Not only because Harper is a shitty liar, but because I've come to know Fai. I'm basically living with him and we spend a lot of time together. I know all the little details about him, everything that others may overlook. He is a guy that hides his truth well. He's learned to contain his feelings and he learned not to show his emotions.

But he can't hide from me. I know what makes him angry, what makes him sad, what makes him happy just by little changes in his expression or just the small changes in the tone of his voice.

I was so mad. So extremely mad at him for lying because I thought he was the person I could trust and rely on.

And then I wanted to hurt him. I wanted to do something to him that'll make him feel the same way.

Now we're here. And I don't regret a single thing. This is his lesson. I hope he's learning it well.

"You came here alone?" Fai asks when he finds his voice again.

"Yes," his mother replies. "It was safer." Her words, I realize, seem carefully chosen. She speaks slowly and uncertainly and I note an accent, but it's as if she's testing the English words out, as if she hasn't spoken the language in a long time. And maybe she hasn't. She doesn't live in America anymore.

She nervously looks at me again. I know she expected a different kind of meeting, but I didn't lie to her. I told her Fai doesn't know about her coming here and it's a surprise and I never lied about him being excited or anything. I knew he wouldn't be.

I put my hand on Fai's thigh. He can't seem to stop staring at her, afraid to even blink, afraid that if he does, she's going to disappear. "You shouldn't be here," he tells her.

Her eyes sadden and she looks down for a moment. "Yes, maybe not. But ... you've grown so much and ... a mother not knowing about their child ... it was killing me, you have to understand."

"It's too dangerous. I'm still not –" he cuts himself off. "It's still not over."

She nods as if she understands, but she looks like she has a hard time accepting it. "I understand. I knew the danger, yet I came anyway, even if to just see you once and never again. I wanted to see that you're okay. You're ..." She doesn't finish the sentence. It seems like she can't.

I suddenly get a lump in my throat from all of the emotions I can feel in the air between them. This just might be one of the saddest things I've seen.

I know Fai will think I did this to deceive him and get him back. And, yes, I did it with that thought in my mind – get him back. Hurt him. But as I'm sitting here and now, I realize I don't want to hurt him. Even though he decided to cold-heartedly do it to me, I don't want to see him in pain because my feelings are way too strong and I'm too soft when it comes to him.

Right now, I'm actually happy I invited his mother here. I know when he talked about her, I felt the sadness radiating off him. The sadness of not knowing where she is, what she's doing, if she's safe. And now he has a chance to reconnect with her.

The loud sound of chair dragging across the floor takes me out of my own thoughts. Fai is standing up now, pent up with energy. "I need a word with you." He points his finger at me. Accusingly so.

"Can't you say it here?" I ask him because, hell, I can't help taunting him.

"No," he says simply, turning around on his feet and walking away.

I let out a sigh. "Excuse me. I'll only be a minute," I say to Laila.

I don't know if she hears me because she stares after where Fai disappeared to as if she's in a daze.

I go after Fai to see what she wants. He's in the bathroom, leaning over the sink. "You wanted a word with me, darling?"

He turns his head, looking at me with the most devilish expression I've ever seen. "Close the door."

I don't know if I want to, but I know that I don't want his mother to hear what's going to go down between us. It'll be ugly. I close the door and wordlessly step further into the bathroom. "What were you thinking, Kadience? What the fuck were you thinking?!" he bellows.

"You don't like the surprise?" I ask, cocking my head to the side.

He pushes backwards, stalking towards me like a panther, ready to attack. "You're playing a dangerous game. Don't play with my fire because you'll not only get burned, but it'll swallow you. You'll come out as ash and nothing more than that."

I give him a defying look. "I love when you talk dirty to me," I say with a completely straight face.

His face twists. And then, all of a sudden, his hand goes backwards and he hits the door right next to my head with such a force, it makes a loud sound that makes me flinch and squeeze tighter against it.

I don't want to show him, but my body suddenly starts trembling. This might be the first time ever I really got scared of him. Scared that I went too far and he's going to lose his mind and hit me.

But when he turns around, his hand pinching his nose, I realize how ridiculous my thoughts are. I know he'd never hurt me. He would never put his hands on me because he knows of my demons. Yet I still can't help my body's involuntary reaction to his anger.

I'm scared to say anything because I'm scared my voice will come out shaky and scared. Because that's what I am, even though I don't want to be.

"It's not safe for her to be here. I told you one little goddamn lie that hurt no one. And you go and put my mother in such a danger that could cost her life." He's not talking to my face, he's staring at the wall.

I'm thankful for that so he can't see how my body is trembling in aftershocks of his fist connecting to the door.

"She's traveling under a fake name and she's alone. No one knows she's here. She was just a normal passenger and she has a hotel reserved under the same fake name, so she won't be staying here."

He's silent for long, long moments. "You infuriate me like no one else. Can raise my blood pressure to the roof."

"Yes, well, before it totally cools down – you'll need to take your mom to the hotel because we can't risk her using public transportation."

Fai turns around this time and he does it before I even finish the sentence. "On what? My motherucking motorcycle? Christ," he says, already taking his phone out. "You really have to go and complicate my goddamn life. I should've never looked at you twice. Knew you were trouble."

"But you could never resist trouble, could you? A little havoc. Trouble makes you feel alive, doesn't it? Runs the blood through your body."

He lifts his eyes to look at me for two seconds. "I didn't know you were also a poet, among other things."

No. but I learned that I am infuriatingly in love with him. And though that doesn't make me want to write poems just yet, it does make me want to scream and curse because our thing has an expiry date that's approaching fast.

"I could be, but have you ever read poems where every third word is fuck? I'd be a terrible poet."

"Fuck do I know? I've never even glanced at poetry, let alone read it."

"Liar. You had to read it in school."

Fai just looks at me with an emotionless expression. "I didn't go to school."

"Really?" But that makes sense, I guess. I didn't really think much about it, mostly because he's too smart for that thought to just pop in your head.

"I was learning how to use a gun and my fists while others were learning all those mathematical equations and read fucking poetry books." He sounds mad about it.

I'd be mad, too. They literally stole Fai's teenage years and forced him into things no person should ever do in their life. I still don't know the full version of his story and I may never find out, but I know that he had to do things he's not proud of.

Yet I still can't see him as a bad person. And I'm not talking about just because he's good to me, doesn't mean he's good in general, because he is. In his own way. We're all villains in someone's story.

"Go to my mom, keep her company while I sort out the shit you created."

"I didn't create any shit," I say defensively.

"Go," he says.

I guess we're still arguing then. "This is your chance to spend some time with your mother. Don't blow it, Fai. See? Even when I go behind your back, I have good intentions somewhere in the back of my mind."

"So did I, Kadie. I didn't lie to you just because I'd want to and because I thought it'd be fun."

"No, you just didn't think at all. Don't do it again. I can hit back twice as hard."

"Clearly," he says dryly. "You hit back without thinking of the consequences."

I shrug my shoulders, just giving in. "I make problems, you deal with them." I send him a wink, catching his scowl just before I turn around and march out of the bathroom.

His mom looks at me with wide, scared eyes, standing up immediately when she sees me. "Are you alright? I heard ... He's mad, isn't he?"

She's looking over my face, probably wanting to see if he hit me. I wonder if Fai's father was the kind to hit women – his mom precisely. I think he was of what I heard about him.

I swing my arm in a nonchalant matter. "He'll be fine. He just likes to be dramatic sometimes." I smile. She doesn't smile back. She's worried. Worried that he turned out to be exactly like his father, maybe? "He's a good guy, you know? Doing bad things, yes, but he has his limits and he has his head on right when he needs to," I find the need to reassure her.

She nods tightly. "How did you two meet? Tell me about that. I'm curious."

"Funny story that," I say, tracking the edge of the table with my hand, my head lowering and a smile appears on my face. It seems so long ago because so many things have happened since then. It seems like I've known him forever.

Fai walks into the kitchen just at the right moment, still looking pissed. "How great that you're here. I was just about to begin telling your mom the story of how we met."

Fai doesn't look any happier at that. He stops when he's beside me, wrapping his arm around my shoulder and looking at his mom. "The night I met her, I thought she was the biggest bitch I've ever met. To this day, my opinion still hasn't changed."

I have to laugh at that, not taking any offense. A lying bastard, that's what you are, my eyes say when I look at him, but what comes out of my mouth is, "Aren't you an asshole?"

He looks into my eyes and whatever snarky comment he had prepared for me, dies on his lips. "The first night I met her," he starts again, still looking deep into my eyes, "I thought she's the most gorgeous, the bravest and the smartest girl I've ever had a chance to lay my eyes on. And I knew I have to have her in any way I could get her."

My smile disappears on my lips and my playful mood is replaced by shock and surprise at his words. I stare at him, speechless. And that is a rare condition for me to be in.

He's the first to break our gentle gaze when he turns back to his mother, removing his arm from my shoulders.

I see his mom smiling, looking reassured now. And ... content. "You found yourself a good girl," she says.

Fai gives her one of those half-smiles. "The good is a little questionable, but I sure did get myself a girl."

"Which is a miracle," I butt in. "Not every girl would be prepared to put up with your ass, so I better see you kneeling and hear you thanking all your lucky stars every night you found me."

"It's your job to be on your knees – not mine."

"I'll take the job as soon as you start paying me for it."

"Can I use the bathroom?" Fai's mom suddenly asks. She can hardly contain her grin.

"Yes, of course. I'll show you. Come with me."

I lead her through Fai's bedroom and she takes everything in. She looks proud, yet a sad smile is marking her face. Before she enters the bathroom, she turns to me, taking my hands in hers. "He loves you," she tells me. "It's lovely when I see him like this, knowing that he has something good waiting on him when he comes back from his ... jobs. That he has something light and not something that'd weigh him down even further."

My throat closes. What is happening to me tonight? Am I going to turn into cry babies? Am I going to be the one who bursts out crying at some cute moments? Shit. I can only manage a nod.

Laila gives me a warm smile and then enters the bathroom. I stand there, staring at the closed door for a few seconds.

Something light. Something that wouldn't weigh him down.

I find Fai standing in the kitchen window. I see his silhouette in the window and see his serious expression. He sees me approaching and he's looking at me, not reacting in any way, just waiting.

I wrap my arms around him from behind, whispering, "I'm sorry I did this. I was too mad to think straight and I just did the first thing that came into my mind, although I did try to be safe about it. But it was unfair and I took it too far. I know you're trying with me. I'm sorry I'm such a trouble-maker for you." I don't care how soapy I sound. I don't care that I'm appearing weak. I left the ego in the other room because it was ruining things from me.

Fai lets out a sigh. He picks one of my hands up and places a kiss on the back of my hand. He doesn't have to say it, but he forgives me.

I place my cheek against his back and close my eyes, letting myself to get lost in him for a few seconds. I find it exhilarating to have someone I can get lost with and lost in because I know he'll always find me and bring me back.

Chapter 40

I work on a drawing, sitting by the window with a cigarette hanging out of my mouth. Fai took his mother to the hotel and I have some time to finish this sketch. I'm working on Fai's tattoo.

Initially, I finished one drawing, but I changed my mind and realized I wanted something else for him. I wanted something that'd remind him of me because I'm too selfish to let him forget me.

I have time tonight because I'm off work. I've been working less and less at the club because it makes me sick to the stomach being around all those men and having their eyes on me. It's never bothered me that much before, but things drastically changed for me in just a few months.

I lay the notebook down on my thighs for a second, rubbing my eyebrow. I lean back and exhale the smoke of cigarette out, feeling the cold air hit the back of my neck.

My finals start next week and I haven't started preparing yet. I don't really care that much because I know I'll get a good grade, but I don't strive for perfection. It just has to be good enough so I get into the university I want and that's it.

I hear the front door open, indicating that Fai came back. I hear him take off his shoes and put the car keys on the table. He had to borrow a car from Jon. He comes to the bedroom and stops when he sees me by the window. He looks visibly tired and I feel all that more guilty for getting his mother here like that.

I'm happy they had a chance to see each other after so much time, but I realize that the circumstances weren't the best and my reaction was too quick. I don't want to hurt Fai.

He sits on the bed, facing me and he lets out a long sigh. I silently offer him my half-finished cigarette because it looks like he needs it more than me and he gratefully takes it. "I'm working on your tattoo," I inform him, but I don't show it to him.

He doesn't react to my words. "I haven't finished yours yet."

I shrug and close the notebook. "That's fine."

I lean forward, putting my elbows on my thighs, noticing how stressed he looks. I get on the bed, sitting close to him and wrapping my arms around his torso, putting my head on his shoulder. "This Stefan guy. Can you tell me what your deal with him is? What do you owe him? Why is he after you?"

Fai turns his head, looking at me.

"I know you don't like talking about him and all this crap," I hurry because I can read the look in his eyes. "But I really want to know. Especially since we all have to look behind our shoulders because of him."

"There's not much to tell. We go way back. He claims he saved my life when I was fighting once, but I think that was intentional and he scripted it. I'd win the fight, anyway, but he showed up. He was more experienced than me in the business and he wanted me to do jobs for him. He told me I'm a natural. I didn't want to do any goddamn jobs, I just wanted to be done with what my father left me and that's it. To this day, he's claiming I owe him for saving my ass, but I refuse to come work for him, so he's been trying to sabotage me and became my enemy because I'm better than him."

I smile at that. Fai's not even trying and he's good at it and he's only doing this because he has to, whereas this is Stefan's job. I'd be mad, too. "When's your last job?"

"No idea. In a few weeks most likely, but I don't know yet. When they'll call me. And then I'm out – for good."

This is the part that worries me. Fai has made some enemies, I'm quite sure. He's made a name of himself and people know of him. I don't think he can quit like that. I don't exactly know how these things work, but I've met gangsters before and once you're in you can hardly get out. Especially when you're good like Fai is.

I lower my eyes, feeling the sinking feeling in my stomach, but I try to ignore it. In a few weeks, things will be different for us. Both of us will be free, both of us will have some more time to spend with each other and then we'll decide what to do with us from then on. If we decided to keep what we have ... it'd be tough.

Fai puts the cigarette out and turns to me, wrapping his arm around my shoulders. "Come and apologize," he tells me, all of a sudden in a very playful mood.

"Whatever for?" I ask him.

"For going behind my back."

"I already apologized. And I meant it – I am sorry."

He nods. "Yes, now show me just how sorry you truly are."

A wicked grin appears on my face as I immediately slide off the bed and go between his legs. "Is this what you had in your mind?"

I get another call from my mother. I don't pick up. She hasn't called me after I told her off the last time, but I guess she felt like trying again, hoping I maybe changed my mind or something. Rest assured – I didn't.

I don't even go to the house anymore. I've basically moved in with Fai and before that, I mostly stayed with Harper.

I'm on my way to visit Harper. Fai gave me a green light to go by myself because he's tracking my phone. I'm carrying a knife with me and I make sure I walk on the streets that aren't too empty.

I'm not really that scared of Stefan. I know that if he wanted to, he'd kill me before. And now I know what he's capable of. I learned his moves. He better not come near me again because I'm prepared to slice his throat if I have to.

Harper has a free evening today, but I have to go to work after. When I come to her place, I hear her giggling. That makes me frown because I imagine Jon is here and that's not how I saw this girl's night going, but alright.

He's not. Harper is by herself, giggling at the TV with a glass of wine in her hand. That makes me stop. Harper. With a glass of wine. "Hello, hello!" I say happily.

Harper moves her head to look at me, her smile faltering a little. She looks me up and down which makes me raise my eyebrows. "Kadience," she greets me and that makes me blink at her. "Are you a stripper?"

I stare at her. We stare at each other for long moments. Harper is not drunk, but she's one, if not two glasses of wine in already. "What kind of question is that?" I ask her, plopping down on the couch next to her, putting my feet on the table.

She gives me an uncertain look, her eyes narrowing. "A pretty good one, I'd say. Jon told me."

Of course he did. Fucking hell. "Told you what?"

"About you. And the strip club. He thought I knew. Why didn't I know?"

Goddamn it. "I work at a strip club, but not as a stripper. I'm fully dressed and just make sure the guests aren't thirsty."

Harper downs a whole glass of wine. It makes me want to have one myself. "All this time ... All this time you've been working there and didn't say a word. Why?" She sounds offended. She sounds hurt.

Now I just feel bad. I turn my body so I'm facing her. "Look, Harp. You know that things have always been a little complicated with me and I hated bringing my shit into your life. You're a worrier – you worry by nature. I didn't want you anywhere near that."

She scoffs. "I deserved to know. Don't sell me this shit."

"You did," I agree. "Truthfully, I just didn't want you to know because you're a little judgmental when it comes to different things like that. At least you used to be."

Her mouth falls open. "That's really not true. I would understand, Kadie. Maybe not at first, but, come on. Lying? All this time ..."

I cross the arms over my chest. "Since we're talking about lying. You have something to tell me, too?"

I see it, then. I see the guilty expression, the panic on her face. She has never been a good liar. "What?" she asks, her voice small.

"You lied, too. Straight to my face. Said that nothing happened the day we thought you were kidnapped. That you just went out to freshen up your mind. I gave Fai so much shit about it, only to hear it was your idea." I didn't want to attack her like this, but since we're doing this right now, I'm not letting her off that easily.

She looks down and I see her bottom lip trembling.

Oh, hell no.

"I'm sorry," she says. "I thought ... You already had so much on your plate already. And you are in danger, too. We were all afraid you'd do something that would put your life at risk."

I sigh and lean my head back against the couch, staring up at the ceiling. "I'm sorry, too. For not telling you about the job."

She leans her head on my shoulder and she wipes the tears off her face. Harper is an emotional drunk. It's one of the reasons she hates drinking. She says it always brings out emotions she's too scared to show sober.

"How are things? How are you and Jon?" I try to change the subject. It's useless fighting about this. I'm tired of it all, too.

Harper sighs happily. "So good. So, so good," she gushes. "I didn't know you could feel like this about someone. It's ... a lot, you know? He's so hot and possessive and he's everything I thought I didn't want once, but it turned out that he's everything I've silently dreamt of having."

I grin because I'm truly happy for her. I was sceptical at first because I was scared Jon would use her and discard her, but if there's any guy I'd have high hopes for, it's him. Harper chose the right one. "You sound in love," I comment.

Harper giggles. "Maybe I am. A little. Tiny, tiny bit."

"Uh-uh," I say, my lips spreading in a wide grin.

We sit in silence for a long time. "You have to work tonight, don't you?" she asks me.

My eyes close. "Yes," I say regretfully. But not for much longer. At least not here.

Fai thrusts inside me again, letting out a grunt. I drag my nails over his back, slightly scratching it. His lips hover over mine when he asks, "You with me?"

I shake my head. I'm not.

Fai puts his hand on my jaw and says, "You have to be with me, bee." Then his hand goes down and he starts playing with my clit, making my eyes roll back. It's still hard for me to come, I realize. I wasn't magically cured the last time we had sex. I was afraid to have it again ever since.

I have to focus too much on where I am and who I'm with. Since it's dark, that's an even harder task. And then I just think too much about how I have to think of only Fai and it's exhausting. I forget to enjoy the act itself in the process.

But Fai doesn't let me forget it. He's pushing me; he's constantly talking to me, kissing me, reminding me that it's him, doing every-thing to make me feel good. He wants to bring me over the edge, even though he has to hold himself back.

"Please," I moan out weakly. I don't even know what I'm begging for, I just want something.

"Come on, baby. Give it to me," Fai says with a strained voice. I feel a few drops of his sweat fall against my forehead, mixing with my own. I grab the back of his head and push him down, kissing him deeply.

We both come at the same time. As soon as Fai feels me squeez-ing him and coming on his cock, he lets himself go, too, burying his head into my neck where he's kissing my neck and my shoulders. It seems like he can't get enough of me.

I close my eyes and bury my head into his neck, too overwhelmed with emotions. Fai doesn't want to let me go, either.

In just a few hours, I have to get up for school. I haven't slept since Fai drove me home from work and it's the first time after many years that I feel really tired.

Fai rolls off me, but he keeps me close to him, wrapping his arm around my body and pulling me close. I smile into the dark, even though he can't see me. I put my hand to his face, blindly searching for it, connecting it to his cheek, my thumb tracing his lips.

I feel him shudder. "You really had to go and do that, huh?" he asks with a croaky voice.

"Do what?" I whisper.

"Made me fall in love with you."

My stomach muscles clench and my eyes close again. "Fai ..." I say weakly. It's too much for me tonight.

"I know," he says and kisses my forehead.

I don't say anything. He knows, anyway. He knows everything.

Chapter 41

When I wake up from my afternoon nap, Fai is sitting on the chair by the window, smoking a cigarette and watching me.

I stretch my arms above my head and stare at him back. "Why are you being a creep?" I ask him with a smile.

A smile that he doesn't return and a question that remains unanswered.

I sit up on the bed. Something is wrong. "What is it?"

Fai exhales the smoke of the cigarette out of his mouth, creating a cloud around his head, moving his eyes away from me. "I got a call."

My shoulders hunch a little, even though I try to stay indifferent and, most of all, brave. "When?" I ask him, grabbing the duvet a little tighter in my hand.

"Two weeks," Fai says, putting the cigarette to his mouth again.

In two weeks, I'll be done with the school, which could mean we'd have the whole summer together with no other obligations. "Last one?" I ask him.

I see his muscles tighten. "Yes," he answers. He doesn't look at me.

He's lying. Maybe not really lying, but he's not convinced in it, either. I look down at the duvet as I slowly release my grip on it.

We sit in silence for long moments before it's me that breaks it. "It's going to be safe, won't it? And it's going to be alright, I hope."

"It won't be much different from all the others, I think, but I'm not sure. I can't be sure about these things because something could always go wrong."

That doesn't really sound comforting. I climb off the bed and walk to him, placing my hands on the chair on either side of him, my face close to his. "It's going to be alright. Do you hear me? You're too good at this for things to go wrong."

Fai shifts his gaze on my face, his eyes looking at me tenderly. He lifts his hand and brings it to my cheek, caressing it softly, before his hand slides to the side of my neck. "I'm just a human, Kadie."

I shake my head, refusing his words. "No. You don't understand – I love you. You're the only one I've ever loved, the only one that understood me on such a level you do. I love you far too much for anything to happen to you. Do you hear me?"

Fai closes his eyes as if in pain. I put my forehead to his, feeling like someone is ripping my soul right out of my body.

"You're going to be alright," Fai says quietly. "No matter what happens."

It feels like he stabbed me just now with his words. "No, Fai. That's not true," I disagree with him, my words quiet, barely there.

Fai places the softest of kisses on my lips, successfully shutting me up. I know he doesn't want me to say anything more. He doesn't want me to make him make promises to me he can't keep.

The days go by too fast. I should be preparing for my finals, but I was too distracted and I found myself not caring about them, even though I should. It's my future here that I should think about, but, deep down, I know I'm going to ace them all.

These days have been filled with tension between Fai and I. He's on edge and that makes me nervous. He's never on edge.

I tried talking to him about it, but he refused. I think he's scared. He's definitely nervous. I know this is going to be huge and this one mission is going to be the most dangerous one out of all of them. That doesn't sit well with me.

I watch the clock ticking on the wall, twirling the pen in my hands. I've been done with this exam, but I can't leave the classroom until everyone's done. It's eerily silent – the clock is the loudest thing in the room. I can hear the pens connecting to the paper, I can hear the sound of writing and here and there, I hear a sigh of despair and nervousness.

I turn my gaze towards the windows, watching the hot sun blasting in, making the room even hotter and making the already nervous students sweat even more.

When the bell rings, I want to bolt out of the class, but that's forbidden. We all have to put our pens down, push the papers to the edge of the desk and wait until the teacher collects every paper in the room, counts them and then we can go. I wait, rather impatiently, my foot tapping on the floor. The murmurs and chattering begin all around me, although quiet.

I stay silent, unmoving in my chair. Waiting.

When the papers are collected and counted and we're free to go, I run out of the classroom. I take my phone out and see that I have a new message from Harper, asking me if I could do her a favor.

What do you need?

Her response comes surprisingly quickly.

Please go and print this picture. I want to give it to Jon and I don't have time today.

She sends me the photo – a selfie of the two of them. It makes me stop in my tracks, in the middle of the crowded hallways, causing a few people to crash into my back and shout profanities.

I just stare at the photo, a little shocked at how much in love they look. I shake my head to myself with a small smile. Ah, young love.

I later show the photo of them both together after I printed it and he raises his eyebrows at it. "Yeah, Jon willingly gave his balls to your girl and she's carrying them around proudly."

I squint my eyes at him. "That's ... an interesting sentence."

He grins. "How are your finals going?" he asks.

I shrug. "They're going."

"Downplaying it, I see. Alright."

I don't say anything back. I don't want to talk about my finals right now. "How's the tattoo for me coming along? Will it be done by the time I'm done with school? I want it as a gift."

"It's done already if you want to see it."

"Please," I say.

He grabs his iPad and unlocks it, searches for the sketch and then puts it in front of me. I stare down at the drawing – simple, yet full of meaning, I believe.

I'm looking at wings – that were once clearly burnt and destroyed, but they're healing now.

I think Fai chose this for a reason.

"Where did you imagine them on me?" I ask him, still looking at the drawing.

"On your back. We can make it as small or as big as you want it. If you want it."

I trace the edge of the iPad with my finger, lifting my eyes to his face. "If I had to pick one for myself, I'd never pick the one that'd be even close to this good of a choice," I tell him. But he knows me too well and he's proving this once again.

He crosses his arms over the chest and leans back in the chair, playing with his piercing. "Now you show me yours."

I have to get up and go to the bedroom for my notebook and when I come back, I sit down on his lap, shifting through the pages until I find the one I've been working on.

"Here," I tell him.

It's simple, too. But full of meaning.

A bee.

Fai lets out a chuckle, looking over my shoulder. "I should've known. Great details, by the way," he murmurs appreciatively. "Where did you imagine I'd have it?"

I turn around and he leans back again, watching me curiously as I place my hand under his shirt and go upwards. I stop when my palm is on his chest, right over his heart. "Here," I say softly.

I count his heartbeats as the silence falls on us. I come to twelve. And then he kisses me.

I visit Harper the next night at the bar. Fai comes with me, of course. He's set on not leaving me out of his sight because he's convinced that Stefan and his men could strike at any moment, especially now. None of us is safe right now and I accepted this prison because it's the only way I can have Fai in my life.

We both had to make some sacrifices for this to work.

I take the photo I printed to Harper and give it to her. She's ecstatic when she sees it in a bigger size. "Aren't we cute?" she asks us with a huge smile on her face.

I give her a half of a smile. "Pretty. Both of you." I send her a wink. "It's a shame my guy doesn't want a photo with me."

"You never asked," Fai butts in.

I turn my accusing eyes on him. "You didn't, either."

He just shrugs, looking around the bar. I make a face at Harper and she has to turn around to hide her chuckle. "Shouldn't you be studying now, by the way?" she asks me.

"For?"

"Your finals?"

"If I have to look at those boring books for one more second, I'll be stabbing someone. Myself, most likely," I grumble.

"How much did you actually study, really?" Harper asks.

Fai answers for me, "Not much. If she says anything else, she's lying."

I give him an offended look. "I studied enough, thank you."

"God," Harper groans as if she's in distress. "If I even had half of your brain ..." She lets out an exasperated sigh.

I throw my head back and laugh. "Shut up," I tell her, still laughing. "You're smart enough as it is."

She doesn't agree with my statement and she shows me that with a grimace. "Where's Jon today, by the way? Isn't he attached to your hip 24/7?"

"He has some work to do," Fai says absently, still looking around the bar.

"Yes, about that. What kind of work exactly? He didn't specify," Harper says, obviously digging. But she's asking the wrong one. If Jon didn't say anything to her, Fai would be even less likely to explain it to her.

"Just normal work. Nothing to worry about."

I turn and look around the bar, too, following his gaze. "Are you looking for someone?"

"What?" Fai asks, still not looking at me.

I pinch his arm, which makes him swiftly turn his head into my direction, moving away from my reach. "What?" he grumbles.

"Are you looking for someone?"

"No, I'm just looking around," Fai says and then stops looking around by turning back around with a grim expression.

"Why are you in a mood?" I wonder. He's been acting weird ever since we came here.

"I'm not in a mood," Fai says with a sigh, bringing the glass of scotch to his mouth.

I make a face at him, but he doesn't see it. Totally in a mood. But I don't bother anymore because I know I'm not going to come far when he's like this. I roll my eyes at Harper and she just shrugs. I grab Fai's wrist and look at the time on his watch. "We'll have to get going," I tell him.

"So soon?" Harper asks sadly.

"I'm working, unfortunately," I say, saddened about it, too. Work these past weeks has been some kind of hell for me. I hate going, but it's necessary because I need the money.

Harper nods. By the purse of her lips, I see she's still not yet quite used to me working at a strip club and she doesn't like it, but at least she's trying to accept it and she understands why I'm doing this.

Money is money.

Fai empties his glass in one swallow and pays for his drink. It's not like him to order something alcoholic when we come here, especially not something this strong. Something is definitely up with him.

I wave at John, the bodyguard, on my way out. "Do you want to drive around?" Fai asks as we get to his motorcycle, grabbing the helmet and giving it to me.

"Why?" I ask as I put it on my head.

"Why not?" Fai says with a grin.

I return the grin.

I climb on the motorcycle behind him, wrapping my arms around his stomach.

We drive around the city, not for a long time, but enough to feel carefree and filled with adrenaline from the fresh air and the starry night.

We've driven many times like this before, but this time, it feels quite different. I can't put my finger on why it is so.

Chapter 42

On the graduation day, the weather is extremely hot, but windy. I sit somewhere in the middle, bored out of my mind, somewhere else in my thoughts completely.

Fai came, even though I told him he didn't have to because even I didn't want to go, but he said that he's going just because he wants to clap and shout when they call me on stage to give me that one piece of paper.

Harper couldn't come, but we're going to have a small celebration in the evening at Fai's place because it's the safest there and. We both took a free evening for this.

When I get called on the stage, I'm surprised to hear the congratulations that my results came out the best of them all. Surprised because I know that Many, the class bitch, was drowning herself in the books. She'd give her arm and leg to be, if not the best, then one of the best ones, at least.

My gaze involuntarily searches for Mandy in the crowd, finding her shocked and furious face. For a moment there, I feel kind of sorry. I didn't deserve this because I know I didn't do much for it and I know others have been giving their all to even pass those tests.

But my thoughts get interrupted and my eyes shoot to Fai who is, true to his word, standing up, clapping, and shouting, "You go, Kadience!"

They put the folder in my hands, shake my hand and we take a quick picture. They ask me to say a few words, making me frown slightly as I get gently pushed towards the microphone. I stare at the small desk and then look at the crowd, wondering what the hell to say. I don't think there's anyone that would be interested in hearing what I have to say.

Besides, I didn't even prepare any speech. I know I should because I was expected to give one since I had the best grades in our class – and generation overall, but truth be told, I just forgot it with everything going on in my life. I didn't care half as much as I should about the school.

I bite down onto my lower lip. I was never much of a talker, especially not for the big crowds. "I'm going to be very short and brief with my speech because, trust me, I know we're all just waiting to be done with this, go home and get drunk." This sentence erupts with laughter amongst the crowd. "My name is Kadience Myers, but that's not important – it does not matter to you who I am, but I hope it matters who you are to yourselves and who you have been in these challenging years. Have you been kind? Easily got angered? Were you a bully? Were you bullied? Were you a fighter?"

I make a pause there, looking at the crowd, making sure I look at every face. "I know most of the answers for most of you. I know who you've been, but do you?" I look down as if I had a paper in front of me from which I was reading. "If I had one wish for you, it'd be for all of you to realize it's not important who you are and what name you're wearing, but it's important how you act towards other people – no matter who they are. Don't care about me and what I think about you – start caring more about who you are and who you want to be. So, to end this extremely boring speech – I wish that whatever path you choose in life, it leads you to success."

I step back from the microphone and avoid looking at any teachers, knowing fully well they're probably not happy about my philosophical approach along with the parents. Well, fuck them. I'm not here to cradle all these babies – they're old enough to accept the ugly truth.

I rub my eyebrow in frustration, walking away from this stupid thing. I don't care about waiting for the final picture or throwing the caps in the air and all that crap. I just want to go. I wait for Fai by his motorcycle, smoking a cigarette in the meantime. I'm sure he's smart enough to notice that I didn't go back to my seat.

And, soon enough, I see him walking towards me at a fast pace and a confused look. "Don't you want to stay until the end?"

"No," I say, my voice empty of all emotions.

Fai studies my expression, clearing fighting an inner battle. "That speech of yours was ..."

"Is going to be written as the worst of them all? Yeah, probably. Or buried somewhere."

Fai frowns. "It was not bad at all, Kadie."

"I completely forgot about preparing a goddamn speech." I smash the cigarette with my foot and then throw it to the nearest trash can. I give Fai a rueful grin. "I bet your bestie would prepare a mind-blowing speech. Too bad she didn't get on the list of the best students."

"What the fuck are you talking about?"

"Mands," I say sarcastically.

Fai lets out an annoyed groan. "Would you stop with her already? It's not like you to be this petty and jealous of someone like her."

His words make me pause and stare at him. The longer I look, the quicker I begin to realize that he's completely right. I'm not a person who gets jealous and bitter. At least I wasn't this person before I met Fai. Now I create enemies out of every girl that looks twice at him. I literally became one of the girls I always despised and was afraid to become. Fucking great. "Let's just go. I'm getting drunk tonight, I deserve it," I tell Fai, not waiting for him to give me the helmet, but grabbing it myself and putting it over my head.

I catch Fai looking at me weirdly and then he grins and shakes his head to himself before climbing on the motorcycle and we're soon on the road. Fai doesn't take us to his place as I thought he would, though. He takes me to a tattoo studio. I don't know whether to laugh or to cry when he stops the motorcycle, but I just know that he made my day so much better.

I've never thought it's possible to feel this much about a person. Everything I feel about Fai is increased – anger, happiness, gratefulness, love ... And I know for sure we're not ready to say goodbye to each other, so why should we? Do we have to?

"Am I getting my graduation gift?" I ask him, putting the helmet on the motorcycle and shaking my hair. I didn't pull it up in a ponytail or a bun today, I left it falling down, coming almost to my butt now.

"I think you deserved it," Fai says with a nod of his head, agreeing with himself. I feel so emotional right now. I'm not used to receiving gifts, so this is something new to me. It makes me happy. And insanely grateful.

I follow Fai inside the studio, looking around with interest. He greets someone, but doesn't stop and continues walking into a room. "Here," he says, closing the door. "You can undress."

"Oh?" I ask, quirking my eyebrow up.

I catch the sides of Fai's mouth pulling up as he checks on the needles and then opens the drawing on his iPad. "Your shirt and bra, Kadie," Fai says, not turning around to look at me.

I grin and pull my shirt off, but leave the bra on and sit on the table. Fai notices this when he turns around. "Bra, too," he says, making it sound more like a command.

"Help me," I say.

Now it's his turn to raise the eyebrows. "Such a hard task you gave me," he muses, walking towards me, but when he stands in front of me, I wrap my arms around his body, hugging him. I feel overwhelmed today and my feelings are all over the place, but Fai always finds a way to make me feel better.

"Are you alright?" Fai asks, hugging me back.

"I'm awesome," I say honestly.

He unclasps my bra then and I move back, putting it off. "Where do you want me?" I ask seductively.

Fai doesn't bite. He's going to be all professional, I see.

"Lay down," he tells me.

I do as he tells me, laying down on my stomach. This almost feels like going to the doctor's where they have these tables with the paper over them they remove after every patient.

"How big did you say you want it?"

I have to grin at his words. "I say as big as you want it."

After the tattoo session, we head home. I'm in a great mood, Fai did a fantastic job and I got to spend almost an extra hour with just him today.

We didn't talk a lot, but Fai mentioned that his mother wrote to him – a handwritten letter, just to let him know that she's back home and she had a safe trip and that it meant a lot to her that she had a chance to see him. Fai said he saved the letter, but he's not going to write. It's still too risky.

We have to get everything ready for this mini party I'll be having for the end of my high school. The more I think about it, the more I find it stupid, but I know Harper would kill me if I didn't celebrate this victory.

So, Fai and I make sure there's enough alcohol and there's enough food. When Harper comes, the first things she shouts is, "I have a cake!" and the second is, "Congratulations, you smart human-be-ing. I can't believe we share the same genes, but holy frick, you're seriously a genius."

"I wouldn't go that far," I say and hug her when she puts the cake down. "And you really shouldn't bother with the cake."

"Nonsense!" she exclaims, horrified. "A cake is a must."

Jon comes after her. They're the first ones to arrive and around 15 minutes later, others come, too – Bastian, Ante, Cruz and Lev. although I'm not the closest to them, they're Fai's friends and they're fun to party with, so they were invited. If it were only us four, this party would be a little sad, anyway.

And it's nice. Nothing revolutionary, it doesn't last until the morn-ing, but we all have fun and we're all laughing a lot. Fai, especially.

I watch him a lot because he seems relaxed and in an element. It's rare for him to smile and laugh so much.

If I knew this would be the last time I'd see him this happy and hear him laugh this much, I would make sure I listened to him even more – just to memorize the sound that's going to haunt me for a long time.

I'm sitting in the dark room, smoking a cigarette, I think it's my fourth one. There's no light on because the darkness calms me.

Fai is out. It's his last mission today. I took the night off work because this is important for us – it'll mean that after this night, he's going to be free. We're going to be free.

Before Fai went, I watched him get ready, sitting in the same chair I'm sitting in now. There's something in watching him get into his bad guy mode. And to think I believed he was some wanna-be gangster when I met him ...

Before he went out, he came for a kiss for good luck, as he said it. And I pulled him down by the jacket and said, "Just see that you come back to me."

He said nothing, but he kissed me. It was a long and deep kiss and it almost felt like we were kissing for the last time – that it was a goodbye. I just want to believe that he was nervous, which made me nervous even more in return.

He knows what he's doing. He's been doing this for years.

I close my eyes and let out a deep breath. It's been hours since he walked out of the front door. I know there would be no way for me to fall asleep, so I didn't even bother. Besides, he asked me to wait for his call because we're going out to celebrate when they're done.

He's been gone for longer than usual now and that's what's making me tense.

But then I hear it. My phone. I pick it up so quickly and clumsily, it almost falls from my hands. It's Fai.

"Yes?" I say when I answer, holding my breath.

"It's done, bee. I'm coming to get you now, get ready for the party."

I close my eyes at hearing his voice. I can hear he's smiling. "I've been ready since you went out," I share with him. I can hear the laughter and the voice of others talking. "Be quick."

"Twenty minutes or so," he promises.

My eyes open and I'm smiling, too. "Fai ... I love you," I say, happy and overwhelmed. It's over. We're done.

There's a pause on the other end. "Me too, Kadie. See you soon, I'm coming right away."

He ends the call and I put my phone down on my lap and wait for him to get here.

Except that he never does.

Fai said twenty minutes and it's now been almost an hour. I'm on my feet, fully freaking out. I've called him at least twenty times, but he never answered. This could mean that he's riding on his motorcycle and, naturally, can not pick his phone up.

I also called Jon and I didn't have any luck with him, either.

What the fuck is happening?

Another 15 minutes go by in silence.

Another 30.

Something's going on. What if they went to the party by themselves?

Fai isn't answering. Jon isn't answering. I don't have the numbers from others.

God damn it.

My hair is a mess, I've been raking my hands through it so many times.

Another 25 minutes go by and then I finally get a call. From Jon.

"Jon! Finally someone. Where are you? What's going on?"

"Kadience ..." It's not Jon. It's Ante, I think – I'm not sure. "Something happened. There was an accident."

I completely stop – stop walking around, stop moving, stop breathing. I think my heart stopped beating, too. "No," I say. "Please, no. He called me before, said you're done."

"You should come to the hospital. I'll text you the address," Ante says, his voice vain and broken. Something I've never heard from him before and I've never wanted to.

"What happened?" I plead with desperation. "Say he's alright. Please."

I hear Ante taking a deep breath. "Just come here, please," he says with a quiet voice.

He ends the call and I scream in pain, agony and fear.

Epilogue

I can count on the fingers on my one hand of how many times I've cried in my life. I guess I could call it an accomplishment, although, at this moment, it doesn't feel like it. When I start crying, I hardly know how to stop. I just don't know how to.

I'm in the hospital, watching the sunrise. I've been crying for hours now, ever since I came to the hospital and was hit with the news.

There was an accident. The words keep echoing in my head. Fai? I asked. It's Harper. I want to scream. I want to scream again because, apparently, I didn't scream enough before.

It's Harper. There was an accident. It's Harper. She didn't make it.

I couldn't believe it. I still can't. It didn't make sense.

How? How could it be her? It can't be her! You're all wrong. Shut up.

But it was her. It was her because they gave me the photo they found there. A photo of Jon and her together, the same one I printed out for her. She put the photo in the frame, but the glass was now broken. I think she wanted to give the photo to Jon today, probably as a gift to their victory.

And their victory never came.

I put my fingers on the window glass, looking at the sunrise through my blurry vision. I think I've never seen a sunrise this beautiful in my life. Funny it chose this day to be this pretty. The day I lost everything and everyone. As if the sun is mocking me today.

There was an accident. It's Harper.

They were on their way back. All of them happy, unsuspecting. Happy it was over. Jon went to get Harper because she was supposed to go and celebrate with us.

But there was an attack. They weren't ready for it, it happened quickly.

Fai was shot three times and is now fighting for his life.

Jon was shot in the leg which made him lose balance and he and Harper fell from the motorcycle. Harper got trapped under it. She couldn't make it. Her head was completely crushed. They said it was a quick death.

When Jon found out, he lost his shit. They had to give him a sedative to calm him down.

When they told me, I wasn't much better, either. Truthfully, I don't even remember my reaction. I know there was a lot of screaming, fighting and crying. Not her. Please, not her. It couldn't be her.

Harper is – was everything I've really had all my life. She's the one person I'd truly die for and, at the end, she died because of me.

Because the attack that happened ... it should've been me that died. Me and Fai. That's what they wanted.

But it was Harper in return.

Her parents are here somewhere. I couldn't talk to them, I couldn't even look them in their eyes.

It should've been. GODDAMNIT, IT SHOULD'VE BEEN ME.

I'm in Fai's hospital room now. It's quiet in here, I can be alone with my thoughts. I can uninterruptedly think, think, think. I still feel a little groggy from the sedative they shot in my veins and I'm irritated that it made me so calm when I know I shouldn't be calm right now. I should be anything but.

I should be screaming in anger and pain because I lost the most important person in my life, yet I just can't because I feel too tired for it.

I don't have the courage to visit Jon. I think he's sleeping, anyway. I wasn't here when he found out, but they later told me his reaction was pretty bad.

I didn't talk to Harper's parents because I just didn't have the nerve. They were completely devastated, completely heartbroken. She was the only child, the beloved daughter and I know they were very proud of her and loved her very much.

I place my forehead against the cold window glass as the sobs overtake me, my body shaking. Everything hurts. It hurts so much that I want to rip everything out from my body so I wouldn't have to feel anything anymore.

I get away from the window and slowly walk towards the bed Fai is laying on, wrapping my arms around myself. Tears are still streaming down my face. I've lost so much already and I'm losing even more. It feels like it's tearing me up inside.

I watch Fai resting. He's so calm, one wouldn't know he's fighting for his life. The doctor said he'll have to do a lot of fighting because he has lost a lot of blood. They could barely save him, but they did. And I know that he's a fighter. He's been one all his life.

I stand by his bed for a long time, listening to the machine, listening to his heartbeat. The sun is already up, the day has started for many people. Not for me. It ended before it started.

The nurses have been here. The doctor came in to check in on him. The guys have been here, except for Jon who's still in the hospital and I still haven't got the nerve to visit him.

Nothing changed with Fai.

Until the afternoon.

I'm reading a book by his bed to think about anything else but my reality right now. It's calm and peaceful in here until the machine suddenly makes a noise that makes me stand up on my feet immediately.

The line is flat. His heart stopped beating.

I don't know what to do, but I realize I don't have to do anything because people come running in the room in seconds. Doctors, nurses. Shouting directions.

I step back, lost. "Please, no," I say quietly, shaking my head. "No, no, no," I say louder. "Save him! You have to save him! He can't die. He can't go."

"Kadie." It's Bastian. He wraps his arm around my shoulders. "Let's give them some space to do their work and wait outside."

I refuse to move. I can't go anywhere. He can't die.

"No." I'm shaking my head. "Don't let him die. I can't lose him, too!"

"Come on," Bastian says calmly and forcefully drags me out of the room. I'm loudly sobbing and, overall, I'm a huge mess, but I keep losing and losing ... how much more? When will life stop taking things and people away from me? Wasn't it enough already?

I have nothing. I have no one.

I lose Bastian's touch. I don't let him comfort him, I don't let anyone comfort me. Everyone is outside, worriedly looking at me, but I don't look back.

I lean back against the wall and slide down, sitting on the cold hospital floor and cry.

Days later, I'm sitting at the kitchen table at Fai's place. In a place that's filled with our memories. Happy memories, mostly. It's suffocating being here, but I came to say goodbye.

Fail will live, the doctor confirmed. He's doing better, but he still hasn't woken up and it might take him a few more days, but he'll come around.

It's Harper's funeral tomorrow, but I won't be here for it.

I came back to this place to get my stuff and to write a letter to Fai so he can read it when he wakes up. I know he deserves to get a better goodbye from me, but I don't have it in me anymore. I had too many goodbyes to say in my life already. I can't do it anymore.

I've been staring at the blank paper in front of me with my hand trembling too much to be able to write anything.

I take a deep breath and wipe the tears from my face and begin.

Fai,

I'm a coward for writing you this letter instead of telling it to your face and you're allowed to hate me for it. But, I can't tell you this face-to-face. Hopefully, you'll understand. It not now, maybe one day in the future.

You're a wonderful person. Despite you not believing it, you are one in a million. And exactly because of that, I'm letting you know that I can not continue to live like this with you. The life you live is not the life I can live any further.

When you met me, I was in love with fear and I made love with it frequently. But falling in love with you meant falling out of love with fear and now fear actually scares me because there are too many things at stake that I could easily lose. I can't be the person to sit at home and let you go out and do things you do anymore because it's not guaranteed you'll come back and I ... learned my lesson this time.

I'm sorry. I thought I was a stronger person and I thought I could be the one for this life, but I'm not. It turns out, deep inside, I'm still just a little girl, trembling with fear of what's going to happen to her.

So, yes. This is a goodbye letter. When you'll wake up, I'll be (long) gone with a changed number. Don't try to reach me and don't look for me and I'll selfishly ask you to not completely forget me either, but move on and stay out of trouble, even though I know trouble fancies you and just won't leave you alone.

Please, don't seek revenge for Harper's death. If you can, go and try to have a better, calmer life. Leaving in constant fear is no way to live.

And, please, find yourself a girl that'll cherish and love you and, most importantly, the girl that'll understand you. You owe yourself that because you deserve it.

I'll love you, probably always and forever, but I'll do it from a distance.

Thank you for loving me when it was hard to do so. And thank you for all of your memories. I'll proudly carry them around in my heart wherever I go.

I'm sorry, but I have to go and chase my dreams. I hope you're going to do the same.

Don't look for me. I'll find you when the time will be right, but don't wait for me, either, because time may never be right.

Forever yours,

Kadie

I let out a shaky exhale, wiping the tears from my face. I've been crying for days now and it seems like I'm not going to stop anytime soon.

I carefully fold the paper and put it in the envelope. I can't imagine what his reaction will be when he wakes up, but he knew I was leaving, anyway. He just didn't know I was going to go this soon. And he also doesn't know where I'm going. I told him what I wanted to study, I just never told him where.

Life threw bricks at me. I'm going to build a house with them.

I go to the bedroom and take the things I already packed. I take one last look around. I feel like I'm going to throw up soon. It hurts so much ...

Now I know how it is to love and to lose. It feels like I'm trying to breathe underwater these days. I've been trying to keep it together so the doctors wouldn't stop me from seeing Fai and to stop them from putting sedatives in me to keep me calm, but inside, I've been screaming and crying the whole time.

It's the kind of pain you can't explain. It just hurts – you don't really know where and you don't know what to do to make it stop. It just hurts. Everything hurts.

My eyes land on the notebook. My notebook with sketches I've kept all this time by the window. I walk to it and pick it up. When I open it, it opens on the page I marked it, the one with Fai's tattoo that he never got.

I rip the page out and put it in the envelope next to the letter. A little souvenir. He can do whatever he likes with it. I might never know.

And then, with one last look around the apartment and with my heart heavier than a ton of bricks, I lock the door and put the key in the envelope. I stand outside the door for a few moments, staring at it, and then put my forehead against it, letting myself sob loudly, putting my hand on the door for support.

I'm not ready to say goodbye and I'll never be, but I need to do this. It's for myself. For my future. Now it's just me against the world all over again.

I got this. I got it once, I can certainly have it again.

I lean back and roll my shoulders, pulling myself together enough so I can leave. I go to the hospital. It's been my home for days now. I didn't talk to anyone, really. Not Jon, not Harper's parents because I'm ridden with guilt.

I'm not going to the funeral because I simply can't. I can't even think about it, having to say goodbye to her forever while everyone stares at me. That should be me.

I'm a coward.

I'm a coward for dropping Fai's letter on the small table next to his bed. I'm a coward for running away.

But I've always been a good runner. All my life, I've been running away from things. It's what I'm good at. It's the only way I know to cope with my feelings.

I don't say goodbye to anyone. Except Fai and he's really not in the state to hear me right now. I don't stay in the hospital for long because I have to go soon. With one more look, one more kiss and one more tear, I go.

The sun is setting when I step out of the hospital, carrying my bags. I take a deep breath and look into the distance.

When the sun sets, I disappear with it.

www.ingramcontent.com/pod-product-compliance
Lightning Source LLC
Chambersburg PA
CBHW070736190726
48292CB00002B/297